A PROBLEM PRINCESS

ANNA HARRINGTON

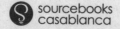

sourcebooks
casablanca

Published by Sourcebooks Casablanca, an imprint of Sourcebooks
P.O. Box 4410, Naperville, Illinois 60567-4410
(630) 961-3900
sourcebooks.com

Printed and bound in Canada.
MBP 10 9 8 7 6 5 4 3 2 1

"Let us follow the corpse of British Liberty slowly and reverentially to its tomb: and if some glorious Phantom should appear, and make its throne of broken swords and scepters and royal crowns trampled in the dust, let us say that the Spirit of Liberty has arisen from its grave and left all that was gross and mortal there, and kneel down and worship it as our Queen."

—Percy Bysshe Shelley, *An Address to the People on the Death of the Princess Charlotte*

One

CLAYTON ELLIOTT STEPPED UP BEHIND THE PORTER IN the dark alley. Around them, the borough lay quiet and still in the early evening shadows, as if holding its breath in anticipation of the nighttime debaucheries to come. "Hello, Burton."

The older man spun around, startled. His meaty hands clenched into fists to defend himself, but Clayton would never let the man come close enough to land a blow. Not with his own fingers curled around the small pistol he held at his side.

Burton recognized Clayton's face in the shadows and relaxed, yet he wasn't at all happy to see him. "*You.*" He spat on the ground. "What the hell do you want?"

"Information."

"About?"

"Scepter."

Burton froze at the name. Then he laughed. "Ain't no more Scepter."

Clayton wished to God that were true. "That's not what I've heard."

"Then ye've heard wrong."

For the past six months, Clayton had been using Burton to stay informed about happenings at the London docks, hoping to hear news of Scepter, a revolutionary group that had pledged to overthrow the British government. If Scepter was attempting to regroup after the execution of their leader, the Marquess of Hawking, then it would certainly be a dockworker who'd have heard. Few people knew the comings and goings of powerful men like the laborers who worked the quays and ships.

"Tell me what you know," Clayton ordered.

"Scepter don't exist no more." Another spit to the ground, this one in capitulation. "Least not like it did."

"You swear on your life?"

Burton croaked out a hoarse laugh. "If I tell ye anythin' about what the men of Scepter are up to, that's what it'll be, all right—*my life*."

"Not if you cooperate. I'll make it worth your while. You know I will."

Burton gave him a hard once-over from hat to boots, most likely to figure out exactly how many guns and knives Clayton had hidden beneath his black greatcoat in addition to the one in plain sight in his hand. Yet he was also assessing the power that Clayton possessed as a Home Office undersecretary to fulfill his promise.

"But if you lie to me," Clayton warned and pointed his pistol at Burton's chest, "I will kill you myself before Scepter's men have the chance to."

Burton was Clayton's last lead in his search for information about Scepter. His Home Office operatives had turned up nothing new about the group since Hawking's execution. The lack of evidence pointed toward what Burton and Clayton's other contacts in London's underworld had told him—Scepter had died along with the marquess.

Clayton had come to believe that the group was a hydra that simply grew a new head whenever an old one was cut off. But how many heads did the monster have left? Or had the men of the Armory truly managed to kill the beast after all?

He needed answers, and damn it to hell that he was left with only Burton to provide them.

"There's a ship at Greenwich leaving at dawn," Clayton told him, "whose captain is looking for a good shipman. He's offering twice the regular pay and might just be persuaded to give you the position of third mate if I ask him." He paused, dangling the reward as bait. "Of course, that all depends on what information you can give me."

Burton's face lit with greed, and he licked his lips. "Haven't heard much at all 'bout Scepter. They've done a few bits of business 'ere an' there in the stews and warehouses, but nothin' organized. Mostly by their old managers tryin' to carry on the businesses without 'em. They're like dogs after scraps, tryin' to pick up what they can while the goin's still good. Others are makin' for the Continent or up north to stay one step out o' Newgate." He gave a ghastly grin of amusement that showed three missing teeth and a lip permanently scarred from an old fight. "Scurryin' 'round like rats, they are, lookin' for holes to run into an' places to hide."

"And their leader?" Hawking's execution would have created the perfect opportunity for an underling to seize control. "Who's attempting to organize them?"

"No one. I told ye. It's done fer."

"But you've heard rumors. What are they saying?" When Burton didn't answer, Clayton clucked his tongue. "Damnable shame if that boat sails from Greenwich without you."

Spurred on by greed, Burton admitted, "Just stories floatin' 'round the docks that a new leader's arrivin' soon from the Continent, ready t' drop in an' scoop up the reins."

"You don't believe them?"

"I don't believe that anyone wi' half a mind would risk findin' his own neck in a noose the same way Hawking done."

Clayton's heart skipped. No one outside the Home Office knew that the late Marquess of Hawking had been connected to Scepter. He'd been arrested, tried, and executed for the kidnapping and attempted murder of Baroness Rowland and her son, along with a litany of other treasonous and murderous acts. But not once had Scepter's name been mentioned in any part of the proceedings.

Clayton kept his voice controlled as he calmly asked, "How do *you* know about Hawking's connection to Scepter?"

Burton's eyes flared at his mistake.

Clayton slowly stalked forward until the tip of his pistol's barrel pressed into the soft flesh under the man's chin. "Tell me."

"I–I know people, an' I hear th-things," Burton rushed out and raised his hands from his sides in a gesture of surrender.

"That's why ye pay me for information, ain't it? 'Cause I got connections."

"Yes, but I never realized how deep your connections ran until right now." Clayton pressed the pistol harder under Burton's chin. The man was forced to tilt his head backward so far that he stared up into the black London sky and the rain that fell in a steady, cold drizzle. "How do you know about Hawking's connection to Scepter?"

Burton swallowed so hard that Clayton could hear the terrified sound from two feet away. "Had me suspicions 'bout the man when he started hangin' 'round the docks, so one day I followed 'im. He weren't careful enough to know I was sneakin' after." The rainwater ran down his face like tears, and his breath emerged in a cloud of fog on the cold evening air. "Followed him all the way t' that fancy house o' his in Mayfair. Asked a servant in the street who lived there—that's how I found 'im."

"Why follow him? Did you plan on blackmailing him? Tell him you'd keep his secret if he paid for your silence?"

Burton nodded, and his flabby chin rocked the barrel of the pistol beneath it.

"You damned fool," Clayton muttered. "You were lucky he was arrested before he killed you."

The man squeezed his eyes shut. "I needed the money. Got sick family an' doctor's bills to pay."

That was a lie if ever Clayton had heard one. Most likely the man had a favorite whore he wanted to spoil, along with all the finery and ease for himself that Hawking's money could have bought.

He stepped back but kept his pistol pointed at the man's chest. Burton was just stupid enough to charge him, but if he tried, Clayton would kill him where he stood.

"What else do you know about Scepter?" Clayton demanded.

Looking relieved to have the gun away from his chin, Burton shook his head. "Nothin.'"

"Don't lie to me, you son of a—"

"*Nothing!*"

Clayton pointed the pistol at Burton's head and stared down the barrel. "One…"

"I told you! I told you everythin' I know. I swear it!"

"Two…"

"All right! All right, please!" Burton put up his hands in a gesture of mercy and shook violently, a coward at heart. "All the men left in Scepter are just waitin', sittin' low an' waitin' for a signal."

Hawking had said the same to Clayton before he was hanged. "What kind of signal?"

"Don't know, but a big one. They'll act then, an' the new man who's comin' from the Continent will step into Hawking's shoes an' lead Scepter, just like Boney coming back from Elba. Then everythin' changes. That's what I heard. *Everything* changes." Burton chuckled nervously. "Like I said, just a bunch of stories."

That didn't put Clayton at ease. Neither did St Mary's bells tolling through the fog and darkness. He counted… seven bells.

Damnation. He was running late.

He eased down the hammer of the pistol and lowered it to his side. It was time to give Burton his reward. "Go see Captain Smith on the *Mercury*. It's leaving Greenwich tomorrow. He's expecting you." But Clayton wouldn't forgive Burton for his betrayal. "Do *not* come back to London."

In reply, Burton spat on the ground again. The glob of saliva landed less than a foot from Clayton's boot.

Clayton laughed at him, turned, and walked out of the alley.

"Don't think you'll be findin' Scepter's new leader 'mong the sailors an' porters on the docks," Burton called out after him. "Or anywhere in the stews or slums, that's fer sure. Look fer him in Westminster wi' the rest of ye snobs an' nobs!"

Clayton didn't slow his steps as he strode over the drizzle-drenched cobblestones toward the thick bank of fog rolling up from the river. He wouldn't let Burton think he cared, even though the comment jarred him to his core.

"Oh, that's right—you ain't no nob. *Yer* pappy was a goddamned murderer!"

Clayton grabbed the knife he kept sheathed up his left sleeve, spun around, and threw it. It sailed past Burton's head so closely that the blade nicked his ear.

Burton slammed his hand against his head with a curse, but he was smart enough not to attack.

"*Never* come back," Clayton threatened in an icy snarl.

He continued to walk away into the dark and damp city. He knew he would never see Burton again. *Good.* Clayton might just kill him if he did.

He took measured breaths to calm himself as he strode

south through the city, but the night air did little to ease the painful clenching of his chest. How dare that bastard Burton mention Clayton's father like that!

But it wasn't the insult that had wounded him. It was the reminder that he'd done little over the past year to uncover the truth about Charles Elliott's arrest and execution.

Until Scepter disrupted Clayton's plans, everything in his life had been focused on uncovering the truth—and proving the world wrong about his father. About himself. About the murders twenty-five years ago. About *everything*. Hell, he'd even joined the Home Office after returning from the wars because the ministry held the resources he needed to investigate, and the position had given him the opportunity to prove his patriotism to a country that thought his father had forsaken it.

He'd been so close to putting the last pieces into place he could taste it. But then he'd had to put it all on hold to stop Scepter.

Yet if Scepter truly was dead and gone, then he could once more turn his attention to those old murders and his father's role in them—if any—even if he succeeded in doing nothing more than exonerating Charles Elliott's ghost.

Around him, the evening was transitioning into a rainy night, helped along by a thick fog that blanketed the streets in eerie white. In the distance, bells clanged from ships bobbing in the Thames, and shouts and laughs went up from the poor who filled the courtyards and derelict buildings in this section of the city.

Yet he didn't dare slow down. Not that he was afraid of

being targeted by some opportunistic footpad who would find himself on the wrong end of a pistol if he attempted it. No, tonight Clayton was being targeted by someone far worse.

The prince regent.

With a roll of his eyes, Clayton hurried toward the Thames and the fastest way through London. His boots clicked on the stone steps as he descended toward the black river and stepped into the waiting boat.

"Westminster." He tossed a coin to the wherry man. "And hurry."

"Aye, sir."

The boatman used the Thames's finicky currents to glide upstream toward the wide bend where the river turned south beneath the new Waterloo Bridge and then on to Westminster. Old hulks appeared like ghost ships from the wall of fog as the wherry passed, and the drizzle and darkness lay so thick across the city that no lights could be seen glowing from any of the buildings on the banks. Only muffled noise from waterside taverns broke the silence, along with the occasional clanging of a ship's bell. Even the lamp that dangled from the wherry's rear pole barely lit up a circle big enough for the boat.

"Charon," Clayton called out over his shoulder to the wherry man. After all, there seemed little difference between this trip down the Thames tonight and one across the River Styx. Both would eventually take him to hell. "What rumors have you heard creeping around in the shadows tonight?"

"None." The boatman snorted. "No one's daft enough to be out in this damp 'cept for fools."

"True enough," Clayton muttered beneath his breath. *He* was certainly acting the fool. Tonight's wild goose chase proved it. He prayed that Burton and his Home Office operatives were correct that Scepter was dead and buried along with Hawking.

His gut told him differently.

By the time the boat glided silently up to the steps at the base of Westminster Bridge and Clayton stepped out, he had convinced himself that Burton knew no more about Scepter's tattered remains than his own Home Office agents and that any tales of a new leader emerging to replace Hawking were just that—fairy tales.

Besides, he had a bigger nightmare to deal with at that moment.

"To the front door of Carlton House," he called out to the jarvey of a hackney stopped on the embankment.

The driver's eyes grew large. "Where?"

"You heard me." Clayton swung inside the compartment, rapped his knuckles against the roof to signal to the man to drive, and muttered, "Onward to hell."

The jarvey cracked his whip over the heads of the horses and started the old rig down the street. He kept them clipping along at a quick pace, possibly because it was his first fare to a royal residence…or more likely because he was convinced Clayton was mad as a hatter and wanted to be rid of him as soon as possible.

"God knows I'd have to be mad to be going to Carlton House," Clayton muttered to himself as he watched the gas lamps pass by in the thickening fog.

But did he have a choice? Since the incident last summer at Waterloo Bridge and Clayton's well-coordinated cover-up that kept the public from learning how Scepter had nearly assassinated the prince regent, Clayton had become one of the regent's favorites, much to Clayton's chagrin and to the suspicions of the prime minister and Home Office secretary. He'd only been half teasing the prince when he'd claimed he wanted to be rewarded with a generalship.

But damn if the royal fool hadn't gone and given him exactly that.

General Clayton Elliott. That unexpected and rapid promotion up the ranks had raised eyebrows across the empire, and it galled him that others thought he hadn't deserved it, that he'd received it not in the heat of battle but in the backrooms of Westminster. Worse—that he couldn't say a word in his own defense to prove he'd earned it because the incident had to remain a state secret. Other gossip had been swirling about his connection to the regent, too, especially as he was now invited to all kinds of events that even a general had no business attending. Like tonight's audience with the visiting royals from Monrovia. No mere Home Office under-secretary and son of a convicted murderer should have been considered special enough for that. The regent most likely knew it, too, and invited Clayton more to aggravate those men who were left off the invitation list than to reward him.

Clayton rubbed at the knot of tension in his nape. Always, what he had wanted most was to prove the true worth of the Elliott name. From the moment he'd left the family brewery and scraped together enough money to purchase a lieutenant's commission, that had been his goal. His path had been grueling—nights spent sleeping on bare ground frozen hard in winters and oozing mud in summers, terror-filled days fighting on the battlefield, his life endangered at every turn, his best friends slaughtered as they fought beside him… He'd worked himself nearly to death in the army camps to earn recognition, then volunteered for every dangerous mission he could, and always with the goal of proving his patriotism and loyalty to England, proving that the Elliott men weren't lawless. *Always.* The wars provided opportunity for quick advancement, and peacetime provided even more with the Home Office.

Now he stood at the pinnacle of his career with all he'd wanted held firm within his grasp.

Almost. He had yet to uncover the truth about his father, and he couldn't stop until he put his father's ghost to rest. In every way.

With a grimace, Clayton pounded his fist against the hackney's roof. The time for his command performance had arrived.

"Stop," he called out the broken window to the driver. They were still several streets from their destination, but he wanted to avoid the tangle of traffic that undoubtedly awaited them. He also wanted to avoid the attention he would draw by arriving at the royal residence in a hired hackney. "Let me out here."

The jarvey pulled the team to a stop at the side of the avenue. Clayton jumped down to the street, tossed up a coin, and headed on foot toward Carlton House.

The traffic was as bad as he'd feared, with a long line of carriages snaking its way back toward Mayfair. Their lamps lit dim halos in the damp fog and gave the entire scene an eerie, unworldly feel, but past experience with the regent told Clayton that the inside of the royal residence would be just as fantastical. The regent would have cut no corners for tonight's festivities. The Monrovian reception was the palace's first public event since Princess Charlotte's official mourning period had ended, and everyone of any importance was attempting to cram themselves into the house's grand reception rooms.

Yet tonight's event wasn't even the grand ball that would take place in a fortnight to mark the culmination of the royal visit. No, tonight's event was only a small welcome ceremony.

Clayton stopped in front of Carlton House's sweeping entrance and stared at the gold cages erected on both sides of the portico that held dozens of swans, the hundreds of guests streaming inside, and an army of servants at the ready to help them.

A small welcome ceremony? *Good Lord.*

He took a deep breath to summon his courage the way he'd never had to before any of the battles on the Continent. Then he hurried up the steps, handed his invitation to the footman guarding the entrance, and stepped inside.

Two

CORDELIA STARED AT HER REFLECTION IN THE MIRROR OF the dressing table that had been brought into the blue velvet drawing room for her use and forced down a deep sigh of boredom as her dresser, Braun, fussed to perfect her appearance.

No. Not boredom.

Utter misery.

She couldn't blame Braun for wanting to make her look beautiful given tonight's momentous implications. After all, her English royal cousins would be laying eyes on her for the first time.

Yet she suspected she could have worn burlap rags and no one would have cared, and not because of poor Princess Charlotte's recent death. Cordelia knew why she was here in England. As an unmarried princess at age twenty-four, she held no delusions about what was expected of her.

She wasn't here for mourning but for marriage, and tonight wasn't a welcome but an audition.

"The ceremony will begin promptly at eight o'clock and is expected to last two hours," Lady Devereaux, her personal secretary, read from the notebook that contained Cordelia's schedule for their visit. "You will be expected to greet all the guests in attendance, and your uncle wants you to pay special attention to the Duke of Wellington and the Duke of Hampton, both former generals and our strong allies in the continental wars."

Well, at least they weren't the royal dukes. That much was a relief.

"As well as the Dukes of Clarence, Kent, and Cambridge."

With a roll of her eyes, Cordelia fought to keep her shoulders from sinking—or shuddering. The royal dukes. She knew they would raise their philandering heads tonight, all three wanting a good look at her as if she were nothing but a brood mare at auction.

Truly, though, wasn't that exactly what she was?

"Supper follows immediately at ten o'clock and will be a private affair in the formal dining room with the prince regent and the royal family. Braun will put you to bed at midnight."

Lady Devereaux paused to glance at the pocket watch she wore clipped to her skirt at her waist. Baroness Devereaux was married to Monrovia's highest ranking general and just as regimented as her husband, which was why Uncle Ernest had selected her to be Cordelia's personal secretary. He'd wanted Cordelia to have the best person available to assist her. Failing that, a drill sergeant.

"Tomorrow," Devereaux continued, "you will rise at eight and dress for breakfast with Princess Sophia at eleven at Buckingham House, followed by a second breakfast with Lord Liverpool at one at St James's Palace."

"A second breakfast?" Her eyes darted to Devereaux's

reflection in the mirror. Good heavens, how much food was she expected to eat?

Devereaux confirmed that with a sharp nod. "At two, you will meet with the royal seamstress to make any necessary alterations to your wardrobe."

Because of all the breakfasts, naturally. Yet Cordelia didn't dare utter a word. She knew her duty, just as she knew the punishment if she refused to carry it out.

Once, shortly after her parents died, she'd had enough of being a princess and refused to cooperate. The thought of one more royal appearance had broken her. In punishment, she'd been stripped down to her shift, locked into an empty room by herself for a week, and given nothing to eat but plain porridge. No one had been allowed to see her, not even Aunt Wilhelmina. When she was finally allowed out of the room, Uncle Ernest sternly lectured her for an hour about the obligations of the royal family, and Lady Devereaux was made her secretary and constant companion to reinforce that lesson. She'd been warned. If she refused to behave like a princess, then the palace would treat her like a commoner, including sending her away to some distant corner of Monrovia where she would never see her family and friends again.

With no other choice, she'd capitulated and gone on to do exactly what was expected of her.

She was still doing it ten years later.

"Your meeting with the War Secretary is at three o'clock, the Home Secretary at four, the Foreign Secretary at five—"

"And a partridge in a pear tree at six," Cordelia mumbled beneath her breath.

Devereaux glanced up from her notes and blinked. "Pardon, Your Highness?"

Oh no—she'd thoughtlessly uttered that aloud! With a smile to cover her slip, she lied, "And another perfect treat at six, I'm certain."

"Oh. Yes." The secretary checked her pocket watch again and waved at Braun to hurry with the final touches to Cordelia's hair and gown. "That is when you'll have your first drawing room with Queen Charlotte at Buckingham House. You'll be dressed at eight for the evening ceremonies with the Royal Society, the Royal Academy—"

"Is there no free time?" Cordelia interrupted yet kept her head perfectly still so Braun could finish securing her curls.

Devereaux flipped through the pages in her book, scanning each one. "Ah yes!" She smiled triumphantly. "On day three. Your uncle requested that we leave time for you to spend with your English family."

Her chest sank. What he meant was more time with the royal dukes. That wasn't at all the type of free time she craved. "If we've planned it already, then it isn't free," she somehow managed to correct without grumbling...too much.

Devereaux's lips pressed firmly together. She had no good response to that except "You know how busy your schedule always is. Everyone desires to meet you and discuss Monrovia's affairs. It's your duty to avail yourself."

Oh, Cordelia certainly knew that! Every day was like this, even in Monrovia, where her schedule was planned down to the minute and filled with endless engagements.

Her life was not her own. When she had turned sixteen

and officially become part of her uncle's court, she had come to the startling realization that she would be told where to be at every moment of every day for the rest of her life.

She hadn't known whether to feel relieved or break down in sobs.

She pulled in a deep breath and announced, "I want to see as much of London as possible while I'm here."

"Of course, ma'am. The planned events will allow you to—"

"Not the events. I want to see London." After all, if she'd be marrying a royal duke and moving here, then she needed to learn about the new country where she'd be living out the rest of her days. "The *real* London."

Devereaux blinked. "Ma'am?"

"I want to see the Tower and the animals I've heard are kept there, visit the art exhibits at Somerset House, ride down the Thames on a wherry—perhaps explore one of the markets—"

"A wherry? A market?" Her secretary gaped, horrified by the idea. "Whatever for?"

"Just to see the city and meet its people." *Just to have a little fun while I still can.*

Devereaux tapped her forefinger against the notebook and reminded her, "You are not here as a tourist on the grand tour, Your Highness. You are here to offer our country's heartfelt support to your English cousins in their time of grief and uncertainty."

No. She was here to be sacrificed in marriage.

When Princess Charlotte died in childbirth, along with

her baby son, the double deaths not only plunged England into mourning but also into a constitutional crisis. Despite a bevy of uncles, Charlotte was the only legitimate grandchild of King George, and none of the royal dukes were in marital positions to produce another. Those royal dukes who were still bachelors would have to marry, and soon, to ensure the continuation of the monarchy, and Cordelia represented everything they wanted in a wife—a continental princess who was young enough to have children and who possessed the fortune of a principality for her dowry.

"That will do, Braun," Cordelia told her dresser as the woman continued to fuss with her chestnut strands, as if attempting to give her a coiffure to rival none in terms of height and perfectly formed curls. When the woman then pulled at the puffed sleeves of her dress, Cordelia raised her hand to stop her. "Please."

"Yes, ma'am." Yet Braun couldn't resist puffing one more bit of fabric before dropping her hands to her sides and moving away.

Thankfully, Devereaux retreated several steps as well, taking that dreadful notebook along with her. When Cordelia had been younger, she'd fantasized about snatching it from the woman's hands and throwing it into the fire. Now she was old enough to know that another notebook would simply replace it.

"You may both leave me," Cordelia ordered softly. "I'm ready."

The two ladies curtsied and left the room.

Cordelia let out a long sigh. She'd never been comfortable

with all the fuss and bother her ladies-in-waiting and staff paid her, and lately they reminded her of a swarm of bothersome gnats.

"You look beautiful," Marie, Comtesse de Marseille, assured Cordelia as she came up behind her. The comtesse looked past Cordelia's shoulder at their joint reflections in the mirror, then swept a critical gaze over her from toes to tiara.

Cordelia nodded at the empty compliment, unable to summon a smile in return.

Marie placed her hands on Cordelia's shoulders and gave them an affectionate squeeze. "You will win the hearts of everyone in attendance!"

It wasn't hearts that mattered tonight. Not when it came to the royal dukes anyway. For those three men, it was a different body part entirely. With them, it was pen—

She bit her lip. Pen*ance*.

The comtesse lowered her mouth to Cordelia's ear and murmured, as if sharing a deep secret, "I am so very proud of you and the woman you have become. Your dear parents would certainly have felt the same."

Grief panged in Cordelia's chest. Yet she smiled because it was expected, and she always did as expected. Her life was nothing if not bound by duty.

Oh, she liked Marie. Well…she liked her well enough. Marie's mother had been Cordelia's mother's companion and most trusted friend. Marie was only a few years older than Cordelia, and the two had practically grown up together within the castle's walls. Always kind, Marie had guided her through the pitfalls of life at the palace, and through the years she had become the closest thing to a sister Cordelia had. Cordelia had even served as maid of honor at Marie's wedding when she married the Comte de Marseille.

Yet Cordelia never forgot the truth. For all Marie's affections and concerns, the comtesse was *not* her sister, and she remained at court only because Uncle Ernest allowed it. As such, Marie could never be completely trusted.

"You look so much like your mother," the comtesse murmured. "The same fine bones, the same hair..." Her eyes softened as she rested her cheek against Cordelia's as if they were both seeing her mother's reflection instead of their own. "You even have the same little flecks of gold and green in your eyes." She smiled at the memory. "When Prince Reginald met your mother, her eyes were the very first thing he noticed. He wanted to stare into them, but the only way he'd be able to do that was if he danced with her. So he asked her for a waltz. By the time the orchestra finished playing, the two of them were hopelessly in love."

Cordelia's chest ached at the familiar fairy-tale story. She missed her parents so much! She'd been only fourteen when they both died in a shipwreck, and their deaths came so unexpectedly that the entire country had been plunged into shock. Thank goodness she'd had Uncle Ernest and Aunt Wilhelmina to become her guardians. They loved her as if she were their own and showed her how to behave at court. At fourteen, what had she known about being a princess?

At *twenty*-four, how little she still knew.

"Theirs was a true fairy tale," Marie continued. "And who

knows what life has in store for you, hmm?" She straightened one of Cordelia's chestnut curls and smiled conspiratorially at her in the mirror. "Perhaps your heart's prince will ask you to dance at the ball, too."

Dread pinched Cordelia's stomach. Oh, she was certain she'd be asked to dance by a prince, all right. *Three* of them. Just as she was certain that her heart wouldn't be in any of those waltzes.

"Try to enjoy yourself this evening." Marie fussed with Cordelia's necklace. "And remember that the British royals are your family."

"*Distant* family." So distant, in fact, that she'd had to consult the historical record to find their connection—and to discover if there might be any impediments to marrying one of them. Any possible impediments at all.

Unfortunately, her hopes at finding any had been dashed.

"Family is family," a deep voice scolded gently from across the room. "Best to remember that while we're here."

Uncle Ernest entered without announcement or knocking. His gold chain of office bounced against his bright white waistcoat with each step he took. The gold medals pinned to the left side of his black jacket shimmered beneath the chandeliers and flapped in time with both his chain and jacket tails.

Good heavens…he looked like a jeweler in mourning. How had she never noticed before how grossly inappropriate those medals were when her uncle hadn't served a single day in Monrovia's military the way her father had? Before he inherited the crown, Uncle Ernest had been appointed secretary of war, but only because Cordelia's father had been too busy running the country to also handle the day-to-day needs of the military. Her uncle had never been close to any battle, army or navy.

"Given our own family history," he reminded her as he approached, "I would hate to think, in a time of grief, that any family member might draw such petty lines of demarcation."

The comtesse smiled at his arrival and curtsied deeply.

Keeping her face carefully neutral at his chastisement, Cordelia rose slowly to her feet and turned toward her uncle. She folded her hands deferentially in front of her and nodded respectfully. "Uncle Ernest."

"Uncle Monrovia." He smiled with that mild correction. "While we are in England, you must address me formally."

Cordelia parted her lips to question that, but after a sideways glance at the comtesse, who faintly shook her head, she knew not to argue. "Of course."

"I came to check on you." He rested his hands on Cordelia's shoulders and placed a kiss on her forehead. It was the same gesture he'd done since she was a child.

She wished she could ask him to stop. She was a grown woman, for heaven's sake! But she also knew how much Uncle Ernest cared for her and how hurt he would be if she did.

He took her chin in his fingers to tilt her head slightly from left to right as he inspected her. "Are you well?"

"Yes." She frowned, slightly bewildered. "Why would you think otherwise?"

He released her chin and stepped back. "Because it was

a long journey, and I am certain it's fatigued you." Concern darkened his face. "I also promised Wilhelmina that I would look after you and not let any harm come to you." His lips curled as he confided, "She'll flail me into next summer if you so much as develop a cough."

Cordelia mustered a smile. The palace had thought it best that her aunt Wilhelmina remained in Monrovia for this trip, claiming it would be too stressful on her aunt's health. Cordelia suspected ulterior motives. In Wilhelmina's absence, she would be forced to interact more with Queen Charlotte and the royal princesses and so give her future in-laws a good opportunity to scrutinize her.

"I am certain no one expects you to linger tonight," her uncle added. "Your formal duties will end once the prince regent makes your introduction to his guests and family."

What Uncle Ernest actually meant was her introduction to the regent's bachelor brothers. After they met her, they would certainly want her gone so they could discuss the rest of her visit among themselves. Or draw straws to decide who would marry her.

She dutifully replied, "Thank you, Uncle. I appreciate the opportunity to retire early." Then, seizing the moment, she dared to ask, "Would it be possible for me to explore London while we're here? I'm certain Devereaux can carve out time between…" When his lips stretched into a patronizing smile, her voice trailed off.

There was no point in finishing her request.

"You are Her Serene Highness Princess Cordelia of Monrovia," he said, although she certainly didn't need to be told that. Every day of her life served as a reminder of who she was. "Your duty is first and always to our country, even when you are out of it."

How well she knew that! In other words, she would be bound to Devereaux's schedule for every moment of her visit and at the side of one royal duke or another.

Duty…sometimes she simply wanted to scream at the thought.

Yet there was nothing she could do about it. Her life belonged to crown and country, and for her, that meant adhering to a grueling schedule of appointments she did not make with people she did not know, dinners and balls, receptions and ceremonies, until she thought she might simply go mad from it all.

But what other choice did she have? She was born a royal, and she would die a royal. The days in between would *never* be her own.

Uncle Ernest squeezed her shoulders. "You must trust me, my dear. I have planned this trip to our best advantage, and I will not risk any threat to our future. The monarchies of Monrovia and England both depend on its outcome."

"I know."

He pulled back and stared down at her with such a somber expression that she trembled. "Do you? Do you fully understand its implications?"

Her heart skipped. He didn't mean a royal marriage. He meant her father's legacy.

If what her father had done during the last years of his reign ever came to light, the scandal would consume

Monrovia and destroy the throne. Her family would become outcasts, considered criminals and murderers, most likely deposed—*if* Monrovia didn't fall into civil war first, because half its people would still lay down their lives in loyalty to her father, despite everything.

Marriage was the best way to save Monrovia. Being seen as a dutiful bride would keep Cordelia and her family in the hearts of the Monrovian people and mitigate any potential scandal. Moreover, marriage into Britain's royal family would be like granting a royal seal of approval to the House of Renaldi from the most important, most powerful monarchy still reigning in Europe.

Of course, she also needed to bear a son, one who might someday assume the crown of Monrovia, and if she married a royal duke, then possibly the crown of Great Britain as well. Their two monarchies would be entwined, both made stronger by the presence of the other. Their continued reign would be ensured for another generation.

Cordelia pushed down a creeping feeling of dread. She knew what was expected of her in marriage and childbirth. She'd resigned herself to it long ago.

She just didn't want it to be with one of the royal dukes.

Yet she answered, "Yes, I understand."

"Good." He squeezed her shoulders reassuringly, as if he knew they were about to sag in resignation. "Our first duty is always to Monrovia, not to ourselves."

"I know."

With a pleased smile, he dropped his hands away, clapped them together happily at her acquiescence, and stepped back.

Cordelia inhaled deeply. She hadn't realized until right then that she'd been holding her breath.

"I came to tell you that the start of the ceremony has been delayed." He retreated toward the door. "Remain here. We'll send word when we're ready for you."

"Thank you," she said quietly. As he left, she turned and caught her reflection in the mirror. As always, her posture was perfect and regal, right down to the way she held her tiara-capped head. Every inch a princess. How many countless hours had she spent walking through the palace balancing books on her head and holding water in spoons to learn perfect poise and deportment? "Far too many."

"Pardon?" The comtesse frowned.

"Nothing." She smiled at Marie and gestured at the door. "You should follow Uncle."

"Are you certain?" The glimmer in Marie's eyes told Cordelia she wanted to do exactly that.

"No need for you to remain here." A thought popped into her head. "And you can tell me what the guests are like when you return for me. Especially the royal dukes."

"That is a good idea." Marie smiled and curtsied. "Your Highness."

No, Cordelia decided as she watched the comtesse leave the room and close the door after herself. What was a good idea was finding a way to carve out a moment's peace for herself.

Cordelia let her shoulders ease down at finally being alone and removed her tiara to set it aside until Uncle Ernest returned for her.

She approached the wide window to take a small glimpse of the city around her. She stared out at the street where dozens of carriages jammed the wide avenue in front of Carlton House. How she wished she were down in the tangled mess with them! How she wished she were *anywhere* but here.

What she wanted… "To be normal," she whispered and reached up to play with her necklace.

She twisted her fingers in the chain as she watched lady after elegant lady and gentleman after grand gentleman exit the carriages and enter Carlton House in a rustle of silks, satins, ostrich feathers, and jewels. They were all coming here to look at her, she knew, as if she were nothing more than an animal in a menagerie.

Just once, just for a little while…*normal*. Or at least not a princess with the weight of two monarchies resting on her shoulders.

For a few minutes, at least, she could put the burden out of her mind and enjoy watching the congested mess unfolding below her. She fiddled with the little clasp on her necklace and laughed at the spectacle. Goodness, were those *swans* in those giant cages? That was exactly how she felt, like a bird trapped in a gilded cage. And that woman in bright pink with ostrich feathers standing three feet—

Snap! The fragile clasp broke. The necklace chain slipped through her fingers as she made a frantic grab for it and landed on the rug at her feet.

She rolled her eyes. "Oh, bother!"

As she bent down to retrieve it, she heard the door open

behind her. Her cheeks flushed with embarrassment. *Perfect.* Now Devereaux or the comtesse would scold her for not being more careful.

"It's only a necklace," she called out as she picked it up from the floor. With a chagrined smile, she straightened. "Thank goodness it happened here instead of in front of—"

A hand clamped over her mouth before she could scream.

Three

Clayton snatched up a champagne flute from the tray of a passing footman and lifted it to his mouth. He scanned the room, searching for any ally in the crush.

The main audience room was filled with aristocrats and politicians of all stripes, including Wellington in his field marshal's uniform and at least two of the royal dukes. Dozens of footmen carried trays of champagne flutes through the jostling crowd, while men stood in groups like gossipy old hens and the women fought to keep bored expressions from their faces. Undoubtedly, though, they were all thankful that the gathering was being held here at Carlton House instead of the palace where court dress was required.

God knew he was.

He spied Marcus Braddock and blew out a grateful breath that he wasn't alone in this sea of serpents.

The former general turned duke—and one of Clayton's best friends—stood in the rear of the room and apart from the crowd as if he, too, were contemplating the fastest route to the nearest exit to slip out unseen. But he would never be able to hide his commanding presence, here or anywhere in the empire.

"General," Clayton greeted him as he arrived at Marcus's

side. He turned to follow his friend's gaze toward the raised dais at the front of the room where the speeches would be made.

"You're late," Marcus commented.

"I'm lucky to be here at all." Clayton swept another glance around the crowded room. "And where are Sinclair, Merritt, and Pearce? Aren't they required to be here, too? We shouldn't be the only ones forced to suffer."

"They weren't invited. The palace is keeping tonight's welcome ceremony to a small, cozy affair of only four hundred or so peers, government officials, and their wives."

Clayton grimaced at that bit of sarcasm, then finished off his champagne in a single swallow and snagged a fresh glass from a passing footman.

"Relax, will you?" Marcus urged quietly. "You're behaving as if this is your first visit to Carlton House."

Clayton looked around the grand room with its red carpets, marble columns, and gold accents. Inside it gathered the most important people in the British empire…and him. He tugged at his jacket sleeves from nervous habit. He'd never felt comfortable at Carlton House, Buckingham House, St James's Palace—well, no place where royals might be lurking in the woodwork, actually. "Hopefully, it will be my last."

"Not a chance. Whitehall is grooming you to be the next Home Secretary."

"Not a chance," Clayton repeated pointedly. Men like him didn't rise to the level of king's cabinet, and everyone in the room knew it, too.

No, he was here tonight for the welcome ceremony for

the royal visit of the princely House of Renaldi for one reason and one reason only—

The regent had forced him.

"Why wouldn't they want you as Home Secretary?" Marcus pressed. "You're perfect for it. You're a general now."

"Exactly." Clayton tapped Marcus on the shoulder with his glass to emphasize his point. "I'm a soldier, not a peer, and the king's ministers are all peers."

"The regent will surely make you one."

"I've done nothing to earn it."

"You think Lord Sidmouth earned his title?" Marcus accepted a glass of champagne from the tray of a passing footman. "Don't think for one moment that every man here isn't wondering who you are and what you've done to snag the regent's attention." Marcus narrowed his eyes on his old friend, the same way he'd done during all those years on the Continent when they'd discussed battle strategy before a fight. "What *did* you do, by the way?"

Stopped Scepter from assassinating the prince regent and prime minister, covered up the incident with a riot, and did it all well enough that no one but the regent and Home Secretary ever found out, including you and the men of the Armory...

Clayton shrugged. "Nothing special."

He hid that lie by looking down to fuss with his cravat. He wasn't allowed to tell anyone how he'd saved the regent's life, not even his best friend. He'd surely end up in Newgate if he did.

When Marcus silently arched a brow at his attempted deflection, Clayton shook his head and added, "I only did my job."

That was the God's honest truth. But just like that, he'd been catapulted in status above half the aristocracy in England.

"If they offer the position to you, you can't refuse it," Marcus reminded him. "You've a duty to accept it."

Duty. An invisible weight settled on Clayton's shoulders. His entire life had been devoted to duty of one kind or another. Duty in providing for his mother after his father's execution. Duty to his country while serving in the army and carrying out his superiors' orders. Duty to the Home Office in carrying out the missions given to him by the Home Secretary. Duty to his father in uncovering the truth. Now duty to the regent in attending his parties when he'd rather have been anywhere else in the world. Duty colored every aspect of his life, every move he made.

Tonight simply epitomized it. The more he succeeded in bringing honor back to the Elliott name, the fewer choices he had regarding his own life. His Home Office career was simply the latest manifestation of it.

Unfortunately, Marcus wasn't wrong. Clayton stood in a prime position to succeed Henry Addington, Viscount Sidmouth, as Home Secretary. It would only take one more grand success—or the death of King George—to put him there. The regent would appoint him then if for no other reason than to annoy the Tories.

"Most likely," Clayton explained, "I was only invited tonight because the Home Secretary is suffering another bout of gout and couldn't attend himself." He grinned and lifted his glass in a mocking toast. "My job tonight is to do nothing more than stand here and look pretty."

Marcus frowned and thankfully ignored that last bit of nonsense. "Since when is the Home Office concerned with royal visits? Why wasn't this duty given to the Foreign Office?"

"I suppose because the visit has little to do with state business. The Monrovian prince has come to England to pay his condolences for Princess Charlotte's death." Clayton was happy to have the conversation anywhere but on himself and added thoughtfully, "Yet I'd bet my last penny that Monrovia will be asking for trade agreements within a fortnight."

"And I'd bet mine that it isn't a trade agreement Monrovia wants but a wedding." When Clayton glanced sideways at him in surprise, Marcus explained, "Prince Ernest brought his niece along for the visit. She'll make a perfect wife for one of the royal dukes."

"So soon after the princess's death?" Even though the official mourning period had ended, one look around the room proved the country was still in mourning. Lavender dresses draped from most of the women, and the men sported black armbands, above the elbow for most but below for those who held military commissions. Clayton knew it wasn't all for show. The English people had dearly loved the young princess. She'd been a breath of fresh air compared to her debauched father and absent mother.

But he also knew Princess Charlotte's death in childbirth had claimed two generations of presumptive heirs in a single blow. Great Britain stood at the edge of a succession crisis if one of the bachelor royal dukes didn't discard his mistress and marry. Soon.

"There's precedent," Marcus answered. "The mourning period for Princess Amelia lasted only from November to March."

"Yes," Clayton murmured, not wanting to be overhead by anyone else as the room grew more crowded around them, "but her death also drove the king completely mad."

Marcus stared into his glass. "I doubt he's been told this time."

And Clayton doubted it would make any difference even if he had, if the rumors of the king's most recent behavior could be believed.

Marcus commented, "There's already been a flurry of bets placed in the book at White's on how many summer weddings the royal dukes will subject themselves to."

"And?"

"I've got the Duke of Clarence by Whitsun."

Clayton smothered a chuckle by raising his glass to his lips.

"And your plans?" Marcus asked.

"Does it matter? I serve at the pleasure of the monarch and his family, whomever they are."

"Even Prince Augustus?"

Clayton paused to reconsider. "Perhaps *not* Augustus."

With a knowing smile, Marcus clarified, "I *meant* what are your plans for the future? You can't keep serving England forever."

"Why not? It's going well so far." Sarcasm lightly touched Clayton's voice. "Haven't you heard? I'm a general now."

All traces of Marcus's amusement faded despite Clayton's teasing. "But it's wearing on you. We've all noticed."

Clayton stiffened, then dismissed his friend's concern with a shake of his head. "I can't retire. I haven't done everything I want to do yet."

"What's left?"

Reform Parliament and how the Commons represented cities like Manchester and Salisbury. Change the army's structure to reward men based on service and success rather than whatever rank they bought their way into. Stop Scepter once and for all, and make certain the bastards never came back...

Redeem my father.

But he deflected by joking, "What would you have me do instead—politics, the church, business?" He laughed and lifted the glass to his lips, mumbling around the rim, "Retire to the countryside and be a gentleman farmer with the sheep and pigs?"

"Marriage."

Clayton choked on his champagne, so startled that he spilled part of his drink down the front of his waistcoat.

"Good Lord," he forced out between coughs. "I'd rather be with the pigs and sheep!"

"Ah, so it's Parliament for you then." The amused glimmer left Marcus's eyes as they fixed on Clayton's waistcoat. "Is that blood on your front?"

Christ. That scuffle with Burton... He lied, "Punch."

Marcus's mouth twisted at the obvious fib. "Better take care of it. You know how the regent feels about clothes." He gestured toward the doors leading out of the reception hall to a series of drawing and retiring rooms beyond. He had the decency to avoid asking Clayton how it had gotten there. "And hurry. The ceremony's about to start."

Clayton blew out a hard breath and left the room. Clearly, he was not made for life at the palace.

He flung open the door of the first drawing room he came to and strode inside.

"Stop!"

Clayton froze. Every muscle in his body tensed instantly.

At the edge of the room, a uniformed footman held a knife to a young woman's throat. A very beautiful young woman.

Four

CORDELIA'S HEART POUNDED SO FIERCELY WITH FEAR that the roar of it in her ears was deafening.

"Please…" She clutched at the arm that wrapped around her upper chest and held the knife blade against her throat even though she knew she wasn't strong enough to push her attacker away. Unable to find her voice in her terror, she whispered, "Please don't hurt me."

The attacker tightened his hold.

"Let her go," the blond gentleman in the doorway said quietly. His voice remained calm despite the way his body tensed, as if he were a spring about to release. He ignored Cordelia and kept his attention fixed on the man behind her.

But her attacker's hold remained as strong as ever. He had no intention of letting her go.

The blond took a single step forward into the room.

"Stay back!" her attacker warned.

Cordelia let out a soft cry as the man pulled the knife away from her throat and jabbed it toward the blond. His arm around her chest slid up beneath her chin and pressed chokingly against her throat as he held her in front of him like a shield.

The blond stranger stopped, but his right hand slid

beneath his jacket. "You haven't hurt her yet," he commented as if discussing nothing more threatening than the weather. "If you let her go unharmed, I'll let you leave. You can get away, and no one will ever know that you were here. I'll let you live."

Her attacker laughed, a maniacal sound that curled icy fingers of terror down Cordelia's spine. "You think I wasn't prepared to lose my life the moment I arrived here tonight?"

Oh God... She was as good as dead! "Please," she begged as hot tears gathered at her lashes. "Please don't hurt me. I won't—"

"Shut up!" Her attacker yanked her against him and tightened his arm against her throat.

The blond man took another quick stride forward and slid his hand further beneath his jacket.

"Stop where you are!" The attacker sliced his knife through the air. "I'll kill her—I promise you!"

"If you do, then I'll kill you. But you'd rather live," the blond gentleman replied, just as impossibly calm as before. He behaved as if he'd faced situations like this so many times in the past that talking to a man with a knife was as easy as negotiating the price for a new pair of boots. "There's no shame in that. I'd want to live, too, if I were you."

He moved forward another step. Not once had his green eyes glanced at Cordelia.

"Events didn't go as planned tonight," the blond gentleman continued. As he inched across the drawing room, Cordelia realized that he was just as large as he'd seemed when he'd filled up the doorway with his broad shoulders and tall frame. "But you can still escape with your life. Just let her go and step away, and I'll let you leave. You won't even have to put down your knife."

The attacker paused at the offer as if considering his options.

"Please," Cordelia begged, her voice hoarse from the pressure against her throat. "Please do as he says…"

Her attacker shook his head and growled out, "I'm dead either way!"

Cordelia flashed numb, and a soft cry passed her lips. This man couldn't be persuaded not to kill her. No one could save her! She had to save herself.

"Scepter," the blond stranger muttered as if the word were a shibboleth.

The attacker froze.

"You're part of it, aren't you?" the gentleman guessed. When her attacker didn't answer, he continued, "Who sent you here tonight? Someone had to have let you into Carlton House and given you a footman's uniform."

The man snarled, "I'll never tell."

"Which peer? Which member of Parliament or Whitehall official? I know it's one of them. It has to be someone connected to the palace, someone high-ranking enough for his orders not to be questioned."

"You know nothing!"

"So much more than you realize." The blond man's voice lowered to an icy drawl. "And if you cooperate and tell me who sent you, I'll make certain they can never harm you."

The attacker paused to consider the offer.

Cordelia needed to act...*now!* She clenched her necklace in her hand, and with a fierce cry, she stabbed it viciously at her attacker's face. The sharp edges of the pendant cut into his cheek and lips.

He let out a shrieking curse as blood seeped from the long, jagged rip across his cheek and shoved her away as she attempted to stab him again.

Freed from his gasp, Cordelia darted away. He lunged and thrust his knife at her. She flung up her arm to block the blow. The sharp blade sliced through her satin glove and into her flesh. She screamed, but the attacker lunged again—

A gunshot rang out.

Her attacker froze, then staggered back a step. A red stain bloomed across the crisp white waistcoat of his palace livery. Slowly, he looked down at it, his face suddenly pale and bewildered. He swayed on his feet, then dropped to the floor, dead.

Behind him, the blond man stood with his arm straight out. Smoke curled up from the end of his spent pistol.

Cordelia sank toward the floor as the blond gentleman dropped his gun and rushed forward to catch her in his arms.

"Who are you?" she managed to choke out. She struggled to keep herself from fainting away completely as the room spun around her and black spots flashed before her eyes.

"No one important." He carried her to the settee and placed her carefully onto the cushions. Then he clawed at his neck to untie his cravat and tore it off. "But *you* must be, or he wouldn't have come after you like that."

She stared blankly at her arm as dull pain began to throb from her elbow to her fingertips. "He wanted to kidnap me..."

When he began to remove her glove, pain shot up her arm and landed in her chest with an alarming thud. She gasped and tried to pull away.

The blond stranger held firm to her arm and persisted in stripping off her glove. The white satin was soaked scarlet with blood. "No," he countered softly. "He had no plans to kidnap you."

Stunned, she didn't try to fight him as he quickly wrapped the cravat around her forearm and tied it off with a tight knot to stanch the bleeding. The pain pulsed through her, growing sharper with every pounding heartbeat. "Then…why?"

His green eyes rose from her arm and seemed to bore into hers. "He wanted to murder you."

"*Oh God!*" She pressed her good hand against her belly and turned her face away. She was going to be sick!

He took her chin in his fingers and gently turned her back to look at him. "Listen to me," he urged in a controlled but intense and insistent voice. "In ten seconds, every guard in Carlton House is going to storm into this room. They're going to arrest me first and ask questions later. You have to tell them exactly what happened and stop them from taking me away, understand?"

Her eyes darted to the dead body lying crumpled on the floor, and her stomach roiled. "I–I can't… They'll never believe…"

"Oh yes, you can." His eyes shone with determination. "A brave woman like you who put up a fight like that—you didn't even faint."

"I might yet."

A deep chuckle rose from his throat. "What's your name?"

"Cordelia," she answered quietly.

"A beautiful name for a beautiful woman." The compliment did little to reassure her, especially as the pounding of running boots in the marble hall grew closer. "Remember, Cordelia. I'm counting on you to save me."

"Why would you—" The aching in her arm began to thump as fiercely as her heart, each pulse of blood shooting agonizingly up her arm and into her chest. She pulled in a deep breath to tamp down the pain and tried again. "Even if they arrest you, you'll be set free in the morning. They'll only question you, and—"

He placed his fingers to her lips to silence her. Intensity radiated from him. "If they take me away tonight, I won't live to see the dawn."

He cupped her face in his hands. Then, stunning the daylights out of her, he leaned in and touched his lips to hers. The gentle kiss jolted her attention back to the urgency of the moment.

"Save me, Cordelia."

Guards burst into the room. They rushed forward, stepping over the dead body to grab the blond man by both arms. He didn't fight them as they yanked him to his feet and pulled him toward the door, yet his eyes never left hers.

Cordelia sat up. Fear and uncertainty gripped her, but so did a blossoming courage. He believed in her, this stranger who had no idea who she was. He'd called her beautiful and brave, said his life lay in her hands…

"Stop," she called out. "Leave him here." She stood,

holding her wounded arm in front of her. Her spine straightened, and she lifted her head with as much imperial dignity as she could summon. "Stop—I order you!"

The guards stopped and turned back to stare at her.

"I am Her Serene Highness Princess Cordelia of Monrovia." She leveled an imperious look at them that brooked no argument or disobedience. "This man saved my life. And I *command* you to release him this instant!"

The blond gentleman smiled with relief as the guards stared at her, blinked with startled confusion, and then hesitatingly let him go. Silently, he mouthed, "Thank you."

Five

Marcus looked down at the dead body at his feet. "I leave you alone for two minutes, and you kill a man in the prince regent's drawing room."

"I tried not to," Clayton returned, mirroring Marcus's low voice and crossed arms. "But he didn't cooperate."

Both men contemplated the dead man who still lay on the floor where he'd fallen. He couldn't be removed until the welcome ceremony was over, all the guests gone, and the servants sent to their quarters. But at least he and Marcus had thought to cover the body with one of the drapes from the window. Thank God the dark blue damask was too thick for blood to soak through.

The ceremony was underway in the main reception rooms, but the guests were oblivious to what had occurred here. The sound of Clayton's pistol had been hidden by the orchestra, and the drawing room was far enough away from the reception area that the guests didn't see the guards come running. Under Marcus's orders, the master of ceremonies announced regretfully that Princess Cordelia was exhausted from her travels and would be unable to join them this evening. The crowd was disappointed, yet the ceremony proceeded on as planned, with footmen lubricating the guests with trays of expensive champagne, claret, and port that further dulled their senses.

At the end of the evening, they would all return home drunk, filled with dreams for power and influence, and none the wiser that someone had been killed tonight only a few yards from where they'd stood.

"Saved the princess, though," Clayton added.

He lifted his gaze to Cordelia as she sat on a settee on the far side of the room.

Two ladies-in-waiting fussed over her in an attempt to ease the princess's nerves, but he could see from even this far away that they were only upsetting her more. One woman in jewels and a fine maroon satin dress that boldly proclaimed rank and privilege sat beside her on the settee and held her hand, but Clayton could tell from the way Cordelia leaned away that the princess didn't want the woman's solace. The other woman—tall and skinny with a notebook tucked beneath her arm and dressed in far less regal attire—stood beside her and attempted to wave a bottle of some noxious-smelling concoction under Cordelia's nose.

To the princess's credit, though, she waved away the unwanted stuff. She was in no danger of fainting, Clayton knew. She hadn't swooned yet at what she'd been through tonight, and the worst was over.

For now.

As if feeling his attention on her, Cordelia lifted her eyes and met his gaze. Her expression was carefully controlled, but she couldn't hide the lingering fear in her big brown eyes or the incredulity that someone would want to kill her.

The well-dressed woman at her side called the princess's attention back to her with a quiet word, and Cordelia lowered her gaze to her arm as it rested across her lap. It was freshly stitched and bandaged by the regent's physician, who hadn't been sworn to secrecy by Clayton and Marcus so much as threatened to within an inch of his life not to speak a word of what he'd seen tonight.

"But I didn't know she was the princess," Clayton mumbled thoughtfully. "And if *I* didn't know, then..."

"Then a footman wouldn't have known either," Marcus finished beneath his breath.

"Unless he was told." Clayton stared grimly at the lump beneath the drape and put words to his deepest fear. "Scepter's back."

"What proof do you have?"

"None." Marcus knew as well as Clayton that everything they'd heard about Scepter in the past few months pointed to its demise. "Yet."

Clayton knelt beside the dead man and pulled back the drape just far enough to search the body. He yanked aside the old-fashioned collar and frilly neckcloth of the regent's household livery to search for the key-shaped tattoo worn by Scepter's men.

He half undressed the corpse as he searched for a key symbol anywhere on the body or hidden in the livery, yet he came up with nothing. No tattoo, no pin...no key anywhere. The man was unmarked.

"Not Scepter, then," Marcus said quietly so the women wouldn't overhear.

Damnation. Clayton tossed the drape back into place and rose to his full height. "He was part of it, I'm certain."

"Did he admit that?"

"No." Clayton bit back a curse at how feeble that answer made his argument sound. "But I saw his face when I mentioned Scepter. He recognized the name." He winced. That argument wasn't any better.

The way Marcus lifted a doubting brow proved it.

"Someone inside the palace is working for them." Clayton tugged at his sleeves. He'd mostly lost that old habit since leaving active service, but standing here beside his former general, once more discussing the enemy and with a dead body at their feet, made him feel as if he were back in the wars. "Someone who was able to hire him as a footman so he would have the uniform and not be noticed, who told him the layout of the rooms and exactly where the guards were positioned." A bitter taste covered his tongue. "Someone who knew when the princess would be alone and that the orchestra would hide her cries for help. Only Scepter could do this."

Marcus tensed. "You're saying someone in the prince regent's own household could have—"

"No. Not staff or servants." Clayton's chest tightened as he remembered Burton's words...*snobs and nobs.* "I'm saying someone much higher than that."

"Who?"

"No idea." He gave his sleeves one final tug. "But I plan to find out."

He turned on his heel and crossed the long drawing room

toward Princess Cordelia. Her pale face was drawn, and her hands trembled as she held them folded in her lap. The grim press of her lips grew firmer as he approached, and her slender shoulders rose and fell as she pulled in deep breaths to steady herself.

"Your Serene Highness." He stopped in front of her and gave a formal bow. "Might I have a word with you?" He looked pointedly between the two ladies-in-waiting. "In private."

The woman in satin and jewels spoke up. "That is not at all—"

"Of course." Cordelia never looked away from Clayton's face as she rested her good hand on the woman's arm and gently silenced her. "Comtesse, if you and Lady Devereaux would give us a moment?" When the woman wasn't convinced, the princess added firmly, "Please."

The comtesse grudgingly relented. "As you wish, Your Highness."

She rose and gave a suspicious glare at Clayton even as she lowered into a curtsy for the princess. Then she backed away to the far side of the drawing room. The skinny woman with the notebook followed in her wake.

"They mean well," Cordelia explained with a chagrined glance toward the two women. They huddled together, surely discussing him and wondering who he was and what he could possibly want with the princess. "They only want to protect me."

"So do I," he returned gently. "And thank you."

She gave a faint shake of her head. "I think they feel guilty that they left me alone and allowed that man to…" Her voice trailed off.

He didn't need her thoughts going to that dark place and changed the direction of conversation. "I *meant* thank you for saving my life tonight."

Her lips parted slightly to question that, but instead she smiled so weakly with relief that he could barely see it. Yet a smile *was* there, and he took hope in it.

She countered, "Thank you for saving mine."

He wasn't certain he was done with that just yet. "I need to ask you some questions about what happened tonight, if you don't mind." He paused. "In *complete* privacy."

She hesitated. He knew what he was asking was wholly inappropriate and simply not done. No respectable unmarried miss would allow herself to be alone in a room with a man unchaperoned. But then, most respectable unmarried misses weren't taken hostage by armed intruders, those empty rooms didn't have dead bodies lying on their floors, the men weren't Home Office undersecretaries, and the young ladies weren't princesses.

In this circumstance, he was willing to bend the rules of propriety. Hell, he was willing to break them to bits and throw them out the window. Her life depended on it.

She must have realized it, too, because she slowly nodded her consent.

Clayton looked over his shoulder at Marcus, then pointedly moved his gaze to the two ladies-in-waiting and jerked his head toward the door.

Understanding the silent communication that had made

them such good comrades in arms across the Continent, the former general approached the two women and very gentlemanly—yet insistently—escorted them from the room. Marcus patiently ignored their protests and concerns and closed the door behind them, leaving Clayton alone with the princess.

"Now then." With his most reassuring smile, he sat on the settee next to her. An inexplicable urge to protect her gripped him, and he carefully reached for her wounded arm. He frowned at the bandage as he examined the doctor's handiwork. "Let's start with this."

Six

CORDELIA TENSED. SHE SHOULD HAVE PULLED HER ARM away, but she simply couldn't make herself. He held it too tenderly and brushed his fingertips across the bandage too soothingly to deny herself that comfort.

The most she could manage was a dubious "My arm is fine."

His eyes flicked up to hers in recognition of that lie, but he didn't challenge her directly on it. Instead, he drew a gentle finger over the bandage that covered her entire fore-arm from wrist to elbow, but one—thankfully—she could cover with long sleeves or gloves. The cut wasn't very long or deep, yet the overcautious physician had tried to mummify her anyway.

"How many stitches?" he asked. A line of concentration formed between his brows.

She winced at the memory of the physician's needle. "*Too* many."

His frown faded into a look of empathy. "Most likely, it will scar, but the wound looked clean. There shouldn't be any infection. The doctor gave you powder for the pain, I assume?" When she nodded, he ordered gently, "Make cer-tain you take it, but only if you need it and not more than necessary. The palace already has one princess addicted to the stuff. I wouldn't want another."

She studied him closely. "How do you know so much about knife wounds?"

"I was a soldier in the wars. Fought at Waterloo, in fact." He absently checked the tightness of the bandage. "I saw more bayonet wounds there than I ever want to see again."

She turned her gaze to the dead body. "Is the army where you learned to...?" Her voice trailed off. She couldn't bring herself to say it.

"Kill a man?" he finished grimly. "Yes."

She swallowed hard to remove the knot in her throat. "Who are you?"

"Clayton Elliott." He smiled, but she could see there was no pleasure behind his expression.

"No," she pressed, searching his face for answers. He was tall and handsome, broad, muscular...*dangerous*. "Who *are* you?"

"I'm an undersecretary for the Home Office." From the way he'd acted tonight, she suspected he was so much more than a mere undersecretary. But before she could question him further, he confessed, "I'm not connected to the palace. I was ordered to attend tonight's welcome ceremony by the prince regent. That's the only reason I'm here."

She sighed out, "Me, too."

He smiled in appreciation at her attempted humor, yet she could easily see he was still preoccupied. She knew why. The reason lay beneath a blue damask drape less than twenty feet away. "Then we have something in common."

"But *I* didn't bring a pistol," she added pointedly.

His smile faded, and she felt the loss of its warmth like the sun disappearing behind a cloud on a summer's day. "Next time, perhaps you should." He paused, and an unspoken warning filled the silence. "He tried to murder you tonight, Your Highness. Why would anyone want to harm you?"

"I don't know." She began to tremble as her fear returned. But Mr. Elliott seemed disappointed by her answer, so she repeated emphatically, "Honestly, I have no idea. No one has ever before tried—" She choked off. "I'm not that important."

His eyes were somber. "He thought you were."

"I don't know why. I've never seen that man before. I–I haven't spoken to anyone since we arrived in England except those who came with me from Monrovia. I swear—I don't know!"

"I believe you. But I still want to keep you safe." He slowly released her arm and trailed his fingertips soothingly across the bandage as he let her go. "Do you mind if we just talk for a bit?"

If he worked for the Home Office, then he worked directly for her cousin the regent, and she had no choice in the matter. Yet she nodded her consent because it was expected.

He stood and crossed the room to a mahogany cabinet in the corner, calling out to her over his shoulder, "Is this your first visit to England?"

"Yes."

"Whose idea was it?" He opened the top cabinet doors and revealed a crowded selection of crystal decanters containing liquor of all colors. The names of their contents were etched into silver tags draped around each decanter's neck on tiny chains. "Yours?"

"No, my uncle Ernest—I mean, Uncle Monrovia." She'd been terrified tonight, wounded, and nearly killed, yet she could never forget who she was or her family's duty to the crown. "He felt we should pay our respects in person since our two families are related."

"How?"

"We're distant cousins through Elizabeth Stuart, daughter of King James the First. My fourth great-grandmother was Princess Henriette Marie, older sister to Sophia of Hanover."

"James the First?" He selected one of the decanters and removed the stopper to splash the dark liquid into two glasses. "That's a long way back."

She shrugged. "It's the same line of succession as the current British royals, actually. Theirs is just a bit further down the family tree." She added beneath her breath, "Low-hanging fruit."

She caught her breath. Oh, she shouldn't have said something like that! But when he chuckled softly at her slip, her unease melted away.

He asked, "Did the rest of your immediate family come with you to England?"

"Aunt Wilhelmina remained behind in Monrovia."

"And the others?"

"I have no other family. Well, none except for distant cousins scattered across the Continent. My uncle and aunt are childless." Her chest tightened with a pang of grief, but she inexplicably felt compelled to tell him, "And my parents died ten years ago. A storm came up unexpectedly while they were on their way to Italy. Their ship wrecked, and they drowned."

He paused as he returned the decanter to offer her a sympathetic glance over his shoulder. "I'm sorry."

"Thank you." Over the years, she'd learned to manage the pain of their loss, if never eliminate it, and gave the dutiful answer, "I'm grateful to have my uncle. When Papa died, he became the sovereign prince and kept Monrovia on a strong path forward."

He closed the cabinet. "Why didn't you inherit the crown?"

"Monrovia follows patrilineal primogeniture. The crown only passes to male relatives."

"But your uncle has no sons." He carried both glasses back to her. "What happens when he dies?"

"The Crown Council will choose an heir. If I'm married and have a son by then, he'll most likely become the sovereign prince."

He stopped in front of her and stared somberly down at her.

She shook her head. "I know what you're thinking, and it's impossible."

"Impossible that the next person in line to the Monrovian throne would want you dead so he can claim it for himself?"

"Yes." That definitive answer brooked no misunderstanding. "The nearest male relative is my father's cousin Maximilian, but he can never become crown prince because his mother married without my grandfather's consent.

Members of the sovereign family must have the reigning prince's consent to marry, or they and their children are removed from the line of succession, the same as if they were born illegitimate." She gestured her hand to indicate the royal residence around them. "You need look no further than your own royal family for examples of that."

That was part of the reason why her cousin the prince regent had thrown over the love of his life for Caroline of Brunswick, why the future of the British monarchy had been plunged into such uncertainty after his daughter's death. And why Cordelia was in London at all. After this generation, there were no legitimate heirs to the British throne. New ones needed to be sired. Quickly.

"Without an heir in the direct line of succession, the Crown Council of Monrovia selects a sovereign prince from more distant members of the royal family," she continued. "It could potentially be any one of over a dozen men. None of them can possibly know if he will be selected." She glanced past him at the corner cabinet and frowned, puzzled. "How did you know there was alcohol in that cabinet?"

"The prince regent lives here," he answered dryly and held out a glass for her. "There's alcohol in every cabinet."

She blinked at that answer, then accepted the drink and gratefully took a sip. She was parched and craving whatever solace the claret might give.

He thoughtfully swirled the dark liquid in his glass but didn't drink it, as if he had no taste for the stuff. "That's what you meant when you said you weren't important enough to be assassinated."

She nodded, then sank against the cushions behind her. "My role here is more domestic than diplomatic. I thought everyone here realized that." She muttered into her glass as she sipped the plum-colored liquid, "Wed, bed, and bred."

His gaze darted to hers.

Self-recrimination flashed through her. Oh, she'd greatly overstepped with that comment! But she found herself saying all kinds of things to this stranger. "I'm sorry," she murmured. "I shouldn't have said that."

"Don't apologize. You can say whatever you'd like to me."

Could she really? Faint excitement tingled through her at that possibility. She'd never been able to say what she truly thought before, not to anyone. Lately, she'd found it harder and harder not to speak her mind.

"I didn't realize an agreement had been formalized." His mouth pulled down glumly.

She much preferred his charming smiles. "It hasn't. Not officially."

"To which royal duke?"

"I don't know yet." Then she seized the wonderful new freedom of speaking her mind with him and added, "But I've heard they all like to gamble. Perhaps they'll cut cards for me."

He narrowed his eyes on her and faintly shook his head. "You seem so...resigned about it."

"I know what Princess Charlotte's death meant—the loss of two generations of heirs for the British throne and my cousins the prince regent and the Duke of York both unlikely to father any more children with their wives. That gives all the younger brothers the opportunity to exchange their mistresses for respectable wives who can give them legitimate heirs. While the royal dukes might never become kings themselves, the continuation of the monarchy would be assured." She traced her finger around the rim of her glass. "More important, so would their government allowances. Your Parliament has already promised funds if they marry." Her mouth twisted. "The Hanoverians are nothing if not self-interested."

He tipped his glass at her. "You're a stranger here. You're not supposed to have more insight into the British monarchy than the English people themselves."

"I know royalty everywhere and what usually matters most to them. Not all of them care about their country as much as the rulers of Monrovia do."

"Lucky Monrovia," he murmured.

"We have much to be grateful for." With the glass resting against her lips, she looked again at the dead body. "That man wasn't Monrovian." A memory triggered inside her head, and she brought her attention back to the undersecretary. "When you were talking to him before, you called him 'Scepter.' Did you know him?"

"I thought I knew," he admitted contemplatively, "but I was wrong."

She shook her head. "It's more than just him, though, isn't it? That's what you meant when you said that if you were taken from this room you would be killed." She straightened her spine to keep her composure even as it crumbled. "He wasn't working alone, and because you saw him and spoke to him, others would be afraid that you'd learned information that might lead to them."

"Beautiful *and* brilliant." His lips curled into a smile. "If you tell me that you know how to use a pistol, I might just lose my heart right now."

Her own heart beat a fierce tattoo at his charming smile. "Your heart is safe." She didn't have it in her to laugh at his teasing. He was only trying to put her at ease, she knew, but she couldn't push down the fear that gripped her. "But why? Why would anyone want to kill me?"

"I don't know. Who in England would want you dead?"

"Who would want *you* dead?" she volleyed back.

"Too many people to count." His mouth twisted in a chagrined smile, but instinctively she knew his flippant answer wasn't a joke.

He set his port aside, untouched. He hadn't wanted a drink, she realized. He'd wanted *her* to have one and knew she wouldn't drink by herself. Uneasiness twined down her spine. What else had he been able to determine about her in such a short time?

Worse—if he was with the Home Office, then what did he already know about her and her family?

"Anyone at all, Princess?" he pressed gently, bringing the conversation back to her.

"I have no idea why—" A thought struck her like a thunderbolt, and she sat up straight. "I'm staying in Princess Caroline's apartments."

He blinked, bewildered. "Pardon?"

Setting down her glass, she rose tremblingly to her feet. He took her elbow to steady her.

"I was given the Princess of Wales's old rooms at Buckingham House because the palace thought I'd be more comfortable there than in one of the regular guest suites." She clutched at his jacket sleeve. "Some of the staff tonight were borrowed from Buckingham House. Do you think that man saw me there and thought I was Princess Caroline? I know how divisive she is, how even her own husband despises her. Wouldn't someone in England have more reason to kill her than me?"

Doubt darkened his face. "You've never met the Princess of Wales, have you?"

"Well…no."

"Trust me," he drawled and dropped a lingering look over her from shoulders to hem. "No one would ever confuse the two of you."

Heat tingled through her beneath his gaze, and she caught her breath. Her earlier perception of him returned… tall, handsome, charming…*dangerous.*

"Then why?" she rasped out, her fear once more returning. "What could I have possibly done to make someone want to harm me?"

"Maybe it's not you," he contemplated.

She released his arm and took a step back. "What do you mean?"

"What secrets are you keeping?"

Her heart skipped. "Pardon?"

"What secrets do you know that someone doesn't want to see the light of day?"

"I don't have any secrets." She forced an uncomfortable laugh. "I told you. I'm not important."

"I never said they had to be *your* secrets."

Unease pulsed through her, and her eyes darted down to her discarded glass of port. She wanted it back. Desperately.

"What do you know?" He reached out and touched her cheek to bring her attention back to him. But once he had it, he didn't drop his hand away. "What are you hiding?"

"Nothing."

His eyes gleamed as if he knew she'd just lied to him. "Someone tried to kill you tonight. I don't want to give them another opportunity." He brushed his knuckles across her cheek in a caress she knew was meant to comfort her but that only made her skin tingle. "You need to trust me. I can keep you safe." He paused. "Who are you protecting?"

"I—I don't know what you're talking about."

"Is it your uncle?"

"No, of course not!"

"Someone connected to your family, then? Or to one of your parents?"

She froze. Even her heart stopped for one brutal moment before it lurched into her throat. He was staring at her as if he could see right through her to the truth, and she trembled.

"What could I possibly know?" she dodged. Her voice sounded completely unconvincing, even to her own ears. "I'm only a princess."

This time, the look he gave her at her obvious lie was one of disappointment. "I can't help you if you keep lying to me."

"Why would I lie?"

"That's what I'm trying to figure out," he answered. "But you should know I'm very good at what I do."

She pulled in a deep breath. "And what do you do, exactly?"

"Uncover secrets." He folded his arms across his chest. "And I'll uncover yours, too. All of them, no matter how long it takes."

That was exactly what frightened her. "No," she assured him, "you won't."

Suddenly, it all became too much—too much fear and grief, too much fatigue, too much duty, too much...*everything*. A tear broke free and slipped down her cheek, and she angrily swatted at it with the back of her hand.

"This is all because of me, and I don't even know why," she rasped out as another tear followed the first. "I put your life at risk." Her tear-blurred eyes slid to the grisly mound on the floor. "And he's dead, too—because of me."

"No," Clayton assured her. "None of this is your fault."

"But it is!" She shook violently, struggling to keep back a flood of tears but failing miserably. "How can I ever—I can *never* forget..."

His strong arms encircled her as he pulled her against him to comfort her.

Cordelia sagged against his front and clutched his lapels in her hands. She desperately needed the strength and reassurance emanating from him, and she craved the protection he offered.

"Tighter," she begged. "Hold me tighter...please."

No mere words could put her at ease, slow the pounding of her pulse, or steady her fast, shallow breathing. She needed his resilience and confidence, his determination and composure. She needed the hero he'd proven himself to be tonight when he'd saved her life and become the only man in this unfamiliar country she could trust.

At that moment, she simply needed...*him.*

"Please," she repeated, so softly barely any sound emerged at all from her lips.

His broad shoulders sagged with capitulation, and he tightened his arms around her. She let out a tremulous breath of gratitude.

"It's going to be all right." He nuzzled his cheek against her hair. "I promise you."

Oh, he was wrong! She would never be all right, never again. Too much had been lost in the last decade, too many crimes uncovered, too many reparations required to ever make amends...

Then she felt it—the light caress of his lips at her temple.

She caught her breath. She'd expected his lips to be as hard as the rest of his muscular body, but to her surprise they were soft, warm, inviting...and as comforting as his strong embrace.

Craving more of his solace, she lifted herself toward him to press into his arms and brought her mouth to his.

He tensed against her for only a moment, then softened and returned the delicate movement of her lips on his.

Her head spun. This wasn't the peck to the lips he'd given her earlier when he'd only wanted to capture her attention and stun her into following his orders. This wasn't one of those fumbling kisses that visiting princes and young diplomats had stolen from her in shadowed gardens when they'd wanted to insinuate themselves into her good graces. No, this kiss was completely for her and given unselfishly, not because she was a princess but simply because she was a woman in need. She could almost taste the strength and protection—

The door burst open.

She gasped and darted away from him, but Clayton was even quicker. He'd put the space of several feet between them within a heartbeat.

"Cordelia!" Uncle Ernest charged into the room.

Behind him followed the Duke of Hampton with the prime minister, Lord Liverpool, hot on his heels. Two palace guards came after. In their wake scurried the comtesse, who had most likely been lingering right outside this entire time, and Devereaux, still clutching her notebook.

Uncle Ernest's face glowed red as he stopped abruptly in front of her. He darted a furious glance at the lump beneath the blue drape.

"What the devil is going on?" he demanded. Then his narrowed eyes landed on Clayton, and he snarled to the room at large, "I demand to know who this man is and what he is doing here!"

"He's Mr. Elliott, undersecretary for the Home Office," Cordelia explained. "He was questioning me about what happened tonight." She forced herself to remain composed and drew herself up as tall and regally as possible. "The man is a hero who saved my life."

"Is he?" Her uncle cast a contemptuous glance over Clayton. "And certainly he was just leaving."

Seven

THE HELL I WAS.

Prince Ernest was damnably anxious to be rid of him, yet Clayton remained right where he was. After months of tracking Scepter's remnants through London's stench-filled taverns and stews, chasing down one false lead after another, he'd been placed straight into the middle of the group's plans for revolution, and he had no intention of going anywhere.

More, he also had to protect Cordelia.

She'd lied to him, but he knew she did it out of concern and affection for someone else. Yet the same person she wanted to protect had placed her life in danger, and whoever wanted her dead wouldn't stop after tonight. He would do whatever he had to in order to prevent England from mourning another dead princess, no matter how many well-intentioned lies he had to sift through.

But he, at least, had spoken the truth. He truly was an expert at uncovering secrets, and he wouldn't stop until he knew exactly what secrets she was hiding.

As for her uncle… Clayton offered a formal bow to the Prince of Monrovia. "Your Highness, on behalf of the Home Office, I want to welcome you to—"

"An *under*secretary has been allowed in my niece's company?" Prince Ernest sneered.

Clayton hid his irritation. He'd dealt with insults like that his whole life and knew how to ignore them. The fact that this one came from a monarch made no difference.

"More than an undersecretary, Your Highness," Marcus explained to soothe the prince's ruffled feathers. "*General* Elliott is the Home Secretary's most trusted man and is here tonight to represent the Home Office in welcoming you."

The princess's eyes darted to Clayton in surprise.

"Your cousin the prince regent also trusts the general and has taken him into his private confidences."

At that, her eyes narrowed.

Wonderful. Clayton bit back a curse. He already had an attempted royal murder to deal with and a revolutionary group once more on the rise. Now he also had a woman who most likely thought he'd hidden his identity and acquaintance with the Prince of Wales just so he could take advantage of her vulnerability. The furthest thing from it! He'd never seen a woman in more need of comfort than the princess tonight, and he'd simply wanted to protect her, in every way he could, including easing her anguish.

"Her Serene Highness was attacked when she was preparing for the ceremony, as you know." Marcus continued the explanation while Lord Liverpool did everything he could to ingratiate himself with Prince Ernest. The prime minister was nothing if not political to the bone. "General Elliott stopped the attacker."

"And saved my life," Cordelia interjected.

The prince turned toward her. "My dear, I had no idea. No one told me the situation was that dire. They only said you were surprised by an intruder and the matter had been dealt with." Concern flashed across his face, and he took her by her shoulders. "Are you all right?"

"My arm was hurt, but that's all." With an embarrassed grimace, she held up her forearm with its thick bandage. "It looks much worse than it is."

"Thank God." He placed a kiss to her forehead, but her expression didn't soften at the affectionate gesture. "I could never have lived with myself if something happened to you."

"It wasn't your fault, Uncle, nor our cousins.'"

"But I was the one who insisted you accompany me on this trip."

He placed a finger beneath her chin and tilted up her face until she had to look him straight in the eyes. Clayton frowned. The prince was her uncle, true, but he treated her as if she were still a child instead of a grown woman.

Cordelia stiffened. Clayton didn't know her well, but he'd seen enough to know she was chafing under her uncle's paternal attentions.

"I promised your father and mother that I would always protect you," Prince Ernest reminded her.

"You are not to blame, Uncle." Despite her forgiving words, her smile appeared strained. "You can't be responsible for a madman."

Her uncle's expression tightened for an instant. Then he released the princess and stepped away, turning back toward Marcus and Liverpool and completely ignoring Clayton.

"I want her guard increased," the prince ordered. "We cannot assume this man was alone in attempting to harm her."

"Of course, Your Highness," Liverpool agreed quickly.

Marcus nodded. "I'll speak to the regent and offer to oversee the princess's protection myself. I'll make certain her personal guard is—"

"No."

The quiet but firm word took all three men by surprise, and they turned toward Clayton for explanation. But his gaze remained locked on the princess.

"*I* am volunteering to protect Her Serene Highness," Clayton announced. That offer was the last thing he should have done, given how he'd lost his mind in his desire to protect her and kissed her. Yet he needed to stay close to her to have any chance of finding Scepter's men and saving her from their next attempt to harm her. The enemy had infiltrated the palace, and the only way to stop them was to put himself right into the vipers' nest. "I believe I've proven myself tonight. Wouldn't you agree, Your Highness?"

Her cheeks pinked with embarrassment, yet he prayed she wasn't daft enough to refuse his protection because of a kiss.

Before she could answer, her uncle smiled patronizingly and held up a ringed hand, silencing her. "We cannot inconvenience the Duke of Hampton and the general. We are guests here, not obligations." He lowered his hand. "Your protection will remain the responsibility of the palace guards." Impossibly, his smile became even more condescending. "We will leave your safety to *professional* soldiers."

At that, Marcus and Clayton exchanged glances. The prince had no idea how much training the two generals in front of him possessed, how many years of experience they'd acquired in the fires of battle. They were professional soldiers to their cores. But both men knew not to correct him.

"Uncle." Cordelia inhaled deeply as if to gather her courage and asserted, "I want General Elliott to lead my personal guard."

Clayton fought back a pleased smile. *Good girl.*

"He is a fine and dedicated soldier who served courageously in the wars against Bonaparte, including at Waterloo." She added, "And I trust him with my life."

From the corner of his eye, Clayton saw Marcus dart him a narrowed glance. Clayton wisely knew not to look back.

Prince Ernest waved that away. "You do not need to trouble yourself, General. I want her safety ensured by the same men who protect the regent."

Clayton fought to keep from rolling his eyes. The prince would never know the irony behind his comment. The only reason Clayton had been invited to Carlton House tonight in the first place was because he had protected the regent. For God's sake, he'd saved the regent's life, and *this* was how he was being repaid?

He definitely needed a new system of royal compensation.

"The guards failed at their task tonight, Your Highness," Clayton countered, softening his voice yet keeping his eyes on Cordelia. For the next fortnight, he had no intention of letting her out of his sight. "Do you truly want to risk a second failure?"

"No, we do not," Cordelia answered. She folded her hands in front of her, but there was nothing demure about the way she held herself, in the imperial lift of her chin and regal hold of her shoulders. Yet her voice was uncertain, as if she were afraid to assert herself in front of her uncle. "I want General Elliott to oversee my guard. I—I insist."

Prince Ernest's jaw tightened, yet he seemed to know when to concede. "Very well, then. If Her Serene Highness *insists*"—any concern for his niece in his order was outweighed by visible irritation—"then General Elliott will oversee her guard."

Clayton gave a low bow. "I serve at the pleasure of the princess."

Judging from the reactions of the men around him, no one except he and Cordelia were pleased by this arrangement. And he didn't give a damn if they weren't. What mattered was protecting the princess.

"Then meet with the captain of the guard," Prince Ernest ordered, "and coordinate the princess's schedule with Lady Devereaux."

The mousey, tall woman curtsied at the order. "Yes, Your Highness."

The prince ignored her. "Now that this evening is at an end, we will say our good nights to our royal cousins and Princess Cordelia will return to Buckingham House under the protection of the captain of the palace guard, where she can rest and recover." He stared down his nose at Clayton. "In the morning, General Elliott will take over her security." The prince held out his hand toward the princess. "Come."

When Cordelia obediently gave her hand to her uncle, all emotion vanished from her face.

The sudden change jarred Clayton. Oh, she was still beautiful, still regal. But she walked stiffly toward the door with her uncle, reminding Clayton of a statue that had come to life and not the warm, soft woman he'd held in his arms.

Liverpool curtly nodded his goodbyes to Marcus and Clayton and followed after. The comtesse gave Clayton an assessing look that clearly found him lacking as she turned toward the door and exited behind the others.

Lady Devereaux popped open her notebook and ran her finger down the page. "I will meet with you tomorrow morning at Buckingham House at eight o'clock sharp." She snapped the book closed and spun on her heel. "Do not be late!"

Once they were gone, Clayton heaved out a sighing curse and ran his fingers through his hair. *Good Lord.* The army didn't prepare a man for nearly enough kinds of battle. He turned toward Marcus and froze.

His friend was staring at him as if Clayton had just sprouted a second head. "Can I ask what the devil you were doing with the princess when her uncle entered the room?"

Clayton rubbed at the knot of tension in his nape. "Questioning her."

"Has the Home Office changed its interrogation tactics, then?" Marcus gestured at the two glasses of port sitting on the end table beside the settee. "I don't think I've ever seen you kiss anyone during your interrogations before."

Christ. "She was upset," Clayton explained as casually as

possible, as if kissing a princess were part of his everyday work responsibilities.

Marcus arched a brow.

"Someone had just tried to murder her. I can't help her if she's too upset to provide answers. That's all."

And *that* made him sound like a callous arse taking advantage of a distraught woman. But the truth would have been far worse. That he'd kissed her because she was in pain and afraid, because she needed to be reassured that she would be safe.

Because he simply couldn't resist.

"That had better be all," Marcus warned. "The last thing the Home Office needs is to start a war with Monrovia."

"The Home Office can go stuff—"

"Or *you* to be accused of treason."

Ludicrous! Clayton laughed at the idea. "It's only treason if a man beds the consort or a princess in the line of succession. And since I have no plans to seduce Queen Charlotte, the Princess of Wales, any of the royal princesses—and *especially* not Princess Sophia—" He shuddered at the thought. "I think I'm safe."

"Is that really the defense you want to present at your court-martial?" Marcus asked dryly.

Oh, for God's sake! "It was only one kiss, and it won't happen again."

"Best keep it that way."

Irritation flared in Clayton's chest at his old friend's overstepping. "I'm not daft enough to pursue a foreign princess." No, apparently he was exactly that daft. Which only increased his irritation, this time at himself. "But I also won't let anyone harm her." Putting an end to their conversation, he called out to the men waiting in the hallway just outside the door. "Guards!"

The door opened, and the same two palace guards who had tried to arrest him slipped nervously inside the room.

"Take down another drape and wrap up that body." Clayton pointed at the lump on the floor. Another layer of damask would keep the blood from seeping through and being visible. "Secure it onto the settee with cords from the drapes as if you're moving nothing more than a heavy piece of furniture and cushions. Then carry the whole lot out the rear service entrance, put it onto a wagon, and haul it ten miles outside the city. Find an isolated spot and dump it in a woods at least fifty yards from all roads and lanes. Dump the drapes and cords somewhere at the edge of London, then take the settee to the regent's upholsterer to be recovered." He added in a mutter, "I'm certain he keeps one on retainer."

Marcus cocked his head thoughtfully as he listened to Clayton bark out orders.

"Tell anyone who asks that wine was spilled on the settee and that it needs to be recovered before the regent sees it. That's why it was removed in the middle of the night, understand?"

"But there's no stain on it," one of the guards foolishly argued.

Clayton snatched up his glass of port and spilled it across the blue brocade settee. He calmly set down the empty glass and nodded approvingly as the dark liquid soaked into the upholstery. "There is now."

Both guards stared, wide-eyed and open-mouthed.

"That man was never here." Clayton pointed at the body on the floor and spoke in a voice so icy cold that the guards turned white. "Do you understand? You never saw him."

The two men nodded, then began their grisly task of removing the body.

Marcus came up close beside Clayton and lowered his voice. "You're awfully good at knowing how to dispose of a dead body. One would think you'd had experience with it."

"Occupational hazard," he returned, deadpan.

He watched the two guards work, but he was still preoccupied with the princess. Why would anyone want to harm a beautiful, intelligent, and warm woman like her, princess or not? What could possibly be gained from her death?

He crossed his arms and faced Marcus. "Tell me everything you know about Monrovia."

Eight

CORDELIA SMILED BRIGHTLY AT A GROUP OF CHILDREN from the Foundling Hospital as they stood on the rear terrace of Buckingham House and sang to the guests gathered on the great lawn for Queen Charlotte's garden party.

For once, the English weather had cooperated and provided a perfect spring day filled with bright sunshine, fluffy white clouds, and a soft breeze. Every lady wore a dress in pale pastel, and the gentlemen all donned light gray or cream-colored finery. Even the children were all dressed in new white clothes that made them look like precious little angels. Knowing children the way she did, though, Cordelia feared their clothes wouldn't stay white for long.

"Wonderful!" she called out as the children finished their song. She clapped out her gratitude, although careful to avoid hurting her forearm, which had been healing nicely since the attack two days ago.

Luckily, her glove hid the much smaller bandage the doctor had put on her arm this morning, and the original pain of the wound had lessened dramatically since the attack. It barely bothered her now unless she thoughtlessly moved her hand the wrong way. Certainly, she wouldn't be joining any games of battledore and shuttlecock or lawn bowling anytime soon, but at least she was well enough to carry out all her engagements.

Not that she had a choice. Cordelia suspected that had she lost an entire arm, she would still have been forced to meet with the Foreign Secretary and Lord Liverpool.

Cordelia pushed the unpleasant thoughts from her mind and hurried forward to greet the children as they stepped off the terrace and into the garden. From a basket held by a footman at her side, she presented each child with a gift bag containing school supplies, soap and flannels, and ripe oranges. They bounced off in excitement with their treasures toward a long row of refreshment tables and their piles of pastries, candies, and sweet fruits.

But it was Cordelia who received the best gift—their beautiful smiles warmed her heart and were the only bright spots in an otherwise dreadful day. From the moment she woke, her day had been a procession of long and boring meetings during which she'd had to pretend that nothing unusual had happened to her two nights ago at the welcome ceremony.

At least today, though, she was in the fresh air and relative calm of the gardens where she could relax. Unfortunately, this moment of escape wouldn't last long. She had an evening full of dinners and receptions ahead of her.

What she wouldn't give to escape it all! Even if only for one day when she could do what she wanted, whenever and wherever the mood struck her, and with whom. For a few precious hours, she wouldn't have to be aware of every word she said, every smile or glance, every time she wanted to roll her eyes or complain.

Sometimes, she simply wanted nothing more than to run away.

Today was made all the worse because she hadn't slept a wink for the past two nights, although only part of her sleeplessness had been due to the attack. She couldn't stop thinking about her father's misdeeds…and about Clayton Elliott, the man who was determined to uncover them.

Was General Elliott right? Were her father's actions the reason someone had tried to kill her? She simply couldn't believe it, especially as no other attempts to harm her had been made. But then, since that night, Clayton had also been guarding her…always in the background, always watching, but thankfully never having the opportunity to speak to her alone and ask her again about her secrets.

For a few precious minutes right now, anyway, she didn't have to worry about any of that. All she had to do was make a child feel special, and *that* she knew exactly how to do.

She lowered onto her heels in front of the last little girl in line, whose big brown eyes practically glowed at meeting a princess. "My! What a beautiful voice you have." Cordelia couldn't help reaching to straighten the girl's hair bow. "What is your name?"

"'Lithbeth," the little girl lisped through a gap of two missing front teeth.

"What a pleasure to meet you, Elizabeth. I'm Cordelia." She ignored the way the footman beside her stiffened at her breach of protocol. Undoubtedly, he would report her improper behavior to her uncle, but a lecture on always maintaining royal appearance would be worth the pleasure of talking to this little girl, today of all days. "I'm so happy that you were able to come to my garden party today. I hope you're enjoying yourself."

The girl beamed from ear to ear. "Here." She jabbed her arms out from behind her back, a yellow dandelion in her small hands. "You can have thith!"

Cordelia's eyes stung at the sweet gesture. It was nothing but a little weed the girl had plucked from the grass beside the terrace, but to Cordelia, it was more special than the dozens of bouquets that had been delivered to her rooms since her arrival.

"What a wonderful gift! Thank you." What did she have to give to the little girl in return? She quickly checked over herself. Her eyes landed on her shoes, and she smiled. "I want you to have this."

She removed the satin bow edged with tiny pearls decorating the tip of her shoe and pinned it to the girl's dress.

Elizabeth stared at the little bow as if it were a priceless treasure, too stunned to remember to say thank you.

Careful of her arm, Cordelia impulsively hugged the girl tightly to her bosom. Then she whispered into her ear, "You are so very special, Elizabeth. Remember that always, will you? Don't let anyone convince you otherwise."

Reluctantly, she released the girl, who collected her gift bag and skipped off to join the other children with one hand protectively guarding the bow. She stopped to look back and waved happily to Cordelia before hurrying on.

Cordelia rose to her feet to start toward the children. She couldn't bear to part from them just yet—

"Good God, the urchins," a tired female voice drawled from behind her, stopping her. "Mama insists on inviting them to every garden party and holiday event she hosts. I think she does it to prove she's charitable. She cannot actually *like* them, for heaven's sake!"

Cordelia forced a tight smile. "Princess Sophia."

"They're foundlings, you know, given up by mothers who didn't want them or couldn't care for them, mothers who most likely delivered them into the world as bastards." Sophia squinted against the afternoon sunshine as she gazed across the lawn where massive tents erected as a hedge against the weather stood unneeded. "Still, I suppose every child deserves a chance at a good Christian upbringing, even the unwanted ones."

Anger flared inside Cordelia. Everyone deserved the chance to have a decent and happy life, *especially* the ones whom Fate had placed into poverty and troubled families. It wasn't the children's fault they were poor and disadvantaged or that the world was fixed against them so they could never rise above the lot they'd been born into no matter how hard they worked.

But Cordelia bit the inside of her cheek to keep from telling the royal princess what she thought. If hugging a foundling child would earn her a lecture, then Uncle Ernest would surely exile her from Monrovia if she did anything to offend her English cousins or put her future marriage in jeopardy.

She also kept silent because she felt sorry for the royal princesses, especially Sophia, even if Cordelia didn't like her very much. Some of King George's older daughters had managed to find husbands and escape their parents' control, but poor Sophia had been left for spinsterhood. Worse— horrible rumors had circulated for years that she'd borne her brother Augustus's incestuous child.

The story was ridiculous, of course, yet it worried Cordelia. Was that the kind of lies the English people spread about their royal family? No wonder the Hanoverians had become the laughingstock of Europe.

"My! What a lovely day." Cordelia swiftly changed topics to the weather, a tactic that served her well when conversing with people she didn't like. "We're so fortunate it didn't rain."

Sophia glanced at the sky. "Hmm."

Cordelia followed the princess's gaze upward. When her eyes came back down, they landed on Clayton Elliott.

He stood at the side of the lawn where he chatted with a small group of ladies. If Cordelia had thought him dashing at the welcome ceremony when he'd come to her rescue, he was impossibly more handsome today in his general's red dress uniform with its gold embroidered collar and cuffs, tight white breeches, and chest full of medals. He wore a dark blue sash diagonally across his left shoulder, gold braids across his right, and a sword at his hip. Other men in military dress uniform stood scattered throughout the gardens and terrace, but none possessed his determined bearing or strong presence.

Her heart ached as she stared at him. The night they met, for a few precious moments he'd treated her like an average woman. He'd called her beautiful and brilliant, teased her, listened to her—truly *listened*, the way the palace courtiers never did. And when he'd kissed her...*oh my*. She certainly hadn't been a princess to him then. She'd simply been a woman in need, and he'd been there to comfort her.

That show of normalcy was why she'd gone along with his scheme to oversee her guard. Oh, she shouldn't have! She should have declined his offer and put as much distance between them as possible so he wouldn't have any chance of uncovering her family's secrets.

But she couldn't help herself. He would protect her, she knew, and right now she needed all the protection she could find.

"The man who's been assigned to head my guard," Cordelia said offhandedly to Sophia. "General Elliott. Do you know him?"

"Not at all," the princess muttered. "But George has taken a liking to him. No idea why." Her frown deepened. "Do you think he's a drunken miscreant like that horrible Brummel?"

Dear God, Cordelia hoped not! "I couldn't say." Although she *had* noticed that he'd not taken a single sip of his drink two nights ago. Surely, that fell in his favor.

"That's usually what my brother sees in his cronies. The worse they are, the better he likes them." Sophia turned to stare boldly at Clayton, not noticing at all that Cordelia wanted their conversation kept private. Or simply not caring that she did. "Makes one wonder what this man has done to earn so much attention from George so quickly, hmm?"

Yes, it did.

"And George placed him in charge of your personal guard, you say?"

"The general volunteered, and the regent agreed." Wholeheartedly, and much to her uncle's irritation yesterday morning when word from Carlton House reached him. Not only had her cousin the regent agreed with her decision, but he'd also insisted in glowing terms that no one could protect her better than General Elliott...and that he would give Clayton a viscountcy for his trouble.

A viscountcy! Cordelia had nearly sobbed with grief at the news.

That extraordinary gift would change everything. Clayton would never again look at her as if she were a normal woman, not as long as he knew personal rewards could be gained by attending on her. In that, she feared he'd prove no different from the other courtiers who fawned over her.

"Well, I suppose he can't be worse than that insufferable Lord Liverpool," Sophia continued. "As I've always said..."

Cordelia let out a long sigh and let her attention wander as the princess rambled on about current political affairs. Her gaze drifted around the gardens right along with it, and once more, it landed on Clayton.

She frowned as two beautiful ladies approached him and engaged him in conversation. Then her frown deepened as he smiled back at them with a casual grin that implied he knew them well. *Very* well. And the way he laughed at something the raven-haired woman said, how his green eyes gleamed—

Oh, bother! Cordelia tore her gaze away, feeling like a complete goose for watching him.

What did it matter who he spoke to...or smiled at? Cordelia needed a competent guard, that was all. He would never learn about her father's past—she would make certain of it—and in a fortnight when the royal visit ended, she'd never see him again. He held no significance for her. *None whatsoever.*

Or at least that was the lie she told herself as she drew in a deep breath and moved her gaze once more around the property to distract herself from him.

Truly, the gardens were beautiful. They were a perfect wild oasis in the heart of congested London, with acres and acres of trees, flower beds, and even a lake stretching out to the ends of the property. How lovely it would be to simply go for a walk across the grounds! Perhaps she could find an excuse to slip away after the party and before she had to be rushed back to her rooms to change, yet again, for the next event she was required to—

"Your Serene Highness! We must chat!"

Cordelia pulled up straight as she came face-to-face with a giant pink turban that had scurried up in front of her. She lowered her gaze to the round woman smiling broadly from underneath it and blinked. "Pardon?"

A second woman beside her wore a hat with so many feathers that it looked as if an entire ostrich was nesting on her head. When she nodded vigorously in agreement with her friend, the thing bobbed so precariously that Cordelia feared the whole construction might go tumbling to the grass.

"Oh, apologies!" the ostrich-feathered woman said. "We must be properly introduced. Sophia!" She waved a gloved hand at Princess Sophia, who was doing her best to make her own escape.

The turbaned woman snagged the royal princess by the

arm and patted the back of her hand as she brought her back to them. "Sophia, do be a dear and introduce us to Her Serene Highness, will you?"

Instead of being furious for being touched or ordered about, Sophia only smiled patiently, the same way one would for a pair of eccentric relatives. "Princess Cordelia, may I introduce you to two dear old friends of my mother? Lady Agnes Sinclair, aunt to the Earl of St James—"

The turban bobbed in acknowledgement.

"And Viscountess Bromley."

The mound of ostrich feathers followed suit. Cordelia resisted the urge to reach out to steady it.

"Ladies, Her Serene Highness Princess Cordelia of Monrovia."

Both women lowered themselves into deep curtsies. Both turban and ostrich feathers teetered precariously.

Cordelia inclined her head. "It's a pleasure to—"

"Thank you very much for your help." The viscountess shooed Sophia away. "You can go."

While Cordelia gaped incredulously at their impertinence toward the princess, who seemed not at all upset by it—or at all surprised, as if such odd behavior happened regularly—Lady Agnes gently took Cordelia's left arm and Lady Bromley her right. Together the two women led her in a slow saunter across the wide lawn toward the far gardens.

"We wanted to personally welcome you to England," Lady Agnes told her. "Isn't that so, Harriett?"

"Oh yes! We both know how difficult it is to be a stranger in a strange land—"

"I had the pleasure of visiting Monrovia in my youth. Such a beautiful—"

"Is it true that the palace is *pink*? I've heard the Mediterranean views are—"

Cordelia's head practically spun as she looked from one to the other, side to side, in a peculiar volley of conversation that felt like she'd fallen into the middle of a tennis match.

"So unlike England that—"

"You must be terribly homesick already and—"

"Are you lonely?"

With that, the conversation crashed to a halt.

Lonely? What on earth…? Cordelia looked toward Sophia to be rescued, but the princess had already fled to safety inside Buckingham House.

Cordelia blinked as the two ladies both stared at her expectantly, holding their breaths as they awaited her answer.

"I—I—" How on earth was she supposed to answer *that*? "My cousins have been very welcoming."

She tried to pull her arms away, but the two women held on and led her farther into the garden and through a long, wide arbor covered with wisteria. She might have suspected the two wanted to kidnap her except they kept wiggling their gloved fingers to greet acquaintances across the gardens.

No, not kidnappers.

Simply mad.

"I suppose they have been." The viscountess's lips pursed into a hard line. "But best to avoid the royal dukes, my dear."

Lady Agnes nodded knowingly. "Especially Cumberland." She added in a mutter, "Never have liked that one."

Cordelia's mouth fell open at her uncensored comment. "You…know the dukes, then?"

Lady Bromley patted her shoulder, carefully avoiding her forearm. "We know everyone at the palace."

"Known most of them for years." Agnes leaned in to say in confidence, "Avoid Lord Worthington as well. His behavior during the wars was questionable."

Heavens.

"But Clayton Elliott's most certainly was not."

Oh, dear *heavens!* Cordelia squeaked out, "Pardon?"

"The general told us that he was placed in charge of your protection," Lady Bromley answered with a knowing smile. "You could not have found a better man for the job."

"Not at all!" Agnes agreed. Then her turbaned head suddenly stopped nodding, and she frowned. "Except…"

Cordelia's heart skipped. "Except?"

"Well, that whole mess with his father, you know."

Lady Bromley clucked her tongue. "Terrible business."

"The man was innocent," Lady Agnes insisted.

"The man was *hanged*," Lady Bromley corrected.

General Elliott's father had been…*hanged*? "For what?"

"Well, smuggling during the wars was—"

"He didn't do it," Agnes interrupted firmly.

"Unfortunately, all the proof—and the late Squire Daniels—said he did."

"But all the proof—and *especially* the late squire—was wrong."

Cordelia stole a glance over her shoulder toward the terrace, searching for Clayton. If she ever needed to be rescued, this was certainly a time. But she couldn't see him. She couldn't see *anything* of the house and terrace. The ladies had steered her behind a thick grove of chestnut trees and to the edge of the lake, neatly separating her from the party. "If he didn't do it… How can you be certain?"

"A man who was supposedly as evil as that could never have raised a son as good as Clayton," Lady Agnes answered with certainty.

Lady Bromley sighed. "Very true."

Cordelia certainly hoped so!

"Anyway, my dear," Agnes reassured her, "you are in competent hands with the general. We've known him for years. He's a good man, a kind soul, and deadly with a pistol."

Cordelia mumbled, "So I've heard."

"This is where we leave you." Lady Bromley squeezed Cordelia's hand. "Enjoy your time in England, my dear."

"And enjoy your time with General Elliott." Agnes winked. "I truly hope you do!" Then, as if in afterthought, she added with a shake of her finger, "But not *too* much."

The two ladies bustled off toward the house and the party, chattering between themselves nonstop and leaving Cordelia alone in the heart of the rambling garden.

She stared after them and rubbed at her forearm and the healing wound beneath the bandage. *Good heavens!* She couldn't have said what on earth their conversation had been about, but she suddenly felt winded.

And warned.

"Hello, Princess."

She spun around and lost her breath.

Clayton.

Nine

CLAYTON STEPPED OUT OF THE EDGE OF THE BUSHES where he'd been waiting for the two ladies to deliver Cordelia, just as he'd asked them to do. He'd hoped her surprised expression would melt into a smile for him, but no such luck. Instead, her chocolate-brown eyes grew impossibly bigger.

"What are you…?" Then her pink lips pressed together and her eyes narrowed as she realized what he'd done. "*You* asked them to bring me here, didn't you?"

Clayton couldn't help but grin at being caught. "They're my best friends' aunties, and they've always taken a liking to me."

Given their bent for all things spy-related, he'd also been able to easily recruit them to help. He'd not been able to talk privately with Cordelia since the attack, and desperate times—he glanced after the bobbing ostrich feathers and bright pink turban as they quickly beat a retreat—called for desperate measures. "We haven't had the chance to be alone since the attack, and I wanted to speak with you."

He'd been in her presence almost constantly since he assumed her guard, standing at the edge of the room or remaining an appropriate distance away. He'd watched her interact with cabinet ministers, members of Parliament, important businessmen, ladies of all rank and position—even the children at today's party. He'd politely greeted her in passing and learned a great deal about her simply by observing her…as she had undoubtedly done with him, if all the times he'd caught her looking at him were any indication. But they'd not been able to have a single word in private.

Always together, never alone. She realized that, too, based on how her irritation drained visibly from her.

"I'm an unmarried princess. I'm never alone." The smile he longed for teased at her lips but never fully blossomed. "Unless I'm with a Home Office undersecretary, it seems."

"The palace only wants to keep you safe." *So do I.* "I'm certain they feel guilty about the attack."

"More likely, their concern stems from worry about almost losing a potential bride." She turned toward a flowering bush on the edge of the lake and touched the pale peach-colored blossoms. "Sometimes," she softly confessed, "I just want…to be left alone."

That stung, although she surely hadn't meant for him to take it personally. "Do you want me to go, then, and let you be alone?"

"After you went to all the trouble of having those two nice old ladies abscond with me?" A teasing gleam lit her eyes, and she gave a gentle shake of her head, which only caused her chestnut curls to show their red and gold highlights in the sunlight. "No. Please stay." She inhaled a fortifying breath. "You wanted to speak with me. It must be important."

"It is."

The afternoon breeze stirred her skirt, a cream undergown

covered with a layer of delicate gauze decorated with tiny pink roses. They were the exact same shade of pink as her lips and the faint flush in her cheeks. An English lady would never have left the shade without the cover of a bonnet the way Cordelia had. It was just another example of how different she was from other women he knew. He'd seen that in the way she'd greeted the children, too. When he watched her hug that last little girl, he'd not been able to hold back a grin even though he knew that type of impulsive behavior wouldn't go over well with the English royals.

But now, he frowned. "I've been questioning people at the palace. Additional staff were sent from all the London palaces to work the event, so many that the master of ceremonies didn't know everyone by sight. When your attacker arrived, he presented work orders for another footman at Kensington Palace, but he wasn't part of the palace staff."

Her fingers stilled against a blossom. "But he wore palace livery."

"He took that from the other man, too. The real footman was found alive but tied, gagged, and stripped bare in a derelict shop a few streets from Kensington Palace." Clayton kept the grislier details of the man's condition to himself, not wanting to upset her further. Even in this, he felt the need to protect her. "I suspect your attacker followed the footman on his way to the palace, pulled him into the shop, and changed places, right down to the work orders he presented at the door of Carlton House."

Her fingertips trembled against the flower's petals. "Thank God he didn't kill the footman."

No, but he'd beaten the man so severely that he'd most likely never walk again. There was certainly no need to share that. Already, the pink color in her cheeks that had captivated him only moments ago had paled.

"But no one working that night recognized him," he told her, "and I haven't been able to turn up any more information about his true identity or why he would want to harm you." *Or who within the palace told him exactly where to find you.*

"You're at an impasse, then, aren't you?" She played with the petals, focusing her attention there. Yet Clayton knew she was keenly aware of him, just as she had been all afternoon when he'd caught her taking surreptitious glances at him from across the lawn. "That's why you wanted to speak with me."

"Yes."

"Because you think I might know something I'm not telling you."

A tingle of suspicion curled up his spine, and he asked carefully, "Don't you?"

"Nothing of significance to anyone in England."

He knew better than to fall for that evasion, no matter how carefully delivered. "Then how about significance to someone *outside* England?" He slowly brushed his hand over hers and down her warm fingers to pluck the flower from its stem. He held it out to her as a peace offering. "I'm trying to protect you. I can't do that without your help."

She accepted the flower and raised it to her nose. A nervous gesture, he guessed, to cover the trembling he'd felt in her fingers. He was right. She was hiding something important.

"I know." She rubbed the flower against her lips. "But I've told you all I can."

"You've told me almost nothing."

Her eyes boldly locked with his. "Which is all I can."

She was foolishly stonewalling him. Worse, she'd brought his attention to her mouth, and he couldn't tear his gaze away from her sensuous lips.

"You supported my request to oversee your protection when you could have refused," he reminded her. Dear God, was his voice truly that husky? He cleared his throat. "So I think it's time you tell me what you know, even if you think it has no significance." He paused. "Unless you don't trust me."

She absently rubbed her forearm, with its bandage skillfully hidden beneath a long glove. If Clayton didn't know better, he never would have suspected it was there. "I trust you as much as I trust anyone in the palace."

He winced. "That little, eh?"

There, finally, was the smile he'd been waiting to see, and when she gave it, his chest warmed the same way it had when he'd watched her interact with the children. "I didn't mean it that way."

When her smile faded, Clayton felt as if the sun had slipped behind a cloud.

"I know I'm little more than a political pawn for our two countries, that everything I say is reported back to the palace, my every move watched—most likely even now, with you." She idly pulled at the petals, slowly plucking them off one by one and letting them fall to the grass at her feet. "Perhaps that's how it should be, given recent events." She let out a long, deep breath. "Unfortunately, that also means I can't trust anyone who works for the Court of St James's. I can't even completely trust those within my own household, knowing they're in my uncle's employ and most likely serving as his spies."

He smiled tightly in anticipation of her answer's sting. "And me?"

She hesitated as she pulled free the last petal. "I haven't decided about you yet, General." She tilted her head to gaze up at him. "Or should I say…Viscount?"

Christ. He still hadn't come to terms with yesterday morning's letter from the regent notifying Clayton of his intentions to grant him a peerage. He didn't know whether he should be proud of reaching such a high pinnacle or humiliated that he'd done absolutely nothing to earn it.

He grumbled, "I'm not a viscount."

"My cousin the regent seems to think so."

He arched a brow. "Your cousin the regent also thinks a man's value in life is dependent on how well he dresses."

"Nice uniform." Her eyes gleamed mischievously as she reached out to pluck at the medals on his chest the same way she'd plucked at the flower petals. "Is this why he made you a viscount?"

"No." He crossed his arms in consternation. "He did that to torture me."

She laughed, and the sound floated soft and lovely on the spring air. It wrapped itself around him like a silk ribbon and tugged him even closer to her. Yet he didn't dare touch her, certainly not here in the open, certainly not after Marcus's reprimand for the first kiss.

But damnation, he very much wanted to.

"If you don't trust me completely," he asked, "then why agree to let me oversee your guard?"

She hesitated and bit her bottom lip. The small gesture had him aching to kiss her mouth until it softened.

Dear God, he was going mad!

"You'll laugh if I tell you the truth," she admitted.

"Try me."

"You put your life at risk for mine when you didn't even know who I was." She searched his face as she gauged her words. "It was the most heroic act I've ever seen."

A man could certainly grow used to hearing such compliments. He fought back a smile. "Well, I—"

"And you were rude."

His head snapped up. "That's not a compliment."

"It is, actually." Amusement curled her lips. "You didn't know I was a princess, and once you found out, you didn't care. You were blunt and direct, and you treated me like a regular woman. You're the only person except for my parents who ever has."

That didn't sound like a compliment either. "I should apologize."

"Please don't. It meant a great deal to me." She sized him up with a direct, honest look. "You might often visit the palace, but you don't know what it's like to be a royal, to lead a life that is never truly yours." She gazed across the lake and blinked against the reflection of the bright sunlight on the water. "Royals belong to their country the same way the army does or the navy—or perhaps more like a fine porcelain vase, passed down from generation to generation, yet little more than a vessel for the state."

"A precious object to be treasured," he countered.

With a grimace at that bit of flattery, she turned and began to walk slowly along the edge of the lake. He fell into step beside her, slowing his long strides to match her shorter ones. How could someone so petite and delicate be so powerful?

"Perhaps not a porcelain vase," she admitted, staring down at the tips of her shoes that poked out from beneath her skirt as they walked through the grass and back into view of the lawn party. "And perhaps not like Princess Sophia either."

"Thank God," he muttered beneath his breath and earned himself an easy laugh from her.

Then her bright smile faded, and she tucked behind her ear a stray curl that had come loose in the breeze. "But we have no meaningful place in the world outside palace walls, and even inside those walls a royal still has to do what is expected. Take my cousin the prince regent, for example. Do you ever wonder why he is the way he is? Or his brothers and sisters?"

"All the time," he blew out in a long sigh.

Thankfully, she ignored his grumble. "It's because of the way they were raised. Strict lessons from dawn to dusk and rapped knuckles for not being faster learners, then paraded out every evening in front of the king and queen to recite what they'd learned that day and always berated for not doing better. Living in cold and austere nurseries and bedrooms with nannies who were told that too much affection and praise would make them weak, taught by tutors who were ordered to withhold dinner if the children didn't do well enough on their studies." She trailed her palm over the leaves and bright pink flowers of a bush as they passed. "It's little wonder that once they escaped their parents' control, they grabbed for all the freedoms and pleasures they could."

He didn't disagree. Being raised by Farmer George couldn't have been easy.

"Still, they don't do anything worse than other royals across the Continent—or even some peers here in England. But because they're royals, they're criticized for it."

He waved a hand to encompass the palace and grounds. "British citizens pay for all this. Aren't they entitled to hold their rulers to higher standards?"

"Yes, for ruling, but not for living their lives. Royals are only people, with the same weaknesses and foibles as everyone else, just on a grander scale." She glanced toward the house and grimaced. "A *much* grander scale. But no one is willing to grant us that consideration. Yet sometimes I wish...I wish royals could give it all up," she admitted in a longing sigh as she turned her face away to stare across the garden. "But I'm not certain that can even be done, if our countries would even allow it. After all, how do you take away royal status from someone who was born to it by the grace of God? And what would our existence be if our duties were abandoned, our very identities lost?" She added softly, "For royals, it *is* duty before all else, even our own happiness."

"A lot of us understand duty, Your Highness. I'm still a soldier, still in service to my country."

She stopped and faced him. "Because you *choose* to be. You carry out your duty because you chose this path, not because it was thrust upon you."

"Don't assume that because I wasn't born into wealth or position that duty wasn't thrust upon me," he countered.

She hesitated, then asked, "Because of your father?"

His heart skipped as the quiet question jarred him. "What do you know about my father?"

"Not much." She gestured toward the house and avoided eye contact. "The aunties said…that he'd gotten into trouble for smuggling."

Gotten into trouble. Well, wasn't that a pleasant way of saying a man had been hanged? "He did." *Among other things*…things Clayton had no intention of sharing with her. "As I said, we have duty in common, Your Highness."

He could tell by the way she hesitated before walking on that she didn't believe him, but he certainly had no intention of telling her exactly where that sense of duty came from. If the prince regent had made him a viscount because a mere general wasn't good enough to guard a princess, what would she think about him if she knew the truth about his father? Would she ever trust that the son of a murderer was good enough to be in her presence, let alone protect her?

"And as for my current duty," he said, injecting a lightness into the conversation he didn't feel, "I serve at the pleasure of the princess."

"But that's why I wanted you to oversee my guard, because

you *don't* treat me like a princess." Frustration heated her voice. "When I was with you the other night, when we were simply talking and you weren't being deferential, I didn't feel royal or duty bound. I felt...*ordinary*, as if I were someone other than a princess." She looked away across the pond as she explained, "The beautiful and brilliant woman you teased me about being."

The floral scent of her perfume reached him on the breeze, and he breathed it in. "I wasn't teasing," he murmured.

She stopped so quickly that she nearly tripped over her own feet as she turned toward him. Her mouth fell open in stunned surprise. "Is that why you kissed me—because you truly thought I was beautiful?"

He crossed his arms and grinned. "I believe *you* kissed *me*."

Her lips slapped shut, and a storm brewed in the warm chocolate depths of her eyes. "Why, you—"

"I'm not saying I didn't enjoy it." His gaze went to her mouth, to those plump, pink lips of hers that had tasted as sweet as ripe strawberries. He could do nothing to satisfy his longing to kiss her again, yet the devil inside him couldn't resist adding, "After all, what man doesn't enjoy having a beautiful woman kissing him? Soft and warm, pliant in his arms..."

She swallowed, and the gentle movement undulated down her throat. A powerful urge gripped him to put his mouth right there against her slender neck, to feel it beneath his lips along with the speeding pulse he knew throbbed through her.

"Trust me," he murmured. "The last thing I cared about at that moment was that you were a princess. At that moment..." Unable to touch her, he swept his gaze over her face, and she trembled as if he'd truly caressed her cheek. "You were just a woman."

And *that* was the problem. He had to stop thinking of her as anything but a royal under his protection. Yet she didn't help when she gazed up at him as she was doing right then, with a look of longing and curiosity. As if he were good enough for a princess.

"If given the chance," she asked breathlessly, searching his face, "would you kiss me again?"

Damn if he wasn't wondering the exact same thing himself. Would he be mad enough? "I think we—"

"Princess!" A loud wail cut through the soft afternoon, followed by the sound of running footsteps.

Startled, Cordelia turned toward the house just in time for a little girl to hurl herself against her skirts.

———

Cordelia stiffened with a gasp of surprise as two little arms wrapped fiercely around her legs. Then she bent down and cradled against her bosom the sobbing child who cried as if her heart had been shattered. She was the same little girl to whom Cordelia had given her bow.

"Elizabeth," she cooed softly and placed a kiss to the top of the girl's head. She lifted her eyes to Clayton and saw his concerned expression. "What's wrong?"

"She—she—" The child sobbed so hard that she couldn't squeeze out the lisped words between tear-strangled breaths. So she pointed in the direction of the terrace.

Too many people lingered in the direction of her pointing finger for Cordelia to understand. "Who, sweetling?"

"N-Nurse B-Beecham."

When Cordelia looked at Clayton questioningly, he answered, "One of the caretakers from the hospital who accompanied the children today."

"I see." Cordelia brushed frizzy strands of hair away from the girl's face. "What did Nurse Beecham do to upset you?"

Elizabeth's lip quivered. "She…she took my bow!"

Cordelia looked down at the girl's dress. The bow was missing. "Why did she do that?"

"She said I stole it." The little girl's voice fell to barely more than a trembling whisper, and shame darkened her face.

Cordelia's heart broke, and it was all she could do to keep her voice from cracking as she said, "Well, she was just mistaken." The nurse was a lot more than that, but Cordelia didn't want to use that kind of language in front of a little girl. "I'll go with you and explain that it was a gift. We'll ask for the bow back, all right?"

"No!" Elizabeth's eyes flared with…*fear*? "No!"

Clayton knelt beside her, placed his hand on the little girl's back, and asked in a reassuring voice, "Why not, poppet?"

"'Cause she…she…" She cast an uneasy glance over her shoulder at Clayton, then put her mouth to Cordelia's ear and whispered, "She slapped me."

Cordelia's blood instantly turned cold. A red streak she

hadn't noticed before marred Elizabeth's cheek. Then the ice inside her sparked into furious fire.

Too angry to speak, she handed Elizabeth to Clayton. Then she rose to her feet and charged across the grounds toward the terrace, her fists clenched. Clayton hurried after her with Elizabeth in his arms, reaching her side just as she stopped in front of a group of hospital workers.

"Which one of you is Nurse Beecham?" Cordelia called out.

The woman turned at her name. When she saw Cordelia, her eyes grew wide, and she dropped into a low curtsy, followed by those around her. "Your Serene Highness, I'm honored—"

"Did you slap this child?"

The nurse's face paled nearly to white against her gray worsted wool dress and white cap. She glanced at her colleagues for support, but none of them stepped forward to defend her. They all lowered their gazes to the ground or looked away. "Yes, ma'am, I did. She'd stolen a ribbon with jewels from one of the—"

"Like this one?" Cordelia stuck out her shoe from beneath her hem, revealing the matching bow. Whispers went up from the guests who were within earshot. "*I* gave that ribbon to her as a gift. Instead of believing her, you accused her of being a thief!"

"My apologies, Your Highness." Beecham's mouth flapped like a fish's as she struggled to find the words to explain. "But—but what else was I to think? If one of the children had something like that in her hand, then obviously—"

"I don't care what she had in her hand or how she got it. *No* child ever deserves to be slapped, especially one in your

care." So much anger boiled inside her that her chest constricted and made breathing difficult. "She should have your patience and kindness, not your abuse."

"Children need a strong hand, Your Highness, if they are to grow into moral, productive members of our society," Beecham explained as deferentially as possible, despite raising her chin.

"Children need to be loved and comforted."

"We do love and comfort them, ma'am." The nurse's face blanked with a lack of understanding. "That's why we scold them when necessary."

Cordelia could barely believe what she was hearing. *Scold?* The woman had slapped a child!

"I did nothing illegal nor anything against the policies of the hospital, Your Highness," Beecham defended herself. "Children need to be disciplined."

"Of course, but discipline does not mean—"

"Your Highness," Clayton said quietly and placed his hand briefly on her arm to capture her attention.

Cordelia's gaze flew to him. His solemn expression took her breath away and jarred an acute awareness through her of where she was, what she had just done. In her anger, she'd made a scene, and everyone knew it, too. Including Clayton.

She was suddenly aware of the people around her, how they stared and whispered, and her face flushed with embarrassment. As the tension grew around her, heads began to turn across the lawn to see what was happening, which only led to more hushed voices and even more stares.

Cordelia wanted to scream with anger, but all she could

do was bite her tongue and back down. She pulled in a long breath that did little to calm her and forced a smile for all who were watching.

"I apologize, Nurse Beecham, for any misunderstanding. I am certain you did what you thought best." The words grated, but what else could she say? It wasn't as if she could speak her true mind, even in defense of a child. "May I ask— where is the bow?"

Beecham reached into her pocket and presented it on her palm with a shallow curtsy. "Here, Your Highness. I planned on giving it to the butler when I left so it could be returned to its rightful owner."

"How thoughtful of you," Cordelia drawled.

She took the bow from the nurse's hand and gave it back to Elizabeth, who closed her tiny fist around it. The little girl held tightly to Clayton for protection with both arms slung around his neck, and her big eyes warily watched the confrontation unfolding in front of her. Cordelia's chest sank. Even little Elizabeth knew she'd gone too far in confronting the nurse.

"Nurse Beecham, perhaps you would enjoy some refreshments," Cordelia said and gestured toward the tables. "Enjoy the rest of your afternoon." *In other words…please leave.*

Cordelia couldn't bear to look at the woman as the nurse curtsied and walked away, her colleagues grouping around her, and all of them thinking she was right to slap a child. Across the garden, guests continued to crane their necks to catch a glimpse of what was happening, and they no longer even bothered to pretend they weren't talking about her.

Cordelia had thoughtlessly created a spectacle, and she

would be punished for it. From the corner of her eye, she could see Marie scurrying across the lawn toward her.

She placed her hand on Elizabeth's head and told Clayton in a low voice so the guests couldn't overhear, "I'll be sent to my room for this. You won't see me again until tomorrow."

If then. Uncle Ernest was already uneasy about their visit. He would send her away before he allowed her to do anything to further endanger her potential marriage. No matter that she'd defended a helpless child.

"Come here, sweetling." She pulled Elizabeth from Clayton's arms and handed her over to Clayton's two aunties as the women bustled up. "Please take care of her, and do not give her back to that hospital. I will find another home for her."

She kissed Elizabeth's cheek, right over the red slap mark.

"Be brave and do as the aunties tell you." She smoothed down the girl's hair before dropping her hand away. "They are both very kind ladies."

The child nodded and clasped onto the viscountess as tightly as she had to Clayton. *Smart girl.* She knew how to recognize those who would protect her.

Cordelia looked at Clayton and bit her lip. Perhaps it was time she learned to do the same.

Clayton saw the fiery determination that had blazed in Cordelia's eyes only moments earlier fade into—was that *fear*? Uneasiness pinched his gut. "Princess? Are you—"

"Your Serene Highness!" The comtesse practically ran across the lawn toward Cordelia, a consternated expression on the woman's face. "You've upset yourself. Let us go—"

"The princess is fine," Clayton assured her as he stepped to place himself between the comtesse and Cordelia. Even now, the need to protect her rose strongly inside him. "I've been watching over her."

"I think you've done enough, sir." The comtesse stepped past him to take Cordelia's arm. "Come, Your Highness. We'll find a quiet room for you to rest." But as she led Cordelia away, she chastised in a low voice Clayton was certain he wasn't meant to overhear, "You've forgotten your place…"

Once again, he saw Cordelia transform into the regal princess who reminded him so much of a lifeless statue. But as the comtesse led her away, Cordelia sent him a parting glance over her shoulder, a look so full of desolation that it nearly undid him.

He could do nothing more than stand and watch her walk away. Cordelia might be so much stronger than she knew, but she also reminded him of the swans the regent kept in gold aviaries in front of Carlton House. Beautiful, trapped in a gilded cage…in desperate need of rescue.

"Clayton." Danielle Braddock, Duchess of Hampton, stepped up to his side and frowned as she followed his gaze toward the departing princess. "Aunt Harriett just left the party, carrying a child. Since that's not the usual kind of party favor the palace hands out to its guests, I thought I'd ask… What on earth just happened?"

"There was a misunderstanding. A nurse at the Foundling

Hospital accused a child of stealing a bow the princess had given her, and the woman struck the child for lying," he explained distractedly, catching one last glimpse of Cordelia before she disappeared inside Buckingham House. "It upset the princess." And for coming to a child's defense, she'd be locked away in punishment. *Madness.* If he could only have found a means to spirit her away, even if only for a few hours, until her family calmed down.

An idea struck him. He sent a sideways glance at his best friend's wife. Only he and Marcus knew the truth about the duchess's past and what she was capable of doing to help women in need. And Cordelia was certainly in need.

"You're good at rescuing people," he said thoughtfully.

"I am." Pride laced her voice.

"I have a favor to ask of you."

"Of course. What is it?"

He turned his back to the house and tugged at his sleeves. "I need you to help pry open a cage door."

Intrigued, the duchess slowly arched a brow.

Ten

CLAYTON STEPPED DOWN FROM THE CARRIAGE AND GRI-maced at the façade of Covent Garden. The opera. *Bloody hell.* He didn't think anything could be more torturous than yesterday's garden party, but this... Yet he wasn't here for his own entertainment.

No. Tonight was purely for Cordelia.

He could have easily passed the princess's protection off to Marcus for the evening. *Should* have done, in fact, and spent the night tracking Scepter. His gut told him the group had been involved in the attack on the princess, but so far he'd turned up no connection. Questioning the palace staff had led nowhere. He might have had better luck simply prowling the streets of London for answers. Even being out in the cold and damp night would certainly have been more fun than suffering through an opera.

Furthermore, being close to Cordelia was damnably disconcerting. He kept forgetting that she was a princess, and that couldn't be allowed to continue.

Pulling in a deep breath to gather his resolve, Clayton strode up the wide front steps. He dismissed the other arriving theatregoers without a thought as he went inside. They would be no threat except to the musicians and performers by the grumbles and mutters they'd unleash when the lights were dimmed. Having spent a small fortune on tickets and finery to stand out from the crowd, they would be disappointed to learn that the prince regent wouldn't be in attendance tonight.

Or perhaps not, given the excitement that the princess's visit seemed to be generating.

As if to prove his point, he heard a lady comment to her husband, "Why can't our royals be more like Monrovia's?"

Indeed. Clayton would gladly substitute Princess Cordelia's striking presence for Princess Sophia's vapidity any day. More—Cordelia was fearless even with a knife pressed to her throat, while Sophia would have fainted a dozen times over at the sight of a spider. Cordelia was compassionate, too. She had come to the defense of that little girl at yesterday's garden party, even knowing she would anger her uncle. That was something none of the British royals would ever have done for a foundling. He'd also seen her at other moments when she'd spoken kind words to servants or complimented those people who were clearly not of aristocratic rank.

She warmed her way into hearts as naturally as the summer sun. So why would anyone want to harm her?

Not knowing the answer kept him up nights.

Clayton spotted his guards positioned inside the theatre lobby. He gave them a curt nod as he slipped through the excited crowd and hurried up the sweeping stairs toward the private boxes. Tonight, the princess would be seated in the royal box at the very center of the theatre where everyone in attendance could see her. He didn't like Cordelia being exposed like that, but he'd taken every precaution.

Tonight, at least, she would be safe, both from outside attackers and her own royal contingent.

A high-pitched voice warmed up backstage, loudly enough to cut through the noise of the arriving crowd. Clayton winced. He, on the other hand, might not survive.

"Clayton! Over here."

He smiled gratefully at Marcus when he spotted his old friend on the landing. Tonight was all due to Marcus and Danielle, who had arranged the evening's excursion to the opera in order to remove Cordelia from the watchful eye of the palace for a few hours. The two had even escorted the princess from Buckingham House to the theatre. A good decision. Marcus would have protected her well if any trouble had arisen, and Danielle would never have allowed the comtesse inside the same carriage with them.

Cordelia's evening of freedom had already begun. Clayton's only concern now was to make certain she enjoyed herself.

He slapped Marcus on the shoulder. "No trouble on the way, then?"

"None. And the two ladies hit it off well."

"Glad to hear it." Knowing the duchess, she most likely carried a pocket pistol in her reticule tonight to surreptitiously help with protection duties. "They're already in the box?"

Marcus nodded. "Along with the Comtesse de Marseille and Danielle's aunt Harriett, who both came in a second carriage. Prince Ernest stayed at Carlton House with the regent."

Clayton was *very* glad to hear that. Having the comtesse here was bad enough. Cordelia wouldn't have had any chance of enjoying herself under her uncle's watch.

"The guards are all placed, I see," Marcus commented quietly so none of the crowd around them could overhear.

"I've taken care of everything." Right down to substituting former soldiers who had served with him on the Peninsula for the box's attendants. The service might be less sparkling than usual, but Clayton trusted them.

Excitement rippled through the opera house as the attendants began to usher the audience members toward their seats. Marcus and Clayton moved slowly down the hall that ran behind the boxes, scanning the thin crowd around them. Even here, jaded lords and ladies lingered in hopes of catching a glimpse of the visiting princess before slipping reluctantly into their boxes. Their curiosity wasn't sparked only because she was a foreign princess but also because they hoped she'd become an English one.

Clayton bit back an irritated curse. In the eyes and hearts of the English, Cordelia had become another version of their beloved Princess Charlotte. Wealthy, antiroyal merchants and troublemaking Whigs had already spilled pamphlets and bills through London's streets in which they offered Monrovia their support and declared their preference for Cordelia and her uncle over their current royals. Caricatures portraying her as an angel and the royal dukes as little devils filled printshop windows.

None of Farmer George's family could have been pleased about that.

Neither was Clayton. The last thing he needed was more attention to be drawn to the princess.

The two men paused outside the door to the royal box. Neither would step inside until the hallway was empty and every lord, lady, and attendant in their places.

"Have you learned anything more about the princess's attacker?" Marcus asked.

"Nothing." And that worried him.

"You still believe he was connected to Scepter?"

"I do."

"Yet you have no proof."

"I have no proof that he wasn't." And one hell of a feeling in his gut that he was.

They fell silent as the remaining crowd in the hall thinned to one last couple who kept casting glances toward the royal box. A frustrated soldier turned attendant tried to convince the couple to take their seats.

Marcus pressed, "Do you have any information at all about Scepter's recent activities?"

"Only what my informants have been saying for months," Clayton grudgingly admitted. He knew exactly how his insistence about the connection between the palace attack and Scepter sounded, even to his best friend. Defensive. And wrong. "That Scepter has stopped all their operations."

"I've never doubted your instincts before." Marcus watched as the lingering couple finally gave up on spotting any royals and made their way, disheartened, toward their own box at the end of the hall. "But perhaps Scepter truly did die on the gallows along with the Marquess of

Hawking, and the attack on the princess had nothing to do with them."

No. Clayton had seen the attacker's face when he'd mentioned Scepter. The fear that had gripped the man was real. "Or perhaps they're simply holding their breath and waiting for the signal that Hawking promised would come."

"But what signal?" The frustration in the former general's voice matched his own.

Clayton grimaced. "No bloody idea."

"So we're back to our original question." Marcus leveled a no-nonsense gaze on him. "Why would Scepter want to kill the princess?"

Clayton shook his head. "I've asked around the palace about her and her family." As discretely as possible, too, using his new position as an excuse. If Scepter had returned and found its way into the palace's inner circle, he didn't want to let them know he was stalking them. "I've discovered nothing credible. Just baseless rumors."

He was at a dead end and frustrated. His only way forward was the princess and whatever secrets she was keeping, but he'd also learned enough about her to know that pushing her would only cause her to dig in deeper.

Marcus reached to open the door and head into the box. "Then best to stay on our guard about everything."

"Agreed." Clayton followed him inside. "I think we should—" His eyes fell on Cordelia, and he froze.

Sweet Lucifer, she was simply stunning.

Except for a small tiara whose diamonds shimmered in the lamplight, she wasn't dressed at all like a princess tonight.

No billowing gown, no ermine wrap, no long strings of jewels dripping from around her neck or bobs dangling from her ears. Tonight, she wore a simple gown of peach satin cut in the current high-waisted style and was all the more striking for it, her dress standing out boldly against the low-cut, jewel-toned velvet gowns draped over the rest of the audience. Her dark chestnut hair was pinned up in casual curls, and a few stray tendrils dared to caress the back of her slender neck and the sides of her oval face. Her eyes were big and bright with excitement at being at the theatre, and she laughed lightly at something one of her companions had said.

The sight of her made his chest clench.

So did another sensation he couldn't name when she rested her hand on the arm of the man standing beside her—

The Duke of Grafton.

Why the hell was *he* here? Clayton forced a smile for the box at large to hide his irritation as he reached for one of the glasses of port offered by the attendant. He couldn't stand the man. Obsequious and self-serving, Grafton had never done a day of hard work in his life. Nor had the dandy served his country in the military, been educated at university, or done anything of merit except be born first to the previous duke, who had done almost as little as his son.

"Why is Grafton here?" Clayton muttered to Marcus against the rim of his glass as he took a long, welcomed swallow. He pretended to ignore both Grafton and Cordelia as he swept his gaze around the box, yet he noticed the far too intimate way Grafton leaned over to say something into Cordelia's ear that made her smile. "He wasn't on the guest list I was given."

"The palace chose him to be Princess Cordelia's official escort for the evening when her uncle begged off."

Clayton knew the princess well enough to know that Grafton's ingratiating, smarmy demeanor was exactly the behavior she didn't like or trust, yet she returned the duke's attentions and flattered him with her smiles, even as she took surreptitious glances in Clayton's direction. Was she attempting to convey the message that she had a different guard to protect her now and no longer needed his watch?

Laughable.

Marcus followed his gaze. "Does it bother you to have Grafton here?"

"It bothers me that I wasn't told about the change." Clayton swirled the port in his glass. "I can't protect her if I don't know what to expect."

"He's the Duke of Grafton," Marcus reminded him. "Not Napoleon."

"I think I'd prefer Boney." Clayton set aside the rest of the port. What he craved tonight was whiskey, and lots of it. "Grafton exemplifies the worst of the English peerage."

"Says the viscount who's one of us."

Christ. "Not yet I'm not." He had until arrangements could be made to introduce him into the House of Lords to find a way to wiggle out of the title. Or to flee England.

"Look on the bright side. At least Grafton's not one of the royal dukes."

That did little to ease the inexplicable knot in Clayton's chest. It also raised a new puzzle. Why *wasn't* one of the royal dukes here to escort her? "Doesn't the palace worry that Grafton might vie for her himself?"

"The exact opposite, I'd wager. Even Grafton isn't daft enough to confuse royalty with aristocracy and overreach himself."

Oohs and aahs went up from the half dozen ladies in the box when Grafton reached into his jacket and withdrew a red rose. With a deep bow, he handed it to Cordelia.

Clayton threw Marcus an I-told-you-so look.

To his surprise—and annoyance—Cordelia accepted the rose with a bright smile.

"What is it with you damned dukes?" Clayton growled beneath his breath.

Marcus grinned and crossed the box to join his wife, but Danielle said something to him that wiped the smile from his face. Then she waved over Clayton, who had no choice but to join the group.

"Wasn't that rose romantic?" Danielle said, squeezing Clayton's hand in greeting. "I just said to Marcus that he never thinks to give me roses at the theatre. Don't you think he should?"

Clayton knew better than to entangle himself in this discussion. "The lamps are dimming." *Perfect timing.* He nodded out toward the stage and the audience seated on the floor of the theatre. "We should take our seats. Wouldn't want to miss the overture."

"A devoted follower of opera, are you, Elliott?" Amusement danced in Grafton's voice at the idea. "You'll have to give us your thoughts on the libretto."

A flash of embarrassment for Clayton crossed Cordelia's face, but her practiced smile returned immediately. "I'm sure the general has more important things to be concerned about tonight."

"At an opera?" Grafton scoffed. "I can't think of a better topic to discuss than music." He gestured his glass of port at Clayton. "Which do you find more awe-striking about opera, Elliott? The libretto or the bravura?"

Clayton knew better than to entangle himself in *this* discussion, too. "The beauty of the ladies in attendance," he dodged, drawing soft laughs from those in the box. "And speaking of beautiful ladies..." With a smile, he bowed smartly to the princess. "Good evening, Your Serene Highness."

"General Elliott." She inclined her head regally, but she couldn't hide the faint smile that touched her lips at his compliment. She paused as if she wanted to say something, but the orchestra struck up the first notes of the overture and interrupted. She turned toward Grafton and gestured toward the front of the box. "Perhaps we should take our seats, Duke."

Grafton didn't move. His eyes remained fixed on Clayton. "Tell me, Elliott. What do you think of Rossini's most recent works?"

"I'm afraid I have no opinion."

Grafton chuckled at Clayton's expense. "Perhaps not so devoted to opera after all."

Clayton refused to let that barb go unanswered, certainly not in front of the princess. Why he should care what she thought of him, he had no idea. But it mattered, damn it.

"I haven't had much time for opera in the past few years,"

Clayton countered with a lazy smile. "I was too busy saving Europe from Napoleon." He cast an assessing look over Grafton, from his overly starched cravat to his highly polished shoes. "What were *you* doing?"

Anger flashed red over Grafton's face. The duke bit out, "You forget your—"

"But I *can* tell you that I find Mozart's, Queen of the Night, aria to be sublime. The dichotomy between the vengeful lyrics and the breathtakingly beautiful rise of the soprano's voice is simply…" He slid his gaze to Cordelia and softened his voice. "Captivating."

Her pink lips parted slightly as she stared at him, her thoughts at that moment unreadable. Then, so softly that her response was almost lost beneath the scattered applause of the audience, she said, "I agree."

Grafton puffed out his chest. "And *I* think you should—"

"Excuse me." Marcus deftly interrupted what Clayton feared might become the first fisticuffs to break out in a royal opera box. "We should take our seats." He held out his hand to Cordelia. "Your Highness, may I have the pleasure of escorting you to your chair?"

"Of course, Duke." She allowed him to lead her out from between the two men and to the velvet chairs in the front of the box, yet the glance she stole over her shoulder wasn't for Grafton but for Clayton. As if she simply couldn't fathom him.

Understandable. At that moment, he had no blasted idea what to make of himself.

Eleven

"I WAS IN ATTENDANCE AT MRS. BILLINGTON'S LAST PER-formance," the Duke of Grafton whispered into Cordelia's ear, ruining the soprano's aria for her.

Cordelia did her best not to roll her eyes, although Grafton's near-constant chatter annoyed her to no end. It was as if he needed to share his knowledge of opera with her at every opportunity, and his interruptions proved so many that she'd lost the plot of what was happening on the stage.

"She deserved respect for her storied career, of course."

Cordelia shuddered at the feel of his breath on the side of her face and neck.

"But by then, her voice had lost its vitality. A shame, really, to see how far her talents had declined. Those of us in the audience gave extra to the charity that night simply out of pity." He paused. "You know how that is, I'm certain."

Not at all. But she certainly couldn't say that here in the midst of the box with the eyes of the entire theatre on her, no matter how much she wanted to.

She gave a silent breath of relief when he leaned away and settled back in his chair beside hers.

Oh, Grafton wasn't so bad, she supposed. She'd suffered through formal events with other men who were far more boring and self-centered and those who had no inkling of cultural awareness at all. He would have been a perfectly adequate escort for tonight's performance, except...

That he wasn't Clayton.

From her seat in the front row, she couldn't see him in the back of the box where he'd taken up his post in his role as her personal guard. But she felt his presence as palpably as if he were sitting next to her, and she knew his eyes had barely strayed from her since the curtain rose an hour ago.

His reaction to Grafton was very out of character. She had no idea what animosities he and Grafton shared for the other, but the two had behaved like opponents sizing each other up before a fight. The general had wounded Grafton's masculine pride, and in response the duke felt the petulant need to prove that he knew more about opera than Clayton.

She groaned inwardly when Grafton leaned toward her again. "I'm hoping to hear Signorina Pasta later this season when she—"

"Duke, please." She smiled to soften her interruption and nodded toward the stage. "The aria."

With a sniff of pique, he shifted away and silently turned his attention back to the stage.

Thank goodness. Free of his immediate attentions, she turned her head to look at the others in the box with her to discover if they were enjoying themselves.

A lie. She simply wanted a glimpse of Clayton.

He lounged on a chair at the rear of the box as if he were nowhere more formal than his own parlor, with his long legs kicked out in front of him and crossed at the ankles and his left arm stretched across the back of the empty chair beside him. His relaxed posture made him appear like a rake instead of a respected government official, right down to the lock of golden hair that fell roguishly across his forehead.

Or perhaps she simply thought that because of how handsome he looked in the shadows, how much more broad-shouldered and solid than the other men in attendance. He wore the same evening finery they did, cut in the same current fashion. But he seemed nothing like the others, nothing like—

His full lips curled into an amused smile.

Caught.

Her breath hitched with a silent gasp, and she immediately turned back toward the stage. Thank goodness the theatre was too dark for him to see her blush.

She hadn't been able to speak with him since yesterday's garden party, having been kept in her room just as she'd feared and only let out tonight due to the insistence of the Duke and Duchess of Hampton that she attend the opera with them. She knew Clayton had been asking around the palace about Monrovia and its monarchy, but she also knew he'd discover nothing incriminating. Uncle Ernest had made certain her father's misdeeds had died with him, even if no reparations had yet been made. *She* would make certain that restitution was paid, however necessary, just as soon as she could.

Until then, she had a different worry on her hands. A very tall, blond, and broad-shouldered worry.

Clayton wanted her to trust him…but how far could she extend that trust?

Alone in her room today, she'd had plenty of time to pace and think. Whatever motive someone had for wanting her dead, it simply could not have been because of her father. She'd traced through every possible reason connected to that, and not one made sense for why anyone connected to the Monrovian military would attack her in England when doing so would have been far easier in her home country. No, there was another reason, and she was afraid she'd figured it out.

She needed to speak with Clayton, and after the incident in the garden, Marie would be more watchful than ever. But she couldn't wait any longer, and she didn't trust anyone to deliver a message for her. She had to do it herself, and she had to do it tonight.

No. She had to do it *immediately*.

With an apologetic smile at Grafton to her left and the Duke and Duchess of Hampton to her right, she stood and waved all the men back into their seats as they rose politely to their feet. Including Clayton, whom she didn't dare glance at as she slipped past him toward the rear of the box and the door leading out into the hall.

"Your Highness." The comtesse was immediately at her side. Concern shown on Marie's face as she reached for Cordelia's hand. "Are you unwell?"

"I'm fine." She lowered her voice to a private whisper. "I simply need to use the retiring room."

"I'll go with you."

"Stay, please. There's no need for you to miss the performance. There are guards in the hallway, and I'll only be gone a moment." When Marie continued to hold her hand, Cordelia pulled hers away. "*I insist.*"

She stepped around Marie and out of the box before the comtesse could stop her—or chastise her again for her behavior as she had with the nurse in the garden. From the way Marie and Uncle Ernest had kept her in her room and threatened to send her home to Monrovia, one would have thought she was a child who had thrown herself into the Thames and attempted to swim for freedom.

Oh, what a sweet escape that would be! But she would make do with tonight.

Once she was in the hall, she leaned back against the wall, closed her eyes, and breathed deeply in a futile attempt to calm her racing heart. She counted to ten in her head as she waited, knowing...

"Princess, it's not safe for you to go off alone."

Clayton's deep voice twined down her spine, and in its wake came the same confusion she'd felt since meeting him...a certainty that she should flee coupled with the inexplicable desire to simply wrap herself around him.

"I'm not alone." She opened her eyes, looked up at him, and lost her breath. "I have you guarding me."

He grumbled, "Try not to sound so aggrieved that I want to save your life, will you?"

Her lips twisted as she fought back a smile at his expense. "I need to speak with you." *And I knew you would follow me.* Her smile faded. "I think I might know why someone would want to harm me."

He stiffened, then glanced up and down the hallway.

They were alone except for two guards turned box attendants standing near the stairs.

"The royal box needs more brandy and claret," he called out to the two men. "Go fetch some."

They nodded and scurried away to do as ordered.

Clayton reached past Cordelia to open the door of the adjoining box. "In here."

He took her arm and led her quickly inside the private box, then closed the door behind them.

The space was unlit and empty. Despite the front curtains hanging partly open to the theatre and stage below, the back of the box was filled with dark shadows that prevented anyone from seeing the two of them together, and the sound of music drifting up to them would keep them from being overheard. Exactly what she wanted.

So why did she suddenly feel nervous? She twisted her trembling hands in her skirt and stepped back against the wall to make certain the shadows obscured her completely from all eyes in the boxes surrounding them. "I've been thinking about the attack, and I think I know why that man did it."

The corners of his mouth curled up. "Have you decided to trust me, then?"

"Yes."

His low chuckle tangled around her in the darkness. "You don't have to sound so aggrieved about *that* either."

In the dim light, she could just make out the gleam in his eyes until she confessed, "You should be pleased about that. There are others in the palace I don't trust at all."

At that, his amusement vanished. "Who?"

"The royal dukes."

He blinked. "Pardon?"

"Rather, that is, someone close to them," she clarified. "One of their mistresses, or a woman who has designs on marriage. She must have hired him to kill me."

"A woman?" he repeated as if he hadn't heard correctly.

"You don't think a woman capable of that kind of plotting?" She lifted her chin. "You're sadly underestimating women, General."

"Believe me, Princess." His soft murmur swirled around her in the shadows and stirred a warmth low in her belly. "I know exactly what kind of spine women possess."

A scattering of applause rippled through the theatre, but instead of intruding on their privacy, it seemed to cocoon them together even more.

"What makes you think someone connected to the dukes wants you dead?" he asked.

"To keep me from marrying one of them." When disbelief crossed his face, she hurried to explain, "I was attacked here, not in Monrovia, so the reason has to be connected to England. But I've no say in any diplomatic or governmental agreements whatsoever—the only value I have here is marriage into the royal family." *The only value I seem to have anywhere.* "If one of the dukes' mistresses or intimates thinks I'm a threat—if some other aristocratic woman or her family thinks I'm a rival in marriage—then she might just be desperate enough to attempt to remove me."

"Which woman?"

"I don't know. I haven't been in England long enough to discover who has designs on which duke."

He asked far too casually for the way he tensed, "It's been settled, then? The palace has selected the duke you're to marry?"

"Not yet." She prayed every night that time would never come, but she might as well have asked the sun not to rise for all the good her wishful thinking did. "But everyone knows that's why I'm here."

"Do you have any say in the matter?"

Very little. "I can't be forced into marriage against my will."

His expression hardened beneath the shadows, as if he recognized her answer for the dodge it was. "Do you have any say in which duke, then?"

Even less. She couldn't bring herself to answer that at all. "I trust Uncle Ernest to make the best match possible for me."

He exhaled slowly and folded his arms across his chest, pulling the kerseymere jacket tight over his broad shoulders. "So you don't know which duke, if any of them, you'll be marrying?"

"No."

"If you don't know, then how would anyone else?"

"Perhaps one of the royal dukes was discussing me, and the woman thought for certain…" Her shoulders slumped in frustration. "You don't believe me."

"I believe you give the royal mistresses too much credit. The people who want you dead are not your rivals for a duke's bed."

Hope seeped out of her, and she slumped against the wall

behind her. "So we're back to the beginning, with no idea who would want to harm me."

"None." He shook his head. "For all we know, your attacker could have simply been a madman. We don't even know if he wanted to target you specifically or if he simply came upon you and acted opportunistically."

She searched his face. "You truly think that?"

"I don't think anyone connected to the dukes was behind it."

She should have been happy for that, but it didn't put her at ease.

Neither did being so close to Clayton in the darkness. She was breaking a thousand unwritten rules by being alone with him like this, and if anyone found them, she'd be placed on the first ship back to Monrovia.

But she needed his comfort. He was her only ally, and she could trust him with her fears and secrets.

Some of them.

"You're probably right," she acquiesced. Then she grimaced. "In any case, after yesterday's garden party, the royal dukes are probably all running away from me as quickly as possible."

A confrontation over a foundling wasn't at all what the British royal family wanted in a bride who should have been demure and never drew unwanted attention to herself. Uncle Ernest had most likely stayed behind tonight in a desperate attempt to repair the damage she'd caused.

Yet she didn't regret what she'd done. The choice between her royal duty and rescuing an abused child... Well, there had been no choice.

"You did nothing wrong," he assured her.

She leveled a disbelieving look at him. "Princess Sophia called that little girl an unwanted urchin. They'll never forgive me for defending her."

He muttered under his breath, "*Princess Sophia* is an unwanted urchin."

Cordelia's hand flew to her mouth to stifle her laugh. Even in the darkness, she saw an impish gleam dance in Clayton's eyes. Oh, that rascal!

"You came to the aid of a defenseless child," he told her. "I thought you were absolutely wonderful for it."

Her heart skipped at that unexpected compliment.

"So does little Elizabeth."

Then her heart stopped completely when he took her hand and gently pulled it away from her mouth to bring it to his to place a kiss to the backs of her fingers before releasing her. A tingle sped up her arm, and she warmed with the possibility of being kissed again. This time not on her hand.

"How is Elizabeth?" Her voice emerged far throatier than she'd intended. *Goodness.*

"The aunties took your wishes to heart and are keeping her with them until a more permanent alternative to the Foundling Hospital can be found." He quirked a grin. "They're spoiling her rotten."

"Good."

"But all she can talk about is the fairy-tale princess who rescued her from the bad witch, how the princess swept in like an angel and flew her away. The aunties are boasting across Mayfair that they're helping 'the angel.'"

She winced. "The palace isn't going to be at all happy about *that*. That's probably why they allowed me to come to the opera tonight, to keep me as far away from the royal family as possible."

"No. You're here because you needed a night of escape."

She shook her head. "I'm here because the Duke and Duchess of Hampton were gracious enough to…" Her voice trailed off as she realized how tonight came to be. "And you're friends with the duke and duchess."

"Best friends, actually."

Her mouth fell open. "*You* made tonight happen, didn't you?"

"I wanted you to have an enjoyable night." He glanced over his shoulder out the front of the box as the soprano onstage reached her highest notes, and he winced. "As enjoyable as possible, that is."

Her chest swelled with gratitude. "I'm having a wonderful time."

"Because of Grafton's attentions?"

Was that jealousy she heard in his voice? *Impossible.* "No. Because of you." Impulsively, she rose up on her tiptoes to kiss his cheek, her hands resting flat against his lapels to keep her balance. "Thank you for tonight," she murmured in his ear. "It means a great deal to me."

As she lowered herself away, her hands remaining on his chest, she looked up into his face. The grin that had been there moments before was gone, and his gaze had dropped longingly to her mouth.

His deep voice wrapped around her like velvet. "I serve at the pleasure of the princess."

"Do you?" Her hands curled into the soft satin of his waistcoat, and her heart pounded as she taunted, "Then prove it."

She heard the soft hitch of his breath. He stood still as a statue, making no move to lower his mouth to hers, but he wanted to, she was certain. So certain she could feel it down in the swirling nervous knots he tied in her belly and the faint ache he stirred even lower.

Her mouth lingered so close to his that his warm breath tickled her lips. "Kiss me, Clayton."

His eyes stared hungrily at her mouth even as he clenched his jaw and refused to kiss her. He was warring with himself. Could she tempt him into surrendering the battle?

She slipped her hand behind his neck and teased her fingers through the silky hair at his nape. "Don't you want to kiss me?"

He laughed, the deep sound rumbling into her. "Of course I do."

"So do I." When he didn't move, she challenged, "You know too much about opera while still claiming to dislike it to attend solely for the performances. Something tells me that I won't be the first woman you've kissed in a dark theatre box."

His mouth tightened with chagrin and proved her right. "But you're not a woman. You're a prin—"

"*Don't* you dare call me that." She put her fingers to his lips to silence him. "Tonight, I just want to be an ordinary woman."

"Trust me," he mumbled against her fingers, looking

terribly aggrieved at the idea. "Princess or not, you could never be ordinary."

Her chest warmed, the compliment pleasing her far more than he would ever know. "Then don't think of me as anything more than a woman who wants to be kissed." She caressed his lips, fascinated by their softness. How could they be part of this otherwise hard, muscular man? She stroked the pad of her thumb across his bottom lip and thrilled when he inhaled sharply. "Show me that I'm not any more special than that."

A low groan of frustration escaped him. "You're asking for the impossible."

"I'm only asking for what you promised tonight would be." She outlined his sensuous lips with her fingertip, and he trembled. "A normal night."

"I don't think I promised that." The husky sound of his voice belied his determination to keep his distance.

Her heart took hope in that. "I'm pretty certain you did."

"That's a poor excuse of a lie."

She wanted to laugh with joy! No one had ever dared before to accuse her to her face of lying. Finally, he was no longer treating her as a princess. *Exactly* what she wanted.

"Well, perhaps you promised only an evening's escape." She trailed her fingertips along his jaw, and his breathing turned shallow and fast. "But I can't think of a better escape than to be kissed by you." She slipped her arms away from him and leaned back against the wall, putting a narrow gap between them. He would have to come to her to complete this fairytale moment, and she prayed with every beat of her heart that he would. "And certainly no better enjoyment."

The temptation became too much for him. With a frustrated groan, he stepped forward to close the distance between them, cupped her face between his hands, and lowered his mouth to hers.

Cordelia relaxed into him and welcomed his kisses. Very skilled kisses, too. No chaste touches, no desire to soothe and comfort as he'd done before—he claimed this kiss for himself, just as he would have with any other woman with whom he'd stolen away into the shadows, and she soared with happiness.

He kissed her hungrily as he shifted to pin her between his body and the wall. As the embrace grew in both heat and intensity, her legs shook, and she realized why he'd pressed against her—to keep her from sinking bonelessly to the floor. His kisses made her feel both weak-kneed and weightless, hot and tingly all the way out to the tips of her fingers and toes. She wrapped her arms around his shoulders and clung to him as though he were an anchor in a storm-tossed sea.

The tip of his tongue teased against the seam of her lips in a plea for her to open for him. Wanting this precious kiss to grow into so much more, she did as he asked. His tongue slipped between her lips, and he hungrily explored her mouth and swirled his tongue over hers in a silky glide that stole her breath.

There was no embarrassment, no uncertainty, in letting him kiss her like this—or in kissing him back just as eagerly. How could there be with a man who had so heroically saved her life, who made her feel beautiful and brave, who saw the woman beneath the tiara? Tonight was her chance to be bold and free, if only for one precious night, and she seized the moment as she closed her lips around his tongue and sucked.

A faint groan tore from him. "Princess…"

"Cordelia," she corrected against his lips. What she wouldn't have given at that moment for him to simply say her name!

His hand slid down the wall to her shoulder, then across to her throat. She was lost in the thrill of him and this wonderful new way of kissing and so had no idea what his hands were doing until—

He dropped his hand away.

She opened her eyes and blinked, confused by the loss of his touch. He'd removed her necklace and reached for her hand to place it on her palm.

"I want to put my mouth right here." He caressed his fingers down the side of her bare neck and lower still to the top of her chest just above her neckline. "But your necklace was in the way. Because if the clasp should unfasten and your necklace slip down beneath your dress," he warned, his voice thick and rough, "I might feel compelled to go after it."

She swallowed. Hard. He wasn't giving a warning; he was asking permission to take his kisses even further—more, he was giving her the freedom to take control. It was her decision, her time to lead in the thrilling dance happening between them.

And she claimed it.

With trembling fingers, she dangled the pendant above the little valley between her breasts. Then she slowly let the chain slip through her fingers and down into her bodice. The invitation was clear...

Go after it.

This time when he leaned toward her, his expression wasn't merely hungry—it was downright wolfish. He devoured her mouth as his hands swept down her body.

His lips moved away from hers, along her jaw to her neck to kiss her exactly as he'd promised. When she shivered, he smiled against her skin and touched the tip of his tongue to the pounding pulse at the base of her throat.

But it was his hands that made her tremble as they stroked along her sides. She felt as if she were falling weightless through space with only Clayton to keep her grounded. He caressed down the curves of her waist and hips, only to change direction and slowly trail his hands upward to her bodice.

She moaned softly when he cupped her breasts. There were three layers of clothing between her flesh and his hands, but the heat of his touch seeped into her, warming her breasts and making them feel heavy. She leaned into him, begging for his touch to soothe away the unexpected tightening of her nipples, and he did exactly as she needed by gently massaging the hard points through her clothes.

His mouth found hers again, and as he kissed her, his fingers moved up to trace over the top swells of her breasts that were just visible above her neckline. Her bare skin tingled everywhere he touched, and when he dared to sweep a finger beneath her bodice and across her hard nipple—

She turned her head away and gasped. "Clayton!"

A soft chuckle rumbled from the back of his throat and into her chest when he lowered his head to kiss the same bare stretch of flesh he'd just caressed. His mouth lingered only inches from her nipple, which ached to be kissed. *All* of her ached for him, yet she somehow knew that whatever kisses he gave her here in the dark box would not be enough to satisfy the longing flaming inside her. The pleasure between her thighs intensified as he continued to caress with his fingers inside her bodice and tease at her tightening nipples.

Thunderous applause roared through the opera house, followed by the stomping of feet. The sound shook the box around them.

His head snapped up.

The intruding noise rushed over them—as did reality. The audience was already spilling out of its seats and boxes for intermission, and an army of attendants moved though the theatre to raise the lamps.

He dropped his hands away from her. Cordelia caught back the breath he'd stolen and looked up at him. But her smile froze on her lips.

He stared at her as if she were a witch who'd tried to cast his soul into the darkness.

"You need to go," he told her.

When she reached for him, he stepped back and widened the distance between them.

He tugged his waistcoat into place and smoothed out the wrinkles. "The comtesse is going to come looking for you, if she hasn't already, and the Duchess of Hampton won't be able to stall her for long."

She blinked in confusion from the sudden loss of his embrace. "But I don't—"

"You have to go." He cast a narrowed glance over her, not out of any kind of longing, she knew, but to assess her appearance and make certain no telltale signs lingered of what they'd just done. "If anyone sees you leave this box, tell them you didn't want to bother the group by returning to the royal box in the middle of the aria and ducked inside here until it ended."

Cold rejection replaced the warmth he'd stirred inside her with his kisses, although she knew their parting had to be this way, for her sake. Once again, he was protecting her. "And if they ask me about you?"

"I guarded the hall while you walked to the retiring room and back, and the last you saw of me, I was giving orders to the box attendants about refreshments. Understand?"

"But where will you truly be?"

"Right here. I'll rejoin everyone in a few minutes."

"They'll expect you to—"

He gave her a hard look. "I am in no condition to follow you into that hallway."

His words registered inside her kiss-fogged brain with a startled thump of her heart. Oh, she didn't dare look down!

"Go," he ordered.

She gave a jerking nod, not knowing whether she should laugh with happiness that such a dashing man had kissed her or break down in sobs that it had ended, and hurried to the door. She felt flushed and frustrated, and her lips still ached for his—

"Princess."

She stopped with her hand on the door handle and looked back. "Yes?"

He bent down and scooped up her necklace from the floor. Wordlessly, he held it toward her. The pearl and diamond pendant dangled from its chain and shimmered in the dim light. As she stared at it, she knew—

Everything had changed again. She was once more only a princess in his eyes.

Her fingers trembled as she took back her necklace and hurried from the box.

Twelve

CLAYTON STRODE DOWN THE DARK CITY STREET. HE'D left Cordelia and her entourage in Marcus's capable hands when the opera ended several hours ago to be safely returned to Buckingham House, then struck out into the night. He wanted to spend what little time he had hunting down more information about Scepter. So far, though…nothing. He suspected Scepter was hiding and holding its breath, but he feared they were holding their breath in preparation for a war cry.

He was also attempting to burn off his frustration over Cordelia. Kissing her like that— *Damnation*. He'd lost his bloody mind.

In the morning, the two of them would have a long talk about inappropriate behavior and how it could never happen again. No matter how much she asked him to kiss her, no matter how warm and soft her body or how deliciously sweet and inviting her lips…

He blew out a harsh breath. A *very* long talk.

He shoved open the iron gate to the Armory's outer yard. He didn't care how much noise he made as he rattled it closed behind himself and loudly crunched the gravel beneath his boots as he walked toward the front doors. Two more teeth-jarring bangs of metal on metal went up as he walked through both doors, beneath the twin portcullises, and into the main room of the Armory.

Like the other men of the Armory, he'd often sought solace here since returning from the wars. Tonight would be no different.

He stopped beneath the metal-studded gas chandelier hanging from the center of the octagonal tower that rose three floors above him and surveyed the familiar space.

The old armory had started a second life two years ago as a place of sanctuary for soldiers returning from the wars who were having trouble adjusting to life back in England. Even then, though, when Marcus oversaw the renovations, he'd provided a training room full of weapons the men could use to hone their fighting skills. But since the execution of Scepter's leader, the Marquess of Hawking, for treason, the training room with its large cache of weapons had barely been used, and the men spent more time lounging on sofas than lunging with swords.

Clayton should have been happy about that. The men were finally settling into their home lives, and the sanctuary the Armory had once provided had become unnecessary for most of them. In fact, he couldn't remember the last time he'd seen Alec Sinclair or Brandon Pearce here, and Nate Reed had permanently moved to the countryside with his new wife and her son.

And yet, with its leather furniture, fully stocked liquor cabinet, and basement kitchen capable of serving up roast pheasant, was this place any different from the private clubs on St James's? Had the men of the Armory turned into the soft-bellied, pampered gentlemen they'd once despised?

He blew out an aggravated breath and called for the former aide-de-camp they'd hired to keep the place for them. "Alfred!"

"He's retired to his room for the night." Merritt Rivers stepped out of the training room, wiping down the blade of a rapier with a soft cloth. "No one here tonight but us street rats."

"I've seen the size of London's rats." Clayton nodded grimly toward the sword. "Don't give them any ideas about arming themselves."

Merritt grinned and stepped back into the training room. Clayton followed.

Based on his clothing—all black from neck to boots, including a tight-fitting tunic—and the discarded black greatcoat slung over one of the sawdust dummies, Merritt had also been out prowling the city streets tonight, but for a completely different reason.

By day, Merritt was a well-respected barrister and King's Counsel, like his magistrate father, who helped victims gain restitution for crimes committed against them. By night, however, he trained a group of women who lived in a derelict warehouse known as the Court of Miracles to patrol the city to prevent crime and keep innocents from becoming victims in the first place. Until recently, his wife, Veronica, had worked at his side, but the baroness could no longer venture out into the city with him. Her leather combat corset didn't fit now that she was heavy with child.

"You're here late," Merritt commented and reached to pull down a second rapier from the wall. Hundreds of weapons covered nearly every inch of the training room, from small pocket pistols to heavy claymores, and every last one of them was a functioning deadly weapon.

"I checked with my contacts in Seven Dials to see if they'd heard anything new about Scepter."

"And?" Like Clayton and Marcus, Merritt had been uneasy over Scepter's sudden disappearance.

"Nothing." Clayton shrugged out of his coat and placed it over Merritt's. "Not one peep." He frowned as he rolled up his sleeves. "It's as if they've simply disappeared."

Merritt tossed him the second sword, and Clayton easily caught it. "Or perhaps, with their leader executed, they've moved into other existing groups. England's full of reformists and revolutionaries these days."

"Don't confuse the two." Clayton slashed the rapier through the air to gain a feel for the blade, then moved to the piste in the center of the room. "I'm all for reform. Love it, in fact."

"Careful," Merritt warned as he took his position in front of him. "Talk like that will get you stripped of your viscountcy."

"Is that all it takes? Then by all means, reform is the way forward into the future." Clayton lowered into the en garde position and added, "But I'm against violence and bloodshed."

Without warning, he lunged, plunging the rapier directly at Merritt's chest.

But Merritt was too skilled as a fencer not to anticipate the attack and easily stepped aside as he parried Clayton's blade and then delivered his own thrust.

"Including that done by my own country," Clayton bit out through clenched teeth as he and Merritt chased each other up and down the piste in a melee of parries and thrusts. The clank of metal on metal reverberated off the thick stone walls. "When the Home Office can't find enough revolutionaries to arrest to appease Whitehall, they send out their spies to create them."

Merritt darted away from the strip and gave chase through the row of sawdust dummies that dangled on chains from the ceiling beams. "You mean the three men who were executed the day Princess Charlotte died?"

"Yes." *Among others.*

When the Home Office spies' reward money dried up because they couldn't easily find true revolutionaries to report, those same spies coerced men into committing suspicious activity to fill the void. Too many good men had gone to prison, Australia, and the gallows during the past year to count.

Clayton angrily slashed the blade at Merritt's chest, but Merritt skillfully parried each attack.

"The palace didn't even have the decency to commute their treason sentences to simple hangings," Clayton blew out between labored breaths.

No, the day the regent's daughter and grandson died, the prince regent showed so-called mercy by reducing their punishment for treason from being drawn and quartered to only a hanging and beheading. For that alone, Clayton had half a mind to tell his newfound friend to take his viscountcy and shove it up his fat arse.

And Cordelia planned on marrying into that family? *Christ.*

He slashed the blade again in anger, but this time he overextended his reach and lost his balance. It lasted only a moment, but he was unbalanced just long enough that Merritt scored a touch by tapping the side of his blade against Clayton's hip.

"Keep your head in the fight," Merritt warned and stepped back, once more falling into his well-practiced en garde stance.

Clayton bit out, "I am."

"Are you?" Another quick slap of the blade against the other hip proved his point.

Damnation. Clayton recovered and charged, chasing Merritt around a rack of dumbbells and a stand of wooden poles and clubs.

But Merritt set the chase most likely just to tire him out, and like a fool he fell for it. *Double damnation.*

"I saw the evidence against those three men, and it was solid," Merritt assured him, once more going on the attack. "They'd raised an army and were marching toward London. That was high treason."

No. It was the work of William Oliver, the Home Office's greediest spy. Merritt might have seen the evidence, but Clayton knew how it had been gathered.

The pressure that Parliament and the crown were exerting

on average Englishmen would come to a head soon, he was certain of it. God help them all when it did.

It was time to change the conversation. Clayton jumped across a bench and called out, "Speaking of judges—"

"We weren't." Merritt followed over the bench, not losing the rhythm of his strikes.

"How's your relationship with your father these days?"

"Fine." He ducked in time to miss Clayton's glancing blow to his left shoulder. "He's proud as a peacock to have a grandchild on the way." Merritt feinted to his right. "How's your relationship with yours?"

Surprise stunned Clayton. He missed a defensive block of Merritt's rapier and cost himself the easiest touch imaginable.

He stopped fighting and lowered the rapier to his side as he straightened out of his fencing stance and heaved hard to catch back his breath. Not all of it was lost due to the exertion of the sparring match.

"My father's dead, remember?" Clayton yanked at the leather fencing glove on his right hand. "Has been for a very long time. There is no relationship between us."

Merritt grimly shook his head and set his rapier down on a nearby table. "Then why are you still trying so hard to prove your worth to the world?" He paused, his hand lingering on the blade, before adding, "And to your father?"

"Is that what I'm doing?" Clayton kept the sudden pain of his tightening chest from registering on his face. "Odd. I thought I was working hard to carve out a good life for myself."

"If that's all it was, you could have stopped two years ago with a successful military career and a commission that would have kept you in luxury for the rest of your life. That alone outshines most men in the British empire, and you were happy. Since then…not so happy, and least of all since you've been back in England."

"Is that why you're bringing this up?" Clayton forced an amused laugh. "Because you're worried I'm not happy enough?"

"*My wife* is worried you're not happy," Merritt explained, "and when my wife is worried, I'm worried."

"Your wife wields a sword," Clayton reminded him, "and my happiness is what worries you?"

"*Especially* when she wields a sword." His old friend arched a brow. "I mentioned that she's with child, didn't I? Being angry at one moment, breaking down in tears the next, eating the most peculiar foods…" Merritt blew out a hard breath, registering all the domestic hell that had beset him recently. "If there's anything I can do to ease her through this, I am going to do it, including checking in on you. Veronica is concerned that you're not happy."

Clayton smiled. "Well, you can tell the baroness I'm just—"

"And *I'm* concerned about you for other reasons."

All his amusement vanished. "No need to be."

Clearly not believing that, Merritt shook his head. "I know why *I* kept pushing myself, why I didn't want to settle for an average career in the Inns of Court, and it wasn't because I had a driving ambition to become a King's Counsel. The wars burned that out of me." His voice turned low and contemplative. Not harsh, not combative…empathetic. "I'd thought they'd burned it out of you, too, yet you haven't rested one moment in the past few years." Merritt studied his old friend. "I was hunting ghosts. What are *you* hunting?"

Clayton set down his rapier, and it rattled on the tabletop next to Merritt's, the sound not jarring into him nearly as much as Merritt's soft words.

That was the problem with living, suffering, and fighting shoulder to shoulder with best friends in the heat of battle and the cold of winters. They came to know each other too well.

"I do it to serve crown and country," Clayton defended himself. "That's all."

Unfortunately, best friends also knew when they were being lied to, just as the look on Merritt's face proved.

"You do it around the clock," Merritt pressed, "passing up rest, running yourself ragged, and associating with men who would eagerly slit your throat if given half a chance."

"Because that's what it takes to protect England and bring reform, and I am dedicated to both."

More—he was driven to change the system so that innocent men wouldn't be arrested in the first place when all they wanted was more say in their government. Even the Americans when they were still colonists half a world away had more representation in Parliament than the entire city of Manchester and far, far fewer taxes than those levied in England. Hell, even the Americans had first tried diplomatic means to avoid conflict.

Not Scepter. They wanted to change the system through cold-blooded violence, ignore the constitution, and seize power by insurrection. They wanted to put in control their own despotic politicians who cared more about keeping themselves in power than in preserving the rights of ordinary Englishmen. In that, they were no better than Napoleon and his minions. Different players, same game.

Reform without tyranny and violence was the only lasting way to create meaningful change. While the English constitution evolved at a glacial speed, it *could* be changed, and over time it would move toward justice.

Lately, though, the pace was damnably slow, even for Clayton. And yet, "I have no intention of stopping."

"Good," Merritt murmured thoughtfully, as if he didn't quite believe Clayton, "because I'd hate to think that you took on the role of the princess's guard only because of fathers."

Clayton frowned, confused. "What do you mean?"

"Prince Reginald, of course."

Cordelia's father. "He died over a decade ago." Wariness clenched its icy fingers around Clayton's chest. "What about him?"

"Rumors have been circulating on the Continent among soldiers and sailors about his behavior during the wars. Those stories followed the Monrovians here to England and are making the rounds in the dockside taverns. I'm surprised you haven't heard yet."

Clayton shook his head. He'd been too busy with Cordelia and tracking down Scepter to pay attention to rumors. "Stories about what, exactly?"

"How he was responsible for the deaths of thousands of his own soldiers."

Clayton's heart stopped.

Thirteen

"I DON'T KNOW WHY I HAVE TO ATTEND TONIGHT'S dinner," Cordelia mumbled as she turned her gaze out the carriage window.

She'd hoped to catch whatever passing glimpse of nighttime London she could as the carriage made its way along the Strand toward the grand town house of Lord Harrowby, Lord President of the Privy Council. But not enough of the street was lit by the handful of gas lamps for her to see anything except footpaths and front doors.

She frowned. "Uncle Ernest should be meeting with the king's cabinet, not me. I know nothing about trade agreements or international relations." In her role as princess, she'd rarely had to do more than smile. The extensive education her parents had insisted on giving her seemed such a waste now. "All the men at tonight's dinner will realize that."

"Your uncle Monrovia is fatigued," Marie answered curtly.

The comtesse had not been pleased with Cordelia since the start of their trip. The confrontation with the nurse and last night's extended absence certainly hadn't helped. But Marie and Uncle Ernest couldn't keep her locked away for the duration of their visit, as tonight's outing proved.

"He didn't want to cancel the dinner at the last moment and knows you will serve well in his place." Marie paused, and then the real reason Uncle Ernest begged off sneaked out. "He also feels that tonight his place is at the palace with the royal dukes."

Ah, so they were back to them. *Again.*

Truly, Cordelia would be glad when they decided among themselves which one would marry her. How long could it take to draw straws or cut cards, for heaven's sake? Then, she could turn her focus to the wedding and…and what came after.

She squelched a shudder. She knew what happened between husbands and wives and how babies were made, but she simply couldn't imagine doing *that* with one of the royal dukes.

"I'd like to go over tonight's guest list again," Marie said.

"No need."

"I insist."

Cordelia sent her a cutting glance, then turned back to the window. "So do I."

The comtesse stiffened at Cordelia's uncharacteristic dismissal. "Is something the matter, Your Highness? You have not been acting at all yourself these past few days."

Cordelia nearly laughed! She'd been brought across Europe to audition for marriage to men who were twice her age, and four days ago a knife had been pressed to her throat. But Marie was concerned that she wasn't behaving like *herself*?

She'd never wanted to flee more in her life than she did at

that moment. Just leap from the rolling carriage, run straight into the night, and disappear into the shadows.

Instead, she was being delivered to a dinner party hosted by one of the king's leading ministers where she would be expected to look like a little doll, hold scintillating small talk about topics that bored her silly, and not show herself to be too intelligent. Men didn't like women who were too competent, intelligent, outgoing…

Except Clayton.

He seemed to like all those things about her. But then, the general turned viscount was proving to be the most unusual man she'd ever met.

"Your Highness, if something is wrong, then—"

"I have been acting exactly like myself," Cordelia interrupted. And *that* was the problem Marie had with her, because down deep, Cordelia didn't feel at all like a princess.

Marie pursed her lips together, knowing not to argue. They were all in an uneasy mood tonight, and the comtesse wouldn't dare stir up trouble, especially since gossip about the garden party was finally quieting throughout the palace. The easiest path forward for Cordelia was simply to push through tonight's dinner and then retire early, smiling brightly all the way.

But when the carriage stopped in front of the grand town house, which was lit as brightly as a Christmas pudding, she didn't feel like smiling.

The tiger opened the door to help her to the ground. She froze as she looked up at the house, her toe poised on the step.

Clayton waited at the bottom of the front steps, arms crossed over his broad chest and his legs wide. It wasn't the way he looked in his evening finery that made her catch her breath, although his black kerseymere jacket and breeches paired with a snow-white cravat and waistcoat were certainly arresting. No, it was the harshness of his narrowed gaze and the tight clench of his jaw that pulled her up short. Stiff, solid, grim-faced...not at all happy to see her.

Oh, this could not be good.

She fixed on a smile, finished stepping to the ground, and breezed toward him. "General Elliott, good evening."

"Your Serene Highness," he bit out and bowed deeply.

She halted in midstep. What on earth had happened since last night to anger him? She'd not seen him all day, being under the careful watch of Marie and the palace guards. Unless...unless it *was* last night that upset him.

Not *at all* good.

Cordelia lingered long enough at the front steps and portico that the comtesse and the rest of the Monrovian escorts in the following carriage went ahead into the house, leaving her behind with Clayton. Without a word, he placed her hand on his arm and led her slowly inside. She could feel the tension in his muscles beneath her fingertips even through his thick sleeve.

Instead of following the others, he stopped in the entrance hall. "Princess, a word about your security detail." He reached past her and pushed open the door of a small reception room. "If you please."

She swallowed nervously. "Of course."

She swept past him into the room. Warm flames glowed from the fireplace, as did those from several oil lamps placed around the room. A silver tray covered with glasses and decanters sat on the low table between two gold brocade sofas, ready for the guests to help themselves after dinner. But for now, the room was all theirs.

Clayton left the door halfway open for propriety's sake, but someone would have to stride completely into the room in order to see them.

"You're upset," she preemptively commented, hoping to minimize any arguments. Or wounded feelings. They hadn't had the chance to talk alone since they kissed at the opera, and she dreaded whatever rationalization of his behavior was coming.

"Damn right I am," he shot back, his voice just as low as hers.

No welcoming smile for her, no soft or kind words—she would have said he was furious with her, but what reason did he have? It was only a kiss…or a dozen or so of them, actually. When she'd been in his arms, she'd been so light-headed that she'd been unable to count, and then when his hands caressed her, she'd been unable to think at all.

"I didn't force you to kiss me." She lifted her chin to appear as imperial as possible, yet she couldn't stop the quiver in her soft voice. "You enjoyed it as much as I did, wanted it as much as I did. There's no reason to—"

"Your father." He closed the distance between them. "And please don't insult either of us by pretending you don't understand what I mean."

The world tilted beneath her, and her body flashed numb. She reached out for the back of a nearby chair to keep her knees from buckling and crashing her to the floor. As she dug her fingernails into the chair back so hard a dull ache shot up her wounded forearm, she could barely breathe. *Breathe! Just keep breathing!* Clayton knew… Oh heavens, he *knew*!

"Tell me the truth," he ordered. "*All* of it."

Guilt and shame pounded through her veins with every fierce heartbeat, and a pain-filled sob escaped her. All the damage her father had done, all the lying and secrets…all the men who had been killed because of it. They were supposed to have looked to her father as a protector and guardian who should have put their lives and safety far above his own. Instead, he'd betrayed them.

So had she for keeping it secret. *Dear God*, what they'd done! How could either of them ever be forgiven?

"What did your father do?" Clayton demanded.

Her eyes blurred with hot tears, and she admitted, barely able to put a trembling voice to it, "Terrible things."

"Things that someone would kill to avenge?"

She rapidly shook her head and choked out, "Things that could end a monarchy."

She squeezed her eyes shut and took deep breaths, but her shoulders had slumped forward until she could barely find the strength to hold herself upright. All her nightmares were coming true. Everything would be destroyed—the royal family, the crown, perhaps even Monrovia.

Her head spun with sickening dizziness that matched the roiling knots in her stomach. She knew this moment was coming, had known for years that a reckoning would arrive. But she never expected it to come like this, and not from the one man in the world she trusted.

Now, certainly, he was a man who also thought she'd betrayed him.

She pressed her hand to her belly as if she could physically calm her pitching stomach. "How…how did you find out?"

"Rumors are being passed among French troops on the Continent, accusations they heard from questioning prisoners of war." The anger had left his voice, but his frustration still rang clear. "None of them would have been credible by themselves. Nothing more than fabrications. Prisoners will say anything they think their captors want to hear just to ease their imprisonment." He paused. "But when I heard what they've been saying, on the heels of the attack…"

"You realized they weren't mere fabrications."

"Yes." His deep voice was closer than before, and she knew he'd come up behind her. "So help me sort through them and separate out the truth so we can figure out how to protect you."

"You can't protect me." A raw, emotional cry came from deep in her throat, and she covered her mouth with her shaking hand. "Not from this."

He took her upper arms in his hands and lowered his head to speak over her shoulder into her ear. "I can, if you're honest with me." He hesitated, then reassuringly brushed his lips against her temple. "Cordelia, what did he do?"

She ached to lean back and bring herself against his hard

front, to have his arms encircle her and hold her safe and protected. But she couldn't. If she did, the tears would fall unchecked, and she'd never be able to get through this.

"He...misappropriated funds that were supposed to have purchased supplies for Monrovia's military."

"How?"

"Monrovia has a secretary of war who oversees the day-to-day military operations of the sailors and soldiers, but we're such a small country that the secretary reports directly to the reigning prince, who oversees the military's finances and materials." She pulled in a deep breath and explained, "The secretary tells the soldiers where to march, but the reigning prince supplies the boots they march in."

"No one monitors the sovereign prince?"

She gave a half-hearted shrug. "The Crown Council, but only if they have reason to suspect misdeeds, and who would have enough spine to challenge their monarch during a time of war?"

"What exactly did he do?"

She paused to take a deep breath to steel herself. "He was supposed to arrange contracts for supplies from merchants and manufacturers so our men would have the best equipment available. Instead, he contracted cheaper, inferior supplies, but he told everyone the costs were the same, only to keep the difference himself." She tightened her hands into fists and dug her nails into her palms, welcoming the pain. "The men were given thin blankets that fell into rags after only a few weeks, uniforms that did the same, boots so poorly made they couldn't march in them, and gloves—" Her voice choked, and she swallowed down the knot of emotion in her throat. "Our men weren't properly equipped, and they suffered for it. Many froze to death in the Alps. Others were killed unnecessarily in battle when they were sent to fight with guns that misfired and artillery that jammed, exploding in their hands and faces…"

She didn't dare turn toward him, too afraid of the condemning expression she'd see on his face. He was a soldier himself, after all, responsible for his men the way her father should have been for his.

"Why would your father do that?" Clayton asked. "He was already a wealthy prince."

"You think men don't want more money simply because they're already rich, that they're somehow incapable of being bought?" She almost laughed at the idea. "All men can be corrupted, even the wealthy, and all men want even more money and the power that comes with it. *Especially* those who already know its benefits. Look around the world— dictators and tyrants are never poor."

"But your father was neither." He squeezed her shoulders, and the soft gesture reassured her more than she had a right to feel. "By all accounts, he'd made several sacrifices of his own power and influence to create reforms for Monrovia."

"He did," she whispered, struck even now by a faint ripple of pride in her father. "Our people loved him. They still do."

Finally, she turned toward him. Thank God it wasn't hatred she saw on his face but concern, and the comforting feel of his hands on her shoulders reassured her.

"I don't know why he embezzled those funds, but he was

going to take responsibility for what he'd done and face punishment by the Crown Council, beg Monrovia's forgiveness, and try to find a way to preserve the principality." She had clung fiercely to that knowledge since Ernest had told her what her father had done. It was a small proof of the honor her father had possessed until the end. "He was going to abdicate, ask the Crown Council to appoint another sovereign prince in his place…"

"But he died before he could."

She nodded stiffly. "When Uncle Ernest came to the throne, he wanted to protect Monrovia and my family's reputation by hiding all the evidence of the crimes. He covered up all he could, but…"

"But the soldiers and sailors knew," he guessed grimly, "and rumors of what happened began to spread."

Her eyes lowered to the floor. "Uncle Ernest hoped that any suspicions would end with the wars."

"That's why you kept this secret." His jaw clenched, and he dropped his hands to his sides. "You'd hoped it would simply go away."

Shame squeezed her chest. "Please understand. If evidence of what my father did ever sees the light of day, the Monrovian monarchy will end."

"Maybe that's exactly what should happen," he muttered coldly.

She raised her chin. "I'd rather die."

"You almost did." He ran his fingers down her forearm to prove his point. "And you didn't think any of this would be reason enough for someone to want to attack you?"

"Not in England, no." Her own frustration mounted as much as his, and she gestured futilely with her empty hands. "I have no power and no control over anything political. My father has been dead for ten years, and killing me would bring no restitution for the men he hurt and their families. Besides, I had nothing to do with it. I was a child when it happened. I barely remember any of it."

His face remained stony. "What do you remember, exactly?"

"Arguments mostly." She shook her head in exasperation as she began to pace and tried to latch on to the memories that mostly eluded her. "My governess often fell asleep when we were at my studies, so I would sneak through the palace to visit my father. If he wasn't busy, I could interrupt his schedule, and I would have him all to myself for a few precious minutes." She trembled as the memories flooded back, and the roiling emotions in her belly twisted into teeming knots. "But sometimes when I went to find him, Uncle Ernest was already in his office with him, and there were raised voices, accusations, curses—I would press my ear against the crack between the doors, but I couldn't hear enough to make out the matter between them. My mother would sometimes be inside, and I could hear her crying." Anguish clenched a fist around her heart. "But whenever I asked about it, they said nothing was wrong."

"Apparently, a great deal was wrong."

She nodded and folded her arms to wrap them around herself as much as possible. "Right before Mama and Papa left for Italy, the arguments intensified, and tensions were so thick within our family that I could feel them before I even entered the room." She bit her thumbnail and continued pacing, the movement the only thing that kept the sickening churning in her stomach at bay. "Uncle Ernest told me later that someone in the government had discovered what Papa had done, that it was only a matter of time until his crimes became public knowledge. Papa had planned on speaking to the Crown Council upon his return."

"But he never returned."

She shook her head and looked away. "Uncle Ernest somehow managed to keep it all hidden. The money was secretly returned to the military's coffers, and the Crown Council never learned the truth. There have been dark rumblings ever since, but nothing that can be proven. We're making amends as best we can."

"Amends?" His voice lowered to a harsh rasp. "Men died because of your father's greed. How can you ever make amends for that?"

She flinched. His words stabbed her with the same force of the knife that had cut her arm. Immediately, a flash of regret crossed his face.

But he wasn't wrong, and she admitted somberly, her eyes boldly meeting his, "In any way I can."

His eyes flared, and she knew he'd put all the pieces together. "That's why you're being offered to the royal dukes, isn't it?" A biting curse left his lips, and he stalked toward her. "Why you're not opposing marriage to selfish libertines twice your age." He stopped in front of her, and his jaw clenched. "Marriage is your way of making reparations."

She didn't expect him to understand, yet she had to try anyway. "Marrying into the British royal family will strengthen the Monrovian monarchy by association."

He asked sardonically, "A royal seal of approval?"

"In a way. News of a royal wedding and the promise of an heir will bring stability to both countries and to Europe as a whole."

"That's your plan—ruin your own life to save a throne?"

"Yes." But the resolve she'd hoped to convey failed beneath the tremble in her voice. "If that is the only choice, then yes."

He stared at her in disbelief, as if she were a stranger. "You would do that, just to keep your family in power?"

It was so much more than that! "Monrovia isn't like England. If our monarchy dissolves, so does our country's sovereignty. We will be subsumed by France and cease to exist." That nightmare had haunted her since Ernest told her the truth about her father. That was why she'd stopped fighting her uncle's wishes and dedicated herself to her duties. *Everything* she did now was for her country, not for herself. "To have the people I love stripped of their sovereignty and rights, of their nationality and identity—potentially all our people's wealth and property stolen away to support a Bourbon king who—"

She cut herself off before her voice could break with sobs and glued her gaze to the floor.

"My duty is to Monrovia, first and always." The frustration seeped out of her, and her shoulders slumped beneath the terrible truth. "Strategic marriage and the begetting of heirs—that's the lot of a princess. What I want doesn't matter."

He said nothing for a long moment, then asked quietly, "And what do you want, Cordelia?"

Slowly, she lifted her eyes until they met his. "I want you."

———

Clayton froze. She couldn't have meant—*Christ*.

He was unable to put together a coherent response. His mind reeled in a way it never had before, not even when facing down the French at Waterloo.

Her lips curled faintly. "Stunned you, have I?"

"You could say that," he muttered, finally catching back his senses enough to speak.

"Don't worry." She crossed to the low table and its tray of drinks. Most likely she needed a drink as much as he did, if the way she inhaled deeply to calm herself after the discussion about her father were any indication. So was the way her hands shook as she reached for two glasses. "I didn't mean that the way it sounded."

Thank God, because the way it had sounded... *Treason*. "How, exactly, did you mean it, then?"

"Well, I wasn't proposing, if that's what you thought." She paused as she reached for one of the decanters. "Tradition says I'm the one who has to propose if I want to marry anyone less than a prince royal. Did you know that?"

"No, I didn't." At that moment, though, he didn't give a damn about tradition.

She pulled free the stopper and splashed the golden liquid into the waiting tumblers. "But I also can't marry without the sovereign's permission. If I do, my marriage will be considered nonexistent and any children I have declared illegitimate. Damned if I do…damned if I don't." She forced a teasing note into her voice, he knew, to distract herself from her anguish over her father and the situation she'd been forced into. He recognized a survival tactic when he saw one. After all, he'd done the same himself countless times with his own father. "Makes courtship complicated, wouldn't you say?"

She held out the glass of cognac to him. A glass… He nearly laughed. What he wanted was to snatch up the decanter and guzzle the entire thing straight down.

"That's what made being alone with you so very special, why I didn't want to ruin that by telling you about my father," she admitted soberly.

He didn't dare let his fingers brush against hers as he accepted the drink. "How so?"

"For the only time in my life, I could be certain that a man wanted to kiss me simply because of me and not because of this." She removed her tiara, and her face fell as she stared at it, as if feeling in it a weight a million times that of its gold and diamonds.

She tossed it unwanted onto the settee.

He stilled, the drink raised halfway to his lips. "Perhaps you shouldn't have done that."

A long sigh escaped her, and this time when her shoulders settled, he knew it wasn't from removing the weight of the tiara or even the crowns of two monarchies. It was pure relief.

"Actually, that felt really good." Then she added breathlessly, "Almost as good as kissing you."

Oh no. This conversation was not going well. If it kept going like this, he'd be in Newgate by midnight.

She removed her ermine-lined cape next and threw it over the sofa arm, revealing the soft-blue silk gown beneath. Its color brought out the pink in her lips and cheeks, the dark chestnut of her silky hair.

He swallowed, hard, yet he hadn't even brought the glass to his lips.

"I enjoyed it," she confessed.

So had he. Far too much. Knowing not to utter a word about that, though, he finally took a mouthful of cognac.

"And I want it to happen again."

He choked. Coughing to clear his throat, he sputtered out, "It can't!"

"Because of what my father did?"

"No." Guilt turned the cognac bitter on his tongue, and he set down his glass. "What happened last night should never have happened. It was wrong of me. I should have stopped—"

"Don't," she bit out. "*Don't* you dare say that kissing me was a mistake."

He said quietly, "A grand one."

"Damn you." Her whispered curse pierced him. So did the wounded expression on her beautiful face.

"Yes, exactly," he agreed soberly. "Damn me." He nodded at her. "And you, Princess, are just the latest reason for that."

Her lips parted with surprise.

"Surely you've heard who I am."

She frowned, puzzled. "You're an undersecretary with the Home Office."

He took a step toward her. "I'm more than that."

"You're also a general and soon to be a viscount."

And another step that closed the last bit of distance between them. "I'm the son of an executed convict." He leaned down to bring his face level with hers. "And *you* are a princess who at this very moment has three royal dukes vying for your hand in marriage and the Duke of Grafton waiting in the wings."

When her eyes flared, a pang of longing shot through him to be any of those four men. What he saw in those warm brown depths that reminded him of melted chocolate— God help him, it was desire.

He bit out the bitter truth. "You're the most challenging, frustrating woman I've ever met."

This time when her eyes blazed, it was with anger. "How dare—"

"But I also find you incredibly alluring and intriguing." His voice lowered until the murmured words almost hummed from his lips. "Be assured that if you weren't who you are and I who I am, I wouldn't hesitate to pursue you."

Her lips trembled. *Sweet Lucifer*, he wanted to lower his head and claim them again beneath his.

"But we *are* those people, and whatever this attraction is between us, it can't lead to anything, so it cannot happen again." He fixed her with a hard look that brooked no argument. "Understand?"

"I'm not asking for it to lead anywhere. I know it can't."

She placed her palm against his cheek, and the satin of her glove cooled his skin even as her touch heated through him. "I just want to enjoy myself while I still can. What harm is there in a few kisses?"

He stifled a groan. Her logic made her even more tempting and this entire situation even worse.

"Oh, Princess." He placed his hand over hers. "If I relented, it wouldn't be for just now, and it sure as hell wouldn't be a few kisses."

She gasped softly when he brought her hand to his mouth and placed a lingering kiss to her palm.

"Do you think I could take a small taste and not crave all of you? That I could simply stand at your side, smelling your perfume and hearing your laughter, and not want to possess you in every way?"

He lowered her hand and folded it in both of his. Her pulse raced beneath his fingertips, her breath coming ragged.

"No matter how much I want that, it can never happen." He continued, needing to drive home this point, "I'm not daft enough to lose my position and reputation over you"— and certainly not his head—"no matter how tempting you are."

She held still for a long moment, then slowly slipped her hand from his and took a single step backward. But she couldn't hide the brutal sting of his rejection that registered on her face. *Damnation.* The two types of women he'd always made a point of avoiding were innocents and royals. God must have been laughing to thrust both on him in the same body…the same soft, warm, and delectable body.

"I understand," she whispered, blinking hard.

The soft flutter of her lashes pierced him as sharply as any blade could have. But he couldn't let her see any weakness, or she would know the effect she had on him. And exactly how much he wanted her.

"Good." He cleared his throat. "Because we have to concentrate on figuring out who wants revenge against your father enough to kill you."

She gave a jerking nod and resignedly folded her hands in front of her. "I'll tell you whatever you want to know."

Her voice emerged so fragilely he thought it might break him. "Then I need to know who—"

Without warning, an explosion ripped through the rear of the house.

Fourteen

CORDELIA GASPED, TOO STUNNED TO SCREAM AS THE house shook around them. Surprised shouts echoed through the rooms, followed by pounding footsteps. Seconds later came the shattering of glass as window after window was broken along the side of the house, the splintering of wood—

Clayton grabbed her by the wrist. "Come on!"

As he pulled her toward the door, she reached back to grasp for her tiara. "I need—"

"Leave it!"

He paused behind the door and cautiously peered out into the entrance hall. Whatever he saw there turned his expression hard, and he shoved closed the door and flipped the lock, then slipped his free hand beneath his jacket where he kept his gun.

"What is it?" Fear coiled through her, and she grabbed tightly onto his free hand with both of hers. "What's happening?"

"We're being attacked," Clayton warned. "Someone's invading the house. We have to get out. *Now*."

Nodding vigorously, she ran to the window. Her fingers shook as they fumbled with the latched shutters.

"Not that way," he corrected. He hurried to the fireplace

and knocked against the wall beside it. With a frustrated grimace, he crossed to the other side of the mantel and knocked there. Around them, the noise of the attack grew with the unfolding chaos.

"What are you doing?" she demanded. Helplessness burned in her chest.

"Finding the latch that—" With a soft click, a hidden latch gave way, and the fake wall swung open. He opened the door wide to the secret passage and held out his hand to her. "This way. Hurry."

She raced forward and took his hand, lacing her fingers tightly through his. But when he tugged at her hand to pull her into the narrow passageway with him, she hesitated at the blackness and the smell of must and mold on the cold air seeping up from the stone foundations.

"Cordelia," he said firmly, "trust me."

She inhaled a deep breath to gather her courage and followed him into the darkness.

He closed the door behind them, and a wave of blackness fell over her.

"Don't let go," she pleaded as terror shook through her so hard she could barely keep her knees from buckling beneath her. "Please—don't let go of me!"

"I'm right here." She felt the soft caress of his lips at her temple, but the passageway was so dark she couldn't see him even though he was only inches away. "I won't let go of you, not for one second. I promise. Come with me."

He led her along the dark passageway. Each blind step she took in the darkness filled her with terror because she couldn't see where she was placing her feet, but so did the noise that continued to pulse from the house around them. More screams, more shouts, the breaking down of doors, and the sound of fire eating at the floors and walls... But Clayton hurried her down the passage as quickly as he dared. The only light came from small holes drilled at unequal intervals along the passage wall, but he didn't stop to look through any of them.

"Where are we?" she asked, her voice low.

"The servants' passage," he murmured over his shoulder but didn't slow his quickening strides. "It will take us to the rear of the house."

"Why didn't we go out the window?"

"Because the attackers are outside the window, waiting for people to come out."

"Why would they be waiting?"

When he didn't answer, she knew—*Oh God!* They were going to be killed! A soft sob bubbled from her lips.

"Don't panic on me, Princess," he ordered. "Where's that commitment to duty you're always bragging about?"

"I left it behind with the tiara," she rasped out as she struggled to shove down her rising terror.

He chuckled beneath his breath, then suddenly stopped. They'd reached the end of the passageway.

He unlatched the door and shoved it open, and they stepped out into the rear servants' stairwell. Sounds of confusion rose up from the basement. Cordelia could see the bright light from the fire flickering at the bottom of the stairs and the moving shadows cast by the servants battling to put it out.

"This way." He pulled her out of the stairwell and burst through the rear doors into the dark service yard behind the house.

She gulped down the fresh air in great mouthfuls, and the rush of blood pounded through her so hard that the roaring of it in her ears was deafening. She needed to rest and catch back her breath, yet he hurried her on, sprinting with her across the rear yard to the dark shadows fronting the brick wall. He ducked down into the shadows, and she followed.

Gunshots rang out from the house behind them. Startled, Cordelia gave a soft cry and bolted upright. She spun around toward the house—

Sharp pain shot through her foot and up her calf, and she pitched forward, falling onto her hands and knees in the muddy gravel with a cry. Her ankle!

"Cordelia!" Clayton grabbed her around the waist and lifted her back to her feet. "Can you walk?"

"Yes, I think—"

"There!" A shout echoed through the darkness. "In the rear! Stop them!"

Clayton looked past the top of her head at the house as two dark figures charged toward them. "Can you run?"

Not waiting for her answer, he pulled her with him across the yard. Each step was agony, but she didn't dare stop. Not with the terrible sounds of fire and struggle still coming from the house, punctuated by the ringing blasts of more gunshots.

The two men were nearly on top of them. Clayton and Cordelia slipped through the gate and into the wall-lined alley only a few strides ahead.

Terror pierced her at the sight of the alley. Stone buildings and tall walls lined both sides, with no place to hide, and the scattering of carriage house doors were all padlocked tight for the night. They were trapped!

"Get behind me," Clayton ordered and let go of her hand.

She made a frantic grab for him, but he stopped in the middle of the alley, shoved her behind him to protect her with his own body, and tossed back the tails of his greatcoat to reach beneath it. He withdrew a second gun and raised both pistols.

———

Clayton tensed, ready to fight. All hell had broken loose tonight, and he would make his stand here. He would protect the princess or die trying.

The gate flung open, and the two men charged into the alley.

"Halt!" Clayton commanded.

The attackers froze in their steps.

"Leave."

The two brutes exchanged a look of resolve, and Clayton knew they were just foolish enough to attack despite the pistols aimed at them—or desperate enough for whatever reward Scepter had promised them for killing everyone inside the house.

The man on the right spat on the ground and started toward them down the alley. The muscular monster raised a cutlass menacingly in the air, then let out a ferocious yell and ran toward them. His partner followed a single step behind.

Clayton fired.

The ball tore through the first man's chest. He staggered back a single step from the force of the shot, then crumpled to the ground.

The other attacker raced on toward them. The second pistol shot caught him in the hip. He screamed with surprise and pain, but his yell was lost beneath the noise that came from the ongoing battle being waged inside the house. He fell back against the brick wall, then to the ground.

Clayton holstered both spent pistols and spun on his heel.

Cordelia huddled on the ground behind him in a little ball, her hands clamped tightly over both ears, her eyes screwed shut. Terror gripped her so hard that she shook in violent spasms.

He had to get her out of here. She wasn't yet safe.

He swept her up into his arms and ran with her down the alley and into the darkness as fast as he could. She buried her face in his shoulder and gasped for breath as she forced down terrified sobs, but she clung tightly to him, so tightly she nearly strangled him. But he wouldn't stop. He turned down alley after alley, taking her through the rabbit warren of streets and passages forming a maze between them and the river. Each stride took them farther from the house.

They could no longer hear the sounds coming from the town house, but already the city around them was alive with people who were coming out of houses and commercial buildings to see what had happened. Shouts and calls echoed off the stone walls, along with the pounding of running feet as people scurried toward the Strand.

Confident that they weren't being followed, he slowed his pace to a walk, but her arms never loosened their hold. He heard her quiet sobs and felt the wet of her tears against his neck as she cried in his arms. But he couldn't stop to comfort her. Not yet. Not until she was completely safe.

When they reached a main avenue, he stopped at the edge of the footpath and slowly eased his hold on her to lower her to the ground. She inhaled sharply when her hurt ankle touched the ground, but she didn't cry out in pain.

"Can you walk?" he asked.

She nodded, unable to speak.

He took her hand and led her, limping, toward the street. He raised his arm to signal for a hackney. A rickety old rig stopped beside them. He flung open the door, scooped her into his arms, and set her inside on the bench.

"King Street in St James's," he ordered the jarvey. He tossed the man a coin and swung up into the compartment. "Hurry!"

He closed the door, then dropped onto the bench across from her. She huddled in the corner, her knees pulled up to her chest and her arms wrapped around her legs. She struggled to fight down her tears and panted hard for breath.

His chest constricted with worry. He wanted to pull her into his arms and assure her that she would be fine, but he couldn't. All he could do was slip his hand up his sleeve for the knife he kept sheathed there in case they were attacked again. As in every battle he'd fought in the wars, he knew not to let down his guard. Time for comforting and grieving would come later.

She lifted her head from her knees, and the terrified expression on her beautiful face nearly undid him. "Why?" she choked out. "Why were we attacked?"

Even in the shadows of the carriage lamp, her eyes haunted him, and he glanced out the broken window. "Most likely it was an assassination attempt."

Or worse—the elimination of all the king's ministers in one fell swoop. His blood froze. Was this the signal the Marquess of Hawking had warned was coming, the same signal Burton confirmed?

Any doubts he had that Scepter was as dead as the marquess vanished in a heartbeat.

"And the others—they're all…" Her voice dropped to a whisper so soft that he could barely hear it above the carriage wheels. "Dead?"

"We don't know that. We escaped. The others might have as well."

"The comtesse." Her hand flew up to her mouth. "Oh, poor Marie!"

"Listen to me." He reached across the compartment and cupped her face between his hands to focus her thoughts away from the horrors swirling through her mind. "We don't know what happened, but based on the noise, they fought back. Liverpool and the others would have made certain she was protected. Just like I protected you."

"But there were gunshots—"

"We don't know who fired them. I fired guns in the alley, too, and we got away safely. Harrowby most likely keeps pistols at the ready throughout his house."

She jerked a nod against his palms, as if she could will herself to believe that everyone inside the house was all right.

Clayton knew better, but admitting to the harsh reality of the attack would serve no good.

Unable any longer to resist the need to comfort them both, he tenderly kissed her lips, then rested his forehead against hers. "You *are* safe. No one will hurt you. I promise."

With that last lie, he pulled back and sank down onto his bench. In the lamplight, he could see glistening tears on her tear-spiked lashes.

"You told the driver to go to King Street." She swiped the back of her hand across her eyes and looked outside at the dark night, even though nothing could be seen beyond the cracked window but the faint glows of gas lamps scattered along the street. "Aren't we going back to the palace?"

"No."

Her watery eyes darted back to him. "Why not?"

"It's not safe for you there. Not until I learn more about tonight's attack."

"Then where are we going?"

They had to stay out of sight until he could reach the men of the Armory and learn what had happened. He couldn't surface with her anywhere, not even within the stone battlements of Windsor Castle, not when the enemy had proven it could strike from within. And certainly not if Scepter's army had been activated by the attack. He didn't even dare take her to the Armory, unable to trust its twenty-foot-thick walls and twin portcullises.

He trusted no one with her life but himself.

"The unlikeliest place in the world to hide a princess," he muttered as the carriage turned onto King Street and stopped. He glanced out the window at the wide, brightly lit town house. "The Château Noir."

Fifteen

CORDELIA STARED OUT THE CARRIAGE WINDOW. AS FAR AS she could discern, the place was simply another London town house, several bays wide and fronting the street. The only oddity was the two large men who flanked both sides of the door. Lights shone from every room, but gauzy curtains and shutters kept her from seeing anything inside.

And yet… "I don't like this place," she admitted warily.

"You wanted to see more of London," Clayton reminded her, "where real people live and work. You can't get more real than this." He cracked open the door just enough to call up to the driver, "Take us around back."

The man cracked the whip, and the old horse plodded onward, pulling the carriage to the end of the street, then around the corner and down the rear alley. Clayton pounded his fist on the roof to signal him to stop.

The structure looked even less appealing from the back, Cordelia decided. A collection of old outbuildings crowded the dark service yard, with piles of refuse waiting for the rag and bone men between two lean-to structures propped up against the back of the house. Another large man guarded the open rear door and laughed with three scantily clad women who stood nearby, all smoking cheroots.

Clayton shed his greatcoat and helped Cordelia into it. "Wait here."

He opened the carriage door and stepped outside to pass a quiet word—and another coin—to the driver. When he came back into the compartment, he held the jarvey's large hat in his hands. He placed it on her head. Its large brim fell down over her forehead and past her eyes, dwarfing her head and face.

"Perfect." He lifted her to the ground. She was so drained from the attack and their flight that she didn't have enough strength—or curiosity—to question his actions.

As the carriage drove away, he buttoned the coat up all the way to her chin. Then he took her arm and led her toward the house.

The guard straightened as they approached. His beefy crossed arms dropped to his sides, but his hands remained fisted as he stepped into the open door to block their way. "All guests go in through the front."

"I'm not a guest." Clayton stopped in front of the man, and even as tall as he was, he had to tilt back his head to meet the guard eye to eye. "I have a knife up my left sleeve and two spent pistols in my holster but am otherwise unarmed. So is she."

The guard slanted a glance down at Cordelia as if he believed she could be hiding a canon under the tentlike coat.

"I need to see Madame Noir. Immediately." When the guard made no move to step aside, Clayton added, "Tell her an old friend from the Home Office is here to interrogate her, handcuffs and all. She'll understand."

Cordelia blinked. What on earth kind of message was that?

Whatever it was, it didn't surprise the guard.

Clayton added, "Tell her I'll meet her upstairs."

Then Clayton scooped Cordelia into his arms, pushed past the guard, and carried her up the rear stairs. He didn't bother knocking before throwing open the servants' door to a set of rooms taking up the front half of the top floor. He kicked it closed behind him and paused only to throw the lock before carrying her across the large room to a gold brocade sofa and setting her down. Immediately, he went to the window and yanked closed the drapes.

She looked around. Gold brocade settees and drapes, yards of purple silk draping the walls, the finest crafted mahogany furniture including what she would bet her life was a Chippendale writing desk and dressing table—*this* was not an average London home. A peal of laughter echoed through the building from the floor below, followed by what sounded like…the crack of a horse whip?

"What *is* this place?" she asked.

"A brothel." He helped himself to a generous pour of liquor from the tray of drinks on a console table near the door. "And the last place anyone would think to look for a missing princess."

A brothel. *Of course it was.* But tonight's attack had numbed her so much that the unprecedented scandal implicit in his explanation barely registered. All she could do in response was nod and sink further into the warmth of his coat, which smelled comfortingly of him.

He carried the glass to her and held it out. When she shook her head, he insisted.

With hands that shook so hard she feared she'd splash the drink everywhere, she accepted it and slowly raised it to her mouth. Whiskey. It burned down her throat, and she pressed the back of her hand to her mouth as she coughed.

She mumbled through her fingers, "What are we going to do?"

He knelt in front of her and rested his hand on her knee. She nearly sobbed again from the sensation of strength and assurance she felt in his caring touch.

"We stay here until I'm able to learn more about what happened tonight," he said. "We need to separate our friends from our enemies and know whom to trust."

He slid his hand slowly down her leg, over her calf to her ankle. Just as with the announcement that he'd brought her to a brothel, she didn't have the wherewithal—or the desire—to slap his hand away.

He gently slipped off her shoe, then slowly circled her foot in the air to test her ankle, his large hands nearly engulfing her foot from toes to ankle. Resting her foot in his left palm, he reached up his sleeve and withdrew a slender knife.

She gaped at him. "You really did have a knife up your sleeve!"

"I never tease about weapons." His grim gaze met hers. "I don't want to risk hurting your ankle further by pulling off your stocking. I apologize for having to do this."

"Do wh—"

He expertly sliced the knife tip through the silk, from toes to low calf. She gasped in surprise.

"The stocking was in the way," he explained. He sheathed the knife and peeled the blue silk away from her leg. He lightly traced his fingertips across her bare skin and once more felt her ankle as he gently turned it.

"Exactly like I was in the way tonight," she said quietly.

He said nothing, but for one heartbeat, his hands stilled.

She shook her head, realizing her mistake. "No, not me. No one would attack a house filled with British cabinet members only to harm me. We know that much at least."

He continued his examination. "I'm not certain we do."

"But it couldn't have been because of me," she reasoned. "Uncle Ernest was scheduled to be the guest of honor. I was a last-minute addition."

"I know. So did others inside the palace."

"Who?"

"I don't know exactly," he answered. "But I don't think your ankle is broken. Just a twist, and a minor one at that. You don't have much swelling and no bruising I can see."

That was a dodge if ever she'd heard one. She leaned forward. "Clayton—"

"We'll wrap it to keep it stable, and you'll have to be careful with it for the next few days. But it shouldn't be too much trouble for you." He nodded at her forearm. "Should I look at that, too, in case you reinjured it when you fell?"

"It's fine." She sat forward, her fingers folding tightly around the whiskey glass. "What aren't you telling me?"

He eased her foot down to the floor and sat back on his

hip, his forearm resting across his bent knee. "If I tell you, I'll only put you in more danger."

More danger? She wanted to laugh at the terrifying absurdity of that. "Someone has tried to kill me. Twice. I don't think there's any worse danger to be placed into."

His eyes narrowed as he studied her carefully, and she could practically see his mind weighing his words. Or how much he could trust her.

"There are groups in England who want to reform the government," he told her. "A few want a complete revolution. They might have used tonight's attack as a signal."

Cold dread tightened her belly. "A signal for what?"

"Declaration of war. The moment for all their members to rise up and overthrow the government."

Oh God... "If they knew I was there," she whispered, so softly her voice was barely above a breath, "if they wanted to..."

"No. Whatever happened tonight—and why—is *not* your fault."

But it was, she knew it. Just as she knew it had nothing to do with her father.

"There's something you need to know." She suddenly felt smothered. She set down the unwanted whiskey on the little side table and pulled at the buttons of his coat to open the heavy collar so she could breathe. "About me."

Concern darkened his face. "What is it?"

"I'm in the line of succession for the British throne. So is Uncle Ernest." She couldn't bring herself to look at him. A confession to a priest about her sins would have felt less damning.

"I know. So are half a dozen royal dukes and half the crown heads of Europe. If Parliament doesn't grant the prince regent a divorce, then the crown passes to his brothers and—"

"*I mean*, if the House of Hanover is excluded, then I am the nearest non-Catholic relative. The Hanoverians descend from Elizabeth Stuart, the oldest daughter of King James the First. So does my family, just from Princess Henriette Marie, Elizabeth Stuart's other daughter, and not Sophia of Hanover." She pulled in a deep breath that seared her lungs and said bluntly, "I'm the *very* next in line after the current king's children. Putting aside the Act of Settlement, my claim is as legitimate as theirs. Perhaps more so." A terrible taste covered her tongue. "If someone wanted to remove the Hanoverians and put their own ruler in place, then..."

"Then they would have to remove you from the line of succession, too."

She gave a jerking nod.

"But they wouldn't have to go that far. They could use your father's misdeeds to exempt you. If he had been deposed, the resulting attainder would have removed his entire line from succession, in both Monrovia and England."

"But it wouldn't exempt my uncle, who is second in line after me." Her fingers tightened around his. "I think that was why the town house was attacked. Those men didn't know my uncle had stayed behind at St James's Palace. I think—" Her voice grew impossibly softer. "I think they wanted to kill us both."

He remained as still as a statue at her feet, for one long moment doing nothing more than staring at her as he absorbed all she'd just confided. Then he wordlessly reached out, snatched up her glass, and downed the remaining whiskey in one gulping swallow.

"Undersecretary Elliott," a husky voice purred seductively from the doorway. "Now *there's* a secretary I'd love to be under."

Cordelia's eyes darted to the main door of the suite. *Who on earth…?*

A striking woman with raven-black hair and a red satin and velvet dress stood in the doorway, one hand resting on the door handle and the other placed provocatively on her hip. Her full lips spread into a predatory smile as her gaze landed on Clayton. Goodness, did she just lick her lips?

With an enticing sashay of her hips, the woman closed the door behind her and slipped into the room. Her eyes never left Clayton as she stepped slowly toward him.

"You naughty boy," she scolded, "showing up unannounced when I would have been pleased to personally welcome you." When he rose to his full height, she raked a hungry look over him from head to boots, sighing heavily when her eyes lingered at his waist on their return back up his body. "*Deliciously* pleased."

Her gleaming green eyes slid down to Cordelia, who was too stunned to do anything more than blink.

"And how thoughtful of you to bring me a gift!" Her lips curled into a smile that reminded Cordelia of a lioness. Right before it devoured a gazelle. "I do so love a new toy."

Warily, Cordelia sat forward and reached to take Clayton's hand as it dangled beside his thigh.

A throaty laugh bubbled from the woman's red lips. "Three is always so much more fun than two, but don't expect…"

Her eyes narrowed on Cordelia in a look of recognition, and she froze. All her teasing flirtation from only moments before vanished, and a look of incomprehension warred on her face with stunned disbelief.

"Dear God," she muttered. "What have you done?"

Sixteen

"Madame Noir," Clayton said with as much formality as he could muster under the circumstances. "May I introduce you to Jane? Jane," he repeated with emphasis and a squeeze of Cordelia's hand to convince her to play along, "this is Madame Noir. She owns this place."

Madame's eyes never left Cordelia's face. "You are *not*—"

"She's Jane," he repeated firmly. "Plain, average, normal Jane Smith."

"And I'm no fool," Madame countered. "I know exactly who she is." She gave Clayton a look so fierce it could have cut glass. "The question is...what the hell is she doing here? Because whatever the reason, it cannot be good."

"It isn't." He crossed to the window, pulled back the drape, and peered out into the street below. Everything seemed normal, right down to the well-dressed gentlemen finding their way to the front door. "The king's cabinet was attacked tonight. I have no idea how many were killed."

"Good God," Madame mumbled.

He dropped the curtain back into place and turned around. He never thought he would see Madame shocked, yet her face had gone ghostly.

"I'm certain you'll hear about it soon from your...guests."

He didn't dare glance at Cordelia for fear of what he'd see on *her* face. "Try to act surprised when you do."

"Don't worry," she recovered herself enough to assure him. "I'm very good at acting surprised with men."

He was certain of that. "We need a room for the night."

She pointed at Cordelia. "You need more than that."

"We'll start with a room. You will, of course, be well compensated by the Home Office for your trouble."

Madame shook her head. "There isn't enough money in all the coffers in Whitehall to pay me well enough for this." She walked to the side table and poured herself a generous glass of brandy. She eyed him over the rim of the glass as she raised it to her lips. "I don't want to know what you had to do with the attack, do I?"

"No." He crossed his arms. "And we were never here, understand?"

"Of course." She smiled and seductively swirled her brandy. "Discretion is my business."

Clayton knew that smile just cost the Home Office an additional five hundred pounds.

"How long will you be staying?" Madame asked.

"As long as we have to." He allowed himself a glance at the princess. She sat huddled in the corner of the settee and absently rubbed her hand over her forearm. "Not until it's safe to leave."

"I don't think—"

"How did you know who I am?" Cordelia's question came quietly, but it stopped both of them in midconversation. She looked up from her arm at Madame. "You recognized me, but I'm certain you haven't been to any of the palace events."

Madame raised a questioning brow at Clayton for permission to answer.

He nodded.

"I read in the *Times* that the Monrovian royal family is visiting London," Madame explained, choosing her words carefully. "And how uncanny, Miss Smith, that you should so resemble the late Princess Marguerite of Monrovia. In fact, one might say, you could be her daughter."

Cordelia rose slowly to her feet. "You...saw her?"

"I *knew* her." Madame traced her fingertip slowly around the rim of her glass. "In Vienna and Paris before the wars. A long time ago."

"And my father?" Cordelia hesitated, and in that moment's pause, Clayton saw a deep vulnerability. "Did you also know him?"

"I did. The prince was a good sovereign and a fine man, and he deeply loved his wife." Madame paused and locked her gaze with Cordelia's. Knowing Madame, Clayton worried about what she would say next until she murmured, "They both would have been very proud to see the fine woman their daughter has become."

Cordelia nodded, satisfied with Madame's answer, and looked away, but not before Clayton saw her blink rapidly.

Concern for her gripped him, along with that ever-present need to protect her. She was exhausted and overwrought by the night's events, and she needed to rest. Desperately.

"A room," he reminded Madame.

"The one next to my suite is available," she informed him as she crossed to her writing desk and opened the drawer. "I keep it for emergencies."

"What kind of emergencies?" Cordelia asked.

Madame tsked her tongue in gentle scolding. "Best not to ask too many questions while you're here. You might not like the answers."

She withdrew a key on a scarlet ribbon and dangled it from her hand as she sashayed back toward Clayton.

"Make yourself comfortable, General." She slipped the key into his hand. Then she leaned toward him to bring her lips to his ear and warned in a low murmur, "But not *too* comfortable."

She patted his chest as she stepped away.

Clayton tightened his jaw. He had no time for games. Ignoring the puzzled expression on Cordelia's pale face, he took her arm and led her toward the door. He snatched up a candlestick as he passed a side table.

"We'll need a tray of food sent up and a pail of hot water for Miss Smith if your kitchen can spare it." He paused to light the candle on the oil lamp. "I also need to send a message. Ask your guard to find a random boy from the street who wants to earn a coin by delivering it."

"You would trust me with that?" Madame asked.

"Not at all." He held up the candle and said as calmly as the flickering of the small flame, "But *you* can trust that I will kill you myself if you dare share one word about this to anyone."

Without waiting for Madame's response, Clayton led

Cordelia to the spare room and closed the door securely behind them. For emergencies all right, he thought. The door had three locks.

The room was dark and cold, but it was also furnished with a well-appointed bed, dresser, writing desk, and chair. Everything they would need to hide here until Clayton could learn more about tonight's attack.

Almost. He released her hand and began to search the room, first pulling open the desk drawer.

"We're staying for the night, then?" Cordelia asked softly, remaining by the door.

"Yes." He closed the drawer and went to the dresser. "We should know more by dawn."

"You're…friends with a brothel madame?"

He frowned into each drawer he opened and searched quickly through the clothes inside. "Not friends, exactly."

"I see."

He shot her a narrowed glance over his shoulder at what she'd implied. "We're not *that* either."

"Yet you trust her?"

"No." He closed the last drawer and turned away from the dresser to scan the room. "But I trust she's self-serving enough to know with which side to ally herself."

She frowned. "What are you searching for?"

"Madame Noir said she keeps this room for emergencies. Knowing Madame, that means…" His attention fell onto the bed, and he squatted beside it. A wooden box had been hidden beneath. He pulled it out, threw open the lid, and found what he'd been searching for. "Weapons."

A small stash of arms of all kinds filled the box, including a brace of pistols, fresh powder, and balls. He quickly reloaded his two pistols.

"Will those be necessary?"

"I certainly hope not." Trusting that Madame kept the other pistols loaded and ready to fire, he snatched them from the box before shoving it back under the bed. "Do you know how to fire a gun?"

When she didn't answer, he looked up at her. She'd gone pale, all of her shaking fiercely, and her arms were wrapped protectively around her middle. She stared at the gun in his hand as if it were a snake about to strike.

He hated frightening her like this, but he couldn't hide the pistols, not when her life might depend on having them at the ready. Instead, he slowly stood and placed one on the bedside table, another on the fireplace mantel, and a third on the dresser. He kept the last one in his hand.

"They're only here in case we need them," he assured her. He laid the pistol flat on his palm to show it to her. "You point it at what you want to hit, cock back the hammer here, and squeeze the trigger there. That's it."

She whispered, "Is it really that easy to kill someone?"

He solemnly met her gaze. "Not at all."

A knock rapped at the door. Startled, Cordelia jumped, and her hand flew to her mouth to stifle a cry of surprise.

He put his finger to his lips to signal for her to remain quiet. Then he approached the door, his pistol raised. "Yes?"

"Madame said t' bring up dinner fer ye," a female voice answered from the landing. "An' water."

"Just leave it outside the door," he ordered.

"Aye."

He waited until he heard her footsteps descend the stairs, then he cautiously opened the door and peered out to make certain the landing was empty. He brought the tray and bucket of hot water inside, then securely sealed them inside again behind all three locks.

He placed the tray on the desk and the bucket by the wash-basin on the dresser. He needed to send a message to the men of the Armory, but first he had to take care of the princess.

He slowly approached her. "You should eat."

She remained by the foot of the bed. "I'm not hungry."

"I know." He slipped her arms out of the greatcoat and tossed it over the desk chair. "But you need to keep up your strength." He took her arm and slowly rolled her glove down and off her fingers. "And you need to rest to give your ankle time to fully recover from your fall."

Careful not to hurt her, he removed the second glove that covered her bandage. He ran his fingers over the white cloth to make certain she hadn't reinjured herself.

No, that was a lie. He simply needed to touch her.

"You're all right, Cordelia," he said in his softest voice, more to reassure himself than her. "You'll be safe here, I promise."

She nodded absently, not because she believed that, he knew, but because he expected it. Even now, her sense of duty permeated her actions. "And we'll find out soon what happened?" she asked, searching his face. "If Marie and the others were harmed or..."

"We'll find out soon that they are all just fine." Another lie. Apparently, he was full of them tonight.

Another knock sounded at the door.

"Who is it?" he called out, not releasing her arm.

"The man downstairs said you need to 'ave a message delivered," the high-pitched voice of a boy answered. "For a good price."

He placed his finger to Cordelia's lips to remind her to remain silent. "Give me a moment."

With a touch of her cheek to reassure her, he went to the desk and quickly scribbled out a message to the only person outside the Armory he would wager his life would never be involved with Scepter—the Honorable Mr. Justice James Rivers. Merritt's father.

Inside the note, he placed a second sealed message for the judge to deliver to Merritt and the men of the Armory, followed by a third message to the Home Secretary. That message was comprised of a single word: *Safe.*

He folded and sealed the note, then wrote the justice's name on the outside. He carried it to the door and slowly opened it.

A towheaded boy covered in a layer of soot and dirt waited with a scowl on his round face. He couldn't have been more than eleven or twelve, but already he'd aged far past his years based on the harsh edge Clayton glimpsed in him.

Clayton held out the note. "Can you read this name?"

The boy's scowl deepened. "Can't read." He spat on the floor. "The man downstairs didn't say nothin' about 'aving to read to earn me coin."

"You don't have to." For the only time in his life, Clayton was thankful a child was illiterate. There would be no chance of the boy putting his life in danger by reading the note. "Take this to Justice Rivers at number ten Sloane Square. He'll pay you a second coin when you deliver it." Clayton reached into his waistcoat pocket and held up a coin. "Repeat that."

"Sloane Square, number ten, Justice Rivers." The boy smirked. "And a second coin."

Clayton gave him both the coin and the note. "Better hurry," he warned, "or Justice Rivers might not pay you."

The boy clenched his teeth with determination and flew down the stairs.

When Clayton came back inside the room, Cordelia was pacing, wringing her shaking hands, and limping on her sore ankle.

Without a word, he scooped her into his arms.

She wrapped her arms around his neck. "What are you doing?"

"I said you need to rest," he reminded her as he carried her to the bed. "Pacing isn't resting."

He set her down gently on the counterpane. Instead of letting him go, however, she kept her arms wound tightly around his neck and forced him to remain leaning over her, half lying on the bed.

He froze even as his heart leapt into his throat.

"What you said before, when you introduced me to Madame Noir…" She searched his face. "Plain, average, normal Jane Smith, am I?"

"Yes." His mouth poised so uncomfortably close to hers

that he could taste her sweet breath as it teased across his lips.

A flicker in her eyes registered that lie. Yet she didn't challenge it and silently let him go, slipping her arms from around his neck. Her gaze never leaving his, she slowly removed her hairpins, set them on the bedside table next to the pistol, and shook out her chestnut tresses. He fought back an aching groan.

Finally—mercifully—she lay back and closed her eyes.

He stared down at her as she lay across the bed in the soft shadows of the candlelight. Even in a rumpled and dirtied dress, she looked more alluring than all the women in jewels and furs at any grand ball. It would only take a small surrender to crawl into bed with her and distract her from her fears. *Sweet Lucifer*, he was tempted. So *very* tempted. Only a small surrender leading to comforting kisses and touches…

And with that, he'd lose everything he'd worked so hard his entire life to achieve. She might as well have been the devil himself asking for his soul.

He blew out a long, silent breath and turned away.

There would be no rest tonight for either of them.

———

The boy returned three hours later.

Clayton traded him a coin for the message and locked the door. This time, he also wedged the desk chair beneath the handle.

He broke the seal. Cold dread pierced him as he read

Justice Rivers's message, one that had been carefully encoded. But even the most difficult encryption couldn't hide the truth staring back at him—he was now considered a rogue agent.

What he held in his hand was notice of his arrest warrant.

He ran trembling fingers through his hair in a futile attempt to keep the rest of him from shaking even harder. *A rogue agent...* No matter that he saved the princess's life—twice—or that he'd placed the guards around the town house who ultimately saved the MPs and peers tonight, the palace blamed him for the attack because they needed a scapegoat, and the Home Secretary wasn't coming to his defense.

Worse, his message to Lord Sidmouth that the princess was safe hadn't reassured the Home Office. Instead, the palace—and her uncle—had taken it as little more than a ransom note.

He was wanted for kidnapping the princess. If he didn't return her immediately, it would be the end of him.

Cordelia sat up and stared at him from the bed. Her soft brown eyes that had always reminded him of warm chocolate were wide and dark with fear, and even from across the room, he could see her holding her breath.

"What does it say?" she asked.

"Very little." How *very* little it took to threaten the end of a man's life. The irony would have made him laugh if he didn't feel like punching the wall. Her uncle had pushed him into a corner. Clayton either had to take Cordelia to the palace, where she'd be placed back into danger, or let his career, his reputation, his search for the truth about his father—*everything* he'd worked so hard to achieve—be destroyed.

"Tell me." Cordelia slipped off the bed and approached him. "Any news of the others?"

"A footman and two guards were killed, but all the peers and MPs escaped with their lives."

She placed her hand on his arm. "And the comtesse?"

He looked down at her hand, sorely tempted to take it and claim what little solace he could in her touch, even such an innocent one. "She's safe at the palace with your uncle. She's shaken but fine."

"Oh, thank God," she breathed out. "Thank God!" The fear she'd worn for the past few hours visibly left her in a rush. She threw her arms around his neck and hugged him tightly in relief. "They're safe…all safe!"

Not even close. He gently took her arms and stiffly set her away.

Her joy at the news vanished, and she frowned with fresh worry. "What's wrong?" She looked at the note in his hand. "What else does it say?"

He could tell her, force *her* to make the decision about how to proceed. Hell, that was exactly what he should do. He'd done his duty to England and saved her life, and now he could deposit her safely back at the palace where the captain of the guards would be responsible for her. He owed her nothing more.

But when she slowly took his hand in hers and laced their fingers together with all the trust in the world that he would protect her even from what was inside that message, he knew he was lost.

He would protect her with his life. *All* of it. He released her hand, crossed to the fireplace, and tossed the note onto the coals.

"Nothing for you to worry about," he told her, watching the flames brighten as they devoured the letter. "Just Home Office business."

"So we can return to the palace?"

The soft question ripped through him. He didn't dare look over his shoulder at her. "Not quite yet."

With that, he'd sealed his fate.

"Then you need to rest." She came up behind him and turned him toward her. Her concern seeped into him when she placed her hand against his cheek. "Take the bed. You need sleep more than I do."

He knew her touch was meant to soothe, but it only wound tighter the coiling frustration in his gut.

He took her hand and gently moved it away. "I'll be fine there." He gestured at the rug in front of the fire. "In the wars, I slept in far worse places than on a brothel floor." He paused thoughtfully. "Although sometimes it *was* a brothel floor."

Unfortunately, he didn't draw so much as a faint smile from her. Even in the short time they'd been together, she'd come to know him too well to let him deflect the seriousness of their situation with teasing.

"You're a princess," he explained quietly. "I'm only a soldier. The bed is yours."

"Then as a soldier, you serve at the pleasure of the princess, correct?" She took his hand and led him toward the bed. "And tonight, it would give me great pleasure if you rest." She stopped by the side of the bed. "After all, I need your strength to save me."

For a long while, he didn't move. He simply gazed down at her in the soft shadows of the fire, knowing she meant far more than what those simple words implied.

"And where will you spend the night?" he asked.

She shrugged. "Plain, old, average Jane Smith can sleep on the chair."

Nothing about her was plain, certainly not old, and not at all average. No, right then, in the glow of the firelight, she looked like an angel. *Almost.* Because an angel wouldn't be tempting him like this. *Go to bed? Certainly...with you.*

She stilled as he reached up to slowly run his hand through her chestnut locks and brush them softly around her shoulders. He bit down a groan as she parted her lips in surprise, then lowered her gaze to his mouth in invitation to be kissed.

He dropped his hand away. She might have taken his life, but he wouldn't yet surrender his soul.

Without a word, he turned away, yanked off his cravat, and stripped out of his waistcoat. He could feel the heat of her eyes on him as she watched him undress, which only intensified the sweet torture. He didn't dare look at her as he pulled off his boots and set them on the floor beside the bed, then lowered his braces to dangle them around his hips. When he crawled into bed, he stretched out his long legs, tucked his arm behind his head, and closed his eyes, yet he didn't expect to sleep a wink.

Only the sound of her slippers against the floorboards told him that Cordelia had found her way to the chair.

Most likely, she'd never seen a man undress before, never seen one stretched out across a bed. *Good*. Maybe the sight would frighten her enough to make her keep her distance.

But that wish dissolved into the shadows when, less than an hour later, he heard the soft rustle of her skirts as she rose from the chair and the pad of her feet as she crossed the room. He didn't open his eyes, letting her think he was deep asleep. The mattress moved beneath her weight as she carefully sat on the side of the bed and then lay down. In her exhaustion, the soft bed had undoubtedly proved too much temptation, even with an undressed man already in it.

Within minutes, he heard her breath grow slow and steady as she fell quickly and deeply into much needed sleep.

Clayton let out a long, silent breath. Thank God. Maybe now he could relax enough to finally fall—

She turned and nestled against his side. The brush of her soft breasts against his chest jolted through him with the force of a lightning strike.

Clayton opened his eyes and stared up at the dark ceiling. It was going to be one hell of a long night.

Seventeen

CORDELIA SLOWLY WOKE AS THE PALE BLUE LIGHT OF dawn began to fall through the window.

For a moment, she didn't move, needing time to remember everything that happened last night and how she had ended up here. Her sleep-fogged mind eventually cleared, but she needed no help to immediately register that Clayton was beside her in bed.

She turned onto her side to study his face in the lightening shadows.

The relaxation of sleep softened his brow and jaw, and his golden-blond hair was mussed from the pillow, with a lock falling boyishly across his forehead. And goodness, how tall and broad he was—there was certainly nothing boyish about his physique. She hadn't fully realized how large he was, how fit and well-built, until he was lying next to her, filling the suddenly small bed that had seemed so big to her earlier.

A smile played at her lips. *My hero.*

She'd never met another man like him. Never one so brave, never one so handsome even with a shadow of morning beard darkening his face. She itched to touch him and feel the scratch of stubble beneath her fingertips. And she could—there was nothing to stop her. After all, he was asleep and would never know…

She held her breath as she slowly brushed her fingers over his cheek. His morning beard scraped lightly beneath her fingertips.

All bristly on the surface, smooth and warm underneath…the perfect metaphor for him, she decided as she trailed her fingers lightly along his jaw. And strong. Even this fleeting touch conveyed to her the strength of him, the solidity, the difference between him and the usual courtiers who were soft and paunchy. *Nothing* about him was soft and certainly not paunchy. How had it never occurred to her before that a man could be as hard and muscular as this yet be even more appealing because of it?

This light touch wasn't enough, so she took full advantage of his being asleep to trace her fingers down his bare neck and across his collarbone revealed by the loose gap at his shirt's neck. Enough of a gap, too, that she could just touch the start of the flat plane of his chest. His skin was warm, and only a sprinkling of golden hair across his chest interrupted its smoothness.

If he felt this good…what would he taste like?

Carefully pulling his shirt collar open, she shifted toward him to bring her lips against his skin.

Without warning, he shoved his hands into her hair and lifted her head away from him.

His eyes opened, and the heated look she saw there stole her breath away, right before he bought her mouth down to his and captured her with a kiss that sent her spinning.

He devoured her lips until she ached. His mouth was insistent and hungry, moving against hers with a need she'd never felt before in a man's kiss, and his hands held her head still even as the tip of his tongue darted out to outline her lips. Cordelia knew what he wanted, and with a sigh, she opened her mouth.

A groan rose from the back of his throat, and he thrust between her lips in a steady, intense rhythm that spiraled a hot shiver through her.

With a gasp, she tore her mouth away from his to regain her breath, but his lips never left her, sliding along her jaw to her ear. There, his wicked tongue did the same as he'd done to her mouth, swirling around her ear and plunging into it.

When he took her earlobe between his lips and sucked, a whimper escaped her. She wanted his mouth on hers again, *needed* it there, giving her ravenous yet reassuring kisses. So she rose up over him and claimed his kiss.

"Princess," he murmured in warning against her mouth.

But she didn't care if what she was doing was proper and dutiful, didn't want to be a princess in his eyes. She knew only her growing need to be close to him.

She lifted her head to look down at him but kept her mouth tantalizingly close to his. "Cordelia," she insisted. Cupping his face between her hands, she lowered her mouth to his and murmured between kisses, "Say my name, Clayton." She took his bottom lip between hers and gently sucked. "Say it."

"Cordelia." Her name emerged as a low rasp, but his desire was clear. So was the trembling in his hand as he moved it down the side of her body. When his hand stroked back up, he brought her skirt along with it to midthigh, then slipped his hand beneath to caress bare skin.

"Please," she whispered as he brushed her outer thigh.

Fulfilling her soft demand, he stroked his hand higher until he touched her bare bottom beneath her dress, until he held her against his large palm. He stroked her buttock in a slow, hard circle that made her feel deliciously feminine.

But even this bold touch wasn't enough to satisfy the growing ache inside her. "More," she murmured against his lips. "I want more."

He rolled her onto her back and brought his body over hers. He caressed her bare thigh above her stocking. "This?"

"Yes," she half moaned. When his hand slipped down to her inner thigh, anticipation shivered through her.

With her hands on his hard shoulders, she felt him tremble as he moved his hand higher. But then, so did she. Tingling waves of electricity passed through her, and the higher he reached, the stronger the tingle grew. The realization of what she needed from him landed with an insistent ache between her legs.

His hand stilled at the junction of her thighs, his fingers resting lightly against her feminine folds. This almost-touch was agonizing.

"Yes?" he murmured.

In that single word, she knew he wasn't asking if she enjoyed it. He was seeking permission.

"Yes." She shamelessly spread her legs, the throbbing ache at her core demanding it. *Oh, yes!*

He lowered his forehead to rest against hers and closed his eyes. Then he murmured something she couldn't discern—and touched her.

She caught her breath. His fingers caressed tenderly between her legs in long, slow strokes across her folds. His touch felt so good…so exciting, yet so oddly comforting. It was the same with his body lying over hers. At that moment, she didn't want to think—all she wanted to do was *feel*, and the feel of his hands on her was simply wonderful.

But then his caresses changed. No longer light touches, each stroke grew harder and deeper until heat balled right there between her legs, just beyond his fingertips. Exactly where she needed him to touch. She couldn't remain still and wiggled her hips against his hand.

He groaned. "Cordelia."

Her heart soared at the sound of her name on his lips, spoken of his own free will. She wiggled again, this time longer and more forcefully, to beg with her body for him to stoke the flames he created in her until they consumed her.

But when he slipped a finger inside her, she gasped against his mouth at the strange sensation…until he began to stroke slowly inside her, which was absolutely divine.

She buried her face against his bare neck. "That feels…"

"Good?" he asked, his voice thick and husky.

"So *very* good," she sighed and earned herself a nuzzle of his stubble-roughened cheek against hers.

His fingers never slowed in their persistent and quickening strokes. Instead, a second finger joined the first, filling her even more completely, and when he began to tease his thumb against the hard bead in her folds, she nearly shot out of her skin!

She wrapped her arms around his neck to keep him close as the pressure mounted inside her. He murmured soft words into her ear that she couldn't understand, lost beneath the delicious feel of his intimate touches and her own whimpers of need. When he touched her again—right there, at that wonderful spot—her hips bucked off the mattress.

"Clayton!"

With an openmouthed kiss, he drank up her soft cries as pleasure spread through her. Electric tingles sparked out to her fingers and toes, and she felt as if she were being swept away on a hot wind. She could do nothing more than cling to him and tremble as her breathing eased and her racing heartbeat slowed.

Even as she sank bonelessly into the mattress, he remained as tense as ever, poised over her on one forearm with his other hand resting on her lower belly. His broad shoulders were taut beneath her hands, and his muscular arms and legs shook. A pained expression darkened his face, with his eyes squeezed shut and his jaw clenched.

"Clayton?" She caressed his cheek, her fingertips trembling. "Did I do something wrong?"

"God no." His head sank between his shoulders. He pulled in a hard breath and muttered, "I did."

"No, you didn't."

A disbelieving sound tore from him, somewhere between a guttural laugh and a groan.

She kissed him with as much reassurance as she could,

yet she tasted the regret in him. How could she make him understand how special this moment was for her? What he'd done to her was simply wonderful. Even now, the warmth of his hand resting on her belly seeped into her and once again stirred the aching need inside her. So did the longing desire she glimpsed in his eyes. He'd given her such delicious pleasures that she would never forget them.

But she also suspected he could give her even more.

"I wanted your touch." She boldly reached down to lace her fingers through his. "And I want it again."

"Cordelia." Her name was a soft warning, yet he didn't stop her as she slowly led his hand back down between her legs. "We can't—*I* can't."

A smile curled at her lips. "Oh, I'm pretty sure you can." Deliciously, in fact.

"I *shouldn't*," he corrected, his hand stilling hers at the top of her thigh.

She searched his face. "You don't want to touch me again?"

A curse tore from him. He brought her hand against his crotch and the hard bulge under his breeches. "Can't you feel how much I want to do just that, and more?"

If he'd meant to shock her, he'd failed. Instead, she brushed her fingertips curiously over him to discover for herself the effect she had on him. He couldn't be comfortable, squeezed into his breeches like that, but she also knew this wasn't the only reason he was pained.

"I'm not made of glass," she said softly as she lifted her head to kiss him and taste the spicy-sweet flavor of his lips.

"I'm not some statue to be placed onto a pedestal and admired from afar." She caressed him harder with her palm, eliciting a low groan from him as his breath turned into shallow pants. "I'm a living woman of flesh and blood. Can't I be only that for you? For this one moment, can't I just be yours?"

A strangled sound tore from him. He grabbed her wrist and stilled her hand.

"You're a princess," he bit out.

When he lifted her hand away, the dark torment she witnessed in him nearly undid her.

"You can *never* be mine."

———

Clayton crawled out of bed and splashed cold water from the washbasin over his face, not caring that he was drenching his shirt and breeches. He still had a chance, however slight, to convince the Home Office and palace that he'd had nothing to do with last night's attack, that he'd fled with Cordelia only to save her life. She would come to his defense, and all would be set to rights—*if* he could keep his goddamned hands to himself.

The water ran in rivulets down his chest and back, and he welcomed the cold. But he could have jumped into the bloody freezing Thames and it still wouldn't have been enough to purge the heat she put into his loins. Or the foolish desire to be so much more to her than merely a bodyguard.

"I wasn't thinking," he explained stiffly. He clasped the sides of the washstand with both hands and somehow managed to resist the urge to dunk his entire head into the basin. "You surprised me, and I..." *I lost my mind.*

If he hadn't stopped when he had, he would certainly have also lost his soul.

"Don't," she ordered softly. "Don't you dare apologize for what we—"

"My *deepest* apologies," he rasped out.

For a long while, only silence responded to that. Then, softly, "I thought you cared about me."

Cared? A tight laugh tore from him. He more than cared. He'd give his life for hers, and he'd come to realize that pledge had little to do anymore with the fact that she was a princess in England's care. She'd found her way under his skin—worse, into his heart—and he knew that she would be a singular event in his life.

He'd never meet another woman like her again.

He swept his hands over his face and hair to wipe the water away, took a deep breath, and faced her.

The sight of her hit him like a punch. She was still in the rumpled bed where he'd left her with her hair cascading around her shoulders like a silk curtain, her raised skirts showing her bare legs from her thighs down, and her bodice pulled scandalously low across her breasts.

God help him, he'd never seen a more alluring woman than Cordelia at that moment. She had no idea the kind of knots she tied him in, what threats she posed, or all he was sacrificing for her.

But a self-destructive urge inside him made him confess, "More than you'll ever know."

A sharp knock came at the door. They both froze, and Cordelia's eyes locked fearfully with his.

Clayton placed a finger to his lips to signal for her to keep her silence. "Who is it?" he called out.

"A woman who's going to become very wealthy in only a few days when you pay your bill," Madame Noir answered, as flippant as ever. "For *every* service you owe me."

Cordelia scrambled out of bed and yanked her dress back into place. But there was no help for her mussed hair, the wrinkles in her skirts, or the telltale puffiness he'd kissed into her red lips.

With a grimace, he went to the door and picked up the pistol he'd placed nearby. He flipped the locks and opened the door a crack to peer out at the landing—empty except for Madame, who didn't look at all happy.

He let her inside and locked the door after her. He didn't set down his gun.

Madame glanced at Cordelia on the other side of the room, but she gave no reaction to the princess's disheveled appearance before returning her attention to Clayton. "You need to leave," she said quietly so Cordelia couldn't overhear. "Immediately."

"What have you heard?"

"Nothing good. Information and rumors have been filtering in from my guests."

In other words, she'd had the women who worked here casually ask their customers what was happening tonight and report back to her.

"Parliament has called for an emergency meeting," she

told him, "and Whitehall is in an uproar. No one knows who's alive, who's dead, and if more attacks are coming. It's taking the Home Office too long to summon the militia, and the palace is refusing to let the War Office send in soldiers to keep order in the city." She added, "I think the regent is afraid of where the army's loyalties might lie these days."

So was Clayton. "And Lord Liverpool?"

"The prime minister hasn't been able to rally the MPs or lords to his side yet to make any kind of statement about the attack or declare support for the current government. The prince regent hasn't acted, and no statement has been made from Windsor or St James's Palace regarding the security of the monarch, the regent, the royal dukes…" She looked past him at Cordelia. "Or the missing princess."

"And Westminster?" If a coup d'état was underway, its flash point would be there.

"Riots have broken out, but none have made their way there yet. Most likely they're only people looking to take advantage of the disorder by breaking into shops and warehouses to steal what they can." She paused. "But those who are brave enough to claim to know who's behind the attack all say the same."

"Scepter." His answer wasn't a guess.

Madame gave a tight nod. "It's too dangerous for all of us if you remain here. You need to take *Miss Smith* out of London as soon as possible." She held out a key and directions written on a notecard. "I keep a cottage on Mersea Island for my husband's use."

Clayton blinked. "You're married?"

"I rarely visit it and like it all the more for that," she dodged. "But then, I rarely visit my husband and like him all the more for that, too." Bitterness edged her voice despite her attempt at dark humor. "He's a ship's captain who uses it when he's in harbor, so no one will think it odd if you've suddenly appeared there. If anyone asks, tell them you're a new sailor on the *Cerberus*, expecting to report as soon as she arrives in port. Your captain is Ian Andrews. You've not yet met him."

"Understood." With the grim determination of a man walking to the gallows, he accepted both key and card. His fate was sealed. Cordelia's wasn't. That was all that mattered. "We'll need a change of clothes."

Madame nodded. "Already waiting in my carriage for you. My coachman has orders to drive you out of London. I suggest you go no farther than Chelmsford before switching to the mail coach." She paused. "I'm certain a man like you knows how to hide his tracks."

"Very well."

"Then do it. If anyone comes looking for you after you've gone, I'll lie to hide you."

"For extra money, I'm sure."

She nodded at the princess. "For her mother. I'm repaying an old favor."

"What favor?"

"I haven't always been a businesswoman. I once had ties to the French aristocracy. Her mother helped me escape to England during the revolution, saving my life. Tonight, I'm saving her daughter's. And now all debts have been paid in full."

She smiled at him. Her old pretense of the overly flirtatious courtesan swiftly returned, and she rested a hand on Clayton's arm.

"Except yours," she purred. "Make certain your payment is generous. After all, size *does* matter when it comes to men and money."

Not caring that Cordelia was watching their private conversation from across the room—or, knowing Madame, more likely because she was—she rose up on her tiptoes to bring her bosom against Clayton's chest, slipped her hand far too familiarly behind his nape, and brushed her lips over his in a goodbye kiss.

"Whenever I think of handcuffs and ropes," she promised, "I'll think of you."

She slid her mouth over his cheek, then lowered herself away and swung her hips wide as she sashayed toward the door.

"The carriage is waiting for you in the rear." She allowed herself to cast back a parting look, one that swept longingly over him from head to toe. Then she exhaled a long sigh of disappointment. "Do not ever come back here again."

With that, Madame was gone.

Eighteen

CORDELIA LOOKED ONCE MORE ACROSS THE CARRIAGE compartment at Clayton. He continued to watch out the window for any sign of attack, while his hand remained beneath his greatcoat on his pistol. They'd left London hours ago in the predawn shadows, but he remained ever her watchdog. She should have been terrified, but she wasn't.

What she was…was puzzled.

They'd made good time bouncing along in Madame's well-sprung carriage, rolling quickly through London before the streets became clogged with traffic and out into the countryside. The drizzly gray morning had helped, keeping people inside…including Clayton, who couldn't ride on top with the driver and tigers and so had to remain inside with her.

To distract her from the perils of their flight—and why he always kept one hand beneath his greatcoat—Clayton had told her stories about his life as a soldier and his time fighting in the wars. Instead of tales of glory and gore, as most former soldiers loved to tell to titillate their audience, he shared bits about camp life and training that made her laugh. His anecdotes of his postwar life in London with the Home Office were just as entertaining, and those she enjoyed most of all because she'd met Lord Sidmouth, Lord Liverpool, and several of the other gentlemen who bore the brunt of his jokes.

But she also knew from what he chose to leave out that perhaps he wasn't as happy as he wanted the world to believe, no matter how successful he was.

That was what puzzled her. Why would a man who'd gained success far beyond other men's wildest dreams keep relentlessly driving himself for more?

What was he running toward so very hard…or running away from?

"You've made a great success for yourself at the Home Office," she commented thoughtfully, breaking the silence and rubbing absently at her forearm where the wound had almost completely healed.

"Hmm?" He shot a glance at her, then turned his attention back out the window. "I suppose."

"No," she countered firmly, her statement a declaration, not a question. "You've made a great success for yourself."

"I've been fortunate."

"You've been driven," she corrected.

"Isn't ambition an admirable trait in a man?"

"As long as it's ambition and not obsession."

This time when he flicked his gaze to her, he didn't comment.

"Do you want to become Home Secretary after Lord Sidmouth?" she asked bluntly.

He shrugged a shoulder. "That's the next step upward."

She studied him closely. For a man who claimed not to care about reaching the pinnacle of his career and becoming arguably the fourth most important person in Great Britain, he certainly seemed driven toward it by every action he took. And yet… "You don't seem happy to be made a viscount."

A grimace tugged at the corners of his mouth. "I'm not."

"Why not? Most men would be honored to receive a peerage."

"Because I did nothing to earn it."

"But you did. You saved my life." *Twice.*

Not replying, he kept his attention on the passing countryside. His eyes scanned the horizon in both directions as if he expected a gang of marauders to jump out from behind the nearest tree.

Or perhaps he simply wanted to appear that way so she'd stop asking him questions.

Not a chance. "Have you ever guarded Princess Sophia?"

"No."

She tangled her fingers in her skirt. "Have you ever… kissed her?"

Surprised, he blurted out, "Has anyone?"

"That's unkind."

His brow arched. "So is Princess Sophia."

Cordelia couldn't argue with that.

He turned back to the gray day, and a long stretch of silence weighed on them like the lowering clouds overhead. Only the rumble of wheels and the occasional splash of a mud puddle broke the silent cocoon around them.

Cordelia studied his profile. Strong jaw, high cheekbone, a lock of blond hair that escaped from beneath the brim of his hat and lay rakishly across his forehead—Dear God, how handsome he was…and how troubled.

As if he could feel her watching him, he assured her quietly, "You're not Princess Sophia, if that's what's worrying you." Then, in a low mutter beneath his breath she was certain she wasn't meant to hear, he added, "Not by a goodly ways."

His words would have pleased her if she wasn't already so troubled by other thoughts.

She frowned and asked the question that had been poised on her tongue since the night they met. "But you've kissed other ladies at court, surely." Lots of women, lots of kisses... lots of all kinds of other things she didn't dare let herself contemplate. "Duchesses and countesses...women in positions of influence and power..."

"So have many, many men." He turned toward her and leaned forward, elbows on knees. His gaze narrowed as it fixed on her. "What exactly it is that you want to know about me, Princess?"

"I want to know—" She pulled in a deep breath and began again with a shake of her head, "I don't understand why you're bothering with me, why you're risking your life for mine." *Why you would kiss me the way you did.* She fought back a blush. He'd done far more than simply kiss her, and she feared she knew exactly why. "If not..."

"If not?" he pressed.

"If not for your own personal gain," she finished quietly. Somehow she found the courage to maintain eye contact. "Men often pretend to like me just to earn my favor at court. They flatter and flirt, steal kisses, and claim dances whenever they can." Putting voice to her gullibility embarrassed her, but it needed to be said. "When they learn that I'm unable to grant them titles or government positions, they want nothing more to do with me. I've learned not to take it personally, yet it still stings." She paused, then confessed, "And I'd very much like to avoid the sting of you."

He didn't move, not to laugh off her accusations or become enraged. Instead, he calmly asked, "You think I'm someone who would use you?"

"I think you're ambitious." *Too much so.* "And I don't know what to make of the attentions you've shown me."

"I am ambitious, but I earn the accolades I'm given. And I've shown you attention only because I enjoy your company." His gaze turned piercing. "I am not one of those other men."

Before she could say anything more, he rose up and pounded his fist against the compartment roof. The carriage slowed, and Clayton opened the window to call up to the driver to stop.

"We'll rest here a few minutes," he ordered the driver. Then he returned to his seat and nodded at the small bag that Madame had provided, tucked against the seat at Cordelia's feet. "You need to change out of your gown. We're almost to Chelmsford. We'll leave the carriage there and catch the mail coach the rest of the way to the coast."

She shook her head. "I can't."

"I'll wait outside. You can draw all the curtains, and I'll keep my back to the carriage and the driver and tigers will remain up top." He reached for the door. "No one will—"

"*I can't,*" she repeated and placed her hand on his arm to stop him. "I can't...undress myself."

He froze. He stared at her hand as it rested on his sleeve, then slowly raised his eyes to hers.

"I have a dresser named Braun who puts me in and out of my gowns," she explained, suddenly flushed. "I'm certain the dress Madame provided is a simple day dress, and I should be able to manage it and the—" She choked on the word. "And the undergarments by myself." Heavens, how warm it had suddenly become inside the compartment! "But I can't remove this gown without help." She took a deep breath and forced herself to meet his gaze, although with a touch of embarrassment and through lowered lashes. "Would you... undress me?"

He didn't move, but his muscles tensed beneath her fingertips.

"It will only take a moment," she said nervously. "Besides, I'm certain I'm not the first woman you've helped out of her evening gown."

Her teasing quip fell flat, and his expression remained just as stony as before.

She bit her lip and looked up toward the top of the carriage. "I suppose I can ask the tiger for help, if you're not willing."

His jaw clenched hard. "Turn around."

Her victory gave her no pleasure. She stood, careful not to put too much weight onto her unsteady ankle. Crouching in the small compartment, she turned her back to him.

For a long moment, he didn't move, simply remaining on the seat. Then her heart lurched into her throat when his fingers brushed against her bodice. He carefully slipped free each pearl button, one at a time, and slowly worked his way down her back. Her bodice sagged around her shoulders and bosom, and when the last button came undone, the silk dress slipped down her body. She let it puddle on the floor around her feet, not bothering to catch it or attempt to cover herself.

Behind her, he sucked in a mouthful of air.

The bare skin on her arms and upper back prickled with goose bumps, and not because of the damp, cold day. Suddenly, breathing evenly was impossible, and she could sense his warmth behind her, even from two feet away. She felt his gaze on her back, as surely as if his hands were on her, caressing slowly over her and exploring her body.

"And my stays." She swallowed. Hard. "Would you remove those, too?"

A long moment passed before she felt him reach again for her back, this time for the long lace that tied her short corset. She felt it slip loose as he started at the top and slowly pulled it free, one long and slow pull of his fingers at a time.

She closed her eyes at the torturous nearness of his hands. He was careful not to touch the bare skin above her stays, so careful not to accidentally brush his knuckles against her shift, but he couldn't stop the heat of his hands from seeping through the thin undergarments and into her skin.

Her belly tightened so much with each pull of the loosening tie that it ached…and so did another part of her, from lower beneath her petticoat.

His hand reached the end of the tie, and he hesitated. She could hear his ragged breath behind her, could feel the heat of his fingers against the small of her back. Was he fighting with himself to keep from pulling her into his arms the way she longed for him to do? Did he crave intimate touches and caresses as much as she did?

Then he hooked his finger around the last cross of the tie and pulled the lace free. The stays fell loose and dropped to the floor at her feet.

"There. All unbuttoned and untied." He cleared his throat, shoved himself up from the seat, and moved toward the door. "Take your time."

He was gone before she could stop him, opening the door only far enough to slip outside.

As soon as he was gone, Cordelia sank onto the seat and pulled in deep lungfuls of air to catch back her breath and slow her racing heart. She held up her hands and watched them shake. Blast that devil of a man that he had this kind of effect on her! His rejection only worsened her frustration and embarrassment.

She nudged back the edge of the curtain and peered outside. Clayton stood a few yards away in the cold drizzle near a low stone wall. How humiliating that he'd rather stand in the rain than subject himself to remaining inside the coach with her while she—

He shrugged out of his greatcoat and tossed it onto the wall, then let his cashmere jacket follow after.

Cordelia blinked. And stared shamelessly.

She couldn't look away as he unbuttoned his silk waistcoat and laid it aside, then pulled down his braces and yanked at his shirt to free it from his waistband and pull it off over his head. Her breath hitched as she shamelessly watched the muscles in his bare back flex as he reached for his own change of clothes.

A pang of disappointment struck her when he left his breeches in place, putting on only a different shirt and brown waistcoat and jacket.

In a matter of moments, the gentleman he'd dressed to be was gone; in his place stood a man who resembled a laborer. But nothing could hide his proud bearing and powerful stance or the strength that radiated from him. He might have the muscles to disguise himself as a regular worker, but he'd never pass for a common man. Not him.

He finished tying his plain neckcloth and turned toward the carriage.

Cordelia dropped the curtain back into place before he could see her.

A few minutes later, she was dressed in the calico day dress Madame had found for her, her hair pinned loosely in a knot at her nape. Her appearance told the world she was far from being a princess, right down to the sturdy, dirt-smeared half boots and the wool shawl over her shoulders. She only wished that could be the truth.

She signaled that she was ready.

"Drive on!" Clayton called up to the driver. Instead of riding inside with Cordelia, though, he swung up onto the top of the coach and sat on the bench beside the driver. To more easily see if anyone rushed upon them to attack them. To more easily use the brace of pistols beneath his greatcoat.

To more easily stay away from her.

She blinked rapidly and stared out the window at the falling rain.

Nineteen

CLAYTON TOSSED A COIN TO THE DRIVER AND SWUNG down from the carriage. The inn on the edge of Chelmsford was far too busy for comfort. Several other carriages had already stopped in the innyard to change out passengers and teams, and small groups of travelers gathered around the door of the inn and inside its large public rooms. He prayed they were all too concerned with their own travel plans to suspect that a runaway princess lingered in their midst.

He beat the tiger to the carriage door and held out his hand to help Cordelia to the ground.

She hesitated, and that small gesture of distrust struck him as hard as if she'd slapped him. Then she pulled her hand away as soon as her feet touched the muddy ground.

He didn't blame her. Her snub was exactly what he deserved.

"We'll rest here before traveling on." He took the small bag from her hand. At least in her borrowed dress and shawl, she looked the part of an ordinary traveler, and taking her elbow to guide her to the inn, he purposefully led her through patches of mud to dirty her half boots even more. "We'll use the necessary, buy a bite to eat, and purchase tickets on the next available stagecoach." He lowered his mouth close to her ear so his voice wouldn't carry. "We need to keep to ourselves as much as possible. Try not to talk to anyone, all right?"

She nodded, but her curious gaze swung around her in all directions. "I've never been to an inn before." A touch of excitement tinged her voice. "And I've never ridden in a mail coach before."

He grimly replied, "You probably won't want to ever again."

As if to prove him correct, a palpable stench smacked them when he opened the inn door. Pungent odors of stale ale and cheap whiskey permeated the air, along with the acrid smell of burned stew and the woody scent of mildew and mold. The air was thick with smoke from the poorly vented fireplace, and an old layer of straw had been scattered across the floor, then left there for God only knew how many weeks. In the corner, a hound lifted its leg and peed on a chair.

She halted in the middle of the door, and her mouth fell open, stunned. Then she turned to Clayton and clasped his arm. "Oh, this is simply wonderful!"

Clayton watched as a second dog attempted to compete with the first on marking his territory. He muttered, "If you think this is grand, just wait until I show you the docks."

Her eyes gleamed. "Promise?"

He bit down a chuckle and led her to a small table just inside the door that seemed to be the cleanest spot in the room and pulled out a chair, keeping its back toward the wall. She sat but was so excited at being in the filthy, cramped inn that she perched on the edge of her seat and craned her neck to take in every detail of the dark room.

"Stay here," he ordered. "I'll be back in a few minutes."

He crossed the room to the counter that served as both bar and guest registration desk. The counter was just as filthy as every other surface in the room despite the large man behind it who was wiping it down with a towel, but the layer of stickiness didn't stop Clayton from sliding a coin across the board.

"We're going to need food and drink." Clayton nodded toward Cordelia at the table. "And two seats on the next stagecoach east." He didn't care where the coach was ultimately headed. They'd change at another inn along the way to throw off anyone who might be trailing them from London, although he'd seen no sign of that so far. "When does it leave?"

"In only a few minutes." The innkeeper flipped the towel over his shoulder and jerked a thumb toward the innyard.

"Then bundle up the food so we can take it with us. We'll buy two seats if any are still available."

The man grunted. "Might be, for the right price."

Clayton grimaced and handed over another coin.

The innkeeper snatched up both coins and barked out orders for food to a bar wench who leaned on her hip against the counter, flirting with a coachman. Most likely she was negotiating more than just his lunch bill. Irritated to be interrupted, she stomped away toward the kitchen.

"I need to send a letter to London," Clayton added. "Do you have a groom who can ride as a messenger?"

"Aye, but it'll cost you."

Of course it would. He tossed over a third coin. "Then I need to use your inkwell and stationery."

The innkeeper placed the writing supplies on the counter and walked away to call for a groom from the stables. Clayton dipped the quill into the ink and wrote out a coded message to Justice Rivers.

The weather turned bad in London, so we decided to take a holiday until it clears.

Merritt's father would know exactly what Clayton meant by that. He hoped the judge understood the next bit as well.

The sea looks like a merror here but inn reverse.

In other words, Justice Rivers could contact them via the inn in Mersea.

Write soon to let us know if the weather changes.

—E.

He blotted, folded, and sealed the letter, then scratched out the direction to the Sloane Square terrace house. He handed the note off to the groom who shuffled in from the rear yard and across the straw-strewn floor to the bar.

"Deliver this as fast as you can," Clayton ordered and placed a coin onto the man's hand. "Get it there before dark, and you'll receive a second coin from the man you're delivering it to."

"Aye." With a tug to his cap, the messenger left.

Clayton waited at the counter for the innkeeper to return with news of secured seats on the next stagecoach. He looked around. Pushed up to the bar were men with their tankards of ale and bar wenches with large bosoms that nearly spilled out of their bodices. Laughter and talk boomed through the busy room, but none of it was about recent events in London. Good. That meant information about the town house attack hadn't yet traveled into the countryside. They'd managed to get ahead of the news before people started to think about missing princesses. *Just.*

His shoulders eased down as he relaxed. They couldn't be gone from London for long, and they would have to move on from Mersea before their identities could be discovered. But for now, at least, fate had given them breathing room.

He looked at Cordelia and smiled at the sight of her, although he should have been furious.

Ignoring his orders, she'd slipped off her chair and approached a mother and three children sitting on the wooden bench along the wall. She'd lowered herself down to the children's eye level, and she was asking the little girl about her rag doll and smiling at the tired mother who had her hands full with the little ones.

Even from across the room, Clayton could see the shine in Cordelia's eyes and face and the pure joy she took in that small interaction. He'd seen her at the palace in jewels and silks, surrounded by some of the wealthiest and most important people in Europe, and nothing about that brought her the happiness she found in those children.

His heart ached for her. She wanted nothing more than to be a normal person.

Yet she could never be that. Fate sealed her destiny the moment she was born.

"Here you are." The innkeeper returned and plunked down a bundle of food on the counter. "And two seats are waiting for you on the coach."

"Thank you." With a polite nod, Clayton scooped up the bundle and made his way to Cordelia.

She didn't see him approach, too infatuated with the children to notice. He should have been angry about that, too. She needed to be more aware of her surroundings. But knowing the reason, he didn't blame her.

"Let's go, Jane," he called down to her and extended his hand to help her to her feet. "We're leaving."

Disappointment darkened her face, but she nodded and took his hand to rise. She glanced back to smile at the children and their mother as he led her toward the door.

"Do you think they'll be all right?" she asked, worried. "They haven't been able to find passage to London yet." She stopped and placed her hand pleadingly on his bicep. "Can't we do something to help them?"

Guilt pricked him. So did the overwhelming desire to please her. "Stay here."

He hurried back to the innkeeper and nodded at the mother and her children.

"Make certain they have beds, hot water, and plenty of good food while they're waiting," Clayton ordered the innkeeper and tossed him another coin. At this rate, he'd be out of money by nightfall. "And when one's free, put her into a post chaise to take her to London."

"Aye, sir."

"Make certain you do it," Clayton warned, his eyes boring

into the innkeeper's. "I'm coming back this way in a few days, and if I find out you've mistreated her or cheated me of my coin, there will be hell to pay. Understand?"

The man nodded emphatically and gestured for a barmaid to wait on the mother. "You've nothing to worry about, sir."

Clayton gave a sharp nod and returned to Cordelia to lead her outside into the innyard and the waiting stagecoach. He helped her up into the compartment.

Cordelia stopped in the tiny doorway and turned back to him. "Sometimes, you're just…" She let her shoulders fall, at a loss for words. "Wonderful."

"Well, don't tell anyone," he grumbled, that small compliment warming him through. "I have a reputation to uphold."

Then he helped her into her seat on the wide bench and stepped into the compartment after her.

They were joined by four others inside the crowded compartment, and as the coach rolled away from the inn and across the countryside toward the coast, he breathed a sigh of relief. They couldn't speak privately in the coach, so she couldn't ask him questions he didn't want to answer. Or give him the chance to undress her again, and this time not stop at her stays.

Within a few minutes inside the warm, rocking carriage, Cordelia fell asleep. She was exhausted from the events of the past few days and slumped trustingly against his side.

He slipped his arm around her. She sighed gently in her sleep and nestled against him, and the ache in his gut took his breath away. He would do anything to protect her.

Even from himself.

Twenty

"THERE," CLAYTON ANNOUNCED AS THEY ARRIVED AT THE last cottage on the bluff above the village.

Cordelia nodded, never so happy to see a tiny, old cottage in her life. They'd traveled nearly nonstop since leaving London that morning, which now seemed like days ago, and crossed the causeway just as the tide had turned and was rising once more to cover it and cut off the island from the mainland. The bell in the village church tower had rung ten times as they'd arrived at the inn and stepped down from the coach. The last stretch on foot through the village and out to Madame Noir's cottage had nearly undone her, and with her ankle still sore but usable and her entire body drooping with fatigue, she didn't think she could travel another minute.

But if she was tired, then Clayton must have been purely exhausted. Yet he didn't show an ounce of it as he led her to the cottage in the glow of the small lantern he'd purchased at the village inn to light their way and unlocked the door.

He led her inside, then released her arm and locked the door securely behind them. He held up the lantern to take a good look at the cottage. "This will do."

Unease rose inside her. He didn't mean how comfortable the little sitting room looked with its settee and overstuffed chair, the thick rug in front of the hearth, or the paintings of flowers decorating the wattle-and-daub walls. No, he meant the thickness of the door and the solidity of the locked shutters, which would make defending the place easier in case another attack came.

"No one could have followed us here," he assured her as if reading her worried mind. "We covered our tracks too well."

She nodded slowly. She trusted him to protect her life, if not her heart.

He took a spill from the vase on the fireplace mantel and knelt to start a fire. "No one will suspect a princess is hiding here."

Perhaps not. And this cottage wouldn't be such a bad little place to hide, she decided. True, it was shuttered up tight and currently cold and dark, but it looked inviting despite that, with a main room downstairs serving as both sitting room and kitchen and a set of stairs leading up to what she assumed was a bedroom tucked beneath the eaves.

"But we still need to be wary." He lit the splinter of wood in the lantern, then held it to the nest of kindling already laid in the fireplace. "We shouldn't stay here for more than a couple of days."

"You think someone will find us?"

He looked up from the fire only long enough to glance in her direction. "I think Madame Noir can't be completely trusted."

When a small flame snaked up from the kindling, he blew on it until the fire grew. It caught hold of the dry logs waiting on the rack within moments. He sat back on his heels, pleased with his work.

She watched curiously as he tended the fire with careful stirs of the iron poker and more pieces of wood from the basket beside the hearth. In her entire life, a fire had always burned in whatever room she'd inhabited yet she'd never started one on her own. That was something she planned on changing.

"I don't think there's any food in the cottage," he commented, "or I'd cook us some dinner."

So was that. She didn't even know how to make tea, for heaven's sake, and her self-recrimination gnawed at her. Shouldn't a person at least be able to feed and warm themselves, rather than expecting servants to always do it? She didn't even know how to purchase a ticket for the coach that brought them here.

She was a fish out of water, utterly helpless on her own. How silly she was to think she could ever be a normal woman! Not even for one day.

"That is," he teased as he rose to his full height and brushed his hands together, "unless I can find an old leather boot in one of the cabinets, although the boiled beef at the last inn was most likely less tender."

An idea struck her, and she reached into her travel bag. "Here!" She pulled out the food bundle he'd purchased for her at Chelmsford, still wrapped in its brown paper and string. She'd not had the appetite to eat it earlier. Now her heart raced that she might be able to put it—and herself—to some good use after all. "Show me how to cook it? I want to learn."

For a moment, he said nothing and stared at the package in her hand, and she feared he might laugh.

Instead, he took it from her. "It's a traveler's lunch," he explained. "It's meant to be eaten on the road." When she looked at him blankly, he explained, "There's nothing in it that needs to be cooked."

"Oh." Disappointment filled that single word.

Seeing her dejected reaction, he added, "But there might be something in it that would taste better warmed up. Let's look, all right?" Despite the late hour—and undoubtedly that he wanted nothing more than to fall into the nearest bed and sleep until noon—he carried the small bundle to the narrow plank table and unwrapped it. "Bread, an apple, some cheese...ah, chicken! We can heat that up and make a picnic of the rest."

"Show me how?"

He nodded at the hearth. "Grab that pan there."

Grateful that he was teaching her, she hurried to the fireplace and lifted the small frying pan from its hook. "This one?"

"Now put the chicken pieces in it and place it over the fire. We don't need to cook it, just warm it. It will only take a few minutes." He tossed her a hand towel. "Use that to hold the pan."

She did as instructed, then knelt beside the fire and watched the chicken intently. After a few moments, she frowned. "Is this all we do? We just wait like this?"

"Yes. Let the fire do the work." As if he knew she wanted—no, *needed*—to do this on her own, he remained where he was, leaned back against the table, and crossed his ankles. "In a few minutes, take that small fork hanging from the mantel and turn the pieces over."

She waited for five minutes, counting off each second in her head, then did as instructed: took the fork and attempted to turn the pieces.

"For God's sake, don't burn yourself," he warned as he watched her. "I already have enough explanations to make to the palace. I don't want to have to explain a singed princess on top of it."

With a small laugh, she carefully turned over the chicken. Its savory scent floated up to her along with a soft sizzling, and the pieces glistened in the firelight.

"Is it warm?" he called out after a little while longer.

"I—I think so."

"Then bring the pan here—carefully."

She set it on the table beside him, her eyes never straying from the chicken as it continued to sizzle. "Now what?"

He shrugged, not moving from his spot to help her. *Good.* "Set the table. Use those plates in the Welsh dresser over there." He nodded toward a cabinet in the corner. "There should be a knife and napkins in the drawer. Bring those, too."

Excitement bubbled inside her as she hurried to the dresser and took down two plates from the shelf, then searched through the drawer and snatched up what she needed. She carefully placed the plates on the table in front of the two chairs, along with the napkins.

She waved the sharp knife in the air. "Now what?"

"Give me that." He took the knife from her hand. When she opened her mouth to protest, he explained, "The man always carves."

She didn't believe that for a moment—more likely he feared she'd flay herself—yet she slid onto her chair without argument. She was too happy to be insulted. She'd cooked! Well, she'd *warmed* at least, and that by itself was a feat. Perhaps he wouldn't think her completely worthless after all.

As if realizing her fledgling kitchen skills had come to a decisive end, he poured water into a large pot himself, hung it on a hook, and swung it out over the flames to heat. Then he snatched up two mugs and a corked bottle from the dresser and joined her at the table. He cut up the chicken and handed her a slice from the tip of the knife. She took it and watched him, waiting for him to try the first bite.

"Delicious," he said around the piece of chicken in his mouth.

She covered her pleased smile by nibbling a bite herself. Oh, it *was* delicious! She nearly laughed.

He cut up the apple and placed half on her plate, followed by half of the small loaf of bread. He didn't look at her as he reached for the chunk of cheese and asked casually, "Why was it so important to you to cook tonight? I could have heated it for us if you didn't want to eat it cold."

"I wanted to do something productive. I'm enough of a burden to you already." She gestured a hand at the cottage around them to indicate…well, to indicate *everything* about their situation. "You're doing all this because of me, and I can't even cook you dinner in appreciation."

He set down the knife and leaned back in his chair. "You're not a burden." He pulled out the cork from the bottle and splashed the golden liquid into the two mugs. "You faced down two sets of attackers who wanted to kill you and you didn't scream. Not once." He lifted his mug in a toast to her and murmured, "You're the bravest woman I know."

A warm blush spread up from the back of her neck and across her cheeks.

His eyes sparkled mischievously. "But if you want to become domestic, tomorrow I'll let you wash my clothes." He winked. "You'll love it."

With a scowl, she threw a piece of cheese at him. He caught it and popped it into his mouth.

His low chuckle faded, and he repeated solemnly, "You're not a burden."

"Then I'm a duty."

His eyes locked with hers. In that moment's pause, she desperately wanted him to deny that, too. Her heart wanted to be far more to him than an obligation.

Instead, he answered, "You're one of the most important people I've ever met."

Her heart sank at that clever dodge. She didn't press for the truth. At that moment, she couldn't have borne it.

"We'll stay here for a few days," he told her. "Just until I'm certain I can ensure your safe return. We should have a message back from Justice Rivers by tomorrow afternoon."

She nodded absently and studied him as she nibbled on a slice of apple.

"We'll be able to make plans then."

"You mean, you'll return me to London," she corrected quietly. "To the palace."

And I'll never see you again.

She had no idea how she would bear it. In the few days they'd been together, he'd captured her heart and made her yearn for so much more than a royal life could ever provide. Now she wanted a true home, one in which her husband would consider her an equal partner and not just a vessel to bear heirs, and children who would be cherished, every last one of them and not just the oldest male.

Most of all, she wanted love. *Will I ever have that?*

"You're a princess." His eyes locked solemnly with hers. "You belong in a palace."

A palace was the very last place she wanted to be! "But what if…what if I don't want to be a princess anymore?"

He shook his head. "God's anointed, remember? You were born a princess and you always will be."

Before she could protest, he shoved back from the table and tossed more logs onto the fire. He snatched up the lantern and set it in front of her on the table.

"We should turn in for the night." He nodded from the lantern to the stairway door. "You'll be safe upstairs."

Her chest tightened. Safe…but alone. "All right."

"We both could use a good night's rest." He hesitated. "You don't need help undressing, do you?"

Forcing a smile, she slipped off her chair and picked up the lantern. "Not at all."

"Do you need this?" He took one of the pistols from beneath his jacket and laid it on the table.

Her smile vanished. "Not at all," she repeated in a whisper.

"Knowing Madame, there are probably a dozen night rails in the dresser or armoire to change into." He grimaced.

"On second thought, knowing Madame, the ones you find won't do much to keep you warm."

She couldn't find the strength to muster even a faint smile at his teasing. He was rejecting her—again—and they both knew it. All the jokes in the world couldn't hide the prick of it. "I'll be fine."

He nodded and made his way to the settee where he would spend the night, removing his jacket as he went. "Good night then, Your Highness."

Not trusting herself to speak for fear of what she might tell him about where he could shove his Your Highnesses, she turned away without a word and climbed the stairs to the bedroom. She undressed, easily undoing the short row of buttons between her shoulder blades, but even then she foolishly hoped he would come to her.

But he didn't. He remained downstairs and a world away.

She put out the lantern and crawled into bed.

Twenty-One

CORDELIA HELD TIGHT TO CLAYTON'S HAND AND GAZED in wonder at the sight before them in the heart of Mersea. "Is that...*a fair*?"

He grinned down at her. Her excitement was contagious. "Unfortunately, just a weekly market."

"Oh." Her face fell with disappointment.

"But we still need to visit it for food and supplies." He squeezed her hand reassuringly. "What do you say, Princess? Is your ankle sound enough to do some shopping?"

She nodded and tightened her hold on his hand, speechless yet with eager anticipation.

He led her forward onto the village green. It was only a tiny market, not at all as grand as the ones in London or Edinburgh, but the rapidly changing expressions of joy and curiosity on her face couldn't have been more special if he'd led her through the Khan el-Khalili bazaar in Cairo. But then, the cultural divide between her and the fishermen and farmers who sold their goods here was just as wide.

She held on to him to keep from stumbling because her wide eyes weren't looking where she was going. She was too busy taking in the busy activities around them, the calls of the merchants, the music, the quick bartering, and the exchange of coins for goods.

When she passed a stack of wooden cages, one of the roosters within let out a loud cock-a-doodle-doo. She jumped, startled.

"Chickens," he explained.

Her lips formed a round O. "They're for sale?"

At the gleam in her eyes, he said firmly, "We are *not* buying you a pet chicken."

She laughed at the idea, the sound light and lovely on the warm spring air. Of course, though, they had to stop so she could peer into each cage at the chickens. There were piglets, too, that she made him stop to look at and lambs she couldn't resist petting, including one she cuddled in her arms.

The whole market fascinated her, and what should have taken them fifteen minutes to explore soon stretched to over two hours.

Clayton didn't mind. He'd never seen her so happy and curious, and she practically glowed beneath the warm afternoon sun. No one here might ever suspect she was a princess, but one look would convince anyone that she certainly wasn't one of them.

"Come on." He took her elbow to lead her away from the large griddle of cockles frying over a fire that had snagged her attention. "We need to buy food."

She gestured at the griddle as she glanced over her shoulder. "But that's—"

"Too close to snails. We need real food."

She laughed at him but tightly held his arm. "Don't let the

French hear you say that! Some of the most delicious dishes I've ever had were at the French court, including snails."

"Well, thank God you're in England, and here we eat good, hearty food." He winked at her. "Black pudding and kidney pie."

She wrinkled up her nose in disgust. "I'd rather have snails!"

He couldn't help but laugh at her expression. Or keep himself from leaning closer just so he could smell the light fragrance of her perfume on the soft spring air. "Then how about a basket of boring old picnic food and wine?" He gestured toward the last stall and handed her a few coins. "Buy whatever you'd like. They might just have chocolate and orange biscuits."

Her eyes softened on him. "Those are my favorites."

"I know."

He knew more about her than he wanted to admit, and little of it had to do with protecting her. He'd simply wanted to learn more about her—why she chewed her thumbnail when she was nervous, what she did to make her chestnut hair so shiny, how she made everyone around her feel comfortable in her presence—so he'd paid attention to her the way he never had to any other woman. He couldn't help himself. With the way she looked at him, with an obvious appreciation that warmed his chest, he certainly didn't regret it.

"Go on," he urged quietly. "Buy us some food."

Cordelia practically bounced as she hurried up to the stall with its piles of wrapped foods. She took her time to make up her mind about what she wanted and gestured for the woman attending the stall to put all of it into a large basket for her.

But when she went to pay, a troubled expression darkened her face.

The woman behind the stall gestured in frustration at the food and the coins. Finally, Cordelia jabbed out her hand toward the woman, the coins resting on her outstretched palm.

Then the woman said something that made Cordelia's shoulders slump and her hands fall to her sides.

Oh no. Clayton started forward, only to halt in midstep when Cordelia raised her chin in that imperial way of hers, forcefully slapped the coins onto the wooden plank counter, snatched up the basket of food, and triumphantly marched away from the stall.

He frowned warily as she returned to him. "What happened?"

"That woman insulted me," she explained, her voice a mixture of anger and bewilderment. "She said I must be daft not to know what coins to use to pay her, how much food costs, or that the basket isn't free. She called me a fool for not bringing my own shopping basket to the market."

Even now the vendor glared at Cordelia and gestured angrily in her direction as she complained to the woman in the stall next to hers.

"She insulted me." Cordelia beamed. "Oh, it was wonderful!"

She handed him the basket as if presenting a trophy.

"No one would ever have dared to say something like that to me before!" Her face glowed. "She thought I was just a normal person visiting the village—well, a *daft* person visiting the village. But she didn't treat me at all like a princess, and that's what matters."

"If that made you happy, then I know what will really make your day." He lowered his mouth to her ear and teased, "Let's go back and barter for a goat."

With a lilting laugh, she stretched up onto tiptoes and placed a kiss to his cheek before he could duck away.

Part of him was glad he'd been too slow.

"I've never bought anything before," she confided as she wrapped her arm around his and allowed him to lead her slowly back through the market toward the high street. Her ankle was almost completely healed and no longer bothered her, but he didn't want to reinjure it by walking too much. "I've never had to. Anything I've ever wanted or needed was provided by the servants and palace staff or by Devereaux. I've never even been to a market before."

Then a thought struck her, and the joy that had been on her face faded, along with the bounce in her step. She stopped.

"You must think me a complete goose," she said quietly. "A woman who doesn't even know how to buy anything, who vaguely knows how money works." She glanced back. "Perhaps that woman in the stall was right and I am just a daft fool."

Oh, she was so very wrong about herself. "I *think*," he chose his words carefully, "you have the brilliance to run this entire market in only a few weeks if you truly did live here, and the woman who insulted you would soon be forced to come to you for lessons on how to conduct business."

His words weren't mere flattery meant to put a smile back on her face, although he was glad they did. He truly meant it. Cordelia was far more competent than she gave herself credit for. But that was what came from being treated as nothing more than a pretty doll, he supposed, to be dressed up and paraded out when the palace needed her but locked in a closet when they didn't.

That was just another example of how far apart their two worlds truly were.

He glanced up at the front of the coaching inn, then set down the basket on the footpath next to her half boots. "Wait here." He leveled a warning look at her. "I mean it. Do *not* wander off."

The impertinent woman had the nerve to look offended.

With a chuckle beneath his breath, he hurried into the inn and retrieved the message waiting for him. Justice Rivers had replied quickly. Clayton couldn't decide if that portended good news or bad, but he did know they would have to relocate in the morning to another village. Somewhere they couldn't be traced.

For now, though, they were safe here, and he didn't want to ruin the day by letting the outside world invade. Not just yet. So instead of opening the letter, he tucked it into his brown workman's jacket.

Cordelia was waiting right where he'd left her, thankfully, but she'd been craning her neck to see every inch of the high street and its busy market day activity.

"It's a beautiful spring day," he commented. "Let's have a picnic by the sea."

With an excited nod, she fell into step beside him.

Around them, the town was lively with villagers coming and going, ships bobbing at anchor in the harbor, and rowboats making their way to and from the docks. Cordelia did her best to take it all in, and Clayton let her, purposefully slowing their walk. He knew how much seeing the village meant to her. But he also knew it distracted her from the danger surrounding them.

They chose a spot on the bluff above the harbor with a sweeping view of the coast and the village below. He shed his greatcoat and spread it out on the ground as an impromptu blanket. When he reached for the basket to unwrap the food, she snatched it out of his hand.

"I want to cook," she announced and began to sort through the basket to find the best foods for their picnic.

"This isn't cooking." He bit back a grin as he settled onto the coat next to her. "It's unwrapping."

"Close enough." She popped a dried apricot into his mouth to silence him.

He chuckled around the bite as he chewed it and lay back on his elbow to watch her set out the food.

"I know I'm just a joke to you, but I never get to do anything like this," she confided as she set down the small bag of dried apricots and apples.

"You're never a joke to me," he corrected quietly.

She paused for a beat, the only outward sign she'd heard him.

"You never picnic?" he asked and brought the conversation back on point.

She continued with unwrapping a chunk of cheese and

putting the bread next to it on its wrapper. "Oh, I go on picnics quite often, but I'm accompanied by ten footmen who set up tables, chairs, and a buffet with chafing dishes to keep the truffle cream sauce warm and ice buckets to keep the champagne cold." She gestured toward the simple orange biscuits in their basket. "It's not the same."

"No, I don't suppose it is," he murmured, noting the frustration in her voice.

She let out a long sigh. "I know what you're thinking— what everyone thinks—that I have no right to complain. *Poor princess*," she drawled sarcastically with a roll of her eyes, "distraught that she has an army of servants at her beck and call to do everything for her, the finest foods to eat and the softest beds to sleep in, and every room heated like a summer's day even during the coldest winters."

Clayton said nothing. That was exactly what he'd thought of every royal…until he met her.

"I know how fortunate I am. I live a life of luxury that most people can never imagine, and I have done nothing to deserve it. I know that I should be grateful, but…" She played with the short length of twine that held together the package of cold boiled beef. "But I'm never alone, never allowed to argue or show any emotion in public, never allowed to make my own decisions—even the colors of my gowns are chosen for me by Lady Devereaux. My life is regimented, and I will be told where to be every moment for the rest of my life." Her voice lowered to barely more than a breath. "Sometimes I feel like a prisoner."

Clayton had no words of comfort to offer. In his heart, he knew she was right.

"I want to be useful," she confessed. Frustration thickened her voice. "Is it so wrong to simply want to be *useful*?"

Silently, he reached out and covered her hand with his.

With a faint nod of resolve, she gestured with her free hand at the spread of food in front of them. "At least I can be useful in setting out our picnic. What do you think—enough for us?"

It was enough for a small army. "It's perfect."

She smiled at the compliment with the same pride as if she'd actually made the food herself and pulled her hand free of his. "Then let's enjoy it."

He looked at her solemnly. "Cordelia, if you—"

"Enough about me," she interrupted. She picked up a dried apple and gestured with it at the wide view of the coast in front of them, covered in sunshine and the fresh scent that only a warm spring day could bring. "I want to know more about village life. You grew up in a town similar to this. What was it like?" When he hesitated, she pressed gently. "I want to know more about the people who live here and what comprises their day-to-day lives. Today, I'm one of them."

He looked at her dubiously. "Even the woman in the stall who insulted you?"

"*Especially* her."

Clayton stifled a laugh and did as she asked. As they ate, he told her about what it was like to live in a coastal village that depended on the fickleness of the sea to provide a living, about everything from the smell of the day-old fish to the fun of holiday festivals of all kinds.

She listened raptly, mesmerized by even the most common part of existence in a typical village.

As the sun slid toward the horizon, their bellies grew full, yet they'd barely made a dent in the food. She pressed him for more stories and details even as he helped her wrap up the leftover food and place it back into her basket.

Then they fell silent and simply watched the deepening reds and purples of the sunset behind them as the shadows lengthened over the countryside and harbor. The tide once again covered the causeway for the night, and once more they were on an island, fittingly cut off from the world. Below, lights were slowly struck across the village and shone through windows of the cottages lining the streets, the shacks on the piers, even the ships sleeping in the harbor.

"I'm sad to see the day end." Her voice was as quiet as the dusk settling around them. A stray lock of her chestnut hair came loose from her chignon in the soft breeze, but instead of simply tucking it behind her ear, Cordelia reached up to remove all the pins and toss them into the basket. She ran her hand through her hair to let it stir free around her shoulders, not caring that she was being far too casual. "For the first time in my life, I was simply myself, and not one person cared who I was."

She reached out to place her hand over his where it rested on his coat, but her gaze remained on the scene below.

"Today was a special gift for me." She squeezed his hand. "I'm more grateful for it than you'll ever know. Thank you."

Then she kissed him.

He caught his breath and froze beneath the warm temptation of her lips, the silkiness of her hair as it brushed gently against his cheeks on the lilting breeze, the softness of her body as she leaned into his. For an instant, the world froze around them, and he was aware only of her sweet scent that reminded him of strawberries and cream and the feather-light caresses of her lips. It was only a kiss of gratitude, only a small touch of her lips to his. But it shook him to his core because he wanted so much more.

How easy it would be to pull her into his arms and onto his lap, to ravish her mouth and claim every forbidden taste of her kisses, then lay her down on the grass and claim even more—

How easy to lose everything over a woman who could never be his.

He climbed to his feet, then cleared his throat and forced a smile. "You're welcome."

Damnation, he felt like an utter idiot for saying that. But something had to be said, and he sure as hell couldn't utter the truth… *If you kiss me like that again, I will no longer care that you're a princess and I'm a soldier. I will make you want me as much as I crave you. I will strip you bare, lick over every inch of you, and take my pleasure between your thighs until you cry out in shuddering release.*

But she continued to stare up at him, an unreadable expression on her shadow-darkened face. She waited for the explanation he couldn't give without breaking her heart.

Somewhere amid palace garden parties, opera arias, and all the miles between London and here, he'd begun to care about her. She'd become far more to him than a princess.

The blasted woman had burned her way into his heart. And if he wasn't careful…

We will both be destroyed by the flames.

Twenty-Two

CORDELIA SAID NOTHING ON THE LONG, SILENT WALK back to the cottage, nor when Clayton securely locked them inside for the night and then began to search the little house to make certain no one had sneaked in while they'd been out.

But when he went upstairs to search the bedroom, she couldn't simply wait silently down in the sitting room. No, the long walk from the bluff had given her time to make a decision. The most important one so far in her life.

Her heart pounded so hard that each beat reverberated against her chest as she followed him silently upstairs, and her hands trembled no matter how tightly she wrapped them in her skirts to keep them still. She stood at the top of the stairway in the shadow of the lamplight and watched as he opened the armoire and then grimaced at Madame's collection of not-so-warm nightgowns.

"I don't want this day to end," she said quietly.

"Sunset says otherwise, I'm afraid," he replied dryly and shut the armoire doors.

"I mean that it's too special to me to let go of it so soon." She stepped out of her slippers and left them at the top of the stairs, then slowly came forward into the room. "So I've made a decision."

"Oh?" He knelt beside the bed to look beneath it.

"I want to be just an ordinary woman for the night." Her trembling hand went to the short row of buttons at the back of her dress, and she slipped them free. "And I want to be that woman...with you."

He sank back on his heels and watched, stunned, as her dress fell to the floor.

She stood before him in only her undergarments, trembling in nervousness. He'd liked her kisses, had told her she was beautiful. Yet she couldn't help but worry about what he truly thought of her. A man like him had surely been with dozens of beautiful women far more alluring than she was, far more sophisticated, while she...she simply needed him.

But when he drifted his gaze over her, the heat she saw in his eyes emboldened her. She wrapped her fingers in the front tie of her short corset, tugged it free, and dropped it to the floor.

"Stop," he ordered, his voice suddenly hoarse. He remained squatting on the floor, as if he didn't have the wherewithal to remember to stand.

"Why?" She reached down and untied her petticoat. It spilled onto the floor with her dress.

"You damned well know why." Yet it wasn't anger that filled his voice but desire.

"Because I'll be ruined? That doesn't matter." She reached beneath her shift to untie her right garter. "I could run naked through Paris and no one would care as long as I still possess the ability to produce male heirs. Let's be honest. That's all I'm good for as far as the world is concerned." She rolled the stocking down her leg, over her foot, and off, then mumbled thoughtfully as she let it slide through her fingers to the floor. "But you've always thought so much more of me."

When she removed the second stocking and dropped it away, he rose to his full height but remained where he was. Tension radiated from him so intensely that the air pulsed with it as she slowly approached him on bare feet.

She stopped in front of him and trembled when he took another slow rake of his gaze over her body. Surely the lamplight turned her thin cotton shift translucent and revealed every silhouetted inch of her to his eyes. *Good.*

When he made no move to touch her, she taunted softly, "Don't you serve at the pleasure of the princess? I can think of no greater pleasure than sharing the night with you."

She lifted her shift over her head and off. She stood completely naked in the shadows of the flickering lamp.

A loud gasp tore from him as his breath left his lungs. His gaze darted up to hers and fixed there.

"Stubborn man," she chastised when he refused to allow himself a glimpse of her.

She would have laughed at his restraint if the air between them wasn't crackling with electricity, if she couldn't feel the tension radiating from him even from a foot away.

"You're meant for a prince," he told her, as much to convince himself as her. "You're not meant for someone like me."

"Someone brave and heroic, kind, intelligent?" she challenged quietly. "Someone who brings out the best in me?"

"A common soldier," he fired back.

"A general."

His dark laugh hitched in his throat when she placed her hand on his chest, right over his racing heart. "That was supposed to have been a joke," he told her, "but your damned cousin took it seriously and made me one."

"And a viscount."

"Also a joke."

"Far from it," she countered and began to unbutton his waistcoat. His breath came more ragged with every button she slipped free, yet he made no move to stop her.

"The son of a murderer," he rasped out.

She froze. No...that—that couldn't be. The aunties had said *smuggling*, and when she'd asked him about it, he didn't deny it... His father was a smuggler, that was all. He couldn't have been—

But the grief that darkened his face told her the anguished truth.

"I can never be the man you deserve." He shook his head. "No matter what military rank and titles I'm given, for my past alone I will *never* be good enough for you."

How she wished he could see in himself the hero she knew him to be! "I don't care what your father did or what rank you possess—or don't. I care about *you*, Clayton. You're a much better man than you think."

She rose up on tiptoe and brought her lips gently to his. It was a kiss of absolution, yet he groaned beneath it as if she were torturing him.

Moving his mouth away from hers, he covered her hands with his to stop her from undressing him, but he didn't push her away. "You're asking me to commit treason."

"I'm asking you to make love to me." Without any resistance from him, she slowly peeled his jacket over his shoulders, down his arms, and off. "If I weren't a princess, if I were just an ordinary London lady, would you still refuse me?"

He squeezed his eyes shut as the confession tore from him. "No."

"Then don't refuse me tonight." She gave a faint shrug of her bare shoulders. "Underneath, I'm only a woman. Can't you see that?"

He raked a look over her so heated that a shiver swept up from her toes and straight out the top of her head. "I can see plenty."

"Then let me have tonight, with you. Let me have the most special night of my life with a man who cares about me…who truly cares about *me*." She paused. Although she wanted desperately to strip off his waistcoat, the brace of pistols he wore stopped her. "You've always protected me."

He choked back a strangled laugh. "And if you get with child?"

"I trust you to protect me from that, too." Summoning her courage, she unbuckled the holster with shaking fingers and gently lowered it to the floor. "I trust you, Clayton, more than I trust anyone else in my life." She slipped her arms around his neck and pressed herself against him. "I trust you with tonight, too. You're the only man I do." She brushed his lips along his jaw. "Please, Clayton. Give me tonight."

"Cordelia." A low groan of surrender came from the back of his throat, and he captured her mouth beneath his.

———

In a single heartbeat, Clayton lost his restraint, his control, and his mind, and he simply didn't care.

All that mattered was the taste of her lips as he plundered her mouth and the softness of her warm body pressing against his. All the reasons he needed to stay away from her vanished like the mist beneath the light of dawn until there was only Cordelia, a woman who needed him.

The woman who needed him.

He cajoled her into parting her lips beneath his, and when she opened to him with a soft sigh, he pulsed his tongue between her lips in a heady rhythm that left no mis-understanding of how thoroughly he meant to learn all her body's secrets tonight. His hand brushed through her long hair that fell across her bare shoulders, then cupped the back of her head against his palm and held her still as he increased the intensity of the kiss, until every deep thrust of his tongue into her mouth brought soft whimpers from her lips.

She tore her mouth away from his to gasp back the air he'd stolen.

But he refused to give quarter and placed his mouth against her throat to lick at her spiking pulse. Her heart raced so furiously that he could feel it beating into his own chest as she pressed her breasts against his front, and the delicious sensation whipped through him, right down to the tip of his hardening cock. Unschooled need practically dripped from her as she trembled in his arms, and the fact that she desired him nearly undid him.

She trusted him. He would never break that trust.

He scooped her into his arms and carried her to the bed. With a lingering kiss, he slipped out of her arms and stepped back.

He stared down at her. *Sweet Lucifer*, she was glorious. Her brown eyes watched him, fascinated, as he yanked off his neckcloth and finished removing the waistcoat she'd left open. He peeled down his braces to let them dangle around his hips and pulled his shirt off over his head.

Her lips parted at the sight of his bare chest. Certainly, she'd never seen a naked man before.

Not wanting to overwhelm her, he turned down the lamp until the flame sputtered out and the room was cast into dark shadows. In the slant of faint moonlight that fell through the open shutters into the room, he removed the rest of his clothes, then slowly crawled onto the bed and stretched his tall body alongside hers. Her skin was soft and warm, her arms welcoming, and when he leaned over her, her fingertips trembled as she reached up to caress his cheek.

She couldn't be his beyond dawn. He knew that and accepted it. But he could give her tonight, and he would make it as special for her as possible.

"If you want me to stop at any time," he told her, turning his head to place a kiss to her fingers, "you only have to—"

"I don't want to stop." She lifted her head from the pillow to kiss him, and he surrendered beneath her spell.

The kiss grew in urgency and heat. As he kissed her, he caressed her body and reveled in the soft feel of her. He cupped her left breast in his hand and felt her breath catch against his mouth, only for her to let out a long sigh when he began to massage her. His thumb circled her nipple, whose taut arousal gave proof of her growing desire.

Unable to resist, he lowered his head to take her nipple between his lips and suckle.

She arched her back to push herself deeper into his mouth, her fingers digging through his hair and scraping at his scalp. She might have been innocent in matters of sex, but she wasn't afraid to take the pleasures he offered.

With a soft chuckle at her eagerness, he bit lightly at the sensitized nipple and elicited a shuddering moan from her. The sound reverberated into him, and he gave her nipple a soothing lick before moving his attentions to her other breast and beginning the sweet torture all over again.

Cordelia wiggled beneath him as the world spun around her. Having his mouth on her was the sweetest, most decadent pleasure-pain she'd ever experienced in her life because each wonderful kiss and touch left her feeling oddly frustrated and empty, inexplicably craving more. His mouth and hands on her body grew the ball of tingling frustration tightening low in her belly instead of easing it away as she'd thought he would.

"Clayton, I want you to…" Her plaintive whisper trailed off. She didn't know how to ask for what she wanted, but she trusted him to know what she needed.

"Do this?" His hand fluttered down her body and caressed between her legs.

"Yes," she cried out. Taking a deep breath, she moved her legs wider apart. "Oh, yes."

He groaned, and the caresses grew harder and faster, the ache inside her pounding away just beyond his fingertips.

"And this?" He slipped a finger inside her.

She gasped, and her eyes flew open at the unexpected caress. Immediately, he stilled and gazed down at her. The concern in his eyes warmed through her, and she smiled to reassure him. "And that." She buried her face shyly against his shoulder as she fought back a begging whimper. "I like that…a great deal."

"So do I." His lips curled into a lazy grin, and he began to stroke inside her. Soon, a second finger joined the first, and she closed her eyes, both to enjoy the sensation of being filled by him and to prevent any embarrassment by showing how much she enjoyed it.

But even that wasn't enough.

"More," she begged and wiggled her pelvis against his hand. "Oh please, more!"

With one last touch of his lips to hers, he slowly slid down her body and trailed his lips down her front in hot, openmouthed kisses that seared her skin. Down across her breasts, lower to her belly, lower still…

When his warm breath tickled the damp folds between her legs, she realized what he planned to do and stiffened—

"Cordelia," he murmured and placed his lips right *there*.

The air rushed from her lungs in a sharp breath. She tensed like a tightened spring, except for the ache between her legs which throbbed wildly as his lips tenderly teased her folds. Soft and warm and gentle… She eased out a low moan and relaxed beneath his ministrations.

But his mouth didn't remain soft and gentle. Soon, he was taking greedy kisses and long licks, and when his tongue dared to delve—

"Clayton!" She arched herself off the mattress, and his name faded into a whimper.

He chuckled at her response. The sound vibrated into her and stoked the growing tension he created inside her with his mouth, with the way his tongue thrust into her the same way his fingers had done only minutes before. But this was so much more than before, so much more wanton and decadent, and when he nudged at her thighs with his shoulders to widen the spread of her legs, she eagerly complied.

"You're beautiful," he whispered against her and traced a fingertip along the outer contours of her feminine folds.

"Not…there…I'm not," she countered breathlessly as his fingertip circled the throbbing nub at the center of all her aching frustration.

"*Especially* here." He placed a lingering kiss against her. "And here." Another kiss followed. "And very much here."

His lips closed around the aching point buried in her folds and sucked.

Raw need flashed through her like a lightning strike, and she let out a gasping moan. His lips were relentless, and instead of releasing her he sucked harder, even as he slipped his fingers back inside her wet warmth and once again gave her those intimate strokes that knotted her belly.

Her hands desperately clenched at his shoulders—*all* of

her clenched as the throbbing ball of frustration beneath his lips threatened to consume her.

"Let it come, my brave beauty," he murmured against her. "And enjoy it."

When he sucked again, pleasure shot through her, and this time it triggered all the tension that had been building inside her to release in one great, shuddering wave.

She cried out, then collapsed bonelessly against the mattress as joy pulsed through her with every pounding beat of her heart. She panted hard to regain the breath he'd ripped from her and could do nothing more than clench and unclench her hands at his shoulders as he placed soothing, lingering kisses against her. Oh, it was heavenly! Simply divine. She never wanted to move a muscle again for the rest of her life.

Until he brought his tall body up over hers. The bare solidity and hardness of his muscles were too tempting to ignore, and she ran her hands over his warm skin everywhere she could reach. But when she slid her hands down between their two bodies and touched—

He flinched and sucked in a mouthful of air between clenched teeth.

She jerked her hand away. "I'm sorry—"

He grabbed her wrist and stopped her. "I'm not."

The dark desire in his eyes sparked into her as he brought her hand back to his erection and guided her in stroking her palm along his length from the nest of hair at his abdomen to his large, round tip.

He groaned, shaking hard. For a long moment, he did

nothing more than enjoy her hand on him, the long and slow caresses up and down his length.

Then he shifted over her and settled himself in the cradle of her thighs, gently moving her legs farther apart to make room for his hips. He reached down and guided himself against her folds, then lowered his hips in a smooth thrust that buried his hard length inside her.

She felt a faint pinch, and a rasping groan sounded from the back of his throat. He froze like a statue, not moving except to breathe, and let her body become accustomed to having him inside her.

She bit her bottom lip. This wasn't at all as wonderful as she'd imagined it would be. She was stretched uncomfortably around him, with her thighs spread wide beneath his hips and her arms wrapped around his neck. His eyes were squeezed shut, and a pained expression gripped his face.

So if *she* wasn't enjoying this, and if *he* wasn't, then why would *anyone*—

He began to move in slow, controlled slides in and out of her tight warmth, and then she knew why. Oh, she knew! It was simply... *bliss*.

Each glide forward brought him deep inside her, and each retreat created a feeling of such great loss that she nearly cried out to stop him until he pushed forward again and brought himself back inside her. What he'd done to her before with his fingers and mouth had been nice, but this... this was absolutely magical!

She clung to him as he continued to rock into her and once more woke the ache inside her. It tingled out to the ends of her fingers and toes, and she welcomed it by wrapping her legs around his waist and locking her ankles together at the small of his back.

A soft growl came from him in response, and the sinking and retreating grew faster and deeper until he was thrusting against her so intensely that every push ground his pelvis against hers and pressed down on the already sensitized nub hidden in her folds. Short bursts of electricity sparked through her with every thrust, and she panted hard to keep her breath as the growing ache tightened into a demanding heat.

Her folds clenched down hard around him, and her thighs shook as she clasped them to his hips. Her back arched off the mattress, and she clung to him for dear life, never wanting to let go—

She cried out as the joy of release swept over her again, even more intensely than before.

He smothered her cry with his mouth and drank up the sound. Then he raised himself away from her just far enough to slip his hard length free of her tight warmth. He pressed it against her abdomen between their bodies and gathered her tightly against him in his arms. With a jerk of his hips and a groan, a warm wetness spilled across her lower belly.

He held himself still for a moment, then fell onto his side next to her and pulled her over into his arms. Perspiration slickened his body, and his bare skin was hot everywhere it touched hers. His heart pounded so hard that she could feel the echo of it inside her own chest. But it was the whispers that fell from his lips that undid her, repeating over and over again how beautiful she was, how brave and utterly special, as if he didn't even realize he was saying them.

Unable to put any words herself to the turmoil of emotions she felt for him at that moment, she silently placed a kiss to the center of his chest and right over his heart. She blinked hard, thankful that his eyes were closed so he wouldn't see what a goose she was to be on the verge of tears.

She couldn't help it. Despite the joy he'd given her tonight, nothing had changed between them. When dawn came, she would still be a princess, her future still destined to belong to another man.

But her heart knew she would never be the same again.

Twenty-Three

CORDELIA SAT IN HER SHIFT ON THE THICK RUG IN FRONT of the hearth in the main room of the cottage, her shawl wrapped around her shoulders. She took a dried apricot from the food basket sitting on the floor next to her and nibbled at it while she watched Clayton stir up the fire with the iron poker in one hand and a mug of wine in the other.

"You're staring," he said into the fire.

"Of course I am." She smiled and held the apricot coyly to her lips. "The view's too spectacular to ignore."

Truly, it was. He'd pulled on his trousers when they'd decided to come downstairs for a late picnic dinner in front of the fire, but nothing else, and the growing flames cast flickering shadows across his warm skin.

It should be illegal for a man to look that good, she decided as she slowly chewed the apricot. And the way he felt...*that* was surely a sin.

Before dawn came, she hoped to sin again. Repeatedly.

"You're still staring."

"Your fault," she countered.

"How is that my fault?"

"If you don't want me to stare, then you shouldn't look so handsome in the firelight."

He chuckled and tossed in another piece of wood.

After making love, he'd suggested they come downstairs for fortification and the warmth of the fire, although she was perfectly happy with the warmth of the bed. Yet she'd agreed. They were both famished, and after all, they couldn't spend the entire night making love…could they?

"I've ruined your sleep schedule, haven't I?" she commented, feeling not at all sorry. "Before you met me, you were probably set in your ways, early to bed and early to rise."

His lips curled in a faint smile, and he murmured, "Something like that."

"Or are you the Home Office's resident night watch who prowls the city streets after midnight, looking for spies and ruffians?"

"That's closer to the truth, I'm afraid." He stirred at the coals again. "My schedule is not my own. I do whatever needs to be done, whenever I'm needed."

She watched him curiously. "What would you have done when you came back from the wars if not for the Home Office?"

He leaned the poker against the side of the hearth, then sat back on his heels, still watching the flames. "I'll find out soon enough."

His comment puzzled her. "Pardon?"

"I'll be…retiring. Sooner than I'd planned."

That wasn't at all the answer she'd expected. "What will you do then?"

"I have no idea."

She inexplicably felt a distance grow between them, even

though they remained right where they were, less than three feet apart. What had she said wrong?

"Well, you *are* a viscount now, so there is that," she reminded him. He hadn't been happy to be granted the peerage, but it might be helpful in retirement. "No more worries about money or rank."

He sent her a defeated look. "Is there really no way out of that?"

"I don't think so. But why wouldn't you want it? You *have* earned it, you know."

He lifted the mug to his lips for a swallow of wine. "The same reason you don't want to be a princess, I suppose."

She lifted a brow. "Because you're tired of state balls and diamond tiaras and don't want to marry a royal duke?"

"Exactly," he muttered with mock sincerity. Yet in the moment's pause that followed, he turned serious. "Where's the valor in being a peer? What's the purpose of that kind of life?" He shook his head as he stared down into his mug. "Knowing your cousin, Prinny also gave me a large estate to go with it, thinking he was doing me a grand favor by bestowing it."

"Wasn't he?"

"Torture, more like, by making me have to worry about tenant farmers, building repairs, maintaining good relations with the local village... That life isn't for me."

"Then hire an estate agent to oversee it and move to London where you can be a man about town."

He gave a dark laugh at that idea. "Whose biggest concern is the cut of his waistcoat and whether he'll be blackballed at White's? No, thank you."

"You'd never be like that," she assured him. "But you *will* become a voting member of the House of Lords. You'll be able to speak your mind about all kinds of affairs, from political representation to international relations and trade. You'll be able to argue for reform."

"I'll be laughed out of Westminster."

"Perhaps at first. But eventually, they'll stop laughing and start listening." She envied him that. She was never allowed to speak her true mind about anything. Except with him.

"You don't know the British Parliament very well if you think they'll ever start listening to reason."

"I think you could convince them." With the warmth of the fire enveloping her, she let the shawl slip from her shoulders and puddle around her on the rug. "I'd support you."

He quirked a grin. "Even with your support, Princess, it's going to take a long, dragged-out, knockdown fight before England has any kind of constitutional reform." His grin faded. "Perhaps that's how it should be, though. Steady and gradual instead of rash and revolutionary." He stared into the flames and admitted, "I don't know what will become of me."

Her heart skipped. That didn't sound at all like a man set on starting a new life. "Clayton, what's—"

"Something will come along," he interrupted and gave her a charming smile. "It always does."

She frowned. But before she could press for more, he stretched out on his side on the rug beside her, leaned over, and took the piece of apricot from her fingertips with his lips.

"And what would you do, Miss Plain Jane Smith," he

asked around the bite in his mouth as he chewed and deftly changed the subject, "if you could find a new purpose in life?"

She gave an exaggerated scowl of irritation at losing her apricot, even though the act sent heat spiraling low in her belly and had her wondering how long they had to wait before they could make love again. "I don't know for certain." She reached into the basket to fish out an orange biscuit. "But I do know that I'd like to help children."

She snapped the biscuit in two, then laughed as he opened his mouth for half. Dutifully, she placed it on his tongue, and he winked at her as he chewed it.

"I want to provide protection to children like little Elizabeth who have no one in the world to fight for them." She paused, resting the piece of biscuit against her lips. "Do you think she's doing all right with the aunties?"

His eyes gleamed. "I think the aunties have most likely adopted her by now and given her a pony and a toy shop."

She laughed, certainly hoping so!

Cordelia studied him as he refilled their mugs with wine. Sometimes, Clayton was simply an enigma. What she wouldn't give to be able to dig beneath the surface and discover who he truly was beneath, what drove him to risk his life the way he did.

Before she could stop herself, she blurted out, "What makes you so dedicated to England?"

He shrugged as he set down the wine bottle. "I love my country."

Was that…a lie? Something she glimpsed deep in his

green eyes made her suspicious. "Most people love their countries, but they don't risk their lives for it the way you do."

"I'm a soldier. It's what we do."

Another lie. This time, she was certain of it. And this time, she wouldn't let him dodge the truth. "You're also the son of a wrongly convicted father."

He froze for a beat with the mug halfway to his lips for another drink. Then he continued to bring the mug to his mouth. "That's where you're wrong."

She blinked, confused. "I don't understand."

"My father *was* convicted, of both murder and smuggling," he corrected. "But I'm not certain the conviction was wrong."

"But the aunties said..."

"Ah, so that's where you heard it," he muttered. "I should have known."

She set the biscuit aside, no longer wanting it. "They said he was innocent."

His mouth twisted into a grim smile that didn't reach his eyes. "Because those two old ladies love me as if I truly were their own nephew, and they don't want to face the truth that I might have been sired by a murderer."

He finished his wine, then shoved himself to his feet and went to the cupboard in the corner, ostensibly to search for last night's bottle of whiskey. But Cordelia knew the real reason he'd walked away. Her questions had finally struck too close to home for comfort.

Suddenly chilled, she pulled the shawl back on over her shoulders. "I'd wager that *you* don't want to face that truth either." She paused. "But *is* it true? Did he really...?"

"Slit the throats of three excise men who came across him while he was illegally smuggling goods from the Continent, dump their bodies in a rowboat, and then anchor it offshore as a warning to any other excise men who might decide to arrest him?" he finished for her, most likely attempting to shock her. Then he snatched down a fresh bottle of whiskey from the shelf. "The court said he did."

She held her breath. "But what do *you* believe?"

"I don't know." He blew out a long sigh and crossed back to the fireplace. "Honest to God, I don't."

He raked his fingers through his hair. The frustration and pain in that small gesture nearly undid her.

Cordelia rose from the rug and went to his side. She placed her hand on his bicep and felt the muscle flinch beneath her touch, but she didn't pull away. For once, she wanted to share her strength with him, the same way he had always done with her.

"Tell me," she urged.

He shook his head. "I was only a boy when it all happened," he said, staring into the fire. "I looked up to my father—worshipped him, in fact. The actions I heard in the courtroom could never have been committed by the man I knew. Yet everyone there believed them, said that the evidence was overwhelming, the witnesses credible. Even my own uncle said so." He stifled a low curse. "What was I supposed to believe?"

Her heart skipped. "You were in the courtroom?"

When he gave a jerking nod, she slid her hand down his arm and laced her fingers through his.

"I wasn't supposed to be there, but I sneaked inside. I was living with my uncle then, and he didn't care what I did." He paused. "He didn't care that I went to the execution either."

Dear God... He was at his father's execution? Cordelia tightened her hold on him to keep from crying out in grief at the hell he'd gone through.

"After that, I ran away every chance I could until I was old enough to join the army. I sold my portion of the family brewery and scraped together every ha'penny I could beg, borrow, or steal to buy a commission. That was when I left Margate for good. Haven't been back, not even to visit my uncle's grave."

Her heart broke for him.

"I've been searching for the truth about my father ever since. That's why I took a position with the Home Office after the wars, so I could gain access to the documentation about my father and the men who accused him of murder."

"And did you?"

"No. Most of the records have been sealed away, including the court records." His eyes remained fixed on the fire. "Per order of the Duke of Portland, who was Home Secretary when the murders took place, under Lord Sidmouth's ministry." He pulled out the bottle cork with his teeth and spat it into the fire. "Now Sidmouth is Home Secretary and just as unwilling to unseal the documents."

She frowned, puzzled. "Why would they have done that?"

"It's the Home Office," he muttered and took a long swig of whiskey straight from the bottle. "God only knows why they do what they do. It could be anything from protecting their operatives to a personal grudge. But whatever reason, it sure as hell can't be good." He pulled in a ragged breath, then released her hand and leaned against the wooden beam serving as the mantel above the hearth. "There's no doubt in my mind that my father was a smuggler. Lots of men traded illegally with the French in those days to avoid excise taxes and customs fees, and my father certainly wasn't alone." He shook his head. "But murder… I simply can't wrap my mind around it."

"Then he might have been innocent after all."

Finally, he raised his gaze from the fire and leveled a hard look on her. "He might very well have been guilty, for all I know."

She watched him take another long, gasping swallow of whiskey. Her chest ached for him and the little boy who so brutally lost his father and his hero.

But there was something else that bothered her about all this, something else he wasn't admitting.

She ventured softly, "All the years you've pushed yourself, the way you've sacrificed everything for your promotions and recognition, how you're risking your life even now—" She held her breath. "That wasn't done to access court records. There's far more behind all that, isn't there?"

The deep flicker in his green eyes told her she was right.

Her mind put together all the pieces of what she knew about him, what she'd been told by the aunties and her cousins, what she'd witnessed herself of his behavior that was always both selfless yet somehow also always drawing recognition—

And she *knew*.

"Dear God…you're still putting him on trial." Her voice was little more than a breath. "After all these years, you're still weighing the evidence and trying to decide whether to find him guilty or innocent in your own heart."

He scoffed and shoved away from the hearth. "Nonsense." But his reply lacked conviction. "He's been dead for years. I can't try him."

"You can't save him either."

He froze, the bottle halfway to his lips. For a moment, the world seemed to crash to a stop, all except her pounding heart.

Then, instead of bringing the bottle the rest of the way to his lips, he set it down on the mantel with a loud thud and stepped back. "I'm not trying to do that."

"But you are," she argued. "Without the information to decide one way or the other, you're doing it the only way you can—by showing the world exactly how patriotic you are, how loyal to English law and rule." She remembered the aunties' words and repeated them. "After all, how could a murderer raise a man whose life is so clearly dedicated to crown and country? To helping people rather than harming them?"

"Or perhaps I simply wanted to be successful, with a good career and fortune." As he stared at her, she could see the agitation rising inside him, the frustration and pain that had most likely plagued him since he was a helpless boy. "You'd fault a man for chasing money and position?"

"No."

A smile began to pull at his lips at her answer. "Then you can't—"

"But you're not just any man."

His smile faded, and he stilled, his expression stony as he returned her gaze. Silence surrounded them, broken only by the crackling of the fire at their feet.

She continued quietly, "Every promotion, every success, every daring risk of life and limb only work to prove the court—no, to prove *all* of England—was wrong about your father." There was no anger in her, no judgment—only grief for the pain he carried. "You're risking your life to redeem his, but you never can. You'll never be able to save him, no matter how much you try."

His eyes narrowed. "You don't know what you—"

"*I know.*" She closed the distance between them and placed her hand to his cheek. "I know because I've been attempting to do the same for my father. I would give anything to save his reputation, including my own future. So would you for yours." She tenderly brushed her thumb along his jaw to his lips. "But you can't—*I* can't. We can never change what others have done in the past, and we shouldn't sacrifice our own lives for their redemption when it will never come. When it *can* never come." She choked back sobs, both for their fathers and for Clayton. "We cannot change the past."

"Cordelia, if I give up—"

Rising up on tiptoes, she silenced him with a kiss of absolution to his lips. "We have to stop fighting wars we can *never* win."

He squeezed his eyes shut and shook his head. "You're asking me to surrender."

"I'm asking you to choose the future over the past." A tear slipped down her cheek. "I'm asking you to pardon that little boy who lost his father all those years ago and could do nothing to stop it." She cupped his face between her hands. "And I'm asking you to forgive the man he's become."

He didn't speak, didn't move, but the look of anguish on his face undid her.

"And if you can't do it for yourself," she urged, barely louder than a trembling breath, "then do it for me…because I want you just as you are."

She buried her face in his chest as the dam of emotion broke, and sobs tore from her. He wrapped his arms around her and pulled her tightly against him. Only after her cries subsided did she hear his soft, deep voice whispering words of reassurance to her. The same words he needed to hear himself.

Their shared pain over their fathers would never go away completely, she knew that, just as she knew they would need strength and resolve to exorcise the ghosts that haunted them and find peace with the past.

But for now, they could at least find acceptance. Together.

He tenderly kissed her, and the pain-filled kiss tasted of hope for the future.

She melted against him as the kiss grew in intensity and need. He lifted her into his arms and gently laid her down on the rug in front of the fire, then followed down next to her. This time when they made love, they weren't driven by the desperate need for possession and release that had consumed them before. This time, it was a joining of hearts and souls, and she came not with a fierce cry but a healing sigh.

When she kissed his cheek, unable to find the words to express what he meant to her, she tasted his salty tears.

————————

Clayton slipped out of bed, careful not to wake Cordelia, who lay wrapped in a cocoon of blankets. She was exhausted, and he'd done little to give her the rest she needed.

But he couldn't help himself. Making love to her was more special than anything else he'd ever experienced in his life. He had no idea how long they would be alone together, and he didn't want to miss a moment with her.

He also didn't want to think about the future and forced all thoughts of it from his mind. She was adamant they couldn't live in the past, and she was right. She'd helped him see that it was time to accept that and move on, no matter how deep the cuts to his heart.

But they also had no future together. And *those* cuts might never heal.

He silently pulled on his trousers. He saw his jacket lying discarded on the floor where she'd dropped it in her rush to undress him last night, picked it up, and pulled from its pocket the letter from Justice Rivers. This was as good a time as any to read it, he supposed, especially with Cordelia waiting warm and soft in bed to help ease away any bad news it might bring him.

He headed downstairs. He picked up the basket of food still sitting on the floor in front of the fire where they'd left it and carried it to the table. He rummaged through it, selected a small chicken leg, and popped it into his mouth. Good lord, he was famished! He grinned around the chicken at the reason and crossed to the hearth. He snatched up a candle from the mantel shelf and lit it on the banked coals. The small flame was just bright enough to read the letter.

He checked the red wax seal—unbroken. Then he cracked it and unfolded the paper. A piece of newsprint fell out and fluttered to the floor.

Dear Son—

Clayton's lips twisted, bemused. He'd always considered Merritt and his father to be like family, but this salutation was meant to hide their friendship, not testify to it.

The book you borrowed needs to be returned right away. I hear the library is as good as a fortress.

His grin faded. The letter was cryptic in case it fell into the wrong hands, but the message was clear. Cordelia needed to be taken back to London, and not to the palace but to the Armory.

We've had a patch of bad weather here in London. The reign is causing problems in your home, and you should avoid it for fear the damage might be irreparable.

Bad weather…Justice Rivers was referring to riots and confusion in London. More—his home referred to the

Home Office, which still blamed Clayton. The judge's warning was obvious. If Clayton encountered anyone from the palace or Whitehall, he was as good as dead.

> *I saw this piece in the Times about the benefit for the hospital and thought you would be interested.*
>
> —*R.*

Clayton bent down and picked up the piece that had been cut from the *Times*. He scanned it. It was an advertisement for a benefit concert for the Royal Hospital in Chelsea, just as Justice Rivers had written. But the inclusion of it in the letter was a ruse.

He turned it over, and a second announcement caught his attention. A special meeting of Parliament had been called in the wake of the attack on the king's council and Princess Cordelia's disappearance. Amid swirling doubts that she was still unharmed and alive, His Serene Highness Prince Ernest of Monrovia had asked to address a joint session of Parliament in Westminster Hall. Two days from now.

Then his eyes fell onto the drawing of Monrovia's royal coat of arms, and his heart stopped. He stared at it, unable to believe…

He'd been such a damn fool! All along, right in front of him in plain sight and staring back at him—

He tossed the newsprint into the fire and watched as the flames devoured it. The paper blackened to ash until all that remained was the coat of arms, and on the shield, the symbol of a key. The same secret symbol used by Scepter.

His blood turned cold. The attack on the king's council at the town house wasn't the signal that Scepter had been waiting for. This announcement was.

The revolution had begun.

Twenty-Four

THROUGH THE FOG OF SLEEP, CORDELIA HEARD A SOFT shuffling in the bedroom, and her eyes fluttered open. The pale blue predawn light fell coldly through the window and lit the room just enough for her to make out a broad, tall form in the shadows.

She smiled. *Clayton.*

"It's still early," she purred in a sleepy voice. "Come back to bed where it's warm."

"I wish I could." He buttoned his waistcoat as he approached. "But we have to leave for the village at dawn."

A chill that had nothing to do with the cold room moved over her, and she sat up, pulling the blanket up to her shoulders to cover herself. "Why?"

He held his back ramrod straight as he tugged at his shirt-sleeves to bring them into place at his wrists. "We need to leave Mersea. We'll hire a carriage at the inn and leave as soon as possible."

Her belly tightened. "Is something wrong?"

"You're needed back in London, Your Highness."

Icy fingers trailed down her spine, and she shivered. He was putting more than the barrier of his clothes between them, she realized. Cold, distant, painfully polite…the affectionate man she'd spent the night with was gone, once more replaced by the loyal patriot who put his duty to England before all else.

She'd known this magical time with him would have to end eventually, but she hadn't expected it to come so soon. Or how her heart would tear so painfully.

"What happened?" she whispered, unable to find her voice.

"I received a message from Justice Rivers. He advised bringing you back to London. The world—and your family—think you've been kidnapped, possibly even killed."

So much confusion swirled through her sleep-dulled mind that she could barely sort through it all. "But you wrote to the Home Secretary before we left London. You assured him I was safe."

"I did." He reached for his jacket on a nearby chair. "But Parliament and your family need to see you for themselves."

She swallowed. Hard. "Is it safe for me in London?"

"I promise to protect you, Princess." He added a heartbeat later, "With my life, if necessary."

Fear began to lick at her toes at his dodge, and she repeated, "Is it safe for me there?"

"It will be." His gaze locked with hers in the shadows. "I will make certain of it."

But his assurance did little to alleviate the growing trepidation in her knotting belly or the new fear that struck her— "Is it safe for *you*?"

He froze, the jacket halfway on. Then he finished pulling it on and repeated, "It will be."

Her heart skipped as she remembered the earlier threat

to his life, the night they first met, when he'd been convinced that if he were arrested, he'd be killed. She'd protected him then. She could do it again.

"Whatever's the matter, I can help you." She leaned toward him. "I won't let them harm you."

He looked at her grimly. "You can't protect me. Not from this."

She slid out of bed and wrapped the blanket around herself to cover her naked body. She stopped in front of him. They stood less than a foot apart, but he felt a world away.

"What exactly was in that message from your friend?" she asked.

"Your uncle has asked to address Parliament." His face remained stoically solemn. "He wants to speak to concerns regarding the town house attack and your disappearance."

Her shoulders lowered in relief. "Of course he does. Everyone in London must think I was killed that night, including him."

He gave a curt nod. "For some reason, Lord Sidmouth hasn't told him about my message about you, or if he has, your uncle isn't willing to believe it."

"So you have to produce the princess and show everyone I'm all right," she guessed, "before my disappearance becomes an international crisis."

"Something like that," he muttered and sat on the chair to put on his boots.

A chill curled down her spine. "No." She knelt on the floor beside the chair and placed her hand beseechingly on his knee. "Tell me *exactly* what you think he's going to do."

His expression grew impossibly grim. "Most likely, he's going before Parliament to announce that you're dead."

The puzzled question fell breathlessly from her lips. "Why would he do that?"

"Because if you're dead, then your uncle takes your place in line for the British throne."

"But that doesn't matter if…" Her voice trailed off as the realization of what Clayton was implying hit her. She sank back on her heels, stunned, and watched as he continued to pull on his right boot. "My uncle would *never*…" Dear God, she couldn't even say the words to deny it!

Yet his bleak expression didn't break into a grin to show he was teasing; it didn't change to show that he had any doubts at all about what he thought. He simply reached for the second boot and stomped his foot into it.

"What you're implying—that's not—it's simply mad!"

"Is it?" He leaned forward, elbows on knees, and brought his eyes level with hers. "The first time you were attacked was at the palace. Whoever hired that man to kill you told him exactly where to find you—information that a footman hired for the evening wouldn't have been privy to—and told him when you would be alone."

"It could have been a coincidence." Yet she felt the blood begin to drain from her cheeks. She didn't even believe that herself.

Apparently, neither did Clayton. "The second time was at the town house."

"But I wasn't even supposed to have been there! My uncle was the guest of honor who—"

"Who begged off and sent you in his stead. I didn't know of your change of plans until the last minute. Neither did the captain of the palace guards, I'd wager, which made it harder to protect you."

She pushed herself to her feet and wrapped the blanket tighter around herself as she stepped away from him. "No one knew I was going to be there."

"Your uncle knew, and he told the men who were sent to attack you." When she began to protest how ludicrous that was, he interrupted, "Your carriage arrived late due to traffic, yet the house wasn't attacked until after you arrived." His expression darkened. "Those men who chased us into the alley were there to kill you, not any of the lords or MPs inside the house or they never would have chased after a fleeing woman."

Oh God. Her hand pressed against her mouth. She was going to be sick! "You're wrong," she breathed out between her fingers. "Simply *wrong!*"

"I wish I were."

"No." She shook her head and, agitatedly, began to pick up her clothes, which still lay scattered across the floor where she'd dropped them last night. "No! My uncle loves me. He treats me as if I were his own daughter. He would *never* do as you're saying."

Clayton remained sitting in the chair and calmly watched as she gathered up her things in the lightening shadows, saying nothing to defend himself.

"He let you guard me, for heaven's sake!" Her hands fell to her sides in exasperation. "Why would he do that if he wanted to harm me?"

"Because he thought I wasn't capable of protecting you," he answered. "Because he thought I was nothing more than the regent's drinking companion who was being rewarded far beyond his capabilities."

Oh dear God! "None of this makes sense." She vehemently shook her head. "Why? *Why* would my uncle do as you're suggesting? Even if he wants to replace me in the line of succession—" She shook her stocking at him. "And I am *not* saying that he even wants to." She threw the piece of silk onto the bed and crossed her arms. "There are at least ten members of the current British royal family in line ahead of me, and the royal dukes will all scramble to sire as many children as possible before death works its way through them. The odds of the British crown going to a foreign prince are astronomical."

He countered quietly, "Not nearly that large, in fact."

She stilled and returned his stare. "What aren't you telling me, Clayton?" When he hesitated to answer, she pressed, "You're always saying I need to trust you. It's time you trusted me."

Slowly, he stood. He joined her beside the bed and picked up her stocking, then gestured for her to sit on the edge of the mattress.

Cordelia knew she'd gain no answers unless she did as he asked, so she sank onto the bed and steeled herself.

He knelt in front of her and reached beneath the blanket for her leg. He carefully slipped her stocking over her toes and began to roll it up her leg, and her heartbeat increased the closer his hands came to her bare thighs.

"There's a secret revolutionary group in England known as Scepter," he explained. His warm fingers brushed over her calf as he smoothed out the stocking.

The name triggered a memory. "Scepter...you've mentioned them before." Her voice emerged as a throaty whisper as his hands continued to caress her leg long after the stocking had been rolled into place. "When that man attacked me at Carlton House... You called him Scepter, but you said you were wrong."

"I lied."

The word barely formed on her lips. "Pardon?"

"That man worked for Scepter. I'm certain of it." He tied the ribbon garter securely into place, then paused with his hand on her thigh. "For the past five years, they've been leading all kinds of criminal enterprises to raise money and discover secrets they can use to blackmail people in important positions." The warmth of his palm seeped into her skin and once more stirred the ache low in her belly. "Brothels, smuggling, black markets—God only knows how far their network reached, but it was far enough to blackmail and bribe officials at all levels of the military and all levels of the government, including the Court of St James's and the palaces."

"Why would they do that?"

He slid his hand down her leg and reached for the other stocking to commit that same slow torture to her again. "Because they want to overthrow the government."

Her breath caught. This time, it wasn't because his hands were sliding provocatively up her legs and pushing the blanket out of the way.

"Their goal is to start a second Glorious Revolution, remove King George and his progeny from the throne, remove all his ministers, and establish their own puppet regime whom they can control to do their bidding." He rolled the second stocking up her leg and into place above her knee. "They don't care about reform or helping those who have no voice." He tied the ribbon. "They care only about gaining and keeping power for themselves."

He leaned over and placed a lingering kiss to her thigh. Her pulse spiked. So did the ache throbbing between her legs. If he wanted to distract her from the seriousness of what he was telling her, he was doing a fine job.

"That's—" She cleared her throat, but the raspy tone he'd put there didn't go away. "That's not possible. How could they…"

Her voice trailed off when he reached up to undo the blanket she'd wrapped around herself. It slipped off her shoulders and fell to the bed, revealing her naked body to his gleaming eyes.

"By using those same blackmailed and bribed officials to call out in unison for a new monarch, a new governmental structure." He rose to his feet and gently pulled her up to hers. "One they can control." His voice lowered to a thoughtful murmur. "Perhaps one who's been leading Scepter all along."

She lifted her arms over her head as he raised the shift into the air and slid it down over her body. His hands caressed her far too lightly. She arched her back toward him to cajole him into caressing her harder, but he only smoothed the cotton down over her hips and reached for her petticoat.

"But the regent, all the royal dukes and princesses—" She caught her breath when he put his arms around her waist to draw the string tight and tie it at the small of her back. She swallowed hard. She was used to being dressed several times a day but never facing her dresser so closely as this. Certainly never by a man. And certainly not by one who slid his hands down her backside and cupped her bottom against his palms. "Ten of them...between the throne and...a new ruler."

"A monarch who's gone mad, a regent who cares more about his own pleasures than he does about the British people, royal dukes and princesses whom the entire empire considers scandalous and immoral, none of them able to assure the security of the government, and all of them likely just as mad as their father?" He stepped back to pick up her discarded corset, and Cordelia felt instantly cold at the loss of his nearness. "If enough high-ranking people in the government call out for change, their cries will be echoed by average citizens across the empire."

He helped her into her short stays and began to tie up the front closure, careful not to draw it too tight. She reminded him, her breathing coming shallow and fast, "Calls for reform are a long way from revolution."

"Not so long," he continued in a murmur. He tied the lace and paused, his fingertips only inches from her taut nipples. "Soldiers will refuse to take up arms to defend King George and his family, and Parliament will vote for their removal. The royals will be run out of England the exact same way James the Second was, and a new monarchy will be put in place."

"I don't understand." She leaned toward him to beg with her body to be caressed the way he'd done last night when they'd made love. "What does any of it have to do with me?"

"Because it seems that Scepter is more than just a group of revolutionaries." He absently traced his fingertips over her nipples through the thick fabric and frowned, distracted. "I believe Scepter is a man, the same man who has been leading and plotting the revolution all along."

She grabbed his wrists and stilled his hands, her heart skipping. "And you think that man is my uncle?"

"I know so." His expression turned grim. "The only way he can have himself named king of Great Britain is to remove the current royal family." He paused. "And any other heir in his way."

Her skin prickled with fear, and she pushed his hands away. "You're wrong." She stepped back and snatched up her dress herself before he could put it on her. She couldn't have borne it. "Uncle Ernest would never do anything like that. How could he?" She shook out the dress, then yanked it on over her head to cover herself from his eyes as quickly as possible. "Monrovia is at least a fortnight's travel away by fastest carriage or ship, and this visit is the first he's made since he inherited the crown. Logistically, it's impossible."

"The wars made it possible. Soldiers coming and going who could ferry messages, diplomatic envoys crisscrossing the Continent, secret dispatches that anyone who saw would think were related to the fighting. If those paths failed, then Monrovia also keeps an ambassador in London who brings sealed dispatches to England all the time. Those men probably didn't even know they were sending along information and orders from Scepter."

She clenched her teeth and shoved her arms into the dress sleeves, too upset to reply to that. What he was telling her was *absurd*...wasn't it?

"He also had loyal men inside England," Clayton continued. "Once they'd maneuvered into positions of power, he wouldn't need as many dispatches. And believe me, Princess, they were loyal beyond measure."

As she fumbled to button up her bodice, he somberly approached her, turned her back to him, and buttoned her up himself. She shivered, this time not from arousal.

He lowered his mouth over her shoulder to her ear. "They blackmailed, bribed, raped, and murdered their way into power and into having others do their bidding. I have seen such atrocities committed by them that it would sicken you just to hear about them."

She didn't doubt that. Her stomach was already roiling.

"And they attempted to kill you twice, for no other reason than you're standing in their way."

"*None* of that proves my uncle is the one behind it." She stepped away and faced him. "There are displaced monarchs and dukes all over the continent since the wars." Her hands shook so hard she could barely straighten the dress and pull it into its proper place. "Why, all the Bonapartes themselves would love nothing better than to come back to power. For God's sake! This Scepter person could be any one of them. You have no proof that Scepter is my uncle."

"The Monrovian royal coat of arms," he said evenly.

She blinked, unable to follow that abrupt change in conversation. "What about it?"

He reached into his coat pocket and withdrew a small pendant. It dangled from its chain as he held it out for her.

She recognized it. "The key from our crest."

"I took that from a general last year who had organized a riot to storm Westminster. It's Scepter's symbol. A shibboleth they use to recognize each other."

She stared at the necklace as if it were a snake about to strike. She didn't dare touch it.

"This symbol has been found on all of Scepter's most important operatives," he explained. "When your uncle announced plans to address Parliament, the Monrovian coat of arms was published in all the newspapers and broadsheets right next to the announcement. Scepter's army has been waiting for a signal to start their revolution. *That* is what they've been waiting for."

He put the necklace into her hand and closed her fingers around it.

She stared down at her fist, her vision blurring with disbelief and anger.

"They'll descend upon London for his address, in which your uncle will most likely announce that you have been killed because the government and crown couldn't keep you safe. He'll make it clear exactly how inept and incompetent the current royal family has become, filled with madness and corruption." He released her hand and dropped his arm to his side. "Before his speech ends, there will be peers and MPs at all levels standing up in Parliament and calling for the renouncement of the current royal family and their replacement by Parliamentary decree." He paused to let that sink in. "And how convenient that when the MPs look around to find a new monarch, the next non-Hanoverian heir is standing right there in Westminster, in front of an empty throne."

"No." She shook her head and shoved the necklace at him. She pounded her fist against his chest until he had no choice but to take it back. "My uncle is a ruling prince! Why would he go to the extremes you're accusing him of when he's already a monarch?"

His countenance darkened with sympathy. "Even men who are already rich and powerful want more money and power. You once said so yourself," he reminded her quietly. "The *very* worst among them will do anything to have it, including destroying a government."

No…no, no, no! Shaking her head hard, she stepped back to put distance between them, then squared her shoulders and lifted her chin as imperiously as possible.

"I know why you're doing this." She wanted to sound forceful, but her voice emerged as little more than a trembling breath. "You're still trying to prove yourself to your father and the men who executed him, even now, even after last night." She swallowed hard to keep back the overwhelming emotions whirling inside her. "You still have to be the most loyal, most patriotic man in England, don't you? But to go so far as to accuse my uncle of this, just to prove yourself to a dead man…oh, you are wrong. You are so *very wrong*!"

Clayton said nothing, his green eyes looking back at her without reproach.

"When we return to London and my uncle sees I am unharmed," she announced as firmly as possible, "then you will know exactly how wrong you are."

"Princess," he agreed quietly, "I certainly hope so."

Beneath his somber gaze, her heart ripped in two.

She knew at that moment she'd lost him.

Twenty-Five

Eighteen hours later, Cordelia let out a long breath as their hired carriage finally arrived in Mayfair and stopped in front of a narrow town house. The bells of St George's rang out the late hour across the dark streets.

"Oh," Lady Agnes Sinclair said in surprise as she climbed into the compartment and dropped onto the seat across from Cordelia and Clayton.

"Oh *my*," Viscountess Bromley agreed as she plopped down next to Lady Agnes.

Both aunties gaped as they slid their gazes back and forth between the two. Then they turned to look at each other. Two sets of brows rose knowingly, and the ladies nodded in silent agreement. Then, with their surprise at finding Cordelia alone with Clayton over, they eased back against the squabs in the shadows cast by the light of the single carriage lamp and smiled like two cats who'd gotten into the cream.

No, Cordelia decided as her chest tightened with trepidation, like two cats who'd gotten into both the cream and the meat larder, then stumbled into a basket of yarn.

Clayton pounded his fist against the roof to signal to the jarvey to drive on.

"Ladies." He turned politely to the aunties. "You remember Princess Cordelia."

Viscountess Bromley nodded deferentially, although she frowned at the state of Cordelia's clothes. "Of course. Your Serene Highness, how wonderful to see you—"

Lady Agnes clamped a hand over Lady Bromley's knee to silence her friend and interrupted. "You've dragged us out long past the dinner hour and surprised us in a dark carriage, one in which you are alone with a princess who has been missing for three days, and both of you are wearing unkempt clothing that is not your own."

Cordelia winced at how that sounded. Yet it was the God's truth.

"Yes, ma'am," Clayton answered, "we have."

"Then there isn't time for pleasantries. Where have you been—" she began.

"And what have you been doing with the princess?" Lady Bromley finished.

Oh heavens. Cordelia was in no condition for this half-mad interrogation and rolled her eyes, wanting to crawl under the carriage and disappear.

She was exhausted from the day of travel in the hired carriage, mostly spent in grim silence while Clayton kept watch out the windows for any sign of danger and Cordelia kept from screaming for the driver to stop, for Clayton to listen to reason, for...for *anything* that would have brought back the magic of last night in his arms. Instead, the past pressed in upon them across every long mile and hour between the coast and London, with only short breaks from the thick tension between them when changing teams and drivers before hurrying on.

Thankfully, Clayton interceded gently, "We were safely hiding in the countryside near Windsor. That's all I can tell you." The tone of his voice brooked no argument. "And that's all you need to know."

The two older women exchanged another knowing look. They knew he'd just lied to them.

"We need your assistance. And your silence."

That caught their attention, and the two women sat eagerly forward at the possibility of intrigue.

"I removed the princess from London for her safety when Lord Harrowby's town house was attacked," Clayton explained. "But it's time to bring her back." He paused pointedly. "Along with the two respectable society ladies who served as chaperones and provided proper supervision and companionship at every moment. You never let her out of your sight, not once the entire time. Understand?"

"But we attended our London Ladies meeting last night," Lady Bromley said. "And had tea with the Duchess of Hampton the day before that."

Lady Agnes narrowed her eyes on Cordelia and muttered sideways to the viscountess, "No, Harriet, you are *mistaken*. We were with the princess the entire time. General Elliott collected us immediately after the attack, and we all decided that the best course of action would be to remove Her Serene Highness to Windsor, where she could remain in hiding for her safety yet still be near the castle should additional protection be needed." She rested a ring-laden hand on her friend's knee. "Don't you remember?"

Lady Bromley blinked away the moment's confusion, then her face lit up. "Oh, yes! We never went to the London Ladies meeting or tea with the duchess, and anyone who says they saw us there is mistaken. They must have seen us last week and confused matters."

Lady Agnes's eyes gleamed at their conspiracy. "We spent the past three days doing needlework and sketching, and we told lots of stories to entertain the princess, who never left our sides."

"Not once." The viscountess waved a hand at Clayton. "Certainly not to be alone with you."

Cordelia's cheeks flushed hot with embarrassment. Thank heavens the inside of the carriage was dark!

With a slight hesitation, Clayton slid his hand across the seat to touch hers for reassurance.

She pulled away.

"We will do whatever we can to protect the princess," Lady Agnes declared.

Viscountess Bromley nodded emphatically, as if she'd just been recruited into the Home Office as an operative. "You can depend on us."

That was why Clayton had picked them to be their alibi, Cordelia realized. The aunties would do whatever he wanted if it meant being swept up into the thrill of government intrigue, including lying to the world to protect her reputation.

Lady Agnes glanced out the window at the dark city and

suspiciously arched a brow that reached nearly as high as her peacock-green turban. "If we're returning the princess, then why have we just driven past the palace?"

A very good question. Cordelia glanced at Clayton, who carefully kept an inscrutable expression on his face.

"We're not going to the palace," he informed them. "We're going somewhere far safer than that."

Both ladies held their breaths, caught up in the moment as if they were spies embarking on their first espionage mission.

Clayton eased back on the seat. "We're going to the Armory."

The two aunties exhaled with a burst of barely controlled excitement. Their faces practically glowed in the shadows.

"What's the Armory?" Cordelia asked.

"Oh, my dear," Lady Bromley said with an exhilarated smile. "It's the most amazing place!"

"It's a sanctuary for soldiers," Lady Agnes attempted to clarify, although her statement did nothing to aid in Cordelia's understanding.

"It's the safest place I know," Clayton murmured in a low voice as he leaned toward her to keep the aunties from over-hearing. "I will never let any harm come to you. Trust me."

She nodded because it was expected, and even now, she did as expected.

But she turned away to look out the window and moved her hand out of reach in case he tried to touch it again. *Trust me...* After his accusations about her uncle, she wasn't at all certain she could.

When the carriage finally stopped, she gaped outside at the building in front of them. The aunties were wrong. This wasn't a sanctuary—

It was a fortress made for war.

"Welcome to the Armory," Clayton announced, then opened the door and dropped to the ground to help the ladies out.

The two aunties scurried forward, chatting excitedly to each other as a guard positioned at the front gate nodded deferentially and opened the gate for them to pass. Another guard escorted them inside, through a thick iron door that clanked and screeched as it opened and then down a dark tunnel lit by flickering torchlight.

Following behind, Cordelia paused at the footpath and stared up at the great building.

It looked like a castle, with a central tower that stretched three stories high and crenellated battlements lining the roof where soldiers could defend it from attack. She could even see a portcullis gate positioned above the main entrance. A dozen or more well-armed guards stood watch in the yard, and fires blazed from tall braziers to light the building's perimeter.

Good God. He'd brought her to a fortress.

Without a word, Clayton took her arm and led her past the guards, through the gate and courtyard beyond, and down the narrow entrance guarded by twin portcullises at both ends. The temperature dropped as they passed through the stone tunnel with what seemed like twenty-foot-thick walls, and she shivered, although not from the cold.

They emerged into the main room of the Armory, and she halted midstep. She stared at the large room in front of her—

No, she stared at the men waiting there.

Over a dozen in all, all of them dressed in black and armed, they turned to look as she and Clayton entered. She recognized them—dukes, earls, barons, and officers of all stripes who had been introduced to her at palace events, including the Duke of Hampton himself, General Marcus Braddock, who stood in the center of the group and somberly sketched a shallow bow to her, one followed in turn by the men around him.

Her chest ached as she stared at them. For all these men to gather here like this in the middle of the night, all awaiting orders and prepared to do battle, then they must also believe…

A tear slipped down her cheek as the harsh realization gripped her so fiercely that she couldn't breathe.

Clayton had told her the truth about her uncle.

Twenty-Six

OUT OF THE CORNER OF HIS EYE, CLAYTON SAW ALFRED, the Armory's butler, lead the princess and the two aunties up the wooden steps wrapping around the sides of the central tower and toward the bedrooms above where they would all spend the night. She would be safe from attack here.

The realizations about her uncle, however, were another matter entirely.

The trip back to London had been painfully silent. He hadn't said anything to her about her accusation at the cottage, that he was still attempting to prove himself to the world and to his father. But her words had gutted him.

He hadn't lied to her. He prayed to God he was wrong, but he wasn't. He knew her uncle was Scepter. So did the men of the Armory.

And so did Cordelia from the way she'd stared at the men who'd waited here to greet and guard her. He'd never before seen a woman go so pale so quickly, and somehow the sight of the tear slipping down her cheek was impossibly worse than her penetrating accusation from that morning.

"The announcement is in here." Marcus Braddock opened the *Times* and showed Clayton the same clipping Justice Rivers had sent to him in Mersea. Marcus tossed the paper onto the massive oak reading table at the side of the central room. "And here." He dropped another paper on top of the first. "Here." Another paper. "And more, including the gossip sheets."

The papers spilled across the polished tabletop, but every one of them held an announcement about Prince Ernest's address to Parliament tomorrow and a drawing of the Monrovia royal coat of arms. The large key symbol stood out prominently on every page.

The core group of men of the Armory gathered around the table and stared glumly down at the newspapers. The others had gotten their orders from Marcus to secure the perimeter and keep watch over Buckingham House and St James's Palace until further plans could be made.

"And not just in the newspapers," Merritt Rivers muttered as he crossed his arms over his chest, as always his sword dangling at his hip. "Letters have been sent to all the peers and MPs about the address, and every one of them contains the key symbol from the royal crest."

"It's also been put on bills," Brandon Pearce, Earl of Sandhurst, blew out on a hard breath. "They've been plastered across the squares and markets of London and sent out across England via mail coach."

"The palace staffs have also replaced the usual banners at all the royal residences with the Monrovian crest," Captain Nate Reed informed them as he strode into the room and straight into the midst of their planning. He removed his riding gloves and slapped them against his thigh to knock off the dust. "I just came from Kensington Palace." He frowned.

"None of the staff have any idea what it means. They think the British royals are simply showing their solidarity with Monrovia."

Marcus cursed beneath his breath. "It would be nearly impossible for anyone of rank or position within a hundred miles of London not to have seen that key by now."

"Anyone who's part of Scepter will know exactly what it means," Alexander Sinclair, Earl of St James, interjected.

"The signal to start the revolution," Clayton finished quietly. "They'll use his address to Parliament as a call to arms."

The men stared silently at the pile of newspapers, but tension hung thick in the air around them. It was that same tense mix of anxiety and growing unease that had descended on them before every battle they'd engaged in during the wars. As before, too, they all assumed the same postures as when they'd discussed battle strategy, the same crossed arms and hard-set jaws, the same inscrutable expressions and somber gazes.

They all knew a new fight was coming.

"There are already calls from common Londoners for Monrovia to take action against England for the princess's apparent death," Merritt Rivers informed them.

"And calls for the removal of the British monarch," Nate Reed added glumly. "They're arguing that if King George and Prinny can't keep their own government—and their foreign guests—safe on English soil, then they can never properly lead a global empire."

Marcus Braddock muttered, "Scepter's men will call out in Parliament right after his speech, and they'll put forward an immediate act to place Prince Ernest on the British throne."

"Prinny will refuse to grant the act royal assent, and the wars will begin," Alec Sinclair added grimly. "It won't be a bloodless coup either. Thousands will die in the streets across Britain."

Clayton's chest tightened with dread. "Then we have to stop those events from playing out." Clayton rapped his knuckles on the stack of papers. "We stop the prince from addressing Parliament, and we use our secret weapon to do it."

They all frowned, yet as Clayton swung his gaze between the men, a rash and reckless hope surged through him.

"They're expecting Scepter," Clayton explained. "We send in the princess instead."

Their frowns melted into expressions of disbelief.

"Let Parliament see for themselves that she's alive and unhurt. That will put an end to any potential conflict between Britain and Monrovia, and her claim of support for the royal family should help suppress sedition. Parliament won't have cause to support calls for deposition of the monarch and replacement of key government officials then, no matter who makes them."

Marcus shook his head. "Scepter won't allow her to come anywhere near Westminster."

Brandon Pearce was even more blunt. "If we take her to the palace, she'll be dead before noon."

"Then we don't take her to the palace," Clayton countered. "We take her directly to Parliament, and we make certain Scepter can't give any orders or signals to his army."

The men exchanged knowing glances.

"So let me see if I understand you correctly," Merritt Rivers summarized. "You're saying we should kidnap a reigning foreign monarch, force our way into Parliament, and bring a woman into Westminster Hall to address the country?"

"Yes," Clayton answered firmly. "That is exactly what I'm saying."

The men stared at Clayton as if he'd gone mad. Then Marcus shook his head. "If it goes wrong, we'll all hang."

Clayton folded his arms over his chest. "Then let's not get it wrong."

━━━━━━━

An hour later, the other men left the Armory to put their plans into motion, and Clayton slowly climbed the tower stairs to visit the princess.

The aunties were sound asleep and snoring loudly from their room across the landing. The evening's excitement had caught up with them, and also most likely Lady Agnes's famed spiked tea that they'd surely been imbibing when he whisked them away from the town house tonight.

He'd had no choice but to involve them. Again. Cordelia needed proof she hadn't been alone with a man for three days, and the aunties would lend just enough respectability mixed with convenient absentmindedness to provide a solid alibi. Anyone who had seen the two ladies out and about in Mayfair would simply be told they were mistaken, and certainly, the two older women could confuse anyone enough to cast doubt into even the sharpest minds.

Besides, no one would dare call Lady Bromley and Lady Agnes liars, not when their nephews were the deadliest dueling shots in the land.

He knocked lightly. "Cordelia, it's me."

When she opened the door and stared up at him with red-rimmed eyes, his heart broke.

He pulled her into his arms and gently kicked the door closed behind him. Her arms wrapped around his waist, and she buried her face in his chest. All of her shook as she sobbed.

He lowered his mouth to her hair and whispered, "Don't cry, darling. I can't bear it."

"You're a soldier," she argued, her voice muffled against his waistcoat and choking with tears. "You're supposed to be braver than that."

He smiled against her temple. "Yes, ma'am." He tightened his arms around her, and his smile faded. "It's going to be all right, I promise you."

"No, it's not." She lifted her head and gazed up at him in the candlelight. "My uncle…" Her voice broke, unable to put words to the harsh truth. "You were right about him. I know that now."

He tucked a stray curl behind her ear. "And so the issue becomes what you plan to do about it."

Her slender shoulders sank, and she slipped out of his arms to pace the length of the large bedroom. There were no windows to shutter against the cold, only a narrow arrow slit converted into a window that revealed the rainy black night beyond.

His eyes drifted to the bed that was still made. She wore her shift as a night rail, yet she hadn't bothered attempting to sleep. Too much weighed on her mind tonight, he knew, and he wasn't certain he could ease any of it.

"What *can* I do?" She wrung her hands as she paced. "I don't have enough solid evidence to present to the Crown Council to have him removed from the throne, and even if he were…"

He paused a moment before finishing for her, "Then what becomes of your family and country?"

She gave a sharp nod. "At best, Uncle Ernest will be exiled from Monrovia and Britain, all his titles and fortune stripped away, and a new prince put into his place. Most likely what my father did will become known, and all our treaties with other states will be threatened, all our trade agreements called into question…all the respect we've worked so hard to earn lost. The trust of the Monrovian people in their monarchs will be completely destroyed." She stopped wringing her hands only to worry at her bottom lip with her teeth, but always she paced, as if determined to wear a path through the rug. "At worst…" She halted in midstep and slowly raised her eyes to meet his. "At worst, Monrovia will cease to exist."

"That won't happen." He crossed to her, cupped her face between his hands, and kissed her tenderly. The pain he tasted on her lips undid him, and he allowed himself only a moment to recover before reassuring her. "Your royal cousins will support you, and tomorrow, we stop your uncle. He won't trouble Monrovia or England—or you—ever again."

She clutched at his waistcoat. "And what becomes of me?"

"I'll protect you."

Sadness darkened her eyes. "You can't protect me from this."

"Better than you think."

Her gaze locked with his. "What do you mean?"

"Tomorrow, you're going where few women have ever been allowed to go." When she frowned, he quirked her a half grin he didn't feel. "You're going to Parliament in your uncle's place."

A puzzled frown creased her brow. "Why would my uncle be absent?"

"Because he won't be there to speak as planned." He didn't want to tell her anything more of their plans until he had to. There was no need to upset her any sooner than necessary. "But you, Your Serene Highness, will be there in all your glory to speak to the empire."

Her mouth fell open. "I can't! I never address foreign governments. It's not one of my duties."

"It is now."

She swayed at the idea, and he took her arm to steady her. "Good heavens, what do I say?"

"You'll be able to think of something." He gave her elbow a squeeze. "Just speak from your heart, and tell them exactly what you want."

"Speak from my heart..." She reached down to take his hand in both of hers and whispered, "My heart wants you."

And *his* heart broke.

Dear God, how much he wanted exactly what she was offering! More than one night by the sea, more than a fleeting encounter... He wanted her for the rest of his life.

Yet she could never be his.

He pulled in a hard breath to combat the squeezing of his chest and rasped out painfully, "The heart can't always have what it wants."

He lifted her hand to his lips and placed a lingering kiss to her wrist where her pulse beat warm and strong. He squeezed his eyes shut against the pain. Tomorrow, one way or another, she would be taken from him, and there was nothing he could do to stop it.

"We can't be together." Then he admitted the damning truth. "A general—even one made a viscount—can never marry a princess."

Desolation filled her voice. "But you would…if you could?"

He hesitated, not wanting to hurt her with his answer. But there was no point any longer in denying it. "In a heartbeat."

When she rose up to kiss him, an anguished tear slipped down her cheek. So much longing pulsed from her that he shook from it.

She laced her fingers through his and led him to the bed. With agonizing slowness, she undressed him. Her fingers trembled as she helped him shrug out of his jacket, then unbuttoned his waistcoat that followed the jacket to the floor at their feet.

"I want to remember everything about you," she whispered as she slipped off his braces. She ran her hands over his shoulders and down his arms. "The way you look…"

When she untied his cravat and pulled it away, her mouth went to his bare neck. The soft, lingering kiss she placed there was aching.

"The way you taste."

A groan of restrained desire tore from the back of his throat when the tip of her tongue licked him.

She reached around him to untie the waist band at the small of his back. Then she gently tugged his shirt free and lifted it over his head and off.

She stared at his bare chest as if attempting to imprint every detail into her mind, and he let her, remaining as still as a statue. She might want to brand on her memory every detail of him, but *he* wanted to remember her doing exactly that.

Then she brushed her hands over his chest, and his pulse raced beneath her fingertips. As they curled into the muscle over his heart, she said hoarsely, "The way you feel."

Her hands slipped daringly beneath his trousers.

He sucked in a mouthful of air through clenched teeth as her hand cupped his balls. When she gently squeezed, his cock jumped. A pleased smile teased at her lips at the power she had over him, yet she had no idea exactly how much. He would give his life for her.

When she tickled her fingers down his hardening length, he closed his eyes and surrendered.

Tonight was about finding solace and saying goodbye. He would let her take the lead in whatever happened and be grateful for the precious time he was given with her. So he stood perfectly still when she unbuttoned his fall and gently freed him from his trousers, when she caressed him between both hands, and when she slowly lowered herself to her knees.

He caught his breath as she placed a soft kiss to his tip. Then she hesitated, not knowing what came next.

"Do whatever you want," he encouraged her. "Do whatever feels good to you."

She cast an uncertain look up at him. "Shouldn't I be doing what feels good to *you*?"

A choked laugh fell from his lips. "Trust me, darling." He reached down to caress her cheek. "If it feels good to you, then it will absolutely feel good to me."

With that reassurance, she lowered her head again, but this time she didn't stop with just a chaste kiss to his tip. This time she nibbled her lips along his length, and he couldn't hold back the shaking that gripped him or the soft whisper of her name.

She took a tentative lick over his hot skin. A flood of burning desire rushed through him, and he spasmed against her tongue. *Sweet Lucifer...*

In many ways, she was still innocent in all the pleasures that men and women could find in each other's bodies, but her mouth was simply wicked when she closed her lips over him and sucked. The air left him in a rushing groan, and he had to shove his hands into her soft hair to keep himself from crumpling to the floor at her knees.

He closed his eyes and gave over to the sweet sucking of her lips that took him deep into her mouth, the teasing flicks of her tongue across his head, the soft caresses of her fingers against his balls. The most erotic, most wonderful soft sounds of her wet lips floated up to him as she took pleasure in deliciously tormenting him. When her head began to bob quickly as she pulsed his length between her lips, he dug his fingers against her scalp and fought for restraint.

Just when he thought he couldn't bear the ministrations of her insistent mouth any longer without losing himself, she slipped him free of her lips and slowly stood. With a light push, she tumbled him down onto the bed and followed after, then daringly straddled him despite the nervousness showing on her face.

She needn't have worried. He would let her do anything she wanted to him. Tonight, he was completely hers, in every way.

Lifting her shift out of the way, she rose up, positioned his cock like an arrow at her core, then slowly lowered herself over him. He slid smoothly into her tight warmth, and a long sigh of shivering pleasure fell from her lips at having him once again inside her. She closed her eyes, for a moment not moving, as if she wanted to brand this sensation, too, onto her memory for always.

Then she looked down at him with such affection that it ripped his breath away.

She took the hem of her shift and stripped it up her body, over her head, and off, leaving her completely naked.

His eyes drank in the sight of her as she perched over him, and he could barely believe she was real. Her dark hair tumbling down across her bare breasts and back, her skin golden in the candlelight, the soft warmth of her body enveloping his—

Dear God, she was glorious. And when she began to move...*heaven*.

Placing her hands flat on his chest, she rocked over him in small, tentative jerks of her hips against his. Slowly, her confidence built, and so did her momentum. The gentle rocking soon transformed into galloping thrusts as she raced to claim her pleasure.

Caught up in the need Clayton could feel building inside her, she leaned forward and curled her fingertips into his muscles as she bore down on him. Her legs squeezed against his sides, and he could feel the tension tightening inside her, every tiny muscle clenching hard around him.

"Don't stop," he encouraged and slid his hand down between them to where their two bodies met. He rubbed at the sensitive little nub buried in her folds.

A throaty moan tore from her as she rocked herself against his fingers. His knuckles pressed hard against her with every forward thrust of her hips—

She bit her lip to keep from crying out as her body spasmed with release. She arched her spine, threw back her head, and welcomed the sweet rush of joy that shuddered through her and into him.

Fighting back his own release, he rose up from the mattress, encircled her in his arms, and rolled her onto her back. He yanked himself from her warmth and squeezed his throbbing cock between their two bodies. His arms tightened around her as he thrust his hips against hers, rubbing himself against her lower belly.

With a fierce jerk, he spilled himself against her. The happiness that consumed him was overwhelming. And absolutely perfect.

He held her beneath him, tightly wrapped in his arms. He did nothing more than absorb the wonderful closeness of her and the unfathomable combination of sweetness and unrestrained passion she'd shared with him.

This was the moment he wanted to remember whenever he thought of her in the years to come. This was the moment he would imprint on his mind—the moment she changed him forever.

"Clayton?" she whispered.

With no choice but to let time pass on, he regretfully rolled onto his side and brought her over against his front. His lips rested against her temple as she slipped her arm possessively over his waist and lay her head against his chest. He was certain she could feel the pounding of his heart against her cheek. Could she also feeling the breaking of it? "Yes?"

"I love you."

The soft words shattered him.

He futilely tightened his arms around her, as if he could simply will the two of them to be together beyond the dawn. He squeezed shut his eyes and confessed into the shadows, "I love you, too."

Twenty-Seven

THE MORNING SUNLIGHT WAS JUST PEEKING THROUGH the narrow slit of a window high on the wall as Cordelia stood in front of the dressing table and fussed with her hair. The door of her room stood wide open to give the appearance of propriety, although it had been locked all through the night and during those short hours when they'd held each other in their arms. Emotion knotted in her throat. *Too* painfully short.

From across the tower, she could hear the aunties starting their day. Amusement tightened her chest at how noisy they were being. Most likely, it was because they knew where Clayton had spent the night and were doing their best to cover all noise from her room and to remind the men in the Armory below that they'd kept careful watch on her all night, even though they hadn't.

Clayton was right, she had to admit. The aunties were the perfect chaperones. As if assured by their alibi, he shamelessly leaned his shoulder against the doorframe and watched as she pinned up her hair.

Dear God, how the sight of him took her breath away! Her fingertips itched to brush that rakish lock of hair off his forehead, and her lips ached to kiss him. If she wasn't careful, other places would soon ache for him, too…most of all her heart. But none of them could be satisfied.

Last night had been the last time they would ever be alone together.

She looked away to keep the anguish from overwhelming her. Her fingers trembled as she twisted her hair into a chignon and placed the last pin. "You have a plan." She cast him a glance. "What happens next?"

"The men downstairs will escort you to Westminster and make certain you're presented to Parliament in your uncle's place."

Her heart skipped. "The men…not you?"

His eyes dimmed, although his expression never changed. Both of them were putting up brave faces this morning. "Not me."

Trepidation pricked at the backs of her knees. "But I can't do this without you."

"Yes, my brave princess, you can."

His assurance did little to put her at ease. "I want you there." Her voice lowered as she took a step toward him, ever mindful of not straying too close and of how he had to remain outside her room, even if only by an inch. "Clayton, I *need* you with me."

"I'll draw too much attention."

A lie. One said to protect her, yet still a lie. "We're going into Parliament to prevent one reigning monarch from starting a revolution and overthrowing another by sending me into the hall in his place." Her brow inched up. "And *you* will draw too much attention?"

He admitted quietly, "If anyone sees me, I'll be arrested on sight."

"Not if I protect you."

His lips quirked into a half smile, yet his expression somehow remained as grim as ever. "Even if you try to protect me. That is, if I'm not shot first."

Her breath strangled in her throat. "You mean by Scepter's men?"

"I mean by the Home Office." He pushed himself away from the doorframe. "I haven't told you everything."

She steeled herself for the worst.

"Since the attack on the town house, I've been considered a rogue agent. The palace blames me for your disappearance and claims I was behind the attack. At least that's what they're saying in public to deflect from their failure to keep you safe. God only knows what they're saying in private. But certainly none of it's good." His eyes fixed on hers. "Call me old-fashioned, Princess, but I don't want the woman I love to see me killed in front of her."

Her blood turned to ice, and she sank onto the edge of the bed to keep from sinking to the floor.

"No." She clenched her hands into fists. "I will *not* let that happen. I'll talk to Lord Sidmouth and Lord Liverpool—I'll throw myself at Cousin George's feet if I have to! I'll explain everything."

"They won't listen."

"I will *make* them listen." Determination blazed through her. It was her turn to protect him, and she wouldn't fail him. "They have to believe me."

He faintly shook his head. "Whitehall needs a public excuse for your disappearance, one that doesn't involve Scepter. They can never admit to the country how close we've come to revolution or allow doubts about the royal family to stir in their subjects' minds. Blaming me is their best option."

"Then they can blame *me*." She pushed herself to her feet and gestured in the air, having no idea in what direction lay Lord Harrowby's town house. "They can say a group of Luddites attacked the house, and I'll say I ran away of my own volition and was too frightened to return. That I made you and the aunties stay with me."

"They won't listen to what you say."

She put her hands on her hips. "I'll make them."

"Listen to me." He crossed the room to her and took her shoulders in his hands. Neither cared that he'd just broken all propriety by stepping into the bedroom with her. "What happens to me doesn't signify." His gaze drilled into hers. "What's important is putting you inside Westminster Hall in your uncle's place. The men of the Armory will make certain that happens. That's all you need to be concerned about."

Not by a goodly ways! "And what happens to you?"

"Once you're safely inside Parliament, I'll flee to the Continent and wait there until everything has settled. In a few months, I'll know whether I can return."

In a few months? She wouldn't be able to survive the next *few hours* without him at her side. "Take me with you." She grabbed his lapels. For God's sake, she'd beg if she had to! "Please, Clayton."

Unable to hide his grief, he took her hands and raised them to his lips. "I can't do that. We both know it." Mercifully, instead of reminding her that generals didn't marry princesses, he said, "You'll be needed in Monrovia. You'll need to guide your country forward and assure Europe that the principality is as strong as ever."

She blinked rapidly to clear the stinging anguish from her eyes, then bit her lip and forced a jerking nod. She knew her duty, even now, and even though it was destroying her.

But she couldn't stop a tear from breaking free and falling down her cheek.

His broad shoulders slumped, and he reached up to brush it away. "Cordelia, please believe me. If I could find a way, I would never—"

An explosion reverberated through the Armory.

Cordelia ran into Clayton's arms. Putting her safely behind him to protect her with his body, he yanked his pistol from its holster and pointed it at the door. She flinched and stifled a scream as a second explosion followed the first.

Below, shouts and confusion rose in the wake of the explosions. Then came sounds of running and gunshots echoing against the thick stone walls of the building. Metallic bangs against the front gates and doors were met by the clank of weapons being removed from the training room downstairs and the thumping chains of the portcullises slamming down into place.

"Clayton!" Brandon Pearce raced up the tower, taking the wooden stairs three at a time in great leaps. "We're being attacked! They're after the princess!"

Merritt Rivers charged behind on Pearce's heels, three swords in his hands. "Pearce!"

Merritt tossed Pearce a second sword, and he caught it one-handed in midair.

Lady Bromley and Lady Agnes scurried out of their room to see what was happening. They were wrapped in each other's arms, a mix of excitement and terror flashing across their faces.

"Go!" Pearce ordered. He and Merritt took positions at the top of the stairs, drawn swords in all four of their hands. "Get her out of here."

"But the aunties!" Cordelia cried out as Clayton grabbed her by the wrist and pulled her forward, not toward the stairs that curled down into the octagonal main room but upward toward a ladder at the very top of the tower. "I can't leave them!"

"We'll protect them," Merritt assured her, then flinched as another explosion blasted from the main door. The sound of metal on stone screeched through the Armory, followed by shouts and the clash of swords and axes. The fortress had been breached. "Go!"

Clayton shoved her halfway up the ladder and scrambled up after. He reached over her head to throw open the wooden hatch and pushed her up onto the roof in front of him. He dropped the hatch in place and rotated a metal bar over it to secure it.

Below them in the yard rose the deafening noise of battle—shouts, the clash of metal, the small blasts of pistols.

Clayton led her to the edge of the crenellated roof and peered down at the ground. A fierce curse tore from him.

"This way!" He raced with her to the edge of the tower and down a narrow metal ladder to the roof below.

She struggled to keep up and to ignore the pain rising in her still-tender ankle, and her lungs burned as she gulped in giant mouthfuls of air. But he didn't slow their escape and pulled her to the far end of the roof. He grabbed a rolled-up rope and metal rung ladder, the kind used on tall ships, and unfurled it down the side of the stone building.

He pointed at the ladder and ordered, "Down."

She froze, frightened of heights and terrified of the battle being waged around her. "I can't!"

"You're the bravest woman I know, Princess." He pushed her toward the ladder. "I'll be right behind you. Now go—quickly!"

Gulping down her terror, she placed her shaking hands on the first rung of the ladder and carefully made her way over the wall and down the side of the building, one slow and unsteady step at a time. Pain radiated up her forearm, but she refused to let it or the near-constant ache in her ankle slow her down.

"Faster, love," he urged quietly from above. "You have to go faster."

She nodded and sped up her descent, only to jump the last three feet to the ground and carefully land on her good foot. The air whooshed from her lungs, and she crouched on the ground, her eyes squeezed shut, as she tried to gather back both her breath and her balance.

"Come on!" Clayton grabbed her arm and pulled her to her feet. He ran with her across the narrowest stretch of yard toward a small gate. He lowered his shoulder and rammed into it, bursting it open with a loud crack and splintering of wood.

Shouts went up. Cordelia glanced behind her and shivered with fresh fear. They'd been spotted!

He pulled her into the street and around the corner of the nearest building. She ran as quickly as she could on her sore ankle to keep up as he darted them down street after street, alley after alley, through the mazelike stretch of city around them. The men who'd given chase were too far behind to see where they'd gone.

Finally, they emerged onto a wide avenue. Clayton flagged down a hackney and pushed her inside. "Mayfair—go!"

The jarvey flipped his whip, and the team scrambled forward.

Clayton looked out the carriage windows in all directions, his hand beneath his jacket on his pistol. "They're not following us."

Cordelia sank against the squabs in relief, only for a second terrifying thought to strike—"The aunties!"

"They'll be protected. Pearce and Merritt will make certain of it." The grim look he gave her prickled the little hairs at her nape. "Besides, the attackers were after you, not them."

"How did they know I was there?" Her head sank into her hands as she swallowed great mouthfuls of air to catch back her breath. "No one knew where we were, not even Madame Noir."

He bit out a curse beneath his breath. "The jarvey who dropped us off last night knew. He must have recognized you and went to the palace for a reward."

Which meant her uncle sent men to... *Oh God*, she was going to be sick! She flung open the window and stuck her head outside into the cold morning air.

"Cordelia?" A concerned hand rested on her back.

She nodded, even though she was far from all right, and squeezed her eyes closed. "Your friends at the Armory, if they're hurt because of me—"

"They're well-trained soldiers who succeeded over the best the French could throw at them, and they have an entire arsenal at their disposal inside those walls," he assured her as he slid across the compartment to sit next to her. "They'll survive this, too."

She gave another nod, which was just as unconvincing as the first, and slipped down from the window and into the comfort of his strong arms. Long minutes passed with the two of them saying nothing as the clip-clop of hooves and the rumble of wheels beneath them led them toward Mayfair.

Eventually, he loosened his arms around her and sat back to examine her to make certain she was all right, including her forearm and ankle. His warm hands were soothing, his touch as calming as always, but not even Clayton could tamp down the fear inside her now.

"Where are we going?" she asked.

"To visit your fairy godmother." He left her only long enough to open the door and call up to the driver. "Charlton Place!"

She frowned with confusion as he pulled her back into his arms.

"We're going to visit the Duchess of Hampton. She's

very good with helping women in need." His solemn eyes darkened unhappily. "She's going to turn you back into a princess."

Dear God, that was the very last thing she wanted! Anguish filled her chest as she choked out, "Can't I stay a frog instead?"

Not answering that, he lifted her chin with his finger and placed a soothing kiss to her lips.

———

Danielle Braddock, Duchess of Hampton, didn't blink when Clayton escorted Cordelia into Charlton Place, as if discovering a missing princess in her drawing room were an everyday occurrence.

But then, Clayton knew, little surprised Danielle.

"We need help," he told her. "And we can't go to the palace."

"Of course not," she agreed. "Marcus sent word about Scepter and told me to remain at home."

Clayton leveled his gaze at the young duchess. He knew her too well. "Are you truly going to follow his orders?"

"Not if I'm needed elsewhere." She nodded at Cordelia. "Fortunately, I'm needed here at the moment. How may I be of service?"

"Her Highness is going to Westminster to address Parliament," he explained. "We need you to make her look as royal as possible."

"But not too royal," Cordelia interjected. She murmured to Clayton in a low voice, "I'm still hoping to remain a frog."

Danielle nodded, completely unperturbed at the request; after all, subterfuge was her second nature. Her eyes narrowed as she cast an assessing look over Cordelia. "I have the perfect gown, diamonds, a tiara...and ermine. Lots and lots of ermine. None will be anywhere near as grand as what should grace a princess, but it should work." She flicked her gaze to Clayton. "How much time do I have?"

"Two hours."

"We'd best get started." Danielle linked her arm in Cordelia's to whisk her upstairs. "Clayton, you know the way to Marcus's study. Feel free to use the stationery." She gave him a knowing look. "I'm certain you have messages that need to be sent."

With that, the two women swept from the room, with Danielle chatting a mile a minute about how she planned on costuming the princess. Only a glance by Cordelia over her shoulder before she disappeared from sight told him how uneasy she was.

She needn't have worried. Danielle could be trusted to transform her into the person everyone would recognize. The irony was bitter. He had to save Cordelia by turning her back into the one thing she didn't want to be.

He only prayed that someday she would forgive him for it.

An hour and a half later, the butler rapped on the study door. From behind the massive desk, Clayton signaled to the man to give him just one more moment, then finished his last letter, the most difficult one he'd ever written in his life.

He blotted and folded the letter, then sealed it with a drop of red wax. He wrote Cordelia's name across the front.

Finally, he looked up. "Yes?"

"Her Grace has sent for you," the butler informed him. "May I show you upstairs?"

With a nod, Clayton rose to his feet. He reached for the large glass of cognac he'd helped himself to from Marcus's liquor cabinet and took a long drink to bolster himself. Then he gathered up the many messages he'd written...to Justice Rivers to thank him for his help, to the Home Secretary to attempt to explain his version of events and what he planned to do this afternoon in Westminster Hall, and to a half dozen other people at the Home Office and in the army who needed instructions for what would come next. He'd even penned one to the blasted prince regent, for whatever good it might do.

"I need you to deliver these immediately," he ordered as he handed the stack to the butler. "*Immediately*. And this one." He held up the last letter with the red seal, then placed it in the middle of the desk. "This one is to be left here for His Grace." It was a letter for Cordelia, to be personally delivered by Marcus if today didn't turn out as planned. "He'll know what do it with it."

"Yes, sir."

Clayton followed the butler upstairs through the house to Danielle's sitting room. In the months since Danielle and Marcus married, they'd turned Charlton Place into a family home, which included changing the master suite of rooms from a shared sitting room flanked by separate bedrooms to a shared bedroom flanked by separate sitting rooms. The nursery wasn't on the top floor either. It now sat directly across the hall.

Clayton grinned. General Marcus Braddock, the Scourge of Spain, had become domesticated.

He entered the room and froze. The smile vanished from his face.

Cordelia stood near the window where the late morning sunlight fell gently around her. She'd been transformed, and the stunning difference took his breath away. Oh, he'd never been able to forget she was a princess, had never been able to ignore the stately way she held herself or how she moved with an inherent grace crafted over the years by an awareness of position and duty. *Always* duty. But this…

Good God.

A white and silver gown with a voluminous skirt draped around her, covered in hundreds of tiny pearls and silver threads in an intricate pattern of spring flowers. A diamond and amethyst necklace lay at her throat, and more matching jewels sparkled at her wrists and fingers over the long satin gloves that reached above her elbows. Her chestnut hair had been styled high in a mass of carefully pinned curls to most effectively highlight the tiara placed carefully on her head, and an ermine stole draped across her shoulders. And if all that somehow failed to convey exactly who she was and the power she possessed, then the purple sash draped diagonally across her bosom proclaimed it in spades.

She was a true princess, every inch of her, and the sight of her pieced him. The gap between their lives had never been more evident. Or wider.

"What do you think?" Danielle called out as she fussed with the long skirt.

"Definitely not a frog," he murmured and earned himself a pleased smile from the princess.

"I hope not," Danielle scolded in return. "That's my wedding dress, I'll have you know."

He knew he should have said something to appease the duchess about the sacrifice of her gown, should have at least uttered something about ensuring its safe return. But all he could do was stare…and feel his heart die a little more with each passing second.

Cordelia turned toward him with a lift of her head and pointed her chin into the air, so imperiously and so smoothly he wondered if she even realized she'd done it. "Will I do for a princess?"

He forced a smile and admitted the awful truth, "Gloriously."

Twenty-Eight

COVERED IN A TENTLIKE CAPE AND HOOD TO KEEP HER identity secret as long as possible, Cordelia watched out the window as the Duke of Hampton's coach rolled past the main entrance to the Palace of Westminster and stopped at the west-side corner.

The streets were filled with a crush of people here to hear her uncle's speech to Parliament, but many others who'd not be allowed inside had also gathered to be part of the historic moment. She bit her lip. How many of them were members of Scepter? How many would cry out for revolution when the moment came and proclaim that her uncle should be Britain's monarch? How many would take up arms to bring revolution by force, if necessary?

She shuddered with dread.

"I have that exact same reaction myself every time I think of entering Parliament," Clayton commented from the bench across from her and Danielle.

Of course, he would notice even that small reaction from her, she decided. He noticed everything about her. But then, he'd also come to know her better than anyone else in the world.

Danielle placed her hand on Cordelia's arm. "I'll be at your side every moment."

Cordelia took comfort in that. The duchess's husband had been a powerful officer in the British empire, second only to Wellington in respect and influence, and had become one of the most important peers in England. Everyone knew of her husband, so everyone knew of the duchess. Even Queen Charlotte couldn't have provided a better personal guard than Danielle Braddock.

"How do we slip inside?" Cordelia asked. She wanted to be as brave as Clayton claimed she was, but even she could hear her voice trembling. "Once I step out of the carriage, everyone will see me and know who I am. I'll be mobbed, and if some of those people belong to Scepter, we'll never be let inside."

"I'll create a distraction," Clayton told her. "When I do, you and the duchess will hurry inside. Try not to call attention to yourselves, and keep your cloak wrapped around you as much as possible, especially over the tiara and sash. Let the duchess do all the talking once you're inside. She knows to whom to speak and what to say."

Danielle nodded and patted Cordelia's hand.

"Tell the chamber guard that you're here for the address as special guests of the palace. You'll most likely be seated high up in the women's gallery."

"How do I stop Uncle Ernest from speaking if I'm all the way up there?"

"You don't." He leveled a no-nonsense gaze on her. "Your uncle will not step into the chamber. The men of the Armory will ensure it."

She swallowed hard at the implication behind that.

"When the time comes for his speech, you'll stand up and address the room in his absence."

She blinked. "From the women's gallery?"

"Most likely. But everyone who sees you will know exactly who you are and will listen to what you have to say, no matter where you are."

"Like a ghost rising from the graveyard, since they all think me dead," she murmured. "Where will you be?"

He shook his head. "Doesn't matter where I am. What matters is stopping Scepter."

An icy coldness moved through her. "You said you'd be arrested, possibly— No! I won't let you sacrifice yourself like that."

"It's what good soldiers do," he said quietly.

"No!" she argued vehemently, fear for him trembling in her limbs. "You serve at the pleasure of the princess, remember? And this does *not* please me at—"

He rose up from his seat, leaned across the compartment, and kissed her.

His kiss was intense, filled with longing and affection, remembrance of all they'd shared, and regret of what could never be. Cordelia fought back her sobs, not wanting her tears to be the last memory he would ever have of her.

When he finally broke the kiss and rested his forehead against hers to linger with her a precious moment longer, his eyes remained squeezed shut, and anguish darkened his face.

"I love you," she confessed in a whisper.

"You'd better." He forced a grin for her, but his teasing only broke her heart.

Then he was gone, throwing open the door of the carriage and bounding down to the street. He jogged away from the coach until he stood several yards from the entrance, then belted out in song at the top of his lungs—

"This was the charter! The charter of the land!" His loud voice reverberated off the buildings. "And guardian a-a-angels sang this strain!"

The milling crowd froze in surprise, then all turned to gape.

"Rule, Britannia! Britannia, rule the waves!" Seeking even more attention, he jumped onto a set of steps and waved his arms high above his head. "Britons never, never, never will be slaves!"

"Now!" Danielle latched onto Cordelia's arm and pulled her from the carriage and away from the bewildered crowd who were all craning their necks to see what was happening on the steps and laughing at the spectacle. She sped Cordelia toward a small west-side door.

Cordelia paused to look back at Clayton, desperate for a glimpse of him. But all she could see were guards and yeomen warders rushing toward him to arrest him and the crowd closing in around him. Someone grabbed his arms and yanked him from the steps, and he disappeared in the crush.

"Clayton!" she cried.

"Hush!" Danielle scolded and pulled her inside the chapel attached to the palace. "The only way to help him now is to do exactly as he ordered. Understand?"

"Yes." But this time, Cordelia didn't nod dutifully. Instead, she hurried on with grim determination.

"The great hall is this way," Danielle told her and guided her through the chapel and into a maze of small anterooms and narrow passages beyond. "It's the largest hall in the palace—the largest in Europe, I've heard," she prattled out to distract Cordelia. "It's used for special occasions when both houses of Parliament gather together. It has plenty of space for large crowds and none of that constitutional messiness of when and if a monarch can enter Parliament."

"How convenient," Cordelia mumbled and kept her cape pulled closely around her to hide as much of her costume as possible, yet she kept glancing over her shoulder.

"Don't worry about Clayton," the duchess told her in a low voice. "He's the most resourceful man I know. If we play our parts today, he'll be just fine."

"And if we don't?"

"He will be just fine," she repeated, but this time, she didn't look at Cordelia. "There! A guard." She pointed at a yeoman warder standing at the chamber's rear entrance. "Put a smile in place, Your Highness. It's time to make your stage debut."

Cordelia's pulse spiked as Danielle led her up to the guard.

The young duchess gave him her prettiest smile and waved a hand casually to indicate Cordelia. "We're here to attend today's address. Can you please show us to the ladies' gallery?"

"No, ma'am." He shook his head and remained firmly in the center of the entrance, blocking their way. "No ladies are allowed into the hall today. Important government business is to be discussed." He gave them a patronizing cluck of his tongue for overstepping their places. "Wouldn't want to distress you ladies with all that talk of politics."

The duchess's smile never faltered, although her fingernails dug into Cordelia's arm with suppressed anger. "I am afraid you are mistaken, sir," she corrected. "We are special guests of Prince Ernest of Monrovia. If there is no ladies' gallery today, then show us to the box for the palace's guests."

The man shook his head. "'Fraid I can't do that, ma'am." He nodded behind them at the way they'd come. "Best to leave 'fore the gentlemen throw a fuss at seeing you here."

Cordelia steeled herself for the duchess's fingers to sink even deeper into her arm. Instead, Danielle pulled her spine ramrod straight. The look she leveled on the guard could have cut glass.

"Sir, I am Her Grace, Danielle, Duchess of Hampton." That did little to impress the old soldier until she added, "The wife of General Marcus Braddock, Duke of Hampton. I am certain you have heard of *him*."

He paled. "I'm—I'm sorry, ma—Your Grace." He nodded deferentially with an expression of acute confusion. "But no ladies of any rank are allowed inside the hall today. No ladies at all!"

Danielle's mouth pressed into an irritated line. "Then may I call your attention to my companion? She's here to support her uncle." She gestured at Cordelia. "Her Serene Highness Princess Cordelia of Monrovia."

Taking her cue—and a deep, steadying breath—Cordelia

pushed back her hood to reveal the diamond tiara and dropped her cloak to the marble floor.

The guard's eyes nearly popped out of his head.

"Now, sir," Cordelia ordered gently, "please show us to our seats inside the hall."

He didn't move, except for his mouth, which opened and closed like a gasping fish's. "I—I'm—I…" He swallowed hard and looked around him for reinforcements. Spotting a chamber usher, he held up his finger. "One moment, Your Princess—I mean, Your Highness."

He darted across the hall to the usher and grabbed frantically at the man's arm. He pointed back at the two women as he conferred quickly with the usher, whose brows nearly shot off his forehead in surprise.

Cordelia kept her face calm, but her heart pounded a fierce tattoo against her ribs. Dear God, she was going to faint!

"Steady," Danielle ordered. "We're almost inside. Just one moment more."

The usher's surprise dissolved. He gave the guard a confident nod and moved him aside to approach the two ladies. He bowed low from the waist.

"Your Highness and Your Grace." He clapped his hands together with a beaming smile. "Welcome to Westminster Palace."

"Thank you." Danielle sniffed in false pique at the guard's earlier failure to recognize them.

Cordelia feigned the haughty superiority that ran in royal blood and ignored him.

"I deeply apologize for any confusion and inconvenience. The palace didn't send word that they would be inviting special guests," he explained deferentially. "So we don't have separate seating arranged for you at this time. But if you would please come with me, I'll make you comfortable while you wait for it to be set up. Then I will personally seat you inside the hall myself, if I may do the honor."

Cordelia nodded, then pointed at the floor at her feet. She hated behaving this way! But she had to present what most people expected—royal rudeness. "My cloak."

The usher apologized for the oversight and picked up the pile of cloth. Folding it over his arm, he gestured politely toward the interior corridor that ran beside the great hall and the series of offices and anterooms leading from it.

Playing her part, Cordelia walked as regally as possible in the direction he indicated, not waiting for Danielle, who trailed after a step behind.

"The Office of the Exchequer," he announced as he guided them toward an oak-paneled door. "Today, it's serving as our ready room."

He opened the door with a flourish. Cordelia swept past him and into the room.

She froze. "Marie."

The comtesse startled. Her shocked face paled, and she stared at Cordelia as if she were seeing a ghost. But then, Cordelia considered, she *was* seeing exactly that.

"Cordelia, y-you're...alive." She shrank against the clerk's desk behind her. "But that—that's impossible! The men said they'd killed you..."

Cordelia frowned. "What men?"

"The men at the town house." The comtesse blinked hard, then shook her head to clear it. "The guards—the ones who found your tiara. We believed you'd been kidnapped and killed because I knew you'd never part with it otherwise."

More proof that Marie saw her only as a princess and not the true woman within. Proof that Marie didn't know her at all.

"Oh, thank God they were wrong!"

Recovering herself with a wide smile, Marie hurried across the room and threw her arms around Cordelia. The comtesse pulled her tightly against her and rested her cheek against Cordelia's, pausing a moment to catch back her breath, calm herself, and not give way to her emotions.

"I'm all right," Cordelia assured her.

"We were all so certain you were dead," Marie whispered. "So certain…"

"I'm sorry to disappoint you," Cordelia said, but her teasing fell flat. No matter. She was inside Parliament. Soon, she would play her part, just as Clayton wanted.

The comtesse stepped away and dropped an assessing look over her from tiara to toes. It wasn't approval of her appearance that Cordelia read on her face. It was annoyance. "You tried so very hard to look like a proper princess, didn't you? But no matter. What's done is done."

Before Cordelia could reply, Marie linked their arms and led her through the front reception area toward the exchequer's main office in the back of the suite of rooms. Danielle followed respectfully at a distance.

The usher bowed and left to head back to his original post, his duty to the ladies now over.

"But why are you *here*, Cordelia?" Marie frowned. "Why didn't you go to the palace and see your uncle?"

Because the men of the Armory have most likely already surrounded him. Because I have to stop him before anyone else is hurt. Because Clayton protected me... "Because I came directly here for his address."

"You shouldn't be here." Marie opened the inner door and led Cordelia inside. Then she paused and hissed in a low voice, "You'll ruin everything."

Marie slammed shut the door and threw the lock. Then she leaned back against it so Cordelia couldn't open it and escape.

"What are you doing?" Cordelia demanded. From the other side, Danielle began to knock at the door, then tried the handle. "Open the door."

"No." Fury burned in her old friend's eyes.

Cordelia lifted her chin and pointed at the door. "Open that door this instant and let the Duchess of Hampton inside. I order you!"

But Marie didn't move to step out of the way. On the other side of the door, the frantic pounding increased like drums as Danielle shouted for Cordelia.

"That would not be prudent." Her uncle's voice came from behind Cordelia and slithered down her spine like icy fingers.

Her breath strangled in her throat. Not daring to look behind her, she whispered, "Uncle Monrovia."

He laughed, took her shoulders, and turned her to face him. "Not for long. Soon I will also be Uncle Britain." His face fell with exaggerated emotion. "Oh, but that's right. You'll never be able to call me that because you won't be alive when it happens." Hatred laced his voice. "Because you *can't* be alive for it to happen."

His betrayal pierced her. In the dark corners of her heart, she had still wanted Clayton and the men of the Armory to be wrong. A part of her still wanted to believe that her uncle loved her like a daughter. That last, dark hope shattered.

Cordelia darted toward the door and shoved the comtesse aside. Her hands fumbled to release the lock. She had to escape—she *had* to!

Ernest grabbed her arms to yank her away, but she clung to the door handle. "Danielle," she screamed at the top of her lungs. "Help me!"

The pounding stopped.

The abrupt silence rattled Cordelia's bones, and she sagged forward against the door, even as Marie's traitorous hand clamped over the lock to keep her from opening it.

"The duchess won't be able to save you," her uncle told her so matter-of-factly that it chilled her. "You're causing all kinds of problems for me, Cordelia. Your entire life, nothing but one problem after another... Why couldn't you have simply died like you were supposed to?"

She squeezed her eyes shut as terror rose inside her.

He stood so close behind her that she felt his hot breath tickle the back of her neck. "I would have been next in line after the Hanoverians. I could have blamed the British royal family's incompetence for your death, and in the ensuing outrage, Parliament would have called for the deposition of the current king and placed me on the throne instead—a monarch who will pay back the men who have loyally followed him with high-level positions, lands, titles. A monarch who will marry the comtesse and provide sons to continue a solid royal line, one without madness or corruption. Now you've made it all so messy for me."

A horrible realization sank through her. That was why he'd insisted she come with him on the trip, why he'd insisted the comtesse chaperone her and his own wife remain behind. He planned to rid himself of both women. Once he'd killed Cordelia and assumed the British throne, he could divorce Wilhelmina by royal decree. No one would have been able to stop him.

No one except Clayton.

"You'll never get away with this," she countered.

"Oh, but I will. You see, I have been planning this moment for years. After my speech today, my followers will call out for the removal of King George, and Parliament will place me onto the throne as their chosen monarch. A second Glorious Revolution will unfold, and our English cousins will be powerless to stop it."

"You're mad," she whispered and turned her head to glare at Marie. "Both of you!"

He laughed. "We're in England. They're used to mad monarchs here."

He grabbed her by the back of her dress and yanked her away from the door.

Cordelia stumbled on her weak ankle, only for Marie to catch her before she could fall. Cordelia ripped her arm away in fury. "Do *not* touch me!"

"That's no way to speak to your new aunt and queen of England," her uncle chastised. Then he mockingly corrected, "But you won't be alive for that either."

Cordelia retreated toward the far end of the large office. Her uncle stalked her slowly toward the massive desk in the rear of the room. There was no second door to flee through, only an old leaded-glass window she'd never be able to open or break through.

The only way out was through her uncle and the comtesse. She swallowed down her fear that she would never be able to rush past them and escape and slowly began to circle the desk, hoping he would follow.

"You're Scepter," she accused in a breathless rasp. "I know what you are and what you've done!"

"So clever of me, don't you think?" He paused to smile in admiration at his own designs. "I formed Scepter years ago when your father discovered I'd stolen funds from the Monrovian military."

She halted in midstep. "But—but you—" The world tilted beneath her, and her hand darted out to the desk to steady herself. "You told me it was Papa who…" She couldn't think through the fog of fear and confusion swirling inside her head.

"I lied."

That was why Ernest had to kill her, she realized, why he couldn't simply use her father's misdeeds to have her removed from the line of succession. If he'd tried, he would have been pointing the evidence right back at himself.

He clucked his tongue. "Poor Cordelia, always so gullible and trusting, always so eager to put duty before all else." He shrugged a shoulder. "I've never had that problem. But then, I'm not a weak and frightened woman."

Oh, he was wrong! Clayton had made her realize exactly how brave she was, and she refused to cower. She tightened her hands into fists and straightened her spine.

He continued to pace slowly after her around the room, and she prayed she could come close enough to the door to try to sprint for it.

"I was tired of having to beg my older brother and the Crown Council for my allowance and any position of power, no matter how slight," he explained coldly. "So I took matters into my own hands. You can't fault me for that."

"You caused the death of Monrovian soldiers and sailors!"

"Who would have died in battle anyway," he justified. "It was inevitable. Why not have some good come of it?"

"*Good?*" Dear God, she was going to be sick! "You're a monster!"

"I'm a realist," he shot back. "It was your father who lived in a fairy-tale fantasy about princes being just and caring rulers. When Reginald learned what I'd done, he insisted that I admit to my crimes before the Crown Council and resign from my royal offices. His mistake was giving me time to put my affairs in order while he visited Italy. Thank God he never returned." His eyes gleamed wickedly. "When I became ruling prince, I began to think bigger. Why settle for only one throne when I could have two? The British tired of their mad and corrupt royals long ago, and they will welcome a better alternative. The death of Princess Charlotte and her son only worked to speed plans along."

"No!" She shook her head, summoning all her courage to defy him. "I won't let you do this!"

"Who is going to stop me? You?" He laughingly sneered, "Or that undersecretary of yours, the same man I plan on blaming for your murder?"

Her gaze darted toward the door. It was so close that she began to think she might be able to escape. But the hallway was impossibly silent. *Where* were the guards?

"The only thing standing between the British throne and me was you, Cordelia." His face contorted with hatred as he snarled, "And you still are."

He lunged. He grabbed her by the shoulders and tossed her onto her back on the large desk. Then he leaned over her, his hands clamping around her throat.

Cordelia grabbed at his wrists to push his hands away, but he was too strong. The most she could do was kick at him with her knees and struggle beneath him to free herself, but it wasn't enough. Already, she fought to breathe, and her throat constricted. Black spots flashed before her eyes. But she wouldn't surrender—she *wouldn't*!

She let go of his wrists and began to strike at his face, clawing with her fingernails and jabbing at his eyes with her thumbs.

He arched himself away, but his hold on her throat remained as strong as ever.

Her arms fell away and hit the desk, which was covered with writing instruments and files. She reached desperately for whatever she could grab. *Something* had to be there, something she could use as a weapon or—

Her hand touched a short, sharp object. Her fingers closed tightly around it.

The office door crashed open, shattering the frame and slamming back against the wall. Startled, Ernest looked up in surprise.

Cordelia let out a fierce cry and struck with the silver letter opener. The sharp blade sliced through his clothes and into his soft belly.

Ernest howled in pain and staggered back. Hatred burned from him, and he ran toward her even as scarlet blood seeped from his wound.

A large body hurled through the air and plowed into Ernest, throwing him backward against the stone wall.

"Clayton!" she cried hoarsely from her burning throat, her relief so great that she crumpled onto the desk.

She winced with each hard punch that Clayton pummeled into her uncle. Behind her at the door stood Danielle and two of the men from the Armory…and the comtesse, attempting to slip out the door.

Cordelia cried, "Stop her!"

With an angry glare, Danielle stepped in front of Marie and blocked her way. "Going somewhere, Comtesse?" The duchess pointed at a chair near the wall and ordered, "Sit."

Seething with rage, Marie sank onto the chair.

But it was Clayton who filled Cordelia with fear. He

continued to pound Ernest with his fists even as her uncle fell back helplessly against the wall and sank to the floor, even as he lay on the floor and whimpered beneath Clayton's furious onslaught.

She pushed herself off the desk and grabbed his right arm as he pulled back yet again for another crushing blow. "Clayton, no!"

He stopped. His lungs heaved hard with exertion, and he gasped for both breath and control as he looked over his shoulder at her.

"Don't kill him," she pleaded.

She slid her hand down his arm and laced her fingers through his. He couldn't swing another punch without yanking her with it.

"You are not your father. You're not capable of murder." She blinked back the stinging tears. "You are a man filled with goodness and mercy, even to those who don't deserve it. That's why I love you."

She led him a few feet away from her uncle, then stepped into his embrace.

He wrapped his arms fiercely around her. "Cordelia," he whispered and buried his face in her hair. "Did that bastard hurt you?"

"I'll be fine." And she would be. As long as he was with her.

He blew out a long breath of relief, then signaled for the two men in the doorway. Merritt Rivers and Brandon Pearce hurried forward and roughly detained her uncle. In the corridor beyond the door, Cordelia could see over a half dozen guards.

"Take him to St James's Palace and wait there with him," Clayton ordered. "Do *not* let him out of your sight. Lord Sidmouth and the prince regent will decide what to do with him."

Cordelia turned her head away, unable to watch the man she'd once loved like a second father be dragged from the room.

Only when she felt Clayton's lips at her temple did she turn back. The love and concern shining in his eyes for her nearly broke her.

"I thought I'd lost you," she whispered. "I saw the guards close in on you, and I thought…" Her voice trailed off. She couldn't bring herself to say it… *I thought you'd been killed.* "How did you slip away?"

"I wrote to the Home Secretary and to the captain of the Palace Guard when you were being dressed at Charlton Place. The Home Office knew what I'd planned. I just prayed they'd support me instead of shooting me. Thank God, they did." He grimaced. "That is, after several minutes of argument and fisticuffs." He tenderly caressed his knuckles across her cheek with his left hand. "And now you and I have to make certain Ernest can never hurt you or anyone else again."

She pulled in a deep breath and nodded, knowing what he meant. Their fight had just begun.

He took her hand and led her toward Westminster Hall.

Twenty-Nine

CLAYTON TIGHTENED HIS FINGERS IN CORDELIA'S AS HE led her up to the side door of the great chamber. Two guards blocked their way. Their gazes noted the splotches of blood on his shirtfront and sleeves from the fight and the faint red smudges that had gotten onto her dress when he'd held her in his arms, but they were both well-trained enough to say nothing and simply held their ground.

"Step aside for Her Serene Highness Princess Cordelia of Monrovia," Clayton ordered. "Her Highness is here to address the chamber in her uncle's stead. Step aside and let us pass."

The two guards exchanged uncertain looks, then glanced at Cordelia. The two men froze with recognition. Quickly, they bowed their heads and stepped back.

Clayton threw open the old oak double doors and charged inside with Cordelia before she could lose her courage. Too much depended on this moment to stop now. He prayed that the brave woman she'd always shown herself to be wouldn't falter.

The side door led into the heart of the hall. He pulled her into the middle of the floor before she could realize exactly how large the crowd was around her, before she could freeze like a doe before the hounds.

She stopped in the center of the grand hall and swung her gaze across the room. Hundreds of men sat crammed inside, from chairs on the floor to tall galleries reaching into the wooden rafters high above. Her face paled, but she made no attempt to grab back Clayton's hand as he slowly slipped it from hers and stepped away.

She needed to be the center of attention and the focus of an empire, had to charge into the fray by herself. *Please, God, give her the courage to get through this…*

Then he took a deep breath, cupped his hands around his mouth, and shouted at the top of his lungs, "Her Serene Highness Princess Cordelia of Monrovia!" He paused, then shouted again, "Your attention on Her Serene Highness!"

A hush of disbelief slowly settled over the room as, one by one, the men realized who she was…the princess, alive and well, standing regally before them.

All members of Parliament from both houses stared openmouthed and stunned, with the lords in their ermine and the commons in their long black tails, along with hundreds of other government officials, all dressed in grim blacks and grays. Military officers in their bright reds and blues sat scattered throughout the room. And in her white and silver gown in their midst, the princess stood out like an angel cast into the darkness of hell. Fitting, as she was now England's only salvation.

As she stood there silently, not yet addressing the hall, the disbelief of the crowd turned into whispers that went up in waves. Angry confusion followed, then shouts and curses. Clayton saw her flinch, her shoulders slump—

She looked pleadingly at him for help.

But he could offer only one means of support… "I love you," he mouthed.

The words visibly transformed her. A sparkle lit her eyes and her back straightened as she once again became the imperious princess that was her birthright. This time when she swept her eyes over the great hall, she cast a disdainful expression at having to lift her hand to ask for silence so she could speak.

But Scepter's men kept shouting out to have her removed, to bring in the prince. They wouldn't let her speak—

"My uncle is not able to address you today," she called out over their voices, not letting them shout her from the hall. The more raucous the crowd became, the stronger grew the determination on her face. "Therefore, I am here to speak on behalf of the royal principality of Monrovia."

More shouts echoed through the hall for her to leave, which only raised the princess's hackles.

She shouted back with all the imperial indignation she could muster, "I *demand* your attention!"

Her fierce shout captured the attention of the room, and the men had no choice but to fall silent, even Scepter's pawns, as they were shouted down by others who wanted to hear what Cordelia had to say. For all their numbers and influence, they couldn't control a room this size, and Clayton took hope in that.

Apparently, so did Cordelia. "I am here to announce to you that the reign of the house of Renaldi has ended in Monrovia. Further, we give up all claims of succession to the British throne."

Surprised gasps went up around the hall, followed by bewildered mumblings.

She continued over the grumblings, "I speak for myself, for my uncle Monrovia, and for our entire family."

Clayton kept his eyes fixed on the princess. She was being propelled along by sheer bravado and by her duty to her country. He'd never seen her more courageous.

Buoyed up by the surprised reactions, she walked slowly toward the raised dais at the end of the hall where sat a gold throne, the same throne used by the monarch for the opening of Parliament and the coronation ceremonies. It was a clear reminder of history and tradition and a firm statement of the strength of the British constitution.

"As you can see, I am unharmed, and neither the Home Office, the palace guards, nor my royal cousins should be blamed for any attempts of violence toward my person." Her gaze darted toward Clayton. "*No one* should be blamed."

She stepped onto the dais and held out her arms as she turned in a slow circle so everyone present could see that she was fine. More than that, Clayton decided as he moved down the hall to stand at the edge of the dais to be closer to her, she was simply magnificent.

She cast an imperial glance around the room, one that reached clear up to the men in the upper galleries and far back into the corners. "Monrovia throws its full support behind His Majesty King George the Third, Queen Charlotte, our cousin the prince regent, and all the royal dukes and princesses." She lowered her voice and muttered so quietly that only Clayton could hear, "Well, perhaps not *all* of them…"

Clayton cleared his throat to fight down a laugh.

"I want to be very clear today as I address the representatives of Great Britain, its military heroes, the finest of its gentlemen, and its leaders of tomorrow." She paused to emphasize her words. "Both my uncle and I will refuse all calls to bestow upon us Great Britain's crown, its orb…"

She picked up a banner hanging from a stand on the dais that showed the Monrovian coat of arms with its gold key, and she ripped it in two.

"And especially its *scepter*!"

⸻

A thunderous cry echoed through the great hall, followed by the pounding of fists and feet, but Cordelia kept her back impossibly straight, her head held high. Never had she been forced to make a performance like this before in her life. But she could *not* fail.

She held up her hand to silence them. She wasn't yet finished.

"I also announce to you today that my uncle Monrovia has abdicated the throne of Monrovia," she continued, putting voice to her most hopeful wishes, even if they weren't true. *Yet.* "Our entire family will rescind our royal duties and status as a way to counter the wrongs committed by my uncle that you shall surely hear of in the days to come—"

When the crowd around her began to call out, she held out her hands in a plea for quiet so she could continue.

"And the Crown Council of Monrovia will quickly

appoint a new reigning prince," she shouted over the growing noise of disbelief and shock among the crowd, "one worthy of our friendship with Great Britain, one worthy of leading Monrovia into the future while also honoring its past."

She reached up with trembling hands to remove the tiara. She stared at it in her hands. It wasn't hers, yet all it represented remained the same. *How heavy it was*... How had she never noticed before the sheer weight of it?

She pulled in a deep, ragged breath and summoned what was left of her courage. She had one more announcement to make. One *very* important announcement.

"Today, I entered Westminster Palace as a princess royal to address you on behalf of my country. Now I leave you as..."

Her courage finally failed her, and her voice trailed off.

"As plain Jane Smith," a deep and familiar voice called out from beside the dais.

Clayton. His love for her shone in his eyes. Buoyed by this strength, she cast a beaming smile across the room and finished, "As nothing more than a dear friend of Britain and all her people."

Chaos broke loose across the great hall as everyone in the room began to talk and shout at once. The men jumped up from their seats and poured down from the galleries to crowd onto the narrow floorspace. Angry shouts of all kinds and bursts of applause echoed off the stone walls and wooden beams overhead, along with the stomping of feet and the pounding of fists on the wooden railings. Stunned confusion competed with both anger and approval, and arguments and shoving matches broke out throughout the hall.

The crowd surged toward her and engulfed her on the dais. The guards ran toward her from the edge of the room, but they weren't fast enough. In the melee, she was jostled down to the main floor and fought to remain on her feet. She could just make out a stream of men—undoubtedly Scepter loyalists—fleeing for the doors, while others hurried to her side to ingratiate themselves with her in a blatant show of support for the royals.

Caught on the current in the sea of bodies, she was swept away from the dais and into the middle of the hall. Panic surged through her. She wasn't safe here in the lion's den with enemies all around, enemies who might yet attempt to kill her even in the very heart of Parliament.

"Clayton!" She strained to see through the crowd, but she couldn't find him. Her heart raced with fear, and she desperately held up her hand above the heads of the crowd around her, like a swimmer drowning in the sea—

A gloved hand closed over hers. "I've got you, Princess."

Cordelia gave a soft cry at the rush of emotion brought on by the sight of his grin, by the mix of joy at stopping Scepter and the fear of an uncertain future.

He opened his arms, and she stepped into his embrace. He shielded her with his body from the crush that pressed in around them as he slowly walked her toward the door and safety. She lay her head against his shoulder and closed her eyes to breathe in deep the strength and solidity of him.

He had protected her again, just as she knew he would. *Always.*

Thirty

Three Days Later

CLAYTON GRIMACED WITH DISBELIEF AS HE LOOKED around the main room of the Armory and muttered a curse beneath his breath.

The building was barely more than a shell after the battle that had been waged here in Scepter's attack. The front entrance had been destroyed by explosives that had blasted to bits the twin portcullises and ripped the metal doors from their hinges. The thick outer walls still stood, but the thinner walls of the entrance hall had tumbled; so had the crenellations edging the roof. The tall tower had caved in, bringing down the gas chandelier and stairs with it, and it lay in a tumble of stones just inches from his boots. The fine rugs and leather furniture that had made the place so comfortable had been ripped to pieces and charred by the embers from the explosions. Insult had been added to injury by the torrential rains that fell shortly after the roof had, drenching the stone floor and buckling the walnut wall panels.

But it was the training room that had taken the brunt of the battle. Its display of weapons had been ripped from the walls during the heat of the fight, and all its equipment had been destroyed.

Unfortunately, the damage went beyond the building. While the aunties had escaped unharmed, several of the Armory's men had been wounded during Scepter's attack. Two of them had stab wounds to shoulders and thighs that had needed surgery to stitch up the deep cuts, and two more had arms in slings. One of them was forced to use crutches until his damaged knee could heal, and even then he might always have a limp.

But they were all alive. Clayton thanked God—and the hoard of weapons in the training room—for that. Lesser men would have been killed.

The men of the Armory had prevailed. But could the Armory itself be salvaged? Would the men even want to rebuild it now that Scepter was finally gone for good?

"Clayton," Marcus called out as he emerged from the basement steps. "I'm glad you were able to come to today's meeting."

"Your message was insistent."

Marcus nodded. "We have to decide what to do with this place."

A handful of men followed behind Marcus, all looking as grim as Clayton felt. The scene of destruction around them was much the same as what they'd experienced in the wars. So were their emotions. There was no triumph in victory when so much devastation accompanied it. There was only relief.

Now they all had to decide how to move on.

"Scepter's gone, the organization dead," Clayton reminded him. "We don't need a headquarters from which to fight against it anymore."

"That wasn't the reason I created this place," Marcus countered. This time, when his old friend glanced at the building around him, Clayton knew he wasn't seeing the damage but the promise of what it had once been. "I did it to give former soldiers a place of refuge when returning to their postwar lives proved too much."

"I'm not certain we need that anymore," Brandon Pearce interjected as he approached them hand in hand with his wife, Amelia. "Once, perhaps, but we've all moved on and found other purposes."

"Then perhaps this place shouldn't be only for us any longer," Merritt Rivers added. "Maybe we can put it to better use. After all, Scepter might be gone, but there are still thousands in London who need our help."

"The poor and the downtrodden," Merritt's wife, Veronica, Baroness Rivers, reminded them as she wrapped her arm around her husband's.

She shouldn't have been there, Clayton knew, not as heavy with child as she was. But he also knew she felt a special connection to the Armory and wouldn't have missed today's meeting to decide its future.

"The abused," Danielle Braddock added as she went to Marcus's side.

The former general placed an affectionate kiss to her temple, and Clayton's gut tightened as he watched them. He wanted that same closeness and love with Cordelia, the same promise of a lifetime together. But she'd been separated from him after her address in Parliament and securely ensconced in St James's Palace, waiting for her contingent to return to Monrovia. He had been turned away by the palace guards every time he'd tried to see her, including one last visit to the palace that morning.

He knew he would never have a future with her. They'd both known that truth all along. Princesses didn't marry men like him. No amount of revolution or peaceful reform would ever change that.

But damnation, he would never even have the chance to say goodbye.

"And the children," a soft voice called out from behind him at the battered entrance.

His heart leapt into his throat, and he spun around, not daring to believe… "Princess."

Her eyes locked with his for a moment. Then she smiled with embarrassment as the men all bowed and the women curtsied at her arrival. She shook her head in a gesture for them to forgo all obeisances as she stepped slowly into the main room.

"I hope you can help children," she explained. "They often have no one to support them, especially the orphans and foundlings."

Clayton said nothing, unable to do anything more than stare and attempt to convince himself that she wasn't a ghost. Or an angel. *Sweet Lucifer*, she looked simply stunning, even in a plain muslin day dress and wrap, without both tiara and sash.

How much he'd missed her hit him like a punch to the

gut. How would he ever be able to recover once she was gone from England and completely removed from his life?

"Then I think we're agreed that our work here isn't done," Marcus announced to the group, "and that the Armory will rise from the ashes."

A cheer went up from the group, and Cordelia beamed a smile at the decision, albeit a nervous one, as her eyes returned to Clayton. This time, she didn't look away.

Around them, the women corralled the men toward the training room under the pretense of discussing repairs, leaving Clayton and Cordelia alone.

His chest tightened with an unbearable ache. The time to say goodbye had finally arrived.

———

Cordelia held her breath as Clayton slowly approached her. Not breaking eye contact, he took her hand in both of his and raised it to his lips for a lingering kiss. She trembled.

"What are you doing here?" he asked and squeezed her fingers as if he simply couldn't fathom that she was there.

She didn't blame him. She could barely believe it herself.

"Marcus Braddock arranged it." Instead of slipping her hand away, she curled her fingers around his. *Dear God*, how much she'd missed him! "He sent word this morning that I was needed here, along with Captain Reed and several Horse Guards to escort me. Apparently, not even the palace is willing to thwart the Duke of Hampton." She hesitated. "He also sent me your letter."

The same letter in which Clayton had confessed his love and how much she meant to him, which had made her soar with happiness...until she read the part where he told her to marry another, to find a prince she could love and build a future with, both for herself and for Monrovia. And then he'd asked for the impossible—he'd asked her to forget him.

She would do anything he asked.

Except that.

"Marcus shouldn't have done that." He dropped his gaze to the floor and slowly shook his head. "It was meant only to say goodbye if..."

She finished, "If you didn't survive. But I'm glad he did anyway." She pulled in a deep breath. "You should know... I'm no longer in consideration for marriage to a royal duke."

His eyes snapped up to hers.

"My royal cousins care nothing about me now except for ensuring that I don't die on English soil before they can send me packing to the Continent to become someone else's problem," she explained bluntly. She never would have said such a thing only weeks ago, before she'd arrived in England, before he'd entered her life. "That's why they've sequestered me in the palace. My uncle has already been exiled to Florence, along with the comtesse. He'll live out the rest of his days there, carefully guarded, and my aunt Wilhelmina will return to her family in the Netherlands."

Concern darkened his face. "And you?"

"Back to Monrovia, I suppose, at least for a few months. I'm no threat to anyone there. Until the Crown Council can name a new ruling prince, I should be there to lend my support however I can. My people need me."

"I understand."

Oh, she prayed he did! Because what she had to ask next... "I'll need a trustworthy guard to protect me while I travel. Do you happen to know of anyone you could recommend?" she asked, far more nervously than the teasing question implied. "Perhaps a brave and clever soldier? It would be helpful, I think, if he were also a viscount."

Yet instead of grinning as she'd hoped, he grimly shook his head. "I don't think my peerage will be coming now that I've single-handedly scuttled the royal dukes' plans for a convenient marriage."

"I haven't properly thanked you for that. Yet I think I should—now, and every day for the rest of my life."

Instead of chuckling at her quip, he only grew even more somber.

"I can't go with you to Monrovia," he said, and each quiet word tore into her heart. "We are still who we are, and I could never bear to part with you once we reached the end of the journey."

She slipped her hand away from his and placed it on his chest, right over his heart. She couldn't bear to part from him either. Perhaps she wouldn't have to. *Perhaps...* "You could stay in Monrovia." Her fingers curled into his waistcoat. "With me."

"And continue to serve as your personal guard while you marry a prince? No." His eyes filled with grief. "That's a hell I never want us to suffer."

"Then it's a good thing we don't have to."

His solemn expression never changed. "Only if you want a husband and children, and I know how much you do. The Crown Council will never allow you to marry someone they don't choose, and if you marry without their blessing, your children will be removed from the line of succession."

"That doesn't matter anymore. I won't be forced into a marriage I don't want, no matter what my family or the Crown Council orders me to do. Tradition dictates that I'm the one who has to propose, and I will never propose to a man who doesn't love me." She straightened her spine with resolve. "To hell with princes and kings and dukes! I'm completely done with the lot of them."

"What are you saying, Princess?"

"That's exactly it. I'm not—" She paused to gather her courage, but her words emerged as barely more than a whisper, "I'm not a princess anymore. Or at least not as I was."

Even from a foot away, she felt him tense. "Because of what you said to Parliament?"

"More than that."

When his eyes narrowed on her as he tried to understand, she dropped her hand away and stepped back. She needed to think clearly to explain herself, and she could never do that if she kept touching him. For heaven's sake, just the sight of him sent her mind whirling. She prayed to God it always would.

"I will always be the daughter of a monarch, but—" She fought to control her shaking hands. "But I am resigning my royal duties and refusing all allowances and royal privileges."

His expression remained inscrutable, yet he remained as still as a statue as the ramifications for her—for *them*—sank over him.

He stared at her for a very long time before carefully asking, "Can you do that? Or will the Crown Council refuse to accept your resignation and force you to continue your duties?"

"I don't think they can." She bit her lip. "But no one's ever willingly walked away from being part of a ruling royal family before. I don't think anyone knows what to do, least of all me." That familiar pang of fear and uncertainty struck again. So did determination. "But I'm adamant about it. I no longer want to be a princess. I've spent the last three days writing letters announcing my decision to officials in Monrovia and notifying all the European heads of state." Her mouth twisted with irritation. "And arguing with Princess Sophia, who thinks I'm making a grand mistake."

He asked cautiously, "Are you?"

She wasn't at all certain. The thought of no longer being a princess both thrilled and terrified her. Her life would have a new future for which she hadn't at all been prepared, and she had no idea what she would do to make her way. She had no idea on whom she could depend or who her friends were, no idea how she would live or where…

But her future might also have Clayton, if he still wanted her now that she was no longer a princess. With him at her side, she could do anything.

"*Everything* will change for me," she warned. "I have nothing of my own. No lands, no castles, no titles—no dowry of any kind except whatever my cousins feel piteous enough to bestow upon me, which is likely to be not much at all." She frowned. "But I'll have scandal in spades to pack into my trunks."

She paused to let the severity of that register on both of them.

"Despite all that," she continued, so nervous she couldn't stop shaking, "do you think it's possible that you might still want to be with me?" She was unsure of herself, of her future…of everything except her love for him. She blurted out, "Clayton Elliott, will you marry me?"

He answered quietly, "You can't ask me that."

Her mouth fell open as her heart began to shatter—

"You're not a princess anymore, remember? Proposing is *my* pleasure." He knelt in front of her and took her hand. "Will *you* marry *me*, Cordelia?" He brought her hand to his lips and kissed her palm. "Say yes, love, and to hell with—what was it?—princes and kings and dukes…to hell with anyone who dares try to keep us apart."

"Oh yes." A tear slipped down her cheek. "Yes!"

She rushed down into his arms, and he sat back on the floor and pulled her against him.

"Then yes, Princess," he murmured, resting his cheek against her hair. "I will marry you."

She let out a sob of utter happiness, and her arms tightened around his shoulders. Her future would be filled with love and hope, and she knew she would finally find a meaningful purpose for her life. With him.

Yet one thing still troubled her.

"I'm frightened of the future," she confessed. "I've only ever been a princess, always protected and pampered, never allowed to make any decisions on my own, and always required to put duty before all else. I don't know what to do. I can't be a princess anymore." Then she admitted, barely louder than a whisper, "But I don't think I can ever be plain Jane Smith either."

"You don't have to be anyone but yourself," he assured her. "Because now you're simply the woman I love."

Happiness swelled inside her, and she blinked back tears as she choked out, "There's no one I'd rather be."

Epilogue

Somerset, England
One Year Later

CLAYTON LOOKED UP FROM HIS PAPERS AND GLANCED out the window of his office as a commotion rose from the front lawn.

A messenger in palace livery galloped up the drive, reined his horse to a stop at the portico, and dropped to the ground. He handed over a small satchel to the butler who went out to greet him. Then he mounted his horse and charged away as quickly as he'd arrived.

"That can't be good," Clayton muttered and pushed himself to his feet. He'd learned over the past year that the best way to deal with British royals was to keep them as far away as possible. He pulled in a deep breath as a knock sounded at his door. "Come."

Instead of the butler, Cordelia sailed into the room. She held out the satchel to him.

He placed a kiss to her cheek. She was the only royal he loved to see and the one he wanted to keep close at his side for the rest of their lives.

"A dispatch from London," she announced. "From the palace. What do you think it could be?"

God only knows. He leaned back against his desk, casually crossed his ankles, and drawled, "Your cousins have decided to leave England to us and move to the south of France?"

"Wishful thinking." With a laugh, she leaned up and kissed him.

Then she handed him the satchel and bounced away with a glowing brightness that lit the room.

He didn't think it was possible to love her any more than he already did. Yet every new day proved him wrong.

She was simply lovely. He supposed that was what love and joy—and freedom—did to a person. Even as she craned her neck to look out the window at the group of children playing on the lawn, her face shone with pride at the home they'd created here for themselves and the children whose lives they were working to save.

Clayton had to give her credit. She'd adapted well to country life in England after their return from Monrovia six months ago, when she'd officially abdicated her royal duties and resigned her designation as Her Serene Highness. Her visit to Monrovia hadn't been easy, with half its people wanting her to stay and the other half calling for her exile.

Thank goodness, Lady Devereaux and her husband had come to her aid. Neither of them had been caught up in Ernest's evil machinations, and they were just as shocked as the rest of Monrovia to learn the truth—and determined to help their country weather the storm. The hard-nosed woman with the demeanor of a drill sergeant was exactly what the principality needed. She'd become the assistant for the new princess consort and served as Lord Devereaux's right hand in his new role of making reparations for Prince Ernest's embezzlement. They were further helped by Cordelia herself, who handed over her family's personal wealth and those properties not entailed to the crown.

Making right what Ernest had done would take a long time, but the new sovereign prince and Crown Council were both dedicated to it.

When the Council put her second cousin Albert on the throne, Cordelia made her decision to leave. She wanted to give her cousin the space to rule in his own way without being haunted by any ghosts from the past, and she wanted a new home in England to go with her new future.

Now, instead of a princess, she'd become a patroness. Together, they ran a home for children in need on the country estate Clayton received as part of his viscountcy, which the regent grudgingly granted after all. Clayton resigned his position at the Home Office and gave up all chance of becoming Home Secretary. He never looked back. That part of his life was over. He had a new future waiting for him.

"Maybe they're rescinding their blessing on our marriage," she commented. "And the dowry my cousin the regent gave me." She sent him a knowing look. "Did you really blackmail George into giving us his permission to marry?"

He grinned. "Yes, I did."

The regent's blessing was delivered personally to their wedding at St George's in Mayfair by Lord Sidmouth, the Home Secretary, who had *not* been invited to the small ceremony. But neither man truly had a choice after Clayton threatened to strike the regent where it would hurt most if the blessing wasn't given—his princely pride. Clayton had to admit that the Home Office was good for providing secret information…including that the Prince of Wales's famous London to Brighton four-in-hand drive in just over four hours had actually been a cheat. Prinny couldn't care less what people thought of his marriage or his mistresses, but his reputation as a skilled driver… *That* he would never surrender.

Oh, he and Cordelia would have married regardless. Nothing could have stopped them. But having a royal blessing made their life together much easier, both here and in Monrovia, where they planned to eventually create a second home. Even though she was no longer a princess, her country still needed her, and she still needed it.

Her eyes darted to the satchel, and he knew she was beyond curious to learn what was inside. "Aren't you going to open it?" She bit her bottom lip. "It's probably important."

"No hurry." He bit back a smile at her expense and tossed it onto the desk with the rest of his work supporting the estate.

He'd once feared country life as a landowner, with its mundane chores and responsibilities. Now, he reveled in it because of Cordelia, the children, and their shared mission. Dealing with matters of estate repairs, tenant farmers, and livestock no longer bothered him since he knew it had a greater purpose. Neither did arguing in Parliament since he'd become a firebrand for reform, not caring that his views alienated him from most of the *ton*. He had his friends at the Armory, he had his work on the estate, and he had Cordelia. He needed nothing else.

"How has your day been?" he asked, purposefully growing her curious agitation at the dispatch by ignoring the satchel. "Good news from the dairy and barns? Any word from the tenant farmers about their plantings? Been to the mercantile to see the new ribbons?"

She placed her hands on her hips. "Clayton Elliott, if you don't—"

In one motion, he shoved himself away from the desk, wrapped her in his arms, and kissed her until she melted bonelessly against him.

"We'll open it together, shall we, Lady Elliott?" he murmured and caressed her cheek.

She shifted back to look up at him, and her bright expression darkened as a thought struck her. "Do you think the dispatch is about Scepter?"

"No."

Scepter was dead and gone, and this time for good, its monster's head completely cut off. The men of the Armory and the Home Office were both certain the group had been routed from England with Prince Ernest's exile, and its staunchest followers had fled to the Continent or resigned their positions in Whitehall and the military. They would never call for revolution again.

"If it were anything about Scepter," he assured her, "Marcus would have sent it."

Still, there was no point in waiting to read it. He picked

up the satchel and untied it. He withdrew a message on white linen paper, sealed with red wax, and imprinted with the royal crest. He recognized the handwriting and frowned.

"This is far worse than Scepter." He held it up. "It's from your cousin the regent."

Her curiosity reached its breaking point, and she snatched the letter from his hand. "*Your* cousin now, too."

He groaned. "Don't remind me."

Wisely ignoring his grumbling, she broke the royal seal and unfolded the note.

"It's good news!" A happy smile broke across her face as she read aloud, "The palace and the Duke and Duchess of Kent and Strathearn are pleased to announce the birth of their first child…a daughter named Alexandrina Victoria."

"That *is* good news." This was the second child born to one of the royal dukes since their mad scramble to marry and produce legitimate heirs—helped along less by a sense of duty for the monarchy than by financial incentives from parliament. The country had let out a collective sigh of relief earlier that spring when Prince Adolphus, Duke of Cambridge, welcomed his son George into the world—and into the line of succession. This second child, with another soon to come from Prince Ernest Augustus, Duke of Cumberland, would ensure the continuation of the House of Hanover on the British throne.

More important, though, with every additional royal baby, Cordelia's claim to the monarchy sank farther away. She would be allowed to spend the rest of her life however she chose.

He came up behind her and slipped his arms around her waist, then placed a tender kiss to her nape.

She stiffened as she read the rest of the letter. "Uh-oh." She looked over her shoulder at him in cold warning. "You're not going to like this."

That could not be good. "What is it?"

"My cousin has finally gotten around to giving us his belated wedding gift." Her expression turned grim. "He's making you a duke."

Christ! Clayton took the letter and scanned it.

His shoulders sagged, and he muttered as he reread his punishment, "Why, that worthless, drunken, philandering sack of—"

"Royal cousin," she interrupted with a pointed reminder.

He blew out a harsh breath and threw the letter onto the desk. "Can we refuse it?"

"Not if we want to stay in England." She placed her hand against his cheek. "And I do want to stay here. This is our home now."

"Yes, *Your Grace*," he grumbled. He would do whatever made her happy. Even this. Yet he ran his hand through his hair in disbelief. "Damnation…I'm going to be a blasted duke."

She laughed and rose up onto tiptoes to kiss him. When she reached to retrieve the letter from the desk, she stopped.

"There's more." She reached into the satchel and withdrew a stack of papers bound by string. She frowned. "What's this?"

He recognized the seals and stamps on the papers. "Home Office records."

"But you resigned. Why would any of their records be sent here?"

His gut tightened as he untied the string and looked through them, noting the dates. He knew without having to read them...

"They regard my father," he said quietly, not looking up from the papers. "All the court documents, witness accounts, diary entries, watch reports... The regent and Sidmouth finally unsealed the documents."

Cordelia placed her hand on his arm. "That's good, isn't it?"

Dread clenched his chest as he thumbed through the old pages, scanning them to understand their meaning.

"Sidmouth wants me to know the truth about my father, after all these years..." His eyes stung as he found the Home Office report and read it. "My father stumbled across the murders afterward, saw the man who committed them...a Home Office operative at the heart of their spy network. The man accused my father and made certain the evidence showed him guilty enough to hang." He choked on the words before forcing out, "The Home Office only found out after the execution that their man was involved. By then, it was too late, and they sealed the documents to protect their other operatives." He looked up at her, his eyes blurring, and choked out, "My father was innocent."

She wrapped her arms around him, and he held her tightly to him, taking comfort in her warmth and love.

"Just as you believed." She slid her mouth across his cheek to his ear and murmured, "You were right about him all along."

He nodded, unable to find his voice. The certain knowledge of his father's innocence didn't ease the pain of losing him. Nothing could ever do that. But he could at least find peace with the past now and truly honor his father's legacy.

He collected himself and stepped out of her arms. He picked up the birth announcement.

"A new princess," he said, his voice husky with emotion.

"We'll send the palace a gift right away," she decided. Then she paused. "Is it wrong of me to hope she'll have a brother or that her uncle Clarence has issue so she doesn't have to inherit the crown?"

"Not at all. But I don't think you need to worry. It's very unlikely that little Alexandrina Victoria will become queen." He carefully placed the Home Office documents into his desk drawer. There would be time later to look through them and come to terms with all of it. "What matters, though, is that the English monarchy is secured through another generation."

"A new baby…" A smile tugged at her lips. "Babies are such wonderful things. Such miracles of love, don't you think?"

She took his hand and placed it on her lower belly.

Clayton's heart stopped, and he froze. He stared at his hand on her belly, speechless.

She nervously repeated, "Don't you think…Papa?"

"Are you…you mean…" He could barely form the words. He blurted out, "We're having a baby?"

A beaming smile spread across her face. "Yes." Her eyes glistened. "I was going to tell you tonight, but the announcement from the palace seemed—"

He let out a shout, grabbed her into his arms, and lifted her off the floor to twirl her in a circle with all the love and happiness inside him.

He placed her on the desk and leaned in to bring his mouth so close to hers that her soft breath tickled across his lips. He needed her to understand exactly how much he meant it when he murmured, "I love you, Princess."

She laughed, wrapped her arms around his neck, and saucily repeated back to him his words from that fateful day in Westminster, the day that led them here. "You'd better."

With a grin, he lowered his head and kissed her.

**Read on for an excerpt from
the first book in the
Lords of the Armory series**

Prologue

April 1814

To General Marcus Braddock
Coldstream Guards, 2nd Battalion,
   Household Division
Bayonne, France

Dear General Braddock,

It is with a grieving heart that I write to you to tell you of the passing of your sister Elise.

There was a terrible accident. She was on her morning ride in the park and was thrown from her horse. The horse guards who found her assured me that she did not suffer. While there is nothing I can write that will lessen your pain, I pray you might find some comfort in that.

I know that your attention must now be fixed on your men and on the fight you are waging against Napoleon, but please be assured that I will do everything I can to support your sister Claudia and Elise's daughter, Penelope, while you are away.

Yours in shared grief—
Danielle Williams

June 1814

To the Honorable Danielle Williams
No. 2 Bedford Square, Mayfair
London, England

Dear Miss Williams,

Although the news was bitter, I thank you for your kind letter. It brings me solace to know that Elise was so dearly loved by you. I am more grateful than I can express to know that you are looking after Claudia and Pippa during this time of mourning.

With gratitude—
Marcus Braddock

January 1816

To the Honorable Danielle Williams
No. 2 Bedford Square, Mayfair
London, England

Dear Miss Williams,

My regiment's work in Paris will be ending soon, and I will be returning to London. I would very much appreciate the opportunity to call on you. I wish to thank you in person for the kindnesses that you and your aunt have shown to my family during my absence.

Yours sincerely,
Marcus Braddock

February 1816

To General Marcus Braddock
British Embassy
Hôtel de Charost, rue du Faubourg Saint-Honoré
Paris, France

Dear General,

Your appreciation is more than enough. Please do not feel obligated to call on us, as I know how busy your homecoming will surely be. I wish you the best with your new endeavors. Please give my love to Claudia and Penelope.

Yours in friendship—
Danielle Williams

April 1816

To the Honorable Danielle Williams
No. 2 Bedford Square, Mayfair
London

Dear Miss Williams,

I have returned home but discovered unsettling information regarding my sister Elise. I must insist on meeting with you. Please reply with the best day and time for me to call upon you.

Marcus Braddock

April 1816

To the General His Grace the Duke of Hampton
Charlton Place, Park Lane
London

Dear Duke,

While I wish to congratulate you on your new title, I must decline your offer to receive you. Elise was my dearest friend—in truth, more like a sister. To speak of her death will only refresh our shared grief and remind us of all that we have lost when your return should be met with joy. I could not bear it and wish to grieve for her in peace. Please understand.

Sincerely,
Danielle Williams

May 1816

To the Right Honorable the Viscountess Bromley
& the Honorable Danielle Williams
No. 2 Bedford Square
Mayfair, London

You are cordially invited to attend a birthday celebration in honor of the General His Grace the Duke of Hampton, on Saturday, May 5, at 8 p.m. Please send your acceptance to Miss Braddock, Charlton Place, Park Lane, London.

And the handwritten note tucked inside with the invitation...

Danielle, please attend. The party will not be the same without you. And to be honest, I will need your support to survive the evening. You know how Marcus can be at events like this. That it is for his own birthday will most likely make him all the worse. And Pippa misses you as much as I do.

~ Claudia

Danielle Williams bit her bottom lip as she read the note, dread and guilt pouring through her in equal measure.

God help me.

There was no refusing this invitation.

One

MARCUS BRADDOCK STEPPED OUT ONTO THE UPPER TER-
race of his town house and scanned the party spreading
through the torch-lit gardens below.

He grimaced. His home had been invaded.

All of London seemed to be crowded into Charlton Place
tonight, with the reception rooms filled to overflowing. The
crush of bodies in the ballroom had forced several couples
outside to dance on the lawn, and the terraces below were
filled with well-dressed dandies flirting with ladies adorned
in silks and jewels. Card games played out in the library, men
smoked in the music room, the ladies retired to the morning
room—the entire house had been turned upside down, the
gardens trampled, the horses made uneasy in the mews…

And it wasn't yet midnight.

His sister Claudia had insisted on throwing this party for
him, apparently whether he wanted one or not. Not only to
mark his birthday tomorrow but also to celebrate his new
position as Duke of Hampton, the title given to him for
helping Wellington defeat Napoleon. The party would help
ease his way back into society, she'd asserted, and give him

an opportunity to meet the men he would now be working with in the Lords.

But Marcus hadn't given a damn about society before he'd gone off to war, and he cared even less now.

No. The reason he'd agreed to throw open wide the doors of Charlton Place was a woman.

The Honorable Danielle Williams, daughter of Baron Mondale and his late sister Elise's dearest friend. The woman who had written to inform him that Elise was dead.

The same woman he now knew had lied to him.

His eyes narrowed as they moved deliberately across the crowd. Miss Williams had been avoiding him since his return, refusing to let him call on her and begging off from any social event that might bring them into contact. But she hadn't been able to refuse the invitation for tonight's party, not when he'd also invited her great-aunt, who certainly wouldn't have missed what the society gossips were predicting would be the biggest social event of the season. She couldn't accept and then simply beg off either. To not attend this party would have been a snub to both him and his sister Claudia, as well as to Elise's memory. While Danielle might happily continue to avoid him, she would never intentionally wound Claudia.

She was here somewhere, he knew it. Now he simply had to find her.

He frowned. Easier said than done, because Claudia had apparently invited all of society, most of whom he'd never met and had no idea who they even were. Yet they'd eagerly attended, if only for a glimpse of the newly minted duke's town house. And a glimpse of *him*. Strangers greeted him as if they were old friends, when his true friends—the men he'd served with in the fight against Napoleon—were nowhere to be seen. *Those* men he trusted with his life.

These people made him feel surrounded by the enemy.

The party decorations certainly didn't help put him at ease. Claudia had insisted that the theme be ancient Roman and then set about turning the whole house into Pompeii. Wooden torches lit the garden, lighting the way for the army of toga-clad footmen carrying trays of wine from a replica of a Roman temple in the center of the garden. The whole thing gave him the unsettling feeling that he'd been transported to Italy, unsure of his surroundings and his place in them.

Being unsure was never an option for a general in the heat of battle, and Marcus refused to let it control him now that he was on home soil. Yet he couldn't stop it from haunting him, ever since he'd discovered the letter among Elise's belongings that made him doubt everything he knew about his sister and how she'd died.

He planned to put an end to that doubt tonight, just as soon as he talked to Danielle.

"There he is—the birthday boy!"

Marcus bit back a curse as his two best friends, Brandon Pearce and Merritt Rivers, approached him through the shadows. He'd thought the terrace would be the best place to search for Danielle without being seen.

Apparently not.

"You mean the duke of honor," corrected Merritt, a lawyer turned army captain who had served with him in the Guards.

Marcus frowned. While he was always glad to see them, right then he didn't need their distractions. Nor was he in the mood for their joking.

A former brigadier who now held the title of Earl of Sandhurst, Pearce looped his arm over Merritt's shoulder as both men studied him. "I don't think he's happy to see us."

"Impossible." Merritt gave a sweep of his arm to indicate the festivities around them. The glass of cognac in his hand had most likely been liberated from Marcus's private liquor cabinet in his study. "Surely he wants his two brothers-in-arms nearby to witness every single moment of his big night."

Marcus grumbled, "Every single moment of my humiliation, you mean."

"Details, details," Merritt dismissed, deadpan. But he couldn't hide the gleam of amusement in his eyes.

"What we really want to know about your birthday party is this." Pearce touched his glass to Marcus's chest and leaned toward him, his face deadly serious. "When do the pony rides begin?"

Marcus's gaze narrowed as he glanced between the two men. "Remind me again why I saved your miserable arses at Toulouse."

Pearce placed his hand on Marcus's shoulder in a show of genuine affection. "Because you're a good man and a brilliant general," he said sincerely. "And one of the finest men we could ever call a friend."

Merritt lifted his glass in a heartfelt toast. "Happy birthday, General."

Thirty-five. *Bloody hell.*

"Hear, hear." Pearce seconded the toast. "To the Coldstream Guards!"

A knot tightened in Marcus's gut at the mention of his former regiment that had been so critical to the victory at Waterloo yet also nearly destroyed in the brutal hand-to-hand combat that day. But he managed to echo, "To the Guards."

Not wanting them to see any stray emotion on his face, he turned away. Leaning across the stone balustrade on his forearms, he muttered, "I wish I could still be with them."

While he would never wish to return to the wars, he missed being with his men, especially their friendship and dependability. He missed the respect given to him and the respect he gave each of them in return, no matter if they were an officer or a private. Most of all, he longed for the sense of purpose that the fight against Napoleon had given him. He'd known every morning when he woke up what he was meant to do that day, what higher ideals he served. He hadn't had that since he returned to London, and its absence ate at him.

It bothered him so badly, in fact, that he'd taken to spending time alone at an abandoned armory just north of the City. He'd purchased the old building with the intention of turning it into a warehouse, only to discover that he needed a place to himself more than he needed the additional income. More and more lately, he'd found himself going there at all hours to escape from society and the ghosts that haunted him. Even in his own home.

That was the punishment for surviving when others he'd loved hadn't. The curse of remembrance.

"No, General." Pearce matched his melancholy tone as his

friends stepped up to the balustrade, flanking him on each side. "You've left the wars behind and moved on to better things." He frowned as he stared across the crowded garden. "This party notwithstanding."

Merritt pulled a cigar from his breast pocket and lit it on a nearby lamp. "You're exactly where you belong. With your family." He puffed at the cheroot, then watched the smoke curl from its tip into the darkness overhead. "They need you now more than the Guards do."

In his heart, Marcus knew that, too. Which was why he'd taken it upon himself to go through Elise's belongings when Claudia couldn't bring herself to do it, to pack up what he thought her daughter, Penelope, might want when she was older and to distribute the rest to the poor. That was how he'd discovered a letter among Elise's things from someone named John Porter, arranging a midnight meeting for which she'd left the house and never returned.

He'd not had a moment of peace since.

He rubbed at the knot of tension in his nape. His friends didn't need to know any of that. They were already burdened enough as it was by settling into their own new lives now that they'd left the army.

"Besides, you're a duke now." Merritt flicked the ash from his cigar. "There must be some good way to put the title to use." He looked down at the party and clarified, "One that doesn't involve society balls."

"Or togas," Pearce muttered.

Marcus blew out a patient breath at their good-natured teasing. "The Roman theme was Claudia's idea."

"Liar," both men said at once. Then they looked at each other and grinned.

Merritt slapped him on the back. "Next thing you know, you'll be trying to convince us that the pink ribbons in you horse's tail were put there by Penelope."

Marcus kept his silence. There was no good reply to that.

He turned his attention back to the party below, his gaze passing over the crowded garden. He spied the delicate turn of a head in the crowd—

Danielle. There she was, standing by the fountain in the glow of one of the torches.

For a moment, he thought he was mistaken, that the woman who'd caught his attention couldn't possibly be her. Not with her auburn hair swept up high on her head in a pile of feathery curls, shimmering with copper highlights in the lamplight and revealing a long and graceful neck. Not in that dress of emerald satin with its capped sleeves of ivory lace over creamy shoulders.

Impossible. This woman, with her full curves and mature grace, simply couldn't be the same excitable girl he remembered, who'd seemed always to move through the world with a bouncing skip. Who had bothered him to distraction with all her questions about the military and soldiers.

She laughed at something her aunt said, and her face brightened into a familiar smile. Only then did he let himself believe that she wasn't merely an apparition.

Sweet Lucifer. Apparently, nothing in England was as he remembered.

He put his hands on both men's shoulders. "If you'll

excuse me, there's someone in the garden I need to speak with. Enjoy yourselves tonight." Then, knowing both men nearly as well as he knew himself, he warned, "But not too much."

As he moved away, Merritt called out with a knowing grin. "What's *her* name?"

"Trouble," he muttered and strode down into the garden before she could slip back into the crowd and disappear.

Two

DANIELLE WILLIAMS SMILED DISTRACTEDLY AT THE STORY her great-aunt Harriett was telling the group of friends gathered around them in the garden. The one about how she'd accidentally pinched the bottom of—

"King George!" The crux of the story elicited a gasp of surprise, followed by laughter. Just as it always did. "I had no idea that the bottom I saw poking out from behind that tree was a royal one. Truly, doesn't one bottom look like all the rest?"

"I've never thought so," Dani mumbled against the rim of her champagne flute as she raised it to her lips.

Harriett slid her a chastising glance, although knowing Auntie, likely more for interrupting her story than for any kind of hint of impropriety.

"But oh, how high His Majesty jumped!" her aunt continued, undaunted. As always. "I was terrified—simply *terrified*, I tell you! I was only fourteen and convinced that I had just committed high treason."

Although Dani had heard this same story dozens of times, the way Harriett told it always amused her. Thank goodness. After all, she needed something to distract her, because this evening was the first time she'd been to Charlton Place since

Marcus Braddock had returned from the continent. The irony wasn't lost on her. She was on edge with nervousness tonight when she'd once spent so much time here that she'd considered this place a second home.

"A pinch to a king's bottom!" Harriett exclaimed. "Wars have been declared over less offending actions, I assure you."

Dani had been prepared for the unease that fluttered in her belly tonight, yet the guilt that gnawed at her chest was as strong as ever…for not coming to see Claudia or spending time with Pippa, for not being able to tell Marcus what kindnesses Elise had done for others in the months before her death. But how could she face him without stirring up fresh grief for both of them?

No. Best to simply avoid him.

"Had it been a different kind of royal bottom—say, one of the royal dukes—I might not have panicked so. But it was a *king's* bottom!"

She had a plan. Once Harriett finished her story, Dani would suddenly develop a headache and need to leave. She would give her best wishes to Claudia before slipping discreetly out the door and in the morning pen a note of apology to the duke for not wishing him happy birthday in person. She'd assure him that she'd looked for him at the party but had been unable to find him. A perfectly believable excuse given how many people were crammed into Charlton Place tonight. A complete crush! So many other people wanted their chance to speak to him that she most likely couldn't get close to him even if she tried. Not that she'd *try* exactly, but—

"Good evening, Miss Williams."

The deep voice behind her twined down her spine. Marcus Braddock. *Drat it all.*

So much for hiding. Her trembling fingers tightened around the champagne flute as she inhaled deeply and slowly faced him. She held out her gloved hand and lowered into a curtsy. "Your Grace."

Taking her hand and bowing over it, he gave her a smile, one of those charming grins that she remembered so vividly. Those smiles had always taken her breath away, just as this one did now, even if it stopped short of his eyes.

"It's good to have you and your aunt back at Charlton Place, Miss Williams."

"Thank you." She couldn't help but stare. He'd always been attractive and dashing, especially in his uniform, and like every one of Elise's friends, she'd had a schoolgirl infatuation with him. And also like every one of his little sister's friends, he'd paid her absolutely no mind whatsoever except to tolerate her for Elise's sake.

Although he was just as handsome as she remembered, Marcus had certainly changed in other ways. The passing years had brought him into his prime, and the youthful boldness she remembered had been tempered by all he'd experienced during his time away, giving him a powerful presence that most men would never possess.

Author's Note

I hope you enjoyed reading *A Problem Princess*. It was immensely fun to write it for you.

As many of you know, I like to draw on real historical events for inspiration. This book was no exception, and I had plenty of succession crises and revolutionary acts from British history to work with.

The first of these occurred in 1700. With a succession crisis created by the death of Prince William, the future Queen Anne's last surviving child, Parliament rushed to pass the Settlement Act of 1701. This act excluded all Catholics and anyone married to a Catholic from inheriting the crown. It specifically excluded James II, all his Catholic descendants, and his sister Henrietta, Duchess of Orleans. Parliament had to go all the way back to the descendants of James I to find a Protestant upon whom to settle the throne—Sophia of Hanover, the Protestant daughter of Elizabeth Stuart, who was the only other child of James I to survive into adulthood. Yet Sophia never received the crown, dying a mere two months before Queen Anne, thus passing the succession to her son George. However, the act solidified two important tenets that would impact another succession crisis in 1817, triggered by the death in childbirth of Princess Charlotte of

Wales and her son: first, it significantly limited presumptive heirs, and second, it permanently established Parliament's role in choosing a monarch.

This, of course, got my brain whirling—what would happen if Parliament, spurred on by radicals, decided to take matters into its own hands?

As you may have guessed, Cordelia's line of succession is completely fictional, and the country of Monrovia is based on the real principality of Monaco. Cordelia's family descends from Elizabeth Stuart, the same as all the Georgian kings, but while the Georgians descend from Elizabeth's youngest daughter, Sophia of Hanover, Cordelia's family descends from Sophia's older sister, Henriette Marie of the Palatinate—a potential successor to the crowns of England and Scotland. Yet Henriette was not mentioned at all in the Settlement Act because she died childless in 1651, leaving Sophia of Hanover as the only surviving Protestant descendant of James I.

You probably also guessed the second historical event I drew on for inspiration for *A Problem Princess*: the Cato Street Conspiracy. A group of men, incited and funded by Home Office spy George Edwards, plotted the murders of all the British cabinet ministers, Lord Liverpool, the Duke of Wellington, and Lord Castlereagh by attacking them during dinner at the home of Lord Harrowby, Lord President of the Council. The dinner was a purely fictional ruse created by the Home Office, which went so far as to place announcements about the dinner in newspapers to make the conspirators believe the event was real. On the night of the planned attack, the Home Office enacted plans to arrest the conspirators at their meeting place. However, while waiting for reinforcements from the Coldstream Guards to arrive, Bow Street decided to take matters into their own hands and acted early. Their botched arrest resulted in a hand-to-hand brawl leading to the death of one of their own men. Five men were hanged for treason, and many others were transported or imprisoned. George Edwards, the man who caused it all, was given a new identity in South Africa, where he lived out the rest of his very long life in relative peace and prosperity.

Cato Street was not the only time Home Office spies incited rebellion and treason, and George Edwards was far from its only opportunistic spy. When the government's involvement in these incidents was revealed, the outrage that followed helped lead to the Great Reform Act of 1832. This act sought to give greater representation in Parliament by extending the vote beyond the roughly 3 percent of people who had been able to vote before. The act allowed smaller landowners, some tenants, and men with independent means to cast votes, gave parliamentary representation to cities that had none before (in fact, in 1776, the American colonies had more representation in Parliament than the entire populations of Manchester and Birmingham—"no taxation without representation" is a fun slogan but not at all accurate), and eliminated the corrupt system of pocket and rotten boroughs. Sadly, it also marked the first statuary bar to women's suffrage by explicitly defining a voter as a "male person." Additional reforms would come during Victoria's reign in an attempt to avert in England the revolutionary sentiment sweeping the globe. However, women would not win suffrage until 1918 as part of a wave of social reform following WWI. (Even then, this right was extended only to women over the age of thirty—while men over twenty-one were allowed to vote—thus excluding one-third of all British women, many of whom had bravely participated in the war effort alongside their male counterparts.) Only in 1928 was the voting age lowered to twenty-one for women, finally giving them equal suffrage rights.

And as for Cordelia resigning her position as princess... the Duke and Duchess of Sussex, known affectionately as Prince Harry and Meghan, also resigned their royal status and stepped away from their royal duties to carve out a life they chose for themselves. No one knew if they could do it either...until they did.

About the Author

Anna Harrington is an award-winning author of Regency romance. She writes spicy historicals with alpha heroes and independent heroines, layers of emotion, and lots of sizzle. Anna was nominated for a RITA award in 2017 for her romance *How I Married a Marquess*, and her debut novel, *Dukes Are Forever*, won the 2016 Maggie Award for Best Historical Romance. A lover of all things chocolate and coffee, when she's not hard at work writing her next book, Anna loves to travel, go ballroom dancing, or tend her roses. She is a terrible cook who hopes to one day use her oven for something other than shoe storage.

Also by Anna Harrington

THE CAPTIVE DUKE

A dazzling, sensuous Regency romance from *New York Times* bestselling author Grace Burrowes

Captured and tortured by the French, Christian Severn, Duke of Mercia, lost his wife, his son, and his will to live. He struggles to find a way back to the world he once knew until Gillian, Countess of Windmere, pointedly reminds him that he has a daughter who still needs him.

As Christian and Gilly spend time together trying to heal Margaret, who was traumatized by her mother's death, their attraction slowly begins to grow. But just as life seems to be getting back to normal, Gilly mysteriously refuses Christian's marriage proposal and Margaret's terrible secret threatens to tear them apart forever...

"Lush storytelling... Smart, compelling, and captivating."
—*Kirkus Reviews*

For more info about Sourcebooks's books and authors, visit:
sourcebooks.com

A GENTLEMAN
OUGHT TO KNOW

A sparkling new Regency romance from
beloved author Jane Ashford!

Charlotte Deeping needs something to keep her occupied now
that she's back home after her first London season. She misses
solving local intrigues with her school friends, but they've all gone
off and gotten married. Then Laurence Lindley, the Marquess of
Glendarvon, comes for a visit, and drops a mystery right into her lap.

In an effort to uncover his past, Charlotte contrives subtle ways
to get close to the mysterious marquess—a closeness they find they
both enjoy. That is, until Charlotte's digging rouses an old vendetta
and Laurence has to delve into his own history to help the young
lady he's come to love.

**"An utterly delightful tale of deception and masquerade
that sets a new bar for the Regency romp.**
—Historical Novel Society for *Earl on the Run*

For more info about Sourcebooks's books and authors, visit:
sourcebooks.com

THE ROGUE
STEALS A BRIDE

Enter the glittering halls of Regency England with *New York Times* and *USA Today* bestselling author Amelia Grey

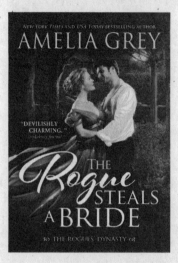

Matson Brentwood has finally met the woman of his dreams. The lovely, red-haired Sophia Hart heats his blood like no other lady. But no matter how attracted Matson is to Sophia, there's no way he can get involved with anyone who is under the watchful eye of the man he's sworn to hate.

"Amelia Grey never fails to entertain."
—Kat Martin, *New York Times* bestselling author

For more info about Sourcebooks's books and authors, visit:
sourcebooks.com

CURLED UP WITH AN EARL

A sparkling new sexy Regency romance series
from award-winning author Amy Rose Bennett

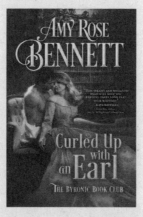

A covert inquiry agent for the Crown, William Lockhart, the Earl
of Kyle, is on the hunt for a ruthless killer—and Sir Oswald, a rare
botanical poisons expert, is the prime suspect. Posing as a groom
in the baronet's household, it shouldn't take Will long to unearth
the evidence Scotland Yard needs. If only the beguiling Miss Lucy
Bertram wasn't so damn distracting.

Miss Lucy Bertram, daughter of the eccentric botanist, is con-
tent to spend her days either writing scientific articles or curled up
with a Gothic romance novel. But when her father insists she accept
the suit of the wealthy industrialist to save the family from penury,
Lucy decides to embark on a search to find her disowned brother
and enlist his aid. But she will need a bodyguard, and that handsome
Will fits the bill nicely...

"Bursting at the seams with delicious drama."
—*Library Journal* for *Up All Night with a Good Duke*

For more info about Sourcebooks's books and authors, visit:
sourcebooks.com